The Courts
of Love

Ellen Gilchrist

The Courts of Love

STORIES

LITTLE, BROWN AND COMPANY

BOSTON   NEW YORK   TORONTO   LONDON

Originally published in hardcover by Little, Brown and Company, 1996
First Back Bay paperback edition, 1997

Library of Congress Cataloging-in-Publication Data

Gilchrist, Ellen
        The courts of love : stories / Ellen Gilchrist.
            p.   cm.
        ISBN 0-316-31478-1 (hc) 0-316-31771-3 (pb)
        I. Title.
        PS3557.I34258C68   1996
        815'.54 — dc20   96-2901

            10 9 8 7 6 5 4 3 2 1

                    MV-NY

Published simultaneously in Canada by Little, Brown & Company
                    (Canada) Limited
            Printed in the United States of America

"... for the lovers, their arms
Round the griefs of the ages,
Who pay no praise or wages
Nor heed my craft or art."

—Dylan Thomas

And for Mike Mattil, friend and counselor, purveyor of commas and common sense, font of knowledge.

"Just remember when you're feeling very small and insecure, how amazingly unlikely is your birth. And pray that there's intelligent life somewhere up in space, cause there's bugger all down here on earth."

—Monty Python

"To hell with elitist fashion; to hell with elitist guilt; to hell with existentialist nausea; and above all, to hell with the imagined that does not say, not only in, but behind the images, the real."

—John Fowles

Contents

The Courts
of Love

I

Nora Jane
and Company

IN WHICH THE FATHERS of the twin girls Tammili and
Lydia Whittington meet again. One would think this was
inevitable. Their DNA had swum together for nine
months, hands touching, legs embracing. In many ways
they are closer than either of them are to the mother.
These three people, caught forever in Indra's net. The net
of jewels, in which each jewel contains the reflections of
all the others. The twins are ten years old. Freddy Harwood is forty-four. Sandy George Wade is thirty-one.
Nora Jane is twenty-nine. The universe is several trillion
million and beginning to coalesce. Nineteen ninety-five
and we are still in orbit. Keep your fingers crossed.

Perhaps a Miracle

IT WAS THE WORST argument they had had in months. Nora Jane almost never argued with Freddy Harwood. In the first place she thought he was smarter than she was and in the second place he always went rational on her and in the third place there were better ways to get what she wanted. The best way was to say she wanted something and then not mention it for a week or two. All that time he would be arguing with himself about his objection and in the end he would decide he didn't have the right to impose his ideas on any other human being, not even his wife. Freddy had not gone to Berkeley in the sixties for nothing. *The Greening of America* and *The Sorcerer of Bolinas Reef* were still among his favorite books. Once a reporter had asked Freddy to name his ten favorite books and he had left out both those books because this was the nineties and Freddy was famous in the world of publishing and independent bookstores and he didn't want to seem too crazy in public. If someone had asked him the ten things he regretted most, leaving *The Greening of America* and *The Sorcerer of Bolinas Reef* off his list would have been right up there with the butterfly tattoo on his ankle.

"It doesn't matter what you take," he said out loud. "It's none of my business."

"You don't care what I take?"

"All I said is that sociology is a pseudoscience and you're too good for that kind of mush. I didn't mean you shouldn't take it. I should never have asked what you are going to take. I'm embarrassed that I asked. All I care about is that you be home by three so the girls won't come home to an empty house."

"You don't want me to go to college. I can tell."

"I want you to go to college fiercely. I wish I could quit work and go with you. My biology is about twenty years behind the field."

"Freddy." She climbed down off the ladder. She had been putting up drapes while Freddy read. She was wearing a white cashmere sweater and a pair of jeans. She was wearing ballet shoes.

"You wear that stuff to drive me crazy," Freddy said. "If they sold that perfume Cleopatra used on Caesar, you'd wear it every day. How can I let you go to college? Every man at Berkeley will fall in love with you. Education will come to a grinding halt. No one will learn a thing. No one will be able to teach. It's my civic duty to keep you at home. I owe it to the culture." He pulled her across the room and began to dance with her. He sang an old Cole Porter song in a falsetto voice and danced her around the sofas. One thing about Nora Jane. She could move into a scenario. "Where are the girls?" she asked.

"In the den doing homework. I told them I'd take them down to Berkeley to get an ice cream cone when they were finished."

"Meet me in the pool house. Hurry." She smiled the wild, hard-won smile that worked on Freddy Harwood better than all the perfumes of the East.

"Yes, yes, yes," he answered, and let her go and she walked away from him and out of the room and down the stairs and across the patio to the guest house beside the swimming pool. She went into the bedroom and took off her clothes and waited. In a moment he was there. He turned off the lights to the pool with a switch on the wall. He locked the door and lay down beside her and began to make love to her.

It was Freddy's theory that the way you made love to a woman was to worship every inch of her body with your heart and mind and soul. This was easy with Nora Jane. He had worshiped every inch of Nora Jane since the night he met her. He loved beauty, had been raised to know and worship beauty, believed beauty was truth, balance, order. He worshiped Nora Jane and he loved her. Ten years before, on a snow-covered night in the northern California hills, he had delivered the twin baby girls who were his daughters. With no knowledge of how to do it and nothing to guide him but love, he had kept them all alive until help came. Nora Jane had another lover at the time and no one knew whose sperm had created Lydia and Tammili. Most of the time Freddy Harwood didn't give a damn if they were his or not. They lived in his home and carried his name and gave his life meaning and kept Nora Jane by his side. The other man had disappeared before they were born and had not been heard from since. It was a shadow, but all men have shadows, Freddy knew. Where it was darkest and there was no path. This was Freddy's credo. Each knight entered the forest where it was darkest and there was no path. If there was a path, it was someone else's path.

Freddy ran his hand up and down the side of Nora Jane's body. He trembled as he touched her small round hip. I cultivate this, he decided. Well, some men gamble.

II

A FOUR-YEAR-OLD boy named Zandia, who was visiting his grandmother in the house next door, had been trying all week to get to the Harwoods' heated swimming pool. He didn't necessarily want to get in the water. He wanted to get the blue and white safety ring he could see from his grandmother's fence. All these days and his grandmother had not noticed his fascination with the pool. Perhaps she had noticed it but she hadn't given it enough weight. She trusted the lock on the gate, and besides, Zandia was such a wild little boy. He could have four or five plans of action going at the same time. His latest fascination was with vampires, and Clyda Wax, for that was his grandmother's name, had been occupied with overcoming his belief in them. "Where did you ever see a vampire?" she kept asking. "There is no such thing as a vampire, Zandia. There are vampire bats. I'll admit that. But they live in caves and they are very stupid and blind and I could kill a hundred of them with a broom."

"They would fly up and eat your blood. They can fly."

"I'd knock them down with the broom. They are blind. It would be easy as pie. I'd have a bushel basket full of them."

"They'd fly up and stick to the trees. What would you do then?"

"I'd get a giraffe to eat them."

"But giraffes live in Africa."

"So what? I can afford to import one."

"What about Count Dracula? You couldn't kill him."

"There isn't any Count Dracula. There's just that vulgar, disgusting, imbecilic Hollywood trash that you are exposed to in L.A. I shudder to think what they let you watch down there. Did the baby-sitter show it to you? Did the baby-sitter tell you about vampires? Vampires are not true. Now go and play with your Jeep for a while. I want to rest." Clyda closed her eyes and lay back on the lawn chair. She didn't mean to go to sleep but she was exhausted from taking care of him. She had volunteered for one week. It had turned into three. He had been up that morning at five rummaging around in her kitchen drawers. "When your mother comes to get you I'm going to a spa," she said sleepily. "I'm going to Maine Chance and stay a month."

As soon as he saw she was asleep he walked over to the fence and undid the latch. He pushed the latch open and disappeared through the gate. There it was, shimmering in the moonlight, the swimming pool with all its chairs and the red rubber raft and the safety ring. He walked under the window of the bedroom where Nora Jane and Freddy lay in each other's arms. He walked around the chairs and up to the edge of the water. He bent over and saw his reflection in the water. Then he began to fall.

"Something's wrong." Nora Jane sat up. She pushed Freddy away from her. She jumped up from the bed. She tore open the door and began to run. She got to the pool just as Zandia was going under. She ran around the edge. She jumped in beside him and found him and they began to struggle. She pulled and dragged him through the water. When she got to the shallow end she pulled him up into the air. Then the lights were on and Freddy was in the water with her and they lifted him from the water and turned him upside down and Freddy was on the mobile phone calling 911.

"How did you know?" they asked her. After it was over and Zandia was in his grandmother's arms eating cookies and the living room was full of uniformed men and Tammili and Lydia had seen their naked parents performing a miracle and were the most cowed ten-year-old girls in the Bay Area.

"I don't know. I don't know what I knew. I just knew to go to the pool."

"You've never even met this kid?" one of the men in uniform asked.

"I've seen him in the yard. He's been in the yard next door."

Later that night, after Zandia and his grandmother had been walked to their house and Tammili had been put to bed reading *The Voyage of the Dawn Treader* and Lydia had been put to bed reading a catalog from *American Girl* and they were alone in their room, Freddy had opened all the windows and the skylight above the bed and they had lain in each other's arms, awed and pajamaed, talking of time and space and life at the level of microbiology and wave and particle theory and why Abraham Pais was their favorite person in New York City and how it was time to take the girls to the Sierra Nevada to see the mountains covered with snow. "We need to do something to mark it. Plant some trees at Willits. Lay bricks for a path."

"You could rearrange the books in the den. It's such a mess in there Betty won't even go in to clean. It's unhealthy to have that many books in a room. It's musty. It's like a throwback to some other age. It doesn't go with the rest of the house."

"Go on to sleep if you can."

"I can. You're the one who doesn't sleep."

"We should both sleep tonight. Something's on our side. I never felt that as strongly as I do right now." He patted her for a while. Then he began to dream his old dream of building the house at Willits. The solar house he and Nieman had built by hand to prove it could be done and to prove who they were. Our rite of passage into manhood house, Freddy knew. The house to free us from our mothers. In the recurrent dream it was a clear, cold day. They had finished the foundation and were beginning to set the posts at the sides. The mountain lions came and sat upon the rise and watched them. "You think I'm nuts to go to all this trouble to make a nest," he told the lions. "Well, you're wrong. This is what my species does."

In that magical house Tammili and Lydia were born and sometimes Freddy thought the house had been built to serve that purpose. To make them so much his that nothing could sever the bond. So what if one or both of them were Sandy George Wade's biological spawn? So what if maybe Tammili was his and Lydia was not? So what in a finite world if there was love? Freddy always ended up deciding.

Next door, it was Zandia's grandmother who couldn't sleep. She was talking to Zandia's mother on the phone. "You just come up here tomorrow afternoon as soon as they finish shooting and spend the night. He's lonely for you. Four-year-old boys shouldn't be away from their mother for this many days."

"I can't. We have to look at rushes every night. It's the first time Sandy and I have had a chance to be in a film together. I'm a professional, Mother. I have to finish my work, then I'll come get him. There's no reason you can't hire a baby-sitter for him, you know. He stays with baby-sitters here."

"He almost died, Claudine. I don't think you understand what happened here. You never listen to me, do you know that? You only half listen to anything I say. The child almost died. Also, he is obsessed with vampires. Who let him see a movie about vampires? That's what I'd like to know. I'm taking him to my psychiatrist tomorrow for an evaluation."

"All right then. I'll send someone to get him. I thought you wanted him, Mother. You always do this. You say you want him, then you change your mind in about four days."

"He almost drowned."

"Could we talk in the morning? I'll call you at seven."

Claudine hung up the phone, then went into the bedroom to find Sandy. He was in bed smoking and reading the script. He put the cigarette out when he saw her and shook his head. "Where have you been?" he asked. "What took you so long?"

"Zandia fell in a swimming pool and Mother's neighbor had to fish him out. They're acting like it was some sort of big, big deal. God, she drives me crazy. This is the last time he's going up there. From now on if she wants to see him she can come down here."

"We'll be finished in a week or ten days. It can't drag on much longer than that. You think we ought to send for him?"

"She can bring him. I'll tell her in the morning. I'll line up a sitter and he can go back to the Montessori school in the mornings. I knew better than to do this."

"How'd he fall in a pool?"

"Mother's neighbors left the gate open or something. The police came. He's fine. Nothing happened to him. It's just Mother's insanity."

Then Sandy George Wade, who was the father of Lydia Harwood, as anyone who looked at them would immediately know, began to flip channels on the television set, hoping to find a commercial starring either Claudine or himself, as that always cheered him up and made him think he wouldn't end up in a poor folks home. He reached for Claudine, to believe she was there, and sighed deep inside his scarred, motherless, fatherless heart. His main desire was to get a good night's sleep so he would be beautiful for the cameras in the morning.

Claudine pulled away from him. She got up and went into the other room to call her mother back. When she returned she had a different plan. "We have to go to San Francisco and pick him up. She won't bring him. Well, to hell with it. She wants me to meet the woman who pulled him out of the pool. I probably ought to sue them for having an attractive nuisance. Anyway, we have to go. Will you take me?"

"Of course I will. As soon as we have a break. Come on, get in bed. I like San Francisco. It's a nice drive. We'll take the BMW. It's driving good since I got the new tires. Get in bed. Let's get some sleep." Then Claudine gave up for the day and climbed into the bed and let Sandy cuddle up to her. Their neuroses fit like gloves. They were really very happy together. They hated the same things. They liked to make love to each other and they liked to sleep in the same bed. It was the best thing either of them had ever known. They even liked Zandia. Neither one of them liked to take care of him but they didn't hate or resent him. Sometimes they even thought he was funny.

Lunch at the Best Restaurant in the World

"So why was I chosen for this? That's what I keep asking myself. It's like a tear in the fabric of reality. Maybe I heard him walking by the window. I have a perfect ear for music. Well, I do. Maybe I saw him by the fence and knew he'd be wanting to get to the pool. All mothers are wary of pools. I've been watching to make sure no one drowns in our pool for years. Maybe there's a logical explanation. I'm sure there is. It only seems like a miracle." Nora Jane was talking. She and Freddy and Freddy's best friend, Nieman Gluuk, were at Chez Panisse having lunch. Nora Jane was wearing yellow. Freddy had on his plaid shirt and chinos. Nieman wore his suit. It was the first time the Harwoods had been out in public since the night Nora Jane pulled the child from the swimming pool. Nieman had been with them almost constantly since the event. Actually he had been with them almost constantly since they were married ten years before. Nieman and Freddy saw each other or talked on the phone nearly every day. They had done this since they were five years old. No one thought anything about it or ever said it was strange that two grown men were inseparable.

"Three knights were allowed to see the Grail," Freddy said. "Bors and Percival and Galahad. They were pure of heart. You're pure of heart, Nora Jane. And besides, you're an intuitive. The first time Nieman met you he told me that. He says you're the most intuitive person he's ever known."

"Maybe this means I shouldn't go to college. It means something, Freddy. Something big."

"You think I don't know that? I was there too, wasn't I? I watched it happen. What it means is that there's a lot more going on than we are able to acknowledge. Thought is energy. It creates fields. You picked up on one. You're a good receiver. That's what intuitive means. Maybe I'll go to school with you. Just dive right into a freshman science course and see if I sink or swim."

Nieman sighed and shook his head from side to side. "I can't believe you had this experience just when you were getting ready to try your wings at Berkeley. It's a coincidence, not a warning. It doesn't mean the girls are in danger or that we are in danger. No, listen to me. I know you think that but you shouldn't. The point is that you saved his life, not that his life was in danger. You will always save lives in many ways. It's all the more reason to go back to school and gain more knowledge and more power. Knowledge is power, even if it does sound trite to say it."

"I wish they hadn't put it in the papers." Nora Jane turned to Nieman and touched his hand. She was one of the three people in the world who dared to touch the esteemed and feared Nieman Gluuk, the bitter and hilarious movie critic of the *San Francisco Chronicle*. "The whole thing only lasted about six minutes. I can barely remember any of it except the moment I knew to do it. Freddy remembers pulling him out better than I do."

"We must never forget it," Nieman said.

"A man who had it happen to him last year called last night. He went through a glass door to get to a pool and saved his nephew. He thinks it has something to do with water. Water as a conductor."

"It proves a lot of theories," Freddy added. "I was there too, Nieman. I witnessed it. I was in bed with her."

"Excuse me." They were interrupted by a waiter, who took

their orders for goat cheese pie and salads and wine. "It was the single most profound thing that ever happened to me in my life," Freddy went on. "I will be thinking about it every day for the rest of my life. A tear in the cover, a glimpse of a wild, or perhaps exquisitely orderly, reality that is lost to us most of the time. Think of it, Nieman. The brain can't stand to consciously process all it senses and knows. We'd go crazy. The brain is a filter and its first job is to keep the body healthy. Occasionally, perhaps by accident, it sees a larger reality as its domain. Altruism. Well, it's so humbling to be part of it." He looked down, afraid they would think he wanted them to remember what he had done in the earthquake of 1986. But they knew better. He had forbidden his friends ever to speak of that. "Well, let's don't talk it all away. It's Nora Jane's miracle. I want to take her up to Willits for a while to think it over but she can't go. She starts school in three days, you know."

The waiter put bread down in front of them, the best French bread this side of New Orleans. Nieman held out a loaf to Nora Jane and they broke the bread. They ate in silence for a while.

"Fantastic about Berkeley," Nieman said at last. "Brilliant. I wish I could go. I feel like a dinosaur with my old knowledge. My encyclopedia is twenty years old. Every year I say I'll get another one but I never do."

The waiter brought more bread. Nieman buttered a piece and examined it, calculating the fat grams and wondering if it mattered. "Our darling Nora Jane," he went on. "Loose on the campus in the directionless nineties. I should write a modern opera for you. The problem is the ending. Shakespeare knew what to do. He poured in outrageous action, tied up all the loose ends, piled up some bodies, and danced off the stage on the wings of language. Ah, those epilogues. 'As you from crimes would pardoned be. Let your indulgence set me free.' Oh, he could lift the language! The modern stage can't bear the weight of so much beauty, so much fun. It's too large an insult to the modern fantasy, boredom, and self-pity. I went to three movies last week that were so bad I didn't last for the first hour. I just walked out. They began hopefully enough, were well acted by fine actors, then you could see the money mold begin to grow, the meetings where the money people in group think begin to decide how to corrupt the script. Well, let's not ruin lunch with such thoughts. After lunch shall we go over to the campus and walk around and get you accustomed to your new domain, Miss Nora? I heard the brilliant translator Mark Musa is here for the semester to teach *The Divine Comedy*. You might want to take that. We could go by and see if he's in his office and introduce ourselves."

"There you go," Freddy said. "Trying to take over what she takes. I pray to God every day to make me stop caring what classes she takes."

"The only answer is for you to go with me. You too, Nieman. Why not? Life is short, as you both tell me a thousand times a month."

"Life is short," Nieman agreed. "We could do it, Freddy. We could think of it as a donation to the university. Pay tuition as special students, sign up for classes, and go as often as we are able. I could take Monday and Tuesday off. I'm going to list the names of seven movies and then leave a blank white space. Think of us back on the campus, Freddy. Freddy was valedictorian of our class, Nora. But you know that."

"His mother's told me a million times. I think it was the high point of her life."

"That's what she wants you to think. The high point of her life was when she flew that jet to Seattle in the air show. No, I guess it was when she played Martha in *Who's Afraid of Virginia Woolf*? You know who she's going out with now, don't you, Nieman?"

"I heard. It's a terrible shadow, Freddy, but you have survived so far. Well, shall we do it then? Register for classes?"

"Yes. I'm taking biology, physics, and a history course. I want to see what they're teaching. It can't be as bad as I've heard it is."

"I'll take Musa's Dante in Translation and a playwriting course. I'll go incognito and write the play for Nora Jane and we'll put it on next year as an AIDS benefit."

"I'll sing 'Vissi d'arte' from the side of the stage while twelve little girls in long white dresses run around the stage doing leaps. Would that be a conclusion? Then a poet can run out on the stage and read part of 'Little Gidding.' Imagine us all going to college together."

"Meeting for coffee at Aranga's. When I was a student I was touched by old people going back to school. We will touch their silly little hearts. At least, Freddy and I will. You'll drive them crazy. I don't know, Freddy, maybe she's overeducated already."

"I want a degree. I'm embarrassed not to have a college degree. I'm the first person in my family in three generations not to have one." She sat up very straight and tall and Nieman and Freddy understood this was not to be taken lightly.

"Then let's go," Freddy said. "If you will allow us, we will accompany you on this pilgrimage." She turned her head to look at him and he fell madly in love with the sweep and whiteness of her neck and Nieman watched this approvingly. After all, someone has to be in love and get married and continue the human race.

An hour later they were on the Berkeley campus, walking along the sidewalks where Freddy and Nieman had walked when they were young. Nora Jane had been on the campus many times but never as a student. It was very strange, very liberating, and she felt her spirit open to the world she was about to enter. "I'll be Virgil and you be Dante and Nora Jane can be Beatrice," Nieman was saying. "The possibility of vast fields of awareness, that's what this campus always says to me. I used to think I could get vibrations from the physics building when the first reactor was installed and all those brilliant minds were here. I used to feel the force of them would dissolve the harm my mother did to me each morning. She would pour fear and anxiety over me and I would step onto the campus and feel it eaten up by knowledge. She was enraged that I was studying theater. She was very hard on me."

"You had to live at home with her?" Nora Jane took his arm to protect him from the past.

"She wanted me to go to medical school and be a psychiatrist, as she was seeing one. I would say to her, Mother, theater is psychotherapy writ large. The actors on the stage do what people do in ordinary life, keep secrets, say half of what they're thinking, manipulate, lie. Because it's writ large on the stage or screen the audience is on to them. They leave the theater and go out into the world more aware of other people's behaviors, if not of their own. Still, she was not convinced. She still thinks what I do is frivolous."

"She can't, after all these years?"

"Can she not? I'm an only child, don't forget that."

"I am too and so is Freddy. We're the only-child league. Like the red-headed league in Sherlock Holmes."

They linked arms, coming down the wide sidewalk to the student union. "This is like *The Wizard of Oz*," Nieman said. "In *The Divine Comedy* they walked single file."

"Well, these are not the legions of the damned either," Freddy added, "although they certainly look the part." They were passing students, some with rings in their ears and noses and lips and some wearing chic outfits and some looking like they were only there because they didn't have anything better to do.

"Let's go to the registrar's office and get that over with," Freddy suggested.

"I will fill out any number of forms but I am not sending off for transcripts," Nieman decreed. "If they start any funny stuff about transcripts I'll drop my disguise and call the president of the university."

"We aren't pulling rank, Nieman," Freddy said. "We go as pilgrims or not at all."

"You go your way and I'll go mine, as always. Yes, it's beginning to feel like old times."

"Don't talk about the sixties or I'll hit you. I was in a convent school kneeling in the gravel before the statue of the Virgin and you were here getting to read literature and hear lectures by physicists. It isn't fair. You're too far ahead. I'll never catch up."

"No competition please. We're in this together."

By five that afternoon it was done. Freddy was signed up to audit World History and Physics I and Biology I. Nieman was taking Dante and had met Mark Musa and promised to brush up on his Italian and Nora Jane had her books and notebooks for

English, History, Algebra, and Introduction to Science. They had sacks of books from Freddy's bookstore and the campus bookstore.

When they were through collecting all the books they went to a coffeehouse across the street from the campus and picked out a table where they could meet. "I don't know if this table will be large enough," Nieman said. "Students will be flocking to us, don't you think?"

"Don't scare me like that," Freddy said.

"Don't turn my education into an anecdote," Nora Jane decreed. "Or I'll get my own table and have my own following." She piled her books up in front of her and looked at them. She was proud of them. She was on fire at this beginning.

The Incursions of the Goddamn Wretched Past

IT WAS THE SUNDAY morning after the wonderful Friday when Nora Jane, Freddy, and their best friend, Nieman, spent the afternoon on the Berkeley campus signing up for classes and being filled with happiness and hope.

It was Sunday morning and Freddy and Nora Jane were on the patio reading the Sunday newspapers and watching Zandia, who was brandishing a plastic sword in the air. He was standing on a ladder by the fence that separated the houses and pretending to poke them with the sword to punish them for ignoring him.

Because Nora Jane had saved Zandia's life he thought he had a claim on her. He thought she was a mean, bad girl to sit there reading the newspapers when he didn't have a thing to do. "I'm killing you," he called out in his annoying, high-pitched voice. "You are Nora Jane Captain Hook. I'm swording you."

"You think I should go get him?" Nora Jane asked Freddy. "Clyda said his mother was coming this afternoon. Can you stand him for a while?"

"Sure. Why not? Did that man call about the new pool cover?"

"He's coming Monday afternoon. Betty will let him in if I'm

not here." Nora Jane got up from her chair and walked down across the lawn to Zandia, who was continuing to threaten her. His grandmother met her at the fence.

"Let me take him for a while," Nora Jane asked. "We like to watch him play."

"If you're sure you want him. I swear to God I'm worn out with him. I'm going to Maine Chance for two weeks the minute that he's gone. I was going to the Golden Door but they're full."

"Let us have him for a while. It will keep Freddy from reading the editorial page. It drives him crazy to read the editorials. Actually he shouldn't even be allowed to read the papers." Nora Jane helped Zandia over the fence and he stood beside her, poking his sword in the direction of his grandmother.

"Claudine ought to be here by three or four. They sent me some stills from the set. You want to see them? She really is a pretty girl. I guess I'm too proud of her." Clyda pulled some photographs out of the pocket of her jacket. She handed them over the fence, still talking. "That's Kevin Kline in the background. That's a Mardi Gras parade. These were made while they were still filming in New Orleans. That's Claudine and the other one's her boyfriend, Sandy Wade. They're pretty handsome, aren't they?"

Nora Jane took the photographs. It was Sandy George Wade, her old lover. Ten years older and stronger looking and wider and twelve times as handsome, if it were possible for anyone that handsome to look any better. It was Sandy, on his way to San Francisco to ruin her life.

"That's her boyfriend?"

"Yes. He's very good-looking, isn't he? They'll be here this afternoon to get Zandia. Claudine wants to meet you and thank you in person. She'll never forgive me if she doesn't have a chance to thank you for what you did."

"I don't know if we'll still be here. We're going to Berkeley starting tomorrow. There's so much we have to do. Well, thanks for showing these to me." Nora Jane handed them back over the fence. "I'll bring him back in half an hour. We have to leave pretty soon." She took Zandia's hand and hurried back across the lawn to Freddy. Tammili and Lydia were with him. Tammili had on a blue and white dress and Lydia had on shorts and a white T-shirt advertising an Amos Oz book.

Lydia is his, Nora Jane said to herself. If he sees her he will know. Anyone will know. We know. Freddy will go crazy when he finds out Sandy's coming. Well, I can't wait. I have to tell him now. We have to leave. What hell is this? That we have to pay for the past forever. The terrible past. The mean past. It's here every moment of our lives, weighing us down, ruining everything we do.

"Take Zandia," she said to Tammili. "Go find him some cookies. I have to talk to your father."

She pulled Freddy up from his chair and led him into the living room. It was a perfect room. High glass walls that looked out onto the bay. White marble floors with soft blue handmade cotton rugs. A long gold sofa. A Japanese tea box for a coffee table. A bowl of white roses beside the fireplace. Nora Jane pushed a button and the music of Johann Sebastian Bach began to play. Freddy had not spoken. He thought she was going to tell him someone had died. He was going over a list in his head. It had to be something Zandia's grandmother told her. It wouldn't be Nieman, or someone would have called.

"Sit down," she said. "Don't go crazy when you hear this. We can deal with this. We are not hopeless in the face of what I'm going to tell you."

"Say it."

"Sandy Wade is the boyfriend of Zandia's mother. They're coming here today. This is real, Freddy. I just saw a photograph of him. We can't let him see Lydia. He's a human being. It would break his heart and then I don't know what he'd do. He's in a film with Zandia's mother. Clyda has photographs of the girls with Zandia at the pool. He'll see them. We can get the girls out of here but what about the pictures? Even if we could do something about that, Clyda will talk about them. He thinks they're his. Both of them. I lived with him the whole time I was pregnant. Don't forget that."

"We'll steal the photographs. That's easy. Say you want to borrow them." He had stood up. He was walking around the room.

"She gave us a set."

"I'm going to get them now. We'll sell the house. We'll move. I'll sell the house tomorrow."

"That's overreacting."

"No, it's not. Call Mother. Tell her we're coming over there for a few days. Then we'll go get the photographs. You keep her busy and I'll steal them."

Twenty minutes later Nora Jane and Freddy were in the kitchen of Clyda's house. "We want to see those photographs you took," Freddy said. "We need to borrow the negatives. We can't find the ones you gave us. The girls must have put them somewhere."

"Oh, they are good, aren't they? I can't believe how well they turned out." Clyda left the room to get the photographs. Zandia stuck his sword into the space between the refrigerator and the wall. The cat climbed up on a counter and sat beside a plate of fruit. The doorbell was ringing. Then the phone was ringing also. Nora Jane started to answer it, then couldn't touch it. Zandia picked up the phone. It was Lydia, looking for her mother. "Put my mother on the phone, Zandia. Zandia, can you hear me? Is my mother there?"

There were excited voices in the hall. Zandia dropped the phone and ran down the hall and then they were there. His mother and his grandmother and Sandy George Wade, moving into the kitchen all talking. Freddy had never met Sandy Wade but he had lived with Lydia for ten years and it was as though she had stepped into the room. The hair, the eyes, the body English, the expression on Sandy's face, quizzical, waiting.

"I have wondered where you were," Nora Jane began. "I'm glad to see you well. This is my husband, Freddy. Sandy is an old friend from New Orleans," she explained to Clyda. "We went to school together."

"We went to the same church," Sandy added. "We knew each other a long time ago."

"We have to be going," Nora Jane said. "We have people waiting on us."

"May I borrow the photographs to show them?" Freddy took them from Clyda's hand and led Nora Jane toward the back door.

"This is who saved Zandia's life," Clyda was saying. "This is Nora Jane."

"I don't know what to say," Claudine put in. "I brought you a present. Sandy, go get my suitcase, will you?" She was very tall, very thin, nervous and excited. She had picked up Zandia but she was not paying much attention to him. She was trying to figure out what was wrong. "Mother," she added, "get that god-damn cat off the counter, will you? I told you Zandia's allergic to them. Has that cat been inside the whole time?"

"We really have to leave. We'll see you later." Freddy put the photographs into his pocket and he and Nora Jane disappeared through the door.

"I'll call you later," Nora Jane called over her shoulder. "We'll get together later."

They made it through the gate and started up the hill to their house. "Get the girls," she said. "Let's get out of here."

They walked back across the yard, holding hands, tight against each other's bodies. Freddy's shoulders barely came an inch higher than Nora Jane's. "Yet I feel the breadth of them," she said, and he did not ask the meaning. They had grown to talk this way when they were alone together. In sentence frag-ments, long hints, musings. Perhaps she had learned it from him, or perhaps she had only learned to do it aloud, since she had always whispered parts of secrets to herself and to her cats. Lonely little only child that she had been, always up in trees with a cat, spinning worlds she could inhabit without fear. Now, into this world she had created with this man, a real world of goodness and light, peace and hope, came this moment and they must bear it and survive it.

"He cannot mean to harm us," Freddy answered. "Still,

she is his and he will know it. What do we do now? First we think."

"He thinks they both are his. We should never have kept this secret. Nothing should be a secret. Secrets are dynamite, weapons-grade uranium."

"Who would we have told? Tammili and Lydia? We can't do that."

"Call your mother and tell her we're coming over there. We'll move if we have to. He knows where we live."

"Leave the house?"

"There are millions of houses. Think of the stuff we could throw away."

"All right. Go get the girls. Let's go. A house on the beach. That's what you've always wanted, isn't it?"

"This is what money is for, Freddy. This is the difference in being rich and being poor." They had arrived at the cobbled path that led to the back door. It was sheltered by azalea bushes and they stopped beneath one and moved into each other's arms. Frozen still, on guard, but moving. This was the thing Nieman envied them, this marriage, this shield they had created, the ability to plan and move as one.

Nora Jane disappeared into the house and began to throw clothes for the girls into a suitcase. Freddy got the station wagon out of the garage and drove it to the side door. He went into the living room and turned on the CD player. Then he called his mother. The strains of the Sixth Symphony were in the background while he talked to her. "It's dire, Mother. Someone who is a threat to us is staying next door. We're coming there, for perhaps a week."

"What will you tell the girls?"

"What do you suggest?"

"Say I need them. Say I was frightened."

"You've never been frightened in your life. They'd never believe that."

"Then tell them they can't know."

"I'll say the air-conditioner's broken. Hell, I'll say the power's going off."

"Come on then. I'm waiting."

"We're going to buy another house. Will you go with Nora Jane this afternoon and help her look?"

"Whatever you need."

Ann Harwood hung up the phone and sat staring out the leaded glass doors into the morning light. Then she picked up the phone and called her lover and told him she couldn't drive to the desert as they had planned. "The children need me," she said. "This is why there's no point in getting married."

"Can I help?"

"I don't think so. I'll call you later." She hung up the phone and walked down the hall and began to open doors to unused rooms.

Sandy George Wade stood by himself in Clyda's pink and white guest bedroom feeling the way he had felt most of his life. Frightened, deserted, in the way, waiting for the next blow to fall. I guess I'd like to see those kids she had, he decided. See how they turned out, but what the hell, nobody offered to show them to me, did they?

Zandia came into the room and brandished his plastic sword. Sandy struck a pose and pretended to fence with him. They moved around the room thrusting and pointing at one another. Zandia began to laugh, he ran in little circles, faster and faster, then he jumped up on the bed and held the sword in both hands and began to jump on the mattress. Sandy picked him up and carried him upside down to his mother. "You've been had, Zorro," he said to him. "You've met your match when you fence with Captain Sandy Hook, the master swordsman of the deep." Zandia whacked him on the leg with the sword, then dissolved in upside-down giggles.

Sandy set him upright and took his hand. "Back to Montessori for you, old buddy," he said. "Tomorrow morning bright and early. And this time don't bring home any colds while I'm filming."

*   *   *

Freddy and Lydia had promised to go to movies with Nieman, so only Tammili went with Nora Jane and Ann Harwood to hunt for houses. "I came to California to live by the ocean," Nora Jane said. "I want to live where breakers beat upon the shore. I want to look out the window and see my girls playing in the sand."

"What's she been smoking?" Tammili dissolved in laughter. They were in Ann's Bentley, going to meet a real estate broker. "It's because Zandia fell in the pool, I bet," she added. "She probably wouldn't let us in the ocean if we lived by it."

At five-fifteen that afternoon they found it. A three-story frame house on a promontory where the Pacific Ocean beat against the shore. Nora Jane stood on a slope and watched the waves break against a tall, triangular rock. She walked to the water's edge and watched her footprints come and go. She thought, I did mean to live by the water, where the land meets the sea. "I was on the ocean's edge when I decided you were about to be born," she said to Tammili. "I think you should be excited by the sound of the waves."

"I know. Then you got on the train and went to Willits and that's why we were born there. How many times do I have to hear that story?"

"But do you like the house?" Ann asked. "We'll restore it and paint it and change the landscaping. But the basic plan, the house, how do you feel about it, Tammili?"

"Who wouldn't want that mansion? But I don't want to move. How are we going to get to school? How will Daddy get to work?"

"It isn't that far. We'll keep the other house too. In case we need it. We won't throw it away."

"I don't see how we'll get to school. We'll have to get up at six o'clock in the morning."

"Details," her grandmother said. "Three months and we can have it done. Paint, new bathrooms, new kitchen. I know just the people. I've been wanting to get them some work. This young contractor who's helpful with Planned Parenthood."

"Do you want to see the other two houses?" the real estate agent asked.

"No, we're mad about this house. We'll go back to my house and talk about an offer. Oh, Freddy has to see it. I forgot about that."

"Can we show him tonight?" Nora Jane asked. "Are the lights on?"

"Yes."

"Why are we getting this house?" Tammili asked. "You can tell me the truth. You can trust me."

"Would you wait a few days and let us tell you then?" her grandmother asked. "Could you trust us?"

"Okay. I guess so. But I know why. I know anyway." She walked off from them and stood looking at the house, smirking to herself. They think I'm so dumb. It's because the people next door are anti-Semitic. Dad's afraid they'll be snotty to us or something. He's so protective it's pitiful. Now Grandmother will have to spend a million dollars or something to move us all out here so we won't have any neighbors. It's ridiculous. If they're snotty to me I'll dump the cat litter in their yard. She walked closer to the house. Actually, it was four houses joined together to make one. A colonial house like one in some faraway country in another time. She was drawn to it. She wanted to go back inside and pick out some rooms for herself and Lydia.

"We aren't ever going to tell them or admit it to them," Nora Jane said. "We made up our mind. Can you live with that, Ann? With never letting them know there is any difference in them to you? You have to leave them the same amount of money in your will and things like that. If we keep this from them and they find it out, the older they are when they find out the madder they are going to be. But it's a chance we have to take. I don't want them to meet Sandy. I don't want him trying that charm on them."

"I always knew this, Nora Jane. I didn't know how exactly. I studied science as a girl, you know. I knew Lydia wasn't kin to me, but it's never mattered one way or the other. I adore her. I would rather be her grandmother than any little girl in the world. She's ten times as lovable as Tammili. Tammili reminds me too much of my mother to be able to pull the strings of my heart. Look at her, she's probably going up there to stake out territory. That's what Big Ann would have done. She was a weaver when she got old, did you know that? She had a loom and made twenty or so rugs and we don't know what she did with them. She never gave us one of them. I think she sold them."

"Are you sure you want to buy this house? It costs so much."

"A sound investment. They don't make any more beaches. It would be a good investment if the lot were empty. I might fix it up for myself if you decide you don't want it or Freddy doesn't like it."

"Oh, he'll like it. He'll go crazy. I know his taste. He'll start wanting to fill it with period pieces."

"Let's go find him. We can send Tammili into the movies if they're still at the Octoplex. Were they really going to three movies?"

"Parts of three. That's how Nieman does it, you know. If he comes to one he likes well enough to stay that one gets a review."

II

OF COURSE NIEMAN started seeing the Harwoods' problems as a play. It had everything. Confused passions (the great overbearing winds of the first circle of the Inferno), uncertain parentage, innocence slaughtered, random ill. He was walking around his house listening to Kiri Te Kanawa sing Puccini and thinking of Nora Jane's amazing singing voice, which she almost never let anyone hear. He was musing on the story of her childhood: a father slaughtered in a senseless war, a mother drinking herself into dementia, the portrait of her grandfather in the robes of a supreme court justice, the grandmother in the blue house with the piano and the phonograph records.

"Unfair, unfair, always unfair." Nieman strode around the living room and waved his arms in the air to the music. *Vissi d'arte,* the consolations of art. There was nothing else. Struggle and death, and in the meantime, beauty. Tammili and Lydia and Nora Jane and his best friend, Freddy, who was born to bear the suffering of anyone who came his way. He bore mine, Nieman remembered, when my own father died within a month of his, both taking their cigarette-scarred lungs to the Beth Israel Cemetery. We were fourteen years old but it was Freddy who became the father. It was Freddy who saw to it that our holidays were never sad, Freddy who sent off for the folders and found the wilderness camp where we could learn the things our fathers would have taught us. Freddy who went to Momma and made her let me go. "I won't let him die, Miss Bela," he told her. "I'll see to it personally that Nieman isn't involved in anything that's dangerous. His safety will be more important to me than my own."

Four weeks later they were stuck all night in a canyon in the Sierra Nevada with half the rangers in the area looking for them.

The phone was ringing. It was Freddy, catching Nieman up on the events of the afternoon. "They bought a mansion on the beach. Up by Mendelin Pass. You wouldn't believe what they bought. It looks like Gatsby's house. Mother's in ecstasy, as you can imagine. She's been trying to get me in a house she understands for twenty years. Well, on a higher note, I'm taking two days off for this education jaunt. You want to meet us somewhere or shall we come and pick you up?"

"We all have to be in different buildings at different times. Let's meet at Aranga's at noon and have lunch. I've got to work all night to get caught up. Is that all? They bought a house? You haven't been home?"

"I'm going over later and see if he's left."

"Can I do anything to help?"

"Not yet."

"He has no legal rights. Your name is on the birth certificate, isn't it?"

"We don't want him to know where they are, Nieman. Hide your treasures. You're the one who taught me that. If he sees them he might want them."

"Perhaps you should confront him. Pay him off. Who is he anyway? You need more information. Call Jody and get him to put a tail on him and do a profile. I thought you read murder mysteries."

"That's the best idea you've had. Tammili has decided we are moving to escape anti-Semitism. It's a sore spot with her that she can't experience prejudice."

"The angel. Well, I'll meet you at noon tomorrow. Call Jody Wattes. Get more information. Don't let your imagination run this. Athena's the goddess you need. Balance, knowledge, cool head."

"See you tomorrow then."

Sandy walked around the perimeter of Nora Jane and Freddy's house. It was eight o'clock at night and there were lights on in the living room and central hall but the garage was locked and no one seemed to be there. "They've run off because of me," he said out loud. "Well, I deserve that. I never sent her a penny. I guess they have a good life, her and her Jewish husband and my kids. I wonder what they look like. She always said they might not be mine. What if they were his kids and I'd been supporting them all these years? Well, things will change for me after this picture is released. I'll come see them then." He shook his head. I'll just go up and look around. See what kind of stuff they keep around. You can tell a lot about someone by the things they keep around. Life never lets up on me, does it? If I get happy for fifteen minutes, something comes along to throw me to the mat. Well, I better get back or Claudine will get worried. She's the best thing to come down the pike for me in years. I even like the little kid. Yeah, Zandia's a kick. He's got a criminal mind. And Clyda's okay for an old lady even if she is a nervous wreck. Yeah, Claudine's good for me.

Sandy walked up on the front porch and listened for guard dogs, then tried the door. It opened. In their hurry, Nora Jane and Freddy had left it unlocked. He walked into the foyer and called out, "Anybody here? I brought a message from Clyda next door." He walked into the living room and came face to face with a huge portrait of Tammili when she was nine years old. Her short black hair, her intense, worried black eyes stared out at him. They were in sharp contrast to the frilly white lace dress Nora Jane had made her wear. It was a powerful, no-nonsense face. A forbidding IQ, an analytical mind, a wide, flared nose, the painter had captured them all. It was a portrait of a Medici.

Not very pretty, Sandy decided. She sure doesn't look like me. The face followed him when he tried to turn away. That is not my kid, he decided. It hardly even looks like a kid.

The painting, the empty house, the strangeness of a life he could not imagine, began to work on Sandy's mind. If they were mine they might not like me, he decided. They wouldn't know anything about me. Maybe when the movie comes out I'll send N.J. a print and she can show it to them if she wants to. If they're mine. That kid's not mine. I'm out of here.

He went back out the way that he had come, wiping his prints off the door handle, locking, then unlocking the door. He walked across the yard and climbed over the fence and let himself down into Clyda's backyard. "Where have you been?" Claudine asked. "Zandia's been looking for you. I want to take him down and rent him a video. You want to go with us?"

"I used to know that woman who lives next door," Sandy said. "I knew her in New Orleans. So what are they, rich Jews or something?"

"They run a bookstore," Clyda answered. "I'll go with you to the video store. I need to get out of the house myself."

Claudine sighed. "Well, Momma, I just wanted to get Zandia off to myself for a while. I don't like to have everyone in one car."

The next morning Claudine and Zandia and Sandy got into Claudine's BMW and started driving back to L.A. "I know she got her feelings hurt," Claudine was saying. "But I couldn't take any more. I don't know how I grew up with her working on me morning, noon, and night. It's a wonder I survived. My analyst says it proves what a powerful personality I have that I got away from her. What was all that shit she was telling you about Scientology?"

"She's just lonely, baby. She's an old lady and she's lonely. It was nice of her to keep the kid so long. Don't go bad-mouthing your mother. You should have seen the one I had. When I had one, which wasn't long. I like your old lady. I think she looks good for her age and she leaves you alone."

"Well, it's over. We did it. Let's go home and get back to our own life. That's what I told her. I said, Mother, I have a life of my own, believe it or not, and I need to get back to it." Claudine bent over the wheel, pulled out onto the eight-lane that runs along the coast. "At least it isn't raining."

III

At five minutes to ten on Monday morning Nora Jane was settling into a seat in the back of the history class. A tall man in a gray shirt came into the room and put his books on the professor's desk. He was overweight and soft in the face but he had intelligent eyes and huge black-rimmed glasses and he rolled up his sleeves as he waited for the class to assemble. There were thirty or forty students when all the seats were filled. Nora Jane got out a notebook and a pencil. She began to write. "Walls and foyer, decorator white. Porch ceilings, French blue. Tammili and Lydia's rooms, sunshine yellow, ask them. Go by Goyer's Paints this afternoon."

"Where to begin to talk about the history of the world? How to begin to sort out the threads that led to the Golden Age of Greece and the first historian, Thucydides? Agriculture, the domestication of animals, the wheel, pots to store food, ways to carry water, the idea that man has a soul. Where does history begin? Is history a concept of the brain? Does time move in one direction? What is a Zeitgeist? What is an inventor? Is he only a sort of point man, the natural next step created by the force or need of many brains, or is he a lone individual stumbling onto a good idea? What is an idea? Who drilled the first well? Was it a pipe in the ground or a boy or girl sucking moisture from the earth with a straw or reed? Tell me the difference in a hat, a roof, and an umbrella.

"Water, food, shelter, keeping the young alive. Are these the things man needs? When there is an earthquake in San Francisco, what are the first things the survivors do? You do not run into the living room to save the video recorder or the Nikonos.

You run to save the babies. . . ." The professor's voice was deep and soothing. Nora Jane got chills listening to him talk. She was thrilled to be here in this class with her books beside her on the floor. If only Sandy doesn't go over to their school today and kidnap them. They wouldn't go with him. The school wouldn't let them go. I have the mobile phone. I could go out in the hall and call the school. I will in a minute. I have to. I can't stand it.

"Our hold on the earth is tenuous at best," the voice was saying. "It doesn't seem so if you are an English-speaking citizen of the United States of America and don't live in a ghetto. We wake up with our automobiles and jet helicopters and computers and video cameras and houses full of every imaginable sort of thing and we know we have gotten rid of the lions and tigers and bears and wolves and bacteria. Unfortunately we have replaced them with the AIDS virus and antibiotic-resistant tuberculoses, by threats to the very air we breathe and polluted lakes and rivers. Also, the same comets that perhaps destroyed the dinosaurs are aiming at us in the sky. . . ."

"Excuse me," Nora Jane muttered to the girl on her right, and leaving her books, went out into the hall and called the twins' school and talked to the receptionist. "Their grandmother is picking them up at three-thirty," she told the girl. "Mrs. Ann Harwood. She has a pale gray Bentley or else a black Porsche. Don't let them leave with anyone else for any reason. Unless you call me first. Here's the mobile phone number. . . . Okay, I know. Well, thank you."

She went back into the classroom and took her seat and listened to the rest of the lecture. Then she put the books into her backpack and put it on her shoulder and struck out across the campus to find Nieman and Freddy.

Nieman and Freddy were at their designated table at Aranga's waiting for her. "I may sell Clara too," Freddy was saying. "Now that he knows where we are. Of course, Nora Jane always told him they might not be his. The whole time she was pregnant she told him that. Isn't that just like her, the darling. Of course the thing is he's AB positive and so am I and so are both of them. It's such a bizarre coincidence."

"Is he bright enough to remember all that and call it into play? I thought he drank."

"Well, obviously he doesn't anymore for what it's worth. He's bright, Nieman. Lydia tests at 130. Just because she's not as smart as Tammili. Of course, psychopathic personalities are never dumb. That's been proven." Freddy played with his coffee cup. "I hope she's all right. Where is she? She got out at eleven."

"It's ten after eleven. Maybe you should prepare to buy him off. I hate to keep bringing this up, but you could just offer him money."

"Solicit blackmail? So we can spend the rest of our days wondering when he'll show up wanting more? It's frightening, Nieman. We can't know what he's thinking. What he's up to."

IV

"I don't know why that woman who saved him never came back to get the present," Claudine was saying. They had stopped at San Jose to get lunch and were still on the road. Claudine was driving and Sandy was watching Zandia and manning the CD player. "Two ounces of Joy I bought her. I wish I'd just taken it home with me. I thought she was rude, didn't you? I keep thinking they think I'll sue for letting him fall in. I keep reading fear of lawsuits, don't you? Did you see the way they beat it out of there?"

"I told you, I used to know her. Maybe there's something she doesn't want her husband to know that she thinks I'll tell him."

"She had a bad reputation, huh?"

"I didn't really know her. She just went to our church. Well, that's over, baby. You're right about one thing. If your mother wants to see the kid she can come and visit us."

"If she ever saw our condo maybe she'd buy me a bigger one. She's got tons of money but her shrink tells her not to give it to me. I hate his guts, the son-of-a-bitch."

"Think about something good. You're making wrinkles, baby, worrying about things like that. We've got plenty going on. I hope that deal down in Mexico works out. We could have a lot of fun living down there for a while. I love it down there. The more I think about it, the more I think it's a breakthrough script for you."

"Sandy, Sandy, Sandy," Zandia yelled from the car seat. "Sandy, Sandy, Sandy."

"He's crazy about you," Claudine said. "I think he likes you better than he does me."

Later that afternoon, while Claudine was at the store, Sandy found a piece of stationery and wrote a letter to Nora Jane.

Dear N.J.,

It was really good to see you looking so happy. Your husband looks like a nice guy. You shouldn't have run off like that. I saw you leave. I thought, there she goes. She always did think she was invisible when she had her head in the sand.

Don't worry about me, baby. I'm glad you got a life. I got one too. We're doing a film in Mexico as soon as we finish this one.

Thanks for saving Zandia. I really like this kid even if I do wish sometimes the little helicopter blade on his hat would fly him off to cloud land for a couple of weeks. Around here we call him IN YOUR FACE.

Take care of yourself. Love always,
                                          Sandy

He carried the letter around for a couple of days, then he tore it up.

Freddy Harwood called his old friend Jody Wattes, who had given up a profitable law practice to be a private investigator, and asked him to put a tail on Sandy. Then he and Nora Jane and Tammili and Lydia moved back into their house while they waited for the new one to be renovated.

"I still don't know why we went over to Grandmother's to begin with," Tammili was saying. "Or why all of a sudden we have to have a house on the beach. It's because the neighborhood is anti-Semitic, isn't it? You just don't want us to know. I don't think people should move because of things like that. So is that what's going on?"

"No, it is not." Nora Jane was doing all the lying on this

matter. Not that she was good at it, but she was better than Freddy was. "I have always wanted a house on the beach. I never really liked this house. This house is pure nineteen seventy. I want to look out a window and see you playing on a beach. If we are going to live near an ocean, we might as well live on it."

"We want room to grow and change," Freddy added. "We might want some foreign exchange students. More dogs. Anything can happen. Besides, think how happy it is making Grandmother Ann."

"I'll have to get up at six in the morning to get to school."

"Maybe you'll want to change schools in the next few years. We'll go and look at some. You might want to go to a different school that's closer."

"You aren't telling me." Tammili stood with her hands on her hips.

"We're evolving," Freddy said. "Rilke said, You must change your life. Are you afraid to live in a different house, Tammili?"

"No. I just want to know what's going on. You all are up to something and I want to know what it is. Grandmother's getting married to that guy, isn't she? Is that it?"

"I doubt it," Freddy answered. "It wouldn't be like her to get married."

Nora Jane went to her daughter and put her arm around her shoulders. "Your college student mother is going to write a report on the new cave they found in France. Come help me pull up the data on the computer. Will you do that?"

"They told us about it." Tammili got excited. "They showed us a picture of the paintings. There was a herd of animals so good no one could paint it any better. I almost fainted. They showed it to us today in art class. You had that too? They talked about it in college?"

"Uncle Nieman knows about it." Lydia had come into the room from the shadow of the door where she had been listening. "Uncle Nieman's been inside the one at Lascaux. He's one of the few people in America who ever got to see it."

"It was a religion." Tammili took her mother's hand, began to lead her in the direction of the room with the computer. "They weren't very big or they couldn't have fit through the crawl spaces. I bet they weren't any bigger than Lydia and me. I can't believe you guys are going to college. It's amazing. Come on. I know exactly where to find it. It was all in the newspapers a while ago. Uncle Nieman made me copies of the stories. I've got them in my room somewhere."

Lydia and Tammili and Nora Jane disappeared in the direction of the computer and Freddy walked out onto the patio and looked up at the stars and started making deals. Just keep them safe, he offered. That's all. Name your price. I'm ready. Don't I always keep my word? Have I ever let you down?

Going to live on the beach, his father answered. Well, that's all right until the big storms come.

What's it like up there? Freddy asked.

I don't know, his father answered. I'm too busy watching you to care.

On the Problem of
Turbulence

*"Where were we ten years ago, that's what I have to remember," Nora
Jane Harwood said to herself many times during those terrible days
of April.*

*"'Natural flowing shapes,'" Nieman Gluuk consoled himself by
musing. "'Great rivers meander in wide curves to the sea. In the sea
itself the Gulf Stream meanders, making loops, swinging east and
west. Great rivers of warm and cold water fight in the sea.' As Schwenk
says, 'the flow wants to realize itself regardless of the surrounding
material.' You cannot fight these powers. But it does not mean we're
doomed. We could learn to ride on the waves as surfers. . . ."*

*"Chaos," Freddy Harwood said to them both, wiping his glasses
on his sweater, then pushing them back onto his face. "Toni Morrison's
house burns down weeks after she wins the Nobel, children are
bombed and starved, Mother goes out with that fool, sects surround
us, so dark and so many, we cannot even discern the enemy. The enemy
is everywhere and is still what it was three thousand years ago.
Ignorance reigns, is fed and breeds. . . . 'The best lack all conviction
while the worst are full of passionate intensity.' Yeats."*

*"Don't wear yellow when I wear yellow," Tammili said to her twin
sister, Lydia. "You always copy me."*

"I didn't see you wearing yellow," Lydia lied. "I was in the other room. It's a coincidence."

"Stop talking like Nieman. You just try to use the words he gives us."

"Well, so what? That's what they're for. Dad said so. He said any word you use belongs to you. I'm not afraid to say coincidence out loud."

Nine-fifteen in the morning. April one, nineteen hundred and ninety-five.

Freddy Harwood sat at his desk in his office at Clara Books and thought about the past. The great days of Berkeley were over and there were those who said they would never come again. Freddy harbored a secret hope that they would come again. They might ride in on a revival of artistic freedom, a cure for AIDS might do the trick, one great stage play, new musical forms, a poet who could break the heart and make the soul sing.

There had been the Stephen Mitchell translations of Rilke, that had seemed a breakthrough, the Danish novels of Peter Hoeg, Kilain Alter's biography of Francis Alter. Other sightings. All was not lost.

Freddy got up from his desk and wandered down into the pre-opening activity of the bookstore. He had dropped his daughters off at school, then gone to the store to begin sorting invoices for the spring books. It was a task he never minded doing. It was what he was doing the night Nora Jane walked into his life. My Nora, he thought, my life, my hope, my meaning. Freddy Harwood adored his wife and children. He loved them in a manner that seems old-fashioned in a cynical world. He lived to serve and protect them. Each act of his day was measured against his concern for their happiness and well-being. In his soul Freddy believed other men felt the same way about their families. He could no longer tolerate the knowledge of cruelty. Stories of wife and child abuse affected him so deeply he had stopped reading newspapers. His secretary, Frances, read them for him and told him what they said.

"I read books," he defended himself by saying. "Sooner or later anything worth reading will make it into a book."

The books that were on his desk at the moment included two translations of the *Paradiso,* one by Mark Musa and one by Charles Singleton, *Fima,* by Amos Oz, *United States,* by Gore Vidal, a book of essays by Robert Penn Warren, and the *Selected Letters of Philip Larkin.*

Freddy Harwood had always been a sweet man. Now, in his forties, he had become a saint. Wise men and women sought him out. On any Saturday night his living room was filled with the best minds who lived in or passed through the Berkeley area. Last week it had been Abraham Pais and his son. Tonight it would be the great editor Sebranek Conrad and his companion, the novelist Adrien Searle. Nora Jane was a big fan of Ms. Searle's writings and had been up all night the night before rereading her books.

Freddy's secretary, Frances, cornered him by a stack of cookbooks. "It's ridiculous to have a reading at noon," she said. "We've tried this before and no one came. I had an appointment at the doctor but I canceled it."

"They'll turn out. Her fans are loyal. Sebranek called last night and said they'd be here about eleven to sign stock. Do you have the reading space set up?"

"Yes. Well, he's the grand old man of publishing now. I want to thank him for not selling out. He's never put his imprint on a book he was ashamed of publishing."

"Now I'm worried no one will come. Go in the office, Frances, and call the list of poets and some of Mother's friends. Do it now."

"There're seventy pre-orders. It'll be fine. We always think no one is coming."

"Someday no one will. This is an idea that has outlived its time. It's turned into souvenir collecting. Well, let's make it as painless for Ms. Searle as possible." He began to straighten the books on a sale table. He set aside some hardback copies of *Brazzaville Beach.* "Put these by the cash register with the new books. People should read this book."

"There's no more room."

"Make room."

In their crazy outgrown glass and timber house overlooking the
bay, Nora Jane was walking around the living room listening to
an Italian grammar tape and picking up things the twins had
left behind. There was a lunch box with a peanut butter sandwich untouched in its plastic bag. There was a fuchsia scarf
Lydia was currently tying around her ponytail. There was a
Barbie doll dressed for scuba diving, a plate of nachos, a copy
of *Little House on the Prairie* with UGH written on the cover by
Tammili. The UGH had been marked out with a red Magic
Marker. Under it Lydia had written EXCELLENT.

Nora Jane gathered all the things into a wicker basket and
carried it to the kitchen and then went into her room to dress
for the day. She was missing two classes at Berkeley today and
she was keeping a crazy, scary secret.

After ten years of never getting pregnant again and wanting
to, she was three days late. Drugstore test kits had confirmed it.
I can't tell him until I know for sure, she decided. I can't even
mention this unless it's certain. He would go crazy. I don't even
want to bring it up. He won't notice. He's involved with Sebranek's coming and Ms. Searle.

She looked at herself in the mirror. Put her hand to her
mouth. Began to chew on her fingers. Then she left the mirror
and began to run water into the tub. Then she began to sing.

A passerby might have thought a great diva was in the
tub as the opening notes of "Quando m'en vo'soletta" began to
fill the room. When Nora Jane sang to herself she was always
alone with her grandmother Lydia, in the long hot days of
summer, in New Orleans, Louisiana, in the part of her childhood that she treasured and could bear to remember. Mirlitons
were growing on the fence behind her grandmother's house. A
morning glory vine twined around the pillars of the porch. It
was fragrant and divine and her grandmother Lydia there beside her to save her from her mother and all the other evils of
the world.

*   *   *

Nora Jane stepped into the tub of hot water and sank down below the waves. Don't think about New Orleans, she told herself. The past is a swamp. Adrien Searle is coming to the store and we get to take her out to lunch. Not to mention telling Freddy about this baby.

Nora Jane sank back into the waves. She was in her first semester at college so the timing would be the way things usually end up happening. The minute you forget about wanting something it shows up.

I have to be careful telling Freddy. If he acts too happy it might make the girls jealous. I don't want them jealous of some little baby before it's even born. What if it was a little boy as crazy as Freddy? Or as handsome as my father. She shook her head and got out of the tub and started drying herself.

Well, I have to tell him today. I have to stop being so secretive about things. I'm as bad as I was when I was young.

She went into the bedroom and pulled on a pair of slacks and a blue and white striped polo shirt. She ran a comb through her hair, found her car keys, and ran. She pulled out of the garage in her little red Miata and headed toward the expressway. I should eat something, she decided. You can't go around skipping breakfast when you're pregnant. She pulled off the highway at McDonald's and ordered a sausage biscuit and a cup of orange juice and ate them as she drove. It was ten-thirty. If she hurried she would have time to tell him before the reading.

He's so crazy, she decided. It's absurd to like your husband as much as I like him. But I wish he wouldn't worry about things. He'll find a way to worry about this pregnancy. He'll read about a hundred books. He'll probably sign us up for some of those dopey parenting courses. Well, I'm not going.

She found a parking place behind the store and went in the back and found Freddy by the cash register, rearranging books.

"Thanks for coming down early. How are you?" He smiled his dazzling smile.

"I have to talk to you right away. Come in the office."

"Oh, God, is it something about the girls?"

"No. It's something good. At least I think it's good. Come on. Hurry up." She took his arm and led him up the stairs to his office. She shut the door and stood holding it. "I'm pregnant," she said. "I'm pretty sure. I did two drugstore tests. I think it's true. I'm pretty sure."

"Oh, God, my darling one." He went to her and took her in his arms. Then he began to cry. Laughing and crying.

"Don't you dare cry. Oh, God, I knew this was going to happen. That's why I didn't tell you last night."

"You knew this last night and you didn't tell me?"

"I wanted to wait one more day. And do a second test."

"I knew this. I dreamed it last night. I had this little boy and I was holding his hand. We were in a valley. At the foot of some mountains."

"You did not. You did not dream this. And we don't know if it's a girl or a boy." Now she was laughing too. They were leaning on Freddy's desk, laughing as if they knew the funniest thing in the world.

Sebranek Conrad had become a great man, almost by accident. He had not sought out greatness. He had just been a scrawny hardworking kid from upstate New York who had dreamed of going into publishing. His neighbor in the village of Rhinebeck, New York, was a publisher, a man whose family owned a publishing house in Boston. When Sebranek was a teenager he had done odd jobs for this man in the summers. He had chopped wood, cleaned barns, groomed horses, planted trees, mended fences, always side by side with the talkative Irishman. Often, as he grew older, the man would have him to the house to meet visiting authors. Sometimes the authors would work by their side. Hemingway had come to the farm and John Fowles had been a visitor one summer. Sebranek had grown up knowing writers and was fascinated by the world they inhabited.

He had worked his way through Yale and done well there, graduating magna cum laude and with other honors. Afterward he had gone to work for a publishing house in New York owned by one of the men he had met on his mentor's farm. By the time he was forty he was a senior editor. By the time he was fifty he was editor in chief.

"I was lucky to be there in those years," he was fond of saying.

"At the end of publishing as we knew it. I was there and I'm still there and will be to the end. Adrien and I are holding on very well, thank you."

He looked across the room at the sleeping body of his lady love, the feared feminist writer Adrien Searle. She was sleeping on her side, curled up like a child. She could sleep anywhere. She never woke at dawn to worry about the day. She lay down beside him and did not stir for eight or nine or ten hours. This fascinated Sebranek and he envied it. When they were younger he would sometimes wake her in the middle of the night and ask her what time it was. She would answer to within a minute of the time and go immediately back to sleep.

"We should be married," he said to himself. "She should give in on that. At least she could have my insurance and my social security." He rubbed his eye with his hand, straightened out a kink in his neck, felt his glasses bearing down on the bridge of his nose. Sixty-four was all right but not as good for traveling as it once had been. Well, she had wanted him along and he had come. *Mission,* her new book was called, and she swore it was her last.

He walked across the room and sat down on the edge of the bed. "We need to get up now," he said. He lay down beside her. He began to caress her arms and breasts. Kissed her soft hair. She woke and started giggling. "You're too old for this," she said. "I know I'm too old for it. Take your clothes off, please. Just this once more and then I'm giving this up forever. Hurry up, it's your absolute last chance to make love to me."

Later, while they were dressing, she brought up the thing they didn't want to talk about. "Do you think Johnnie will come?"

"No."

"Do you think he will even call?"

"It's been in the papers and I had my secretary call and tell him we were here. He knows where we are. He would have called the hotel if he wanted to see us."

"Why didn't you call him yourself?"

"I tried to. He doesn't have a phone. You have to leave messages at some service. He doesn't talk to me on the phone. You know that. If he contacts me at all it's an undated note with no address. He's in full retreat, Adrien. There's nothing I can do."

"Well, this is his territory now. In a way we're invading his territory."

"Ungrateful sons who don't speak to me don't have territory as far as I'm concerned."

"At least he stopped taking drugs."

"We assume he stopped. Don't worry about Johnnie, Adrien. Worry about your poor old starving editor. I need to eat breakfast before I face this crowd."

"Do you think there will be a crowd?"

"Of course there will be. Your fans love you. Well, come along. You look fine. I'm starving. Let's leave this room."

They had a quick breakfast in the hotel cafe, then a car came to pick them up and delivered them at two minutes past eleven to Clara Books. Sebranek took Adrien's arm and they walked into a sea of admiring fans. Adrien was wearing a yellow sweater and gold earrings. Her hair was a riot of dark gold curls. Her smile was honest, her courtesy unfailing. "Thank you for coming here," she was saying. "I'm so pleased to be here. So pleased to get to know you."

Sebranek left her to her fans and joined Freddy by the front cash register. They were old compadres of several battles. When Sebranek first published Salman Rushdie, Freddy had been the only bookstore in Berkeley to display the books in his front window. Clara had been bombed in retaliation for that. Freddy had rebuilt the front windows and put the books back in them. The store had been bombed on Wednesday. By Saturday afternoon the windows were repaired and the Rushdie books were in both of them.

"How's the book tour?" Freddy asked. "Are you sorry you started this?"

"It's only three cities. I'm enjoying myself. It's a revelation, to tell the truth. More publishers should go to bookstores. Maybe I'll start accompanying all my authors."

A line had formed of people trying to get into the room

where Adrien was going to read. Freddy and Sebranek watched the people for a while, stopping every now and then to talk to someone who came their way. There was only one front entrance. Neither of them saw Johnnie come in. He was a familiar figure to Freddy. Just because he was in full retreat from his family didn't mean he had stopped reading books.

Adrien read the first twenty pages of her book. Then the audience asked her questions. They were hesitant, silly questions at first, but, as she seemed to give of herself with good humor, the questions became more serious.

Johnnie walked around the edge of the crowd. He was wearing a coarse beige jacket and a pair of shorts. His hair was cut as short as a Marine recruit's. He had a backpack full of books over one arm. He was taller than Sebranek and handsomer. He looked like Northern California. He looked like Northern California had been invented for him.

"Are you reading any contemporary poets?" he asked Adrien when she recognized him and pointed his way. "Is there anyone new you can tell us about?"

"I should ask you to tell me," she answered. "I don't haunt bookstores as I used to. I used to ferret out writers, find poems. I was looking for them, I was on the prowl for writing and now I am like a domesticated wolf. I eat and sleep and write and watch movies and stay home and wait for things to come to me. Perhaps I'll spend the afternoon searching this bookstore and the next time someone asks me that I'll have a better answer."

"Have you read Michael Atkinson?" a young girl asked. Then the audience joined in and began to tell each other about poets. Sebranek saw his chance and went to his son and embraced him. "Thanks for coming," he said. "I don't know if you got any of the messages."

"I can't stay long. I just came by to say hello. I have a meeting in an hour that I can't miss. I'm involved in something I want to talk to you about soon, Dad. I can't talk about it yet. But I may need your help with it soon." Johnnie moved back into the children's section. His father followed, reaching for his billfold, taking out money.

"Stay and have lunch with us. It's just Freddy and Adrien and myself. Or perhaps we can see you later."

"Don't give me that. I don't want money." Sebranek was pushing a hundred-dollar bill into Johnnie's pocket. "Don't do that, Dad. I'm a grown man."

"I want to give you something. I want to do something. I don't want this rift between us. Your mother and I are on good terms. Why can't you and I be? We need to spend some time together. I'm coming back out here in July. We could go to the Oregon coast or climb a mountain. Will you think about it?"

"Sure. I have to leave now, Dad. I really have to be somewhere in half an hour. I want to talk to you. I'll call you next week when you get back." Johnnie was moving toward the door, still facing his father. Behind them the crowd had surrounded Adrien and she was signing books.

"What are you doing? Are you working? What's going on?"

"No time now, I'll tell you later. When I get it squared away. It's still in limbo. Well, you look great, Dad. So does Adrien. I'll buy the book when I have time and read it." He stopped and allowed Sebranek to embrace him, then he was gone, out the turnstile and onto Telegraph Avenue, and his father followed him and watched him down the street. His youngest son, tall, proud, arrogant, who had once been a sickly, asthmatic child coughing his way around the streets of Brooklyn. It was easy to see how the transformation had occurred. The same hard will had driven the child that seemed to drive the man. We don't know them when they are grown, Sebranek told himself. They go off and become a mystery to us. If they would let us in we would not understand what we were seeing. "For their souls dwell in the house of tomorrow, which you cannot visit, not even in your dreams." *The Prophet.* We cannot walk in their shoes nor save them from sorrow. Parallel worlds, enigmas. So be it.

Johnnie caught a streetcar and took it to the last stop. He got off and walked the next two miles to an abandoned warehouse where he and four other young people had made an after-school hangout for deserted and homeless kids. He threw his book bag into a corner and dragged the ladder out onto the floor and began to put a new net on the basketball goal. He had stopped on his way to the streetcar and bought it with the hundred-dollar bill Sebranek had stuffed in his pocket. The rest he had spent on parts for the stove. "I'll fix that stove as soon as I finish here," he told the redheaded girl who stood with her hands on her hips watching him. "You'll be baking cookies by the time school is out."

"So did you see your dad?"

"Yep. He bought this net. What did you find out about the lease?"

"He'll extend it if we repair the bathroom. It's going to cost six or seven hundred dollars to do that. Connie said she'll put in five hundred from her dividend check but that won't pay for all of it. I'll get a job if I have to."

"You have a job." Johnnie took off his jacket. He reached in the pockets reflexively. There were three more hundred-dollar bills folded together. "That son-of-a-bitch," he said. "That god-damn controlling bastard."

When the last book was signed and the last fan listened to, Nora Jane drove Sebranek and Adrien to Chez Panisse. Freddy was following in his car. "He doesn't like to wait at Chez Panisse," Nora Jane explained. "He has this thing with them that's been going on for years. He can't believe they won't give him a table when they say they're going to. But he loves the food so much he has to eat there. It's better if he comes after we get a table. It's so volatile between him and the maître d'. Well, they have these goat cheese pastries that are worth any wait."

"I've been there," Adrien said. "I used to stay in Berkeley in the fall. I had some friends who lived here."

They were in Nora Jane's convertible. Sebranek was in the front seat. Adrien was squeezed into the back. She picked up a book from the floor. It was *Little House in the Big Woods*. "Is this good? I've never read these books."

"Lydia loves them and Tammili hates them. They're fraternal twins, you know. Do you know about them? Our daughters?"

"I heard that Freddy delivered them in a house in the woods under terrible circumstances and a helicopter came and there was a big rescue and everyone lived. That's Sebranek's version."

"That's it. Then we got married and here we are. Well, Freddy hates the story now. He thinks the girls will hear it when they grow up and think they were in danger because we were counterculture people or something. One minute he's so liberal and the next he's as conservative as the pope."

"Sebranek does that." Adrien laughed.

"Every six months I beg her to marry me in a church."

"Why don't you do it?"

"I don't know why we don't. Maybe I think it would end up in *People* magazine. My love turned into a *People* anecdote."

Nora Jane swerved to avoid a truck, then swerved back to the center. "Don't worry about a thing," she said. "I've never had a wreck in my life." She turned into the street of the restaurant, drove smartly down three blocks, expertly backed into a parking place, and turned off the motor.

They went into the restaurant and settled down to wait in a rattan-furnished lounge. Its windows looked out upon a garden and a street. The smells from the kitchen were subtle, rich, pungent, clean. Light fell down through the shuttered windows and the skylights. Palm fronds moved in the breeze from the air-conditioning vents. "Freddy said you bought Salman Rushdie's apartment in New York," Nora Jane said. "That's so brave of you. I'd like to know about it if it's something you can talk about."

"We benefited from that, not him." Sebranek put his arm around the back of the wicker love seat, uncrossed his legs. "It's a dream apartment, overlooking Central Park. Something I'd never have been able to afford. I had trouble adjusting to that part of town at first, but Adrien loves it. She likes grandeur."

"It's a mixed blessing." Adrien smiled at her. "I feel like we're at ground zero in that place. It's beautiful and comfortable but sometimes it seems we really aren't in New York City. It's the Middle East, in the heart of feuds so ancient and bloody that anything which touches them is spoiled. Too many dead on both sides. Husbands, fathers, brothers, sisters, mothers. I had it redecorated, the old wallpaper removed, floors redone. Still, it's the place where Salman lived. Nothing changes that."

"I couldn't read his books." Nora Jane sighed, her old Southern politeness making her cautious. "I think they're boring and overwritten, or just plain silly. It's terrible that they want to kill him, but if they'd left him alone no one would have read the books. Well, that's just my opinion."

"I wonder what he thinks of his own writings. I don't suppose he has much objectivity. Not that any writer has much."

"Salman is a line drawn in the sand." Sebranek spread his hands on his knees. "I'm going to talk about him at a conference of newspaper editors next week. He's having a hell of a life. They made their point with him, that's for sure. They have killed two of his translators."

"This has made a battlefield of literature," Adrien added.

"Free speech is always a battlefield. Always was, always will be. I wish Freddy was here. I want to talk to him about this while I have it on my mind."

"What do you do, Nora Jane?" Adrien asked. "Do you help Freddy with the store?"

"I've gone back to school to get a degree. I was going to study sociology but I think I'll go on and be in the music department instead. My grandmother was a diva. I took lessons when I was young from a man in New Orleans who was really good. I just never have liked to sing in public. So I decided it was all right to go on and study it for myself. Anyway, I just found out I'm pregnant, so that changes things. We didn't plan it. I guess you think we're crazy, having children in this crowded world. Anyway, we're having it."

"No one should be without their art." Adrien reached over and touched Nora Jane's hand. "Being pregnant shouldn't interfere with music in any way. It might make your voice better. I have a friend in San Francisco who is one of the greatest teachers in the world. She taught Kathleen Battle. She lives out here because she makes money coaching people for the movies. Delaney Hawk is her name. Have you heard of her? If you could pay her, she would teach you."

"God, yes. Everyone knows about her."

"Your speaking voice is lovely. I can imagine how well you might sing. I was telling Sebranek a while ago that your voice was wonderful, wasn't I, my darling?"

"She was indeed. She's mad for accents and voices."

"I'd love to meet Mrs. Hawk. Would you take me there?"

"We'll go tomorrow. I need to see her myself. I'll call her this afternoon."

The maître d' came to take them to a table. As they were being seated, Freddy joined them, carrying more books for Adrien to sign and a box wrapped in white satin paper and tied with a velvet ribbon. "We found these books in my office. I forgot to give them to Frances. Would you mind signing five more for us?" He handed the books to Adrien, then pulled out a chair next to Nora Jane and handed her the package.

"You just didn't want to wait for a table." She took the package and laid it beside her napkin. "What is this? Where did you get a present for me so fast?"

"It was for your birthday. Now it's for the baby. Please open it."

She removed the ribbon and the paper. Inside was a velvet case. Inside the case was a diamond bracelet. Twenty small perfect diamonds in gold links. "Oh, my God," she said. "Freddy, take this back. I don't have any use for this. Where would I wear something like this?"

"They were Grandmother's. All I paid for was the setting. If you don't want it, save it for the girls."

"Of course she wants it." Adrien picked up the bracelet and held it out. "Let me put it on your arm. Diamonds and babies, a cause for celebration. Order some wine, Sebranek. It's a finite world. Let's celebrate this day."

Sebranek signaled a waiter. "I wish Johnnie could have stayed to be with us. He looked fine, didn't you think so? His mother is the passive-aggressive resentment queen of the East Coast," he said to Freddy. "It's driven him to extremes."

"Good wombs have borne bad sons, and vice versa." Adrien touched his arm.

"Don't say that in front of me." Nora Jane laughed. "What if I was carrying a bad one."

"Johnnie isn't bad," Sebranek said. "He's just confused and can't decide what to do with his life. I don't know what he's doing for a living. I guess his mother sends him money. He's always been able to manipulate her. Well, what can I do but love him and wait?"

"You can't fix their lives for them. I wrote a piece for *Elle* last year about parenting grown children. I learned something from writing it. I had a great mother. She liked being a mother and she was healthy and protective. A psychiatrist told me a lovely thing. She said a great mother produces an irrational sense of security in a child. I'm irrationally secure. That's why I can do such an insecure thing for a living. Once I wrote three mediocre, almost bad, books in a row and still I kept on believing I was a good writer."

"They weren't bad." Sebranek laughed. "I liked them enough to publish them, before I fell in love with her."

"You were probably always in love with her," Freddy added, and they all laughed at that. "I was in love with her for weeks when I read *Dark Winter.*"

Nora Jane was quiet, thinking of her own drunken mother, her lonely nights, her dirty house. Nothing like that will ever happen to my children, she thought grimly. I guess I better quit school. I can't do that with this baby coming. I can read books. I don't have to go to college to be happy.

"Nora Jane is the best mother in the world," Freddy said. "She's stood in there and learned and been firm and sweet at the same time. If I'd had her I'd probably be the president by now. Our girls aren't perfect but they do well in school and they're happy, I think."

"They're ten years old," Nora Jane added. "They are so funny. They like being twins but then they have spells of not wanting anyone to know it. Lydia is the one who likes the twin thing. Tammili, who is like Freddy, is always straining against it. They're wonderful to have. We like them a lot."

The waiter brought wine and food. They ate and drank. The conversation moved on to lighter subjects. When they parted, Adrien and Nora Jane made plans to go the next afternoon to pay a call on Delaney Hawk. "You will profit from knowing her whether she accepts you as a student or not," Adrien said. "She adores money and probably won't be able to turn down a student who is sure to pay. I have a premonition about your meeting her. Something portentous in the wind."

"You aren't coming to dinner tonight?" Freddy asked. "My friend Nieman is dying to meet you."

"I promised her the ballet," Sebranek answered. "I do anything for my authors, didn't you know?"

II

The Muslim fundamentalist sect to which Navin Backer belonged was not closely aligned with the group that blew up the World Trade Center but it was sympathetic to it. The old sheikh who was standing trial in New York City was a sentimental favorite with the young men who came each day to the house on Telegraph Avenue and sat around drinking coffee, watching television and reading Iraqi newspapers brought in on the daily planes from Paris and Madrid. The papers were brought in by a service that also supplied them with money and explosive devices.

Navin was in a dark mood. His number two wife was sulky and after three years had not produced a child and his number one wife had become so fat she no longer interested him. He wanted to go home to Baghdad and get new wives and walk along streets where men and women did not view him with disdain. He had been in a dark mood all spring. Now his mood had turned vicious.

"He needs something to do to take his mind off his wives," his mentor, Amir Haven, told his second in command. "We must send him to blow up an airplane or a boat. Is there nothing for young Navin to make him bloom?"

Both men laughed. "Why not two airplanes, perhaps the whole airport, anything to get his mind off women," the second in command jokingly suggested.

"Here is an interesting thing in the newspaper. This Sebranek

Conrad. Isn't he on the list? I've heard him mentioned. Is he the one who is going to publish the books of the whore?"

"Let me see." Amir took up the paper and read the short piece in the Book Talk section. Then he went to his desk and rummaged through his papers and found the name. "What is the bookstore named?"

"Clara."

"We bombed it ten years ago when the heretic published the book he hasn't been punished for yet. Yes, that might interest Navin. We could send him to demonstrate or throw a brick through the window. Something useful but not too daring. Dangerous but not important enough to call attention to us at this time. Bring him in here. Let me talk to him."

Amir sat back in his chair. He had no interest in taking foolish chances, but still, this might be useful in several ways. He considered the idea. A book publisher was not high profile with the general public but it scared an influential group. It was always difficult to decide who to target. A hit should send out waves, like a pebble dropped into a pond. It should be unexpected, fresh, but with the message clear. This might do to remind people they were there, that men of God would not tolerate the insults the godless heaped upon them. Also, it would keep the young men busy. Their lives were not good in the United States. They were spat upon in the eyes of the women. He had felt it himself. Felt his sexual organs shrink at their piggish soft-faced looks, their contemptuous gazes. The community was not organized. They were spread around the city, some in disguise as teachers and Christians, others working at menial jobs. The women were affected also. At first they were frightened by the supermarkets and automobiles, then you could almost hear it happening, as their curiosity began to overpower their modesty and training. This was all a bad thing, this being in America, even if it did ensure a heavenly reward. But I do not always believe that Allah cares, Amir thought. I am not sure Allah exists in this land. Perhaps he cannot see through the smoke that drifts above their houses. Perhaps he is too offended by their ways to turn his head in this direction. Allah be praised. Forgive a humble servant.

Navin came into the room and made obeisance. Then he stood against the wall. Navin didn't like to sit in chairs. Even in America he liked to pretend he was on the desert. He confronted the universe at every moment. He imagined wind and sand in his face.

"I think we will remind them that we are watching," Amir said, spreading the newspaper out on the desk. Pointing to the article. "All the Jews are not in Israel."

"As Allah knows."

"Would you like to be the messenger?"

"If I am needed. The list of enemies is long."

"For now we will not make it shorter but we will frighten them perhaps. Would you like to leave a message for this man?" Navin moved across the room, looked down at the newspaper. "A small explosion in a bookstore window perhaps," Amir continued. "A hotel room in disarray. What do you see happening?"

"Give me a driver. I will disturb their peace before they leave the city."

"Allah is pleased."

"Allah is Allah. I am unworthy to say his name."

After lunch Freddy went back to the store and Nora Jane returned home and sat on the steps waiting for the twins. She was trying to decide how to tell them about the baby. She stretched her legs out in front of her. The sun beat down and bounced off the stone and warmed and soothed her. They are so different, she was thinking, remembering the girls leaving for school that morning, dressed as though they were continents apart. Lydia in tomboy clothes and tennis shoes, Tammili in a serious jumper and starched white blouse.

A station wagon pulled into the driveway and the girls got out. Lydia dragging a pink backpack behind her. Tammili with her pack sitting squarely on her shoulders.

"I'm going to meet a singing teacher tomorrow," Nora Jane said, when they were near enough to hear.

"Then you'll go on the stage and we'll never see you again."

Lydia abandoned her backpack altogether and went to her mother and cuddled up beside her on the stairs.

"That's good," Tammili said. "That's good, Mother. That would be good for you."

"What did you do in school?"

"We had a Spanish festival with this stupid piñata. I'm about sick of this multicultural stuff. Miss Armand had on this long skirt. All we do is waste time. I'll never get into Harvard going to Country Day. If you don't get me in a better school, I'm going to quit and just stay home."

"She asked Miss Armand if she could go to the library while they had the festival." Lydia looked at her mother and raised her eyes as if to say, Only you and I know what this means.

"And did they let you, Tammili?"

"Part of the time they did. They made me stay for the songs. But at least I didn't have to waste my time on the stupid piñata. I'm going to tell Uncle Nieman about it. He thinks it's hilarious the stuff they do." Tammili carefully removed her backpack and got out three papers with A's on them and handed them over. "I got the highest grade in the class in math."

"You always do," Lydia added. "So what?"

Uncle Nieman was their godfather, and he took his godfathering seriously. He saw them at least twice a week, to check, he said, on their spiritual progress, by which he meant what they were reading and what movies they were seeing. He had given them leather-bound editions of the Harvard Classics for their eighth birthday and also kept them supplied with videos he thought suitable. Not only did he buy them books and films, he lectured them on the things he bought. At the moment they were study-ing *Green Mansions*, which he read aloud to them when he came to dinner on Friday nights.

When the girls had eaten a snack and gone off on their bikes, Nora Jane went into the music room and opened the piano and began to play. She lifted her head and began to practice scales. Her voice had lost nothing in the years she had ignored it. If anything it was even sweeter and clearer, with a range that was almost unearthly at times. Since she had never strained it or challenged it, it was still a young voice, as natural and beautiful as a bird's song. It was the one thing she had always kept to herself. She had never let anyone persuade her to use her voice for anything except the joy of singing when she felt like singing. My voice is not for sale, she had always said to herself, even in the darkest moments of her life. It's my voice and no one can hear it unless I want them to.

Now, suddenly, at age thirty, Nora Jane was getting excited about meeting this teacher. I might really be excited about the baby, she tried to tell herself, but she knew it wasn't so. No, the baby is just there. This is because the great feminist writer Adrien Searle is coming to get me and take me to meet Delaney Hawk. Maybe I'll audition for her. Maybe she knew about Grandmother. I bet she knew of her.

What if I really started singing, she was thinking. I would have a concert one day and Freddy and Lydia and Tammili would come and be surprised. They'd say, I don't believe that's our mother.

Navin dressed in blue jeans and a white shirt. He put on a baseball cap to hide his black curls and then added a tweed jacket someone had found for him in a secondhand clothing store. He changed into the new basketball shoes. He put on his flesh-colored gloves. He picked up a knife and held it for a second, then slipped it into his jacket pocket. A small revolver was already taped to his ribs. The marble-sized smoke bombs and explosive devices were in his sleeves. "I will leave the message in the hotel room," he had told Amir. "The closer to home, the more it frightens them. The knife is for the clothes, he told himself, looking into the mirror. Unless better meat presents itself. Amir is too cautious. He has become soft from his time here. He thinks they have power to stop us. He is a bad leader. Then I must lead myself, with Allah's blessing. I must assure my path to heaven, or else perhaps I will be sent home soon. It is in your hands, blessed one, guide me. I am a faithful servant if you show the way.

He went outside and waited for the car to pull up to the curb. A young man named Ali Fava was in the driver's seat. They embraced, then sat back and were quiet. Ali Fava drove him to the Paris Hotel. He got out of the car and went into the hotel through the adjoining coffee shop. He nodded to the man at the desk but did not stop to speak. He got into the elevator and went up to the second floor and found the door to the room and disabled the latch with a wire and let himself into the double room. It was all so quick, so perfect, that if Sebranek and Adrien had been standing by the door they would not have heard it or been able to stop it.

Adrien was in the bathroom. She was dressed and was putting on powder and lipstick. She had meant to spend a long time on her makeup but had been caught up on the phone with an editor at *Harper's Bazaar* and thought she was running out of time. She wanted to talk to Delaney once more before she brought Nora Jane out there. She wanted to stress the importance of not scaring the young woman. Delaney sometimes terrified the young. "She's a special young woman, I will say. From a wealthy and powerful family. Even you need connections, Delaney. So give her a chance. For the sake of our friendship. I've never asked a favor of you, have I?" Adrien practiced the speech, then chided herself for preparing a speech to give to a friend. "Nonsense," she concluded. "I'll just tell her what I want."

She heard the door close. "Sebranek?" she called over her shoulder, still looking in the mirror. "What are you doing back here?" She saw in the mirror the reflection of Navin's face. Like a terrible dream, the beard, the eyes, the knife. Then he was directly behind her and grabbed her head and held her. He stuck the knife into her breast three times. Then he slashed her throat. He was very fastidious and did not like to be bloodied. He let the body drop, then stepped gingerly over her and went to the tub to wash the blood off his gloves. He used a towel to clean his shoes.

He went back into the room and found a plastic bag in a trash can and stuffed the towel into it. He let himself out of the room. He took off the gloves and added them to the bag. Then he went down the back stairs and out onto the patio and through a gate and found Ali Fava waiting with the motor running. He got into the car and threw the bag in the backseat. "Go to the coffeehouse on the corner," he said. "The Peet's. I want to get a pound of coffee. Do as I say. Drive slowly. Roll the windows down. There is no hurry. There is nothing to fear."

"Did you leave a good message?"

"It became complicated. I had to do more than was anticipated. It is unfortunate, but Allah knows all, sees all, directs us. We are servants and must not complain."

"What's in the sack?"

"We'll get rid of it later. Park in front of the coffee shop. You'll go in with me."

Ali Fava did as he was told. He feared Navin. When Navin was in a dark mood, it was unwise to anger him.

At twelve Nora Jane started getting dressed. At one she got into the convertible and drove down the steep driveway and out onto Archer Street, which curves along the bay. The blue-green water and the Golden Gate Bridge were lovely in the hazy noon light. Above the bridge long cumulus clouds moved and gathered, hovering over the bay like angels, waiting for a wind to blow them to the shore.

Nora Jane was sitting up very tall, letting the wind blow her hair. I'm going to meet Delaney Hawk, she was thinking. I might be getting ready to have a career just when I have this baby. Who cares? I can do two or three things at once. It's a new world. I'd never neglect my children. Grandmother used to take Daddy when she'd tour and he grew up to go to Annapolis. I can feel him in me even if I never knew him, even if he did get blown to smithereens in a stupid war. I've got him in me and Grandmother too. I wish she was here today. I was lost and now I'm finding every part of me, that's how I feel today.

She took the ramp off the bridge and went down a side street, then turned onto an avenue. Groups of people were strolling along, shopping, standing on corners, walking dogs. Farther down, in the neighborhood of the hotel where Adrien and

Sebranek were staying, the people seemed older, old hippies and retired rich people, chic little flower shops and coffee shops, art galleries and shoe stores that sold outrageously expensive shoes.

As she neared the hotel she saw police cars blocking the street. Even then I didn't know what it was, she always said later. I didn't have a clue. So if I'm intuitive it sure wasn't turned on that day.

She parked the car and began to walk in the direction of the hotel. I remember hurrying, she would say later. I started walking as fast as I could walk.

As she approached the small front door of the hotel, she saw four orderlies carrying a covered body on a stretcher. Police were everywhere. The people in the adjacent restaurant were lined up at the bar. Their faces were taut and strained. A tear had been made in the fabric of civilized life. Not down in the projects or poor sections of town, but right here, in Berkeley, near Chez Panisse and Black Oak Books, here, where civilization and peace had been worshiped as gods.

"It's a woman," Nora Jane heard someone say. "It's some woman writer."

A policeman was helping the orderlies load the body into an ambulance. Then the doors were shut and the ambulance driver got into the front seat and drove slowly off.

Nora Jane stood for a long moment trying to catch her breath. Then she broke through the crowd and found a policeman and took his sleeve. "Who was it? I was coming here to meet Adrien Searle. Tell me that wasn't who that was on the stretcher."

"That's who it was, lady. Could we have your name? Were you related to Ms. Searle?"

"I was coming to pick her up. She came to do a book party for my husband yesterday. That's why she was here. Where's Sebranek Conrad? Please tell me what happened, what's going on here?"

"Come with me." The policeman led her underneath the wire. He motioned to another officer to take his place, then he led Nora Jane into the hotel. They went past the desk and into a small room where the San Francisco District Attorney's Office had set up a temporary station. "Here's a lady who was coming to pick up the victim," the policeman said, handing her over to a man who seemed to be in charge.

"I'm sorry you walked into this," the man said. "Please sit down. Tell us what you know." He was a nice-looking man with thick strong arms and shoulders that were bulging out of the lightweight fabric of his summer suit. He reminded Nora Jane of the Cajun men in South Louisiana.

"I don't even know what happened. Adrien died? She died here? She was killed?"

"She was stabbed to death. Tell me your name."

"I'm Nora Harwood. My husband owns Clara Books. Ms. Searle came out here to do a reading yesterday. She's the one who wrote that book about the environment that started a congressional investigation. She wrote *End of All Springs*. That was the book, and lots of other books. She changed people's lives. How could she die? Someone killed her?"

"Yes." He waited, as though expecting her to confess.

"I'm pregnant. I just found out. I shouldn't be here like this. Where is Sebranek Conrad? He was with her. I need to call my husband and tell him about this. May I use the phone?"

"Your husband is the reason she came to San Francisco?"

"No, her book is the reason. Sebranek Conrad is her editor. He was with her. Where is he? I need to use the phone, please. What is your name?"

"Jason Hebert. Look, you give me the number. I'll call your husband." She told him the number and he dialed it. He hasn't answered a single one of my questions, Nora Jane was thinking.

"Hebert is a Louisiana name. I'm from New Orleans."

"My folks are from Boutte. I thought I recognized that accent of yours. Wait a minute." He spoke to someone on the phone, then turned back to her. "Get Mrs. Harwood some water, Jake. Sit down, honey. Sit down and drink that water, will you?" He smiled at her then, a sweet smile. He had eyes so brown and kind and worried that Nora Jane settled down beneath their gaze. Then he turned back to the phone. She could only half hear the conversation he was having with Freddy.

She looked down at the glass of water the man named Jake had given her. This isn't true, she decided, this is not happening. That was not Adrien being put into that ambulance. I don't want it to be anyone. Not anyone at all.

Jason Hebert turned back to her. "Your husband's on his way. I wish you'd drink that water. I don't want a miscarriage on top of a murder this afternoon."

"I'd like some bottled water. I can't drink this. The glass doesn't even look clean. Tell me what happened, please."

"Your friend was stabbed to death sometime this morning and was found about eleven-forty-five by the maid, who let herself into the room to clean. That's all we know. It was quick and clean and she didn't put up a fight. Does that help?"

"No, that's horrible. It's terrible. I'm not even sure it's true. How do you know it was her? It might not have been Adrien. It might be someone else was in her room."

He got up and came around the makeshift desk to her chair and took her arm. "Go get some bottled water out of the bar, Jake," he said. "And bring a clean glass." Nora Jane looked up and met those eyes again, extraordinary eyes. The eyes of an altar boy, a darkened church on Poydras or Melepomene. Incense, the mass being read in Latin, death and the smell of death. "You okay?" he asked.

"No, no, I'm not okay at all." Then she began to cry and he reached in his pocket and took out a white handkerchief and handed it to her.

"Can you help us at all?" he asked, when the tears had subsided and she looked at him again. "Tell us who might have done this. Anything you know. Any enemies she had."

"Who knows. Anyone can hate a writer who writes the truth about the world. Anyone can fixate on a writer or stalk them or think they own them because they read their books. Things like that happen. But I never met Adrien Searle until yesterday. She wasn't someone who made enemies. She was this very sweet older lady who was like a mother to everyone. She wasn't some-one who gets killed out of hate. Maybe it was a robbery. Did they steal things?"

"Not that we noticed. She had on a watch and rings, and her pocketbook wasn't touched."

"I don't know. Let me think." Nora Jane was crying again. At the thought of the day that had begun so brilliantly and now had ended like this. This was like her childhood had been, fear and anger and uncertainty. Evil that seemed to come from nowhere and darken the sun. One moment her mother would be sober and trying to get in good with her. The next moment she was crying and begging for help and saying she was going to die. Then I went to Grandmother, Nora Jane remembered. I'd walk over there day or night even when I was so little. I'd walk across Magazine Street by myself at night when I was seven years old. I still don't know why I never got run over.

Then Freddy was there, having parked his car on the street behind the police barricade. "I left my automobile on the street," he told Jason Hebert. "See if you can keep them from towing it. It's a dark blue Honda. Are you all right?" He turned to Nora Jane.

"I don't know. I saw them carrying her out. Where is Sebranek?"

"Mr. Conrad is upstairs with our physician," Jason answered. It was as though he had decided it was all right to answer her questions now that Freddy was here. "He's in shock. He returned after we got here. He identified the body. What do you know about his son Johnnie? Do you know where he lives?"

"What does Johnnie have to do with it?" Freddy asked.

"We don't know," Jason answered. "But we need to talk to him. Do you know where he lives?"

"No. He comes in the store occasionally but I don't think he lives in this part of town. Ask Sebranek. He knows where he is."

"We have asked him. I need the two of you to come down to the station and give us a statement sometime today."

"Johnnie Conrad's not involved in this." Freddy stood up very close to Jason and looked him in the eye. "Don't go running down blind alleys while the murderer gets away. I promise you,

Johnnie Conrad wouldn't kill anyone. He probably doesn't even eat meat. What are you people thinking?"

"Two people saw a young man fitting his description hurrying through the lobby at eleven o'clock. They noticed him because he was in such a hurry. He showed up yesterday at her reading, didn't he?"

"How did you know that? Where are you getting all this information? Johnnie Conrad wouldn't have any reason to kill Adrien Searle."

"She broke up his parents' marriage, didn't she?" It became very quiet in the room. Nora Jane stood up and went to Freddy. A chill went through her. They weren't kidding. This wasn't a television movie. They thought Sebranek's son was involved in this.

A detective entered the room. "We found the Conrad kid," he said. "He's running some kind of after-school program down in Soweto. They took him downtown."

"I want to see Sebranek," Freddy said. "You can't be holding him. He needs us. Take us to him before I start calling lawyers, and that's not an idle threat."

"No need for that. I'm sorry this has been so bad for your wife. Jake, go see if Mr. Conrad can come down here. We'll wrap this up and seal off the room and then we'll get downtown. I wish we hadn't walked on that hall carpet. Roll it up and bring it down."

"I took it up an hour ago. You didn't notice?"

"Good. Start talking, Mr. Harwood. Tell me what you know."

"She had enemies. Every anti-environmental person in the West thinks she's the Antichrist. Also, Sebranek publishes Salman Rushdie. Did anyone tell you that? They both surf the edge. It could be anyone, it could be random violence. What it isn't, is anything to do with Sebranek Conrad's son, who graduated, I'm pretty sure of this, summa cum laude from Cornell. That divorce is old, old stuff. Where did you get the idea that the boy they saw in the hall was Johnnie Conrad? What have you been smoking?"

Freddy was getting mad, a dangerous thing. He was the only

son of an extremely wealthy woman who had indulged his every wish since the day he was born. He had firms of lawyers at his beck and call. A detective from the San Francisco police department was nothing to him. Ninety-nine percent of the time he went about his life as if he were an ordinary person. He cultivated wearing old clothes and never letting anyone see his power, but when the one-quarter Irish blood his mother had bequeathed him rose to the top, he boiled. Nora Jane had not seen it often but she had seen it enough to be frightened by it. For all she knew Freddy might haul off and hit Jason Hebert and then they'd both go to jail.

"Oh, please," she said. "This is not the time for this. Please, Freddy, settle down. We have to talk to Sebranek. Think how he's feeling."

"The maid knew Johnnie," Jason said. "She used to be his girlfriend."

Then Sebranek was there and they surrounded him and embraced him and tried to find a way to comfort him but there was no comfort. "Come home with us," Freddy pleaded. "Come to our house."

"I have to go downtown and see about Johnnie. They saw him here. Of course it's some coincidence, but we have to straighten it out." Sebranek pushed them away. He turned to Jason. "Have they found my son?"

"He's on his way downtown. We'll take you with us. Jake, did you see about Mr. Harwood's car?"

"It's right where he left it. Jim's with it."

They went out onto the street and found Freddy's car. "Let me drive you," Freddy said to Nora Jane.

"No, I don't want to leave the car. I'll follow you."

"I don't want you out of my sight."

"I have to take my car home, Freddy. It might get towed."

They stood in the middle of the police barricade, a uniformed policeman holding the car door open. "This is like Vonnegut's description of space travelers looking down on the earth and thinking the inhabitants are little steel automobiles being served by four-limbed bits of protoplasm. Leave the goddamn car there, Nora Jane. We'll send somebody for it."

"I can drive it. I'm better than you are. At least I didn't threaten a detective."

"I'm going to sue some detectives. That was the most inhumane little meeting of minds I've yet encountered. This woman, his love, is dead, murdered, and they're treating him like a suspect."

"Why would Johnnie have been there?"

"I don't know. But we'll find out, won't we." He let her go then and she got into her car and drove slowly home and he followed her. Once or twice he turned on the radio to see if it had made the news but all he could get was music and an update on the weather.

Two hours later Freddy and Nora Jane and Freddy's best friend, Nieman, and Freddy's bookkeeper, Frances, were in the Harwood living room manning phones. The media had the story now and were playing it for all it was worth. It had been a godsend to the media. There was no foreign news of interest to the citizens of the United States and no new scandals in Washington. What scandals there were concerned money and banks and bond fraud. Americans are too healthy to stay interested for long in theft. Murder and passion and revenge are what the American public likes on a nice spring day, and Adrien Searle's death promised all that and more.

Nieman and Freddy were doing what they could to control the damage. They were calling in their chits with reporters all over the country. The *San Francisco Chronicle*, the *Los Angeles Times*, the *New York Times*, the *Boston Globe*, CNN, the Associated Press, the United Press. All three phones were ringing without stop as reporters they knew called back and forth gathering parts of the story. Johnnie was being held for questioning and the media had gotten hold of the Conrads' divorce and Johnnie's years of therapy and Sebranek's ex-wife's crippling arthritis and her brother's unsuccessful Senate race and Sebranek's rise to literary fame and the Rushdie connection.

"Take a break," Freddy said at dusk. "Turn the phones off and let's eat something. Where are the girls, Nora Jane?"

"They're here. They're fine." She pulled the master phone plug out of the wall and the four friends turned to face each other on the white chairs Freddy had bought when he was in his Scandinavian mood.

"They'll have Adrien's sons in it by night," Nieman was saying. "Didn't you tell me she doesn't talk to one of them? That's pathological enough to occupy a day's news, wouldn't you say? This is turning into a mess, a real mess."

"It's already a mess. Adrien's dead." Nora Jane got up and took Nieman's glass to fill it. He was drinking wine.

"'Things fall apart,'" Freddy quoted, "'the center cannot hold. . . . The best lack all conviction while the worst are full of passionate intensity.' Yeats. This is the tip of the iceberg, Nieman. You and I know Johnnie didn't kill Adrien, and in the meantime whoever did is running the streets of San Francisco. I'm thinking of sending Nora Jane and the girls down to the Baja to Mother's place."

"You are not sending me anywhere. What is it, darling?" Tammili had come to stand in the door.

"May I use the phone now? Tara thinks I'm going to call her. She's going to get mad at me and we just made up. If I don't call her she's going to get mad again."

"Of course you may call her. Come over here. What's that in your hair?"

"Lydia's making dreadlocks. She made me one."

"Come here to me, goddaughter of my heart." Nieman held out his hands to her. "A friend died, Tammili. But it will never touch you in any way. We are calling reporters so they won't write foolishness in their newspapers. We are trying to maintain civilization and that is why the phones have been busy. What's this about your friend Tara? Your friendship is in danger, fraught with people getting mad?"

"Don't laugh at me," she said, but she went to him and let him hug her and he plugged in a phone and helped her dial her friend, having to cut out incoming signals as they dialed.

"She wants me to come over," Tammili said, when she had

hung up the phone. "It's not dark yet. May I ride my bike to her house?"

"Go on then," Nora Jane said. "Tell Lydia to come in here and let me see what she's doing to her hair. Never mind, I'll go in there. Did Betty give you supper? Did you eat supper?"

"Yes."

"Well, go to Tara's until eight o'clock. Then come right back."

"I'll take her," Freddy said. He got up and put down the papers he was holding.

"It's only four houses. Leave her alone. We can't change their lives. Go on, honey. She and Tara are doing a science project. They have to work on it."

Tammili left the room and Freddy followed her. She went to the carport and found her bicycle and wheeled it out onto the long driveway that curved down the acre of land to the street.

Freddy stood by the front steps watching her. Two of his three sheepdogs ran over and begged to be petted. He caressed their fine big heads. An old male named Prospero and his granddaughter, a high-strung beauty they called Cleo. It was growing dark. To the west there was a cloud bank of unearthly blue, so subtle and evanescent that it changed as Freddy watched. Cleo nuzzled his hand. Prospero pushed her away and stood against his leg like a pillar.

Tammili's bike moved down the long drive and out onto the sidewalk and continued down the hill. As she passed a hedge of azalea bushes, a man rose up and stood in her way. Tammili screamed. Freddy and the dogs began to run. The dogs were there before the bicycle finished falling. Then Tammili was on the ground with a dog on top of her and the man was running down the street with the second dog pursuing. He jumped into an old red car and drove away.

Cleo returned to Freddy. She was holding a piece of torn leather in her mouth. She was slobbering and breathing hard when Freddy reached her but would not let go of the leather.

Prospero was with Tammili, licking her and whining. He was making little short breathy whines. Tammili was petting him as she extricated her legs from the bike. She stood up in a rage. "He hit Prospero with a gun," she said. "He hit him on the back.

Poor old Prospero, poor old wonderful dog." She was examining
the animal for wounds. Freddy bent over to look for cuts on her
legs.

Nora Jane and Nieman were running down the yard with
Lydia behind them. "Call the police," Freddy yelled to them.
"Call the neighborhood patrol."

Fifteen minutes later a bomb went off in the front window of
Clara Books. It destroyed an exhibit of first editions of Karsh
and Ansel Adams monographs and took out the entire travel
and poetry sections. There were books there that would never
be in print again. All the Lost Roads and Dragonseed editions
printed on paper made to last a thousand years. All the Faber
and Faber hardbacks. It would be a long time before the extent
of the damage was fully revealed to the staff of Clara Books, the
oldest and least economically successful privately owned bookstore in the Bay Area. But that is a different tragedy. "And
furnished me with books from my own library, which I prize
above my dukedom," as the real Prospero said.

The neighborhood patrol beat the police to the house. Jason
Hebert was right behind them. He had been on his way to tell
Freddy about the bombing. Before he reached the door he got
news of Tammili's assailant.

"We assume this is all related until we find a reason not to
believe it," he said. "I'm really sorry about your store. We have
it cordoned off. I'll take you down there if you want to go."

"I have a piece of the jacket," Freddy answered. "I had a time
getting it from the dog but I tried not to touch it. I wrapped it
in plastic. What do you want me to do with it?"

"Your family will be under our protection," Jason answered.
"It will be a twenty-four-hour watch. I want you to know they
will be safe."

"You're leaving in the morning and taking the girls with you."
Freddy was folding his clothes to leave on the chair overnight.
It was a habit he had gotten into at Exeter and he always fell
back into it when he was thinking. No matter how wrinkled or

dirty the clothes were, if Freddy was thinking hard he folded each piece as he took it off and stacked the pieces on a chair. He took his socks off next to last and his underpants off right before he got into bed. He was taking his socks off now. As he rolled them into a neat roll, Nora Jane knew she was in for it.

"You can go to Mother's house or up to Willits or to Europe. If the house on the beach was finished you could go there. What you can't do is stay in this house with my children and my unborn child until we find out what's going on."

"We are perfectly safe. The police are watching us. Nothing is going to harm us here. I'm not leaving, Freddy. It would scare the girls to death. I don't think that man was after Tammili. It was some sort of coincidence. Besides, I won't be run out of my own house by murderers. I want to go see Mrs. Hawk and ask her what Adrien said to her on the phone. I told Inspector Hebert I was going to help."

"Help! What are you talking about? You don't help in a murder investigation. Good Lord, Nora Jane. I don't believe you said that. This has nothing to do with you."

"It does have to do with me. I liked Adrien so much. Oh, God, do you think she knew they were going to kill her? Do you think she had time to think?"

"You're in denial. They bombed the store. A man was in our azalea bushes. And, yes, she had time, they slit her throat, which is why you're leaving here."

"Come get in bed. I'm scared too, Freddy. But I'm not leaving unless you do. I'd be more scared being away from you than being here." She patted the pillow, tried to pretend to look seductive, but it didn't work.

"I'm going to look in on the girls first."

"Nieman's sleeping in the room next to them with the door open. And you know he never sleeps."

"I'll just look." Freddy padded down the hall barefooted and looked in on the girls. Then he looked in at Nieman, lying on his back in the guest room pretending to be asleep.

Freddy returned to his bed and got in beside his wife. "Can you believe he insisted on staying here? That's just like him. I love Nieman, Nora Jane. He's a pillar. He's never let me down."

"Go to sleep," Nora Jane said. "Come here to me. This is our house. No one can harm us here."

Night settles down upon this house, Nieman was thinking. Night fills the oceans and the valleys and the towns, night falls on this murderer, this sick or benighted person whom it serves no purpose to hate or fear. Only reason can save us now, and reason is slow, so slow. Reason is the turtle in the race, and reason demands that I sleep. I will sleep. Nieman relaxed the muscles in his cerebral cortex, he relaxed the muscles that pump blood to the brain, he relaxed the muscles that control the eyes. He set his sights on Athena and he slept. He was not always this fortunate in controlling his brain's whims.

As soon as they finished breakfast the next morning, Nieman and Freddy went into a small office behind the kitchen to decide how to proceed. It had been a maid's room when Freddy bought the house. Later he had turned it into a reading room. The walls were lined with the books he had owned when he was a student. The sofa was covered with an old blanket he had taken to camp as a child. He sat down upon it now and it seemed to give him strength.

Nieman sat facing him. "Don't talk," he said. "Think."

"Figure out who the enemy is. Who would kill Adrien, then bomb my store. If it was Muslim fundamentalists they would have announced themselves, wouldn't they? Isn't that how they operate?"

"Look for the thing we have forgotten. Is there a money trail? Is it about you or Nora Jane? Someone who works for the store?"

"No. No way."

"Is it Sebranek?"

"It looks that way. But then, if they are after Sebranek, why bomb the store? It would hurt him more if suspicion stayed on Johnnie."

"Are the two things related? That's the real question."

"And what of the man who startled Tammili? That's the thing that's driving me crazy. Right here, in my yard, on my property, while I watched. If the bombing is related to that, we have to leave San Francisco. The house on the beach will be finished in a month. It might be safe there. At least the property is open and could be watched. God, Nieman, is this happening to us? What effect will it have on the girls?"

"I was up half the night pondering that one."

"Tammili's spooked, whether she admits it or not. She's probably listening outside the door right now. Nora Jane kept them home from school." Freddy got up and went to the door and opened it. The only sound was the dishwasher in the kitchen.

"Is it about our being Jews?"

"I don't know." They were silent. Then Nieman raised his arms as though to conduct a symphony.

"Freddy, why didn't we think of it? There's the new Center for Middle Eastern Studies at Berkeley. I met the director the other day. I'd been so derisive and irritated about it and then I ran into the director in Musa's office and he turned out to be rather nice. Affable, trying to make friends. He's a Palestinian Christian, a Doctor Zouabi, something like that. I was struggling so hard to overcome my prejudices so we could talk that I didn't get his name. Let's go over there and get him to give us a reading on it. We can't rely on the police, or even the FBI on this one. We have to make our own assessment. Don't you agree?"

"Call him now. Make an appointment." Freddy got up quietly and pulled open the door and caught sight of Tammili's red shirt disappearing around a corner.

Three hours later they were sitting in a crowded cubicle in the old administration building, part of which had been turned into the new Center for Middle Eastern Studies. Freddy and Nieman told Doctor Zouabi what they knew, including the Salman Rushdie problems of the past.

"Who do you think is after us and why?" Freddy asked. "I want to meet them and talk to them. I'll take his books out of the store if it's still Salman. I mean it. Find out what they want."

"Can you help us?" Nieman added. "Can you find out anything?"

"I can try. I'm more suspect by those factions than you are. They are not happy about our work here."

"Do you have an idea?"

"There are hit lists. Perhaps your Mr. Sebranek Conrad is on one of them." He laced his fingers together. He was an extraordinarily ugly man, wearing very expensive corduroy trousers and fine leather shoes with cashmere socks. A silk shirt, a dark green alpaca sweater. A gold watch. There were rings.

He's got about twelve grand on his person, Freddy decided. Then bowed his head. Don't be prejudiced, he warned himself. You have come for help. Don't project prejudice or hate. Help me, you son-of-a-bitch. Tell me which of your ugly benighted countrymen is after my life and my children.

"If you get information for me I'll make a grant to your foundation in gratefulness," Freddy said. "If they want Salman's books out of the store they can have that." I'm sick of fighting this battle. I don't have to defend free speech for Muslims who don't believe in it anyway. To hell with it. I should have given up when they bombed me last time.

"He's overwrought," Nieman added. "As you can see. We appreciate your seeing us. We're grateful to you already." If you want to veil your women and keep harems, go on with it, he was thinking. But then, you're a Christian, aren't you? So the university believes, anyway. Well, I won't be prejudiced. I'll outgrow my conditioning. I'll rise above it. I swear I will but not today in all probability, not with you wearing those pants and that watch and those rings.

When they were gone, Doctor Hava Zouabi picked up the phone and began to call numbers on two continents. At six o'clock that night he got what he wanted. "Two Jews are being harassed over some book-selling Jew from New York City," he said. "They want to apologize and buy someone off. Do you know who might want an apology from a bookstore in San Francisco?" He listened for a while, then wrote down a name and an address. "Thank you, Saleem, God be with you."

It's good when they learn a lesson, he decided. How much I hate this ugly place, these ugly big people and their heartiness and disdain. Three more years. I will suffer it and cause my little children to suffer it for three more years, then I will go home. I will never set foot in their filthy cities again. Never watch their piglike children slop around the streets all day and night, their whores of women, their television sets.

He closed up his little cubicle and walked the seven blocks to his rented house and went inside and kissed his children and let his wife bathe and feed him and put him to sleep for the night.

III

"We must grow or die," Freddy said, when they were in the car with Nieman driving. "We have read Amos Oz. We have seen the bodies of our children and their children. If this is about Salman, the books go out of the store. I won't put my family in jeopardy for him. Let him apologize to his people or take the stupid book out of print. Who cares? If you think for one moment I'm not serious about this, you're wrong. I hate them. It's true, deep down inside where I can never root it out I hate and fear them and wish them dead. I cannot rise above this, Nieman. There must be a way to ride above it then. A way to constantly know how stupid it is. Hate and war make hate and war. They destroy the reasons men attain the property over which they fight. The idea is to protect women and children and then the women and children end up being killed." Freddy rolled his shoulders into a ball as he spoke. He curled his body into itself. He undid his seat belt so he could think better. His hair was very thick and curly and he was nearly always in need of a haircut. Today it was even dirty.

"You look like an Arab street kid with that hair. Let me put it this way. If you remove Salman's books from the store and apologize to the Arab world it's all right with me. As long as that's the enemy in this case and I'm not sure it is. I'm not blameless in this hatred and you know it. Just because I try to be rational doesn't mean my mother wasn't just as big a bigot and ball- and soul-breaker as yours was. They all are. That's what they do and we must forgive them every morning and move on.

"Freddy, I woke up this morning thinking about what was in the window of the store the day they bombed it. It doesn't make sense. Ansel Adams photographs Then I started thinking. You put that exhibit up the day after Adrien spoke. I was by there the day before she spoke to buy a book about coins for my nephew and the front window was a mess. There were displays of Adrien's books and photographs of her. But that was crowded into a small space. All around it were piles of mess. I was meaning to say something to you about it. I thought it was disrespectful to have her things all crowded in with everyone else's pet agendas. Every rabid feminist of the last ten years was represented, as though Adrien was not a law unto herself with broad-ranging interests. What was all that stuff?"

"Nieman, stop the car. Do you realize what you just said? That was a pro-choice display from the day before. I guess Frances just crowded it to the back to put Adrien's books in the window. The women had a benefit for Planned Parenthood the day before Adrien came. One of the speakers was that Palestinian woman they're all so crazy about who says all men are rapists. What if it was unrelated? What if Adrien's death had nothing to do with the bombing? All these years I pay lip service to the scientific method and when I need it, what do I do? Jump to the first conclusion that occurs to me. Tammili keeps saying the license plate on the car said Alabama. She reads all the mysteries she can get her hands on. She would read a license plate, wouldn't she? We would have when we were her age. Don't stop the car. Go down to Jason Hebert's office and let's talk to him."

"I wasn't going to stop the car. We're on the freeway, Freddy. I thought you wanted to go see about the store."

"Frances will take care of the store. Go to Jason's office now."

Doctor Hava Zouabi was still worrying about the visit Freddy and Nieman had paid to him. He picked up the phone and began to call numbers he should not have been calling from his office phone. He called the cell in New York City and the one in Los Angeles and the man in Los Alamos. "They said Amir might know why a bookstore was bombed and a woman killed," he asked these people.

"Amir is not interested in bookstores," they answered him.

"Is he interested in Salman Rushdie?"

"No one bothers with Salman Rushdie now. Let him stew in his own juice. He has angered the British. He has been ungrateful and the British don't like that. We have other mares to tame, Doctor Zouabi. Don't be involved in things that don't interest you. Do your work. Trust in Allah. Allah be praised."

"Life is good. Allah be praised."

Lydia and Tammili and Nora Jane and two detectives were in the Harwoods' living room. Tammili and Lydia were wearing matching navy blue jumpers and white blouses. They were wearing the gold bracelets they had gotten for their tenth birthday. They were wearing white tennis shoes and new white Nike socks. Lydia had her hand on Tammili's arm.

"It said ALA 540, then I couldn't see the rest," Tammili was saying. "It wasn't dark and I wasn't really hurt and Prospero was on top of me but I could see. I have twenty-twenty vision. The first thing I did was look at the license plate. It said ALA 540. He was as skinny as he could be and he had on that black jacket and Cleopatra tore off a piece of it. How did those dogs know what to do? That's what I want to know. Did they read my mind or did they know he was mean?" She sat up very straight. Tammili wasn't afraid. She lived in the center of a group of people who would kill or die or move to Malibu for her. What did she have to fear?

"Could it have said AR?" the detective asked. "Think very hard, Tammili. Think as hard as you can."

"It might have. There was an A and the plate was white with dark letters. I thought it was ALA but if you put the 5 very close to the A I guess it could. It could. I'll say provisionally it could." *Provisionally* was one of the vocabulary words Nieman had sent her last week on E-mail. She had been looking for a way to use it.

"Then we may be on to something. There's an antiabortion ring we've been watching who have a dark red Chevrolet with Arkansas plates. It's a stolen car. We've been letting them keep it because it makes it easy to track them. Stolen from a used car lot in Fort Smith, Arkansas. One of their favorite targets lately is bookstores. They stole all the feminist books out of a big discount store in L.A. We've been waiting for them to do something we can jail them for. We found the jacket, by the way. It was thrown away several blocks from here. A cheap leather jacket made in Taiwan like ones that are sold in jeans stores everywhere."

"Then it has nothing to do with Adrien's murder, does it?" Nora Jane shook her head from side to side as she spoke. She was becoming terrified at last. "What does any of this mean? If these people scared Tammili and bombed our store, why did they do it? I don't get it. None of it makes sense. Is there anything else you need Tammili to tell you?"

"Not unless she can remember something she didn't tell us yesterday." The detective folded his hands. They were good hands, wide and strong and freckled. Another altar boy, Nora Jane decided, I cannot escape them anywhere. The Church. Its shadows are everywhere. Light and shadow, that's all we know. The past, the past, the past. She saw herself going with her mother into the darkened sanctuary, her mother smelling of whiskey and cigarettes. She would have been better if she'd gone to AA meetings, Nora Jane decided, but then, they have AA meetings at churches, don't they? Good and bad, in constant battle for the world. The goddamn antiabortionists, the fools. And yet, they call it into play. They force the issue, don't they? I didn't abort the girls and God knows, there was no reason to have them. I didn't even know who they belonged to. Still am not sure. Of course we know. We know. Tammili is Freddy's and Lydia belongs to Sandy and I fucked two men in two days and got pregnant like an alley cat. And that's the past and I've been shriven for that a million times for sure.

"What are you thinking?" the detective asked.

"Are you a Roman Catholic?"

"I was."

"Me too. Those groups make you think about it. They may be crazy but it works. It gets our attention."

"If they bombed our store they should be put in prison for the rest of their lives," Tammili said. "They are trampling on our First Amendment rights."

"Who told you that?"

"Uncle Nieman."

"Are you finished?" Nora Jane stood up. The detective met her eye. Realms of discourse passed between them. Nora Jane was especially beautiful this day, with her high cheekbones and wide green eyes and her passion and her fear. She was lovelier now than she had been when she was younger. Lovelier than the night she met Freddy Harwood, when she tried to rob him with a wooden gun and ended up talking to him all night and crying in his arms. Freddy could never remember what they said that night. I am a creature of language, he had told Nieman later. But all I can remember is her face and the way she moved her hands when she spoke. There are Graces, I decided. And they have chosen this woman as their proof.

Now the poor twenty-nine-year-old detective from the San Francisco Police Department was suffering that face and that voice and those graces. He stood up beside her and tried not to let it show.

"That's all," he said. "The D.A. just wanted us to see if there was a chance we'd got it right about the car."

Nora Jane turned to her children. "You all go find something to do for a while. Your grandmother wants to take you shopping later. Did I tell you that? Do you want to go with her?"

"Yes." They looked at each other and giggled. They loved going shopping with their grandmother. Nora Jane and Freddy were contemptuous of malls but their grandmother Ann approached a mall as if it were a carnival. She had even let them ride a centrifugal-force machine.

"Then go on and call and tell her you're ready." Nora Jane watched them leave the room, then moved closer to the detective. "Tell me more about this group of people from Arkansas."

"Actually, they're from Utah. They have a stolen car with Arkansas plates. They're dangerous people. If we could pin this bombing on them, it would be a help."

"I think it's about Salman Rushdie. I don't think it's about Mormon sects. They wouldn't bother to come to where our store is. They wouldn't even know about that part of Berkeley."

"Nuts are everywhere."

"Then where is it safe to live?"

"Not in this city," he answered. "If you knew what I know you couldn't sleep at night."

In the Los Angeles office of the Muslim fundamentalist group to which Doctor Hava Zouabi was attached as a spy and a terrified tool, they had called a meeting to discuss the telephone conversations he had been making in the last few days. "He's beginning to think he's a free agent," Amir was saying. "The university people have spoiled him. He has forgotten the thirty million dollars our country gave them for their school. He has begun to believe they are interested in what he has to say. I think it's time he went home before he loses his usefulness altogether. He made three phone calls from his office to special numbers. We had all the numbers changed, of course, but it was unthinking. We need a more attractive man in the job. He's not presentable with that pockmarked face. It confirms their prejudices. I was thinking Mostapha might be better in the position."

"How could we explain his leaving?"

"An illness. That's easy enough to arrange."

"What of the bookstore people? Has there been any decision on Salman lately?"

"Let Salman stew in his juice. Public opinion in Britain is turning against him. If anyone gets to him, of course, so much the better."

"Will we claim credit for the bookstore?"

"Childish idea. It was bungled, amateur and messy. Abdel says it was a Christian group from Utah. Of no interest to us."

"What of the emir in New York City? It was his disciple who took the woman in the hotel."

"We will rescue them when the time comes. He's an old man. It's good for people to see they have no pity for him. We have made our point. They know we can reach them. The times of jihad will come. Two shipments from Cologne got through the airport. It all goes as planned. There is much we know. Much we cannot know. Allah be praised."

"Allah be praised."

*   *   *

Jason Hebert was in his office staring at a poster that read CONVICTION IS THE ENEMY OF TRUTH. It was covered with a fine layer of dust and he was thinking of getting up and wiping it off with his handkerchief when Freddy and Nieman were ushered in.

"I'm glad you came," he said. "We think we know who your intruder was. He's part of a Mormon sect that broke off from the Church in Utah. Just another bunch of crazies who went to the hills to have four wives. Only this bunch has a leader who's a real nut. Kid from Salt Lake City whose father left them early. His mother ran a halfway house for unwed mothers. All the babies given up for adoption. A couple of the girls committed suicide later. About the time he was nineteen he left home and started collecting followers. He's a good-looking devil, a natural leader. We're pretty sure it was one of them outside your house. Maybe him. But we don't know why. What could you have done to get the attention of that bunch?"

"That's why we're here," Freddy began. "We had a feminist enclave the day before Adrien spoke. They may have thought she was part of that. Her books were in the same window with all the feminist books. Could they have planted the device and it went off the wrong day? Or did they get Adrien mixed up with someone else? She was a feminist too, but that wasn't the main thrust of her books."

"This crowd isn't smart enough to know the difference, but killing women in hotel rooms isn't part of their m.o. I'd have a hard time fitting that in. I think they're doing peyote. I was around in the seventies. I can spot drug behavior. Each drug leaves a trail for me. I can smell it."

"What would I have done?" Nieman asked.

"Nothing. Bottled water."

"That's right. He had the first filter system in Berkeley. So Adrien could have died for a mistake?" Freddy sat down in the chair facing Jason's desk. "All of it could be a mistake. Just being in the public eye. Even being there can endanger someone's life. That's what we've come to?"

"Technology allowed madness to spread," Nieman said. "And yet, most of us would be dead without it. Bill Clinton is the last president who will ever give a damn about the poor, and his days are limited."

"Where is Sebranek?" Freddy asked. "We can't find him."

"He's with his son. We released the body. They are taking it to New York in the morning."

"We haven't heard from him all day. Then Nieman remembered what was in the window and we decided to come down here. Adrien's books were in the window with everyone a Mormon sect would hate."

"We released a statement apologizing for picking up Johnnie Conrad. It's not sufficient, but it will help."

"Was Johnnie at the hotel?"

"No, the girl changed her story. She went out with him a year ago, once. She went crazy because she saw the body. No one's blaming her for anything. She's in bad shape."

"Many harbor madness waiting for an outlet," Nieman said. He put his hand on Freddy's sleeve. "Let's go home, old friend. I've had enough of this day. We'll go by the museum and look at the jade Buddha and try to stop the madness in our own hearts."

"Is my family safe?" Freddy stood up and faced Jason. Jason shook his head. It took him a moment to answer.

"I feel they are. We'll keep a police watch on you for a while. Until we can round up some of the Holy Rollers and question them. I don't think you were the targets. I think it's broader than that, unspecific."

"That's not an answer."

"I know."

"Thank you for the work you do." Freddy shook his hand and then he and Nieman walked silently back to Nieman's car and got into it and drove away.

"Do you want to stop and see the Buddha?"

"Not today."

"I'm scared."

"So am I, old buddy."

Sebranek was talking to Nora Jane on the phone. "I'm with Johnnie," he said. "They're baking cookies. Where do you buy a stove? Do you know somewhere that would have a stove delivered in a hurry?"

"Sure. Call Sears. They're the only ones who service them. Not that I'm prejudiced."

"I forgot. Freddy's grandmother owned it, didn't she? You wouldn't have a number, would you?"

"When are you leaving? What's going on?"

"We'll have the service tomorrow in New York. I'm leaving tonight. Johnnie's going with me. You wouldn't know someone I could hire to come down here and work until he gets back, someone who might be good at fixing things and playing basketball?"

"I don't know where you are, Sebranek. Start at the beginning."

"I'm watching Johnnie work. I didn't know he worked. I've never seen him work. It's a light in the cave. I don't want him to leave it to go with me but he's insisting."

Which is how it happened that Freddy Harwood and Nieman Gluuk ended up spending the weekend overseeing the installation of a stove, a refrigerator, a washer and dryer, and two portable basketball goals in a warehouse in the heart of the most dangerous ghetto in San Francisco. Nieman brought along a young black reporter from the Arts Live section of the *Chronicle*. "He'll get a story out of it," he excused himself to Freddy. "You know I don't use people."

Freddy brought Tammili because she insisted on going along.

In New York City, in a church on Fifth Avenue, Sebranek and Johnnie and half the literary community of the East Coast were burying Adrien Searle.

The Episcopal priest raised the cup, the organ played "Amazing Grace," there was not a dry eye in the packed church. The body of Adrien Searle was now either completely irrelevant to the universe of particles and waves, or else, alive in Sebranek's brain, or else, what had been Adrien was coiled deep within the eggs of her five-year-old granddaughter, waiting for some sperm worth devouring.

*   *   *

In San Francisco Nieman was paying the pizza delivery man for twenty cheese and pepperoni pizzas and Tammili was setting the picnic tables with blue and white paper tablecloths.

The redheaded girl was worrying that Johnnie might never come back and the Sears deliverymen were trying to remember they were being paid time and a half for Saturday work and forget they were in Soweto risking their lives.

The youngest deliveryman finished his work on the refrigerator, then decided, what the hell, he'd do the plumbing for free. "If someone will take me home later," he said to Freddy.

"We'll get you home," Freddy promised. He smiled at the young man and approved of him to the tenth power, something the young man had never gotten at home.

Which is how Milton House came to leave his job at Sears and grow his hair out to his shoulders and spend his mornings getting an M.A. in social work and his afternoons being in love with Johnnie Conrad's girl and having his mind bent by Johnnie's superior mind. But that is another story.

Back at their house Nora Jane and Lydia were having lunch by the pool. They had made pita bread sandwiches filled with sprouts and chopped celery and tomatoes and green peppers. They were drinking iced Sports Tea and talking about perfume and ballet.

"My grandmother would put a drop of perfume on her letters if she wrote to anyone she used to know when she was a diva," Nora Jane was saying. "She didn't have much money by then but she always had that perfume."

"But singing doesn't ruin your feet like ballet does. Maybe Tammili was right to quit. I'm going to quit too. Aurora Morris's big sister had to have her feet operated on because she got these bone spurs and Madame Gautier can barely dance anymore. If I was seventy years old and all I'd been doing was riding my bike I bet I wouldn't be crippled like she is."

"No one cares if you take it or not. You can quit anytime you like."

"What do you want me to do?" Lydia put down her sandwich

and went around the table and put her arms around her mother's neck. "You say."

"I want you to be smart and use your brain and pass math and wear yellow once a week so I can look at you in it." Nora Jane giggled. It was enough. Her child's arms around her neck was sufficient reason to love the earth. The earth was not an evil place. Murder and pain and evil did not rule the earth. Children do, and loving them and watching them and listening to them grow. Amen.

You Must Change
Your Life

In January of nineteen hundred and ninety-five the esteemed movie critic of the *San Francisco Chronicle* took an unapproved leave of absence from his job and went back to Berkeley full time to study biochemistry. He gave his editor ten days' notice, turned in five hastily written, unusually kind reviews of American movies, and walked out.

Why did the feared and admired Nieman Gluuk walk out on a career he had spent twenty years creating? Was it a midlife crisis? Was he ill? Had he fallen in love? The Bay Area arts community forgot about the Simpson trial in its surprise and incredulity.

Let them ponder and search their hearts. The only person who knows the truth is Nieman Gluuk and he can't tell because he can't remember.

The first thing Nieman did after he turned in his notice was call his mother. "I throw up my hands," she said. "This is it, Nieman. The last straw. Of course you will not quit your job."

"I'm going back to school, Mother. I'm twenty years behind in knowledge. I have led the life you planned for me as long as I can lead it. I told you. That's it. I'll call you again on Sunday."

"Don't think I'm going to support you when you're broke,"

she answered. "I watched your father ruin his life following his whims. I swore I'd protect you from that."

"Don't protect me," he begged. "Get down on your knees and pray you won't protect me. I'm forty-four years old. It's time for me to stop pacing in my cage. I keep thinking of the poem by Rilke.

> *"His vision, from the constantly passing bars,*
> *has grown so weary that it cannot hold*
> *anything else. It seems to him there are*
> *a thousand bars; and behind the bars, no world.*
>
> *As he paces in cramped circles, over and over,*
> *the movement of his powerful soft strides*
> *is like a ritual dance around a center*
> *in which a mighty will stands paralyzed.*
>
> *Only at times, the curtain of the pupils*
> *lifts, quietly—An image enters in,*
> *rushes down through the tensed, arrested muscles,*
> *plunges into the heart and is gone."*

"You are not Rilke," his mother said. "Don't dramatize yourself, Nieman. You have a lovely life. The last thing you need is to go back to Berkeley and get some crazy ideas put in your head. This is Freddy Harwood's doing. This has Freddy written all over it."

"Freddy's in it. I'll admit that. He and Nora Jane and I have gone back to school together. I wish I hadn't even called you. I'm hanging up."

"Freddy has a trust fund and you don't. You never remember that, Nieman. Don't expect me to pick up the pieces when this is over. . . ." Nieman had hung up the phone. It was a radical move but one to which he often resorted in his lifelong attempt to escape the woman who had borne him.

Nieman's return to academia had started as a gesture of friendship. Nieman and Freddy had attended Berkeley in the sixties but Nora Jane was fifteen years younger and had never attended college, not even for a day.

"Think how it eats at her," Freddy told him. "We own a bookstore and she never even had freshman English. If anyone asks her where she went to school, she still gets embarrassed. I tell her it's only reading books but she won't believe it. She wants a degree and I want it for her."

"Let's go with her," Nieman said, continuing a conversation they had had at lunch the day before. "I mean it. Ever since she mentioned it I keep wanting to tell her what to take. Last night I decided I should go and take those things myself. We're dinosaurs, Freddy. Our education is outdated. We should go and see what they're teaching."

"Brilliant," Freddy said. "It's a slow time at the store. I could take a few weeks off."

"Here's how I figure it." Nieman stood up, got the bottle of brandy, and refilled their glasses. "We sign up for a few classes, pay the tuition, go a few weeks, and then quit. The university gets the tuition and Nora Jane gets some company until she settles in."

"We have spent vacations doing sillier things," Freddy said, thinking of the year they climbed Annapurna, or the time they took up scuba diving to communicate with dolphins.

"I need a change," Nieman confessed, sinking down into the water until it almost reached his chin. "I'm lonely, Freddy. Except for the two of you I haven't any friends. Everyone I know wants something from me or is angry with me for not adoring their goddamn, whorish movies. Some of them hate me for liking them. It's a web I made and I've caught myself."

"We'll get applications tomorrow. Nora Jane's already registered. Classes start next Monday."

Nieman went to the admissions office the next day and signed up to audit Dante in Translation and Playwriting One. Then, suddenly, after a night filled with dreams, he changed the classes to biochemistry and Introduction to the Electron Microscope.

This was not an unbidden move. For several years Nieman had become increasingly interested in science. He had started by reading books by physicists, especially Freeman Dyson. Physics led to chemistry, which led to biology, which led to him, Nieman Gluuk, a walking history of life on earth. Right there, in every cell in his body was the whole amazing panorama that led to language and conscious thought.

The first lecture on biochemistry and the first hour with the microscopes excited Nieman to such an extent he was trembling when he left the building and walked across the campus to the coffee shop where he had agreed to meet Freddy and Nora Jane. A squirrel climbed around a tree while he was watching. A girl walked by, her hair trailing behind her like a wild tangled net. A bluejay landed on a branch and spread his tailfeathers. Nieman's breath came short. He could barely put one foot in front of the other. Fields of wonder, he said to himself. Dazzling, dazzling, dazzling. If they knew what they are carrying as they go. Time, what a funny word for the one-way street we seem to have to follow.

"This is it," he told Freddy and Nora Jane, when they were seated at a table with coffee and croissants and cream and sugar and butter and jam and honey before them on the handmade plates. "I'm quitting the job. I'm going back to school full time. I have to have this body of information. Proteins and nucleic acids, the chain of being. This is not some sudden madness, Freddy. I've been moving in this direction. I'll apply for grants. I'll be a starving student. Whatever I have to do."

"We don't think you're crazy," Nora Jane said. "We think you're wonderful. I feel like I did this. Like I helped."

"Helped! You are the Angel of the Annunciation is what you are, you darling, you."

"Are you sure this isn't just another search for first causes?" Freddy warned. "Remember those years you wasted on philosophy?"

"Of course it is. So what? This isn't dead philosophical systems or Freudian simplicities. This is real knowledge. Things we can measure and see. Information that allows us to manipulate the physical world."

"If you say so."

"May I borrow the house at Willits for the weekend? I need

to be alone to think. I want to take the textbooks up there and read them from start to finish. I haven't been this excited in years. My God, I am in love."

"Of course you can borrow the house. Just be sure to drain the pipes when you leave."

"It might snow up there this weekend," Nora Jane put in. "The weather station warned of snow."

Two days later Nieman was alone in the solar-powered house Freddy and his friends had built on a dirt road five miles from Willits, California. The house was begun in 1974 and completed in 1983. Many of the boards had been nailed together by Nieman himself with his delicate hands.

The house stood in the center of one hundred and seven acres of land and overlooked a pleasant valley where panthers still hunted. In any direction there was not a power line or telephone pole or chimney. The house had a large open downstairs with a stone bathroom. A ladder led from the kitchen area to a loft with sleeping rooms. There were skylights in the roof and a wall of glass facing east. There was a huge stone fireplace with a wide hearth. Outside there was a patio and a deep well for drinking water. "This well goes down to the center of the earth," Freddy was fond of saying. "We cannot imagine the springs or rivers from which it feeds. This could be water captured eons ago before the crust cooled. This water could be the purest thing you'll ever taste."

"It tastes good," his twin daughters, Tammili and Lydia, would always answer. "It's the best water in the world, I bet."

Nieman stood in the living room looking out across the valleys, which had become covered with snow while he slept. He had arrived late the night before and built up the fire and slept on the hearth in his sleeping bag. "It was the right thing to do to come up here," he said out loud. "This holy place where my friends and I once made our stand against progress and the destruction of the natural world. This holy house where Tammili and Lydia were born, where the panther once came to within ten yards of me and did not strike. I am a strange man and do not know what's wrong with me. But I know how to fix myself when I am broken. You must change your life, Rilke said, and now I am changing mine. Who knows, when I come to my senses, somebody will have taken my job and I'll be on the streets writing travel articles. So be it. In the meantime I am destined to study science and I am going to study science. I cannot allow this body of information to pass me by and I can't concentrate on it while attempting to evaluate Hollywood movies."

Nieman moved closer to the window so he could feel the cold permeating the glass. Small soft flakes were still falling, so light and small it seemed impossible they could have turned the hills so white and covered the trees and the piles of firewood and the well. I can trek out if I have to, he decided. I won't worry about this snow. This snow is here to soothe me. To make the world a wonderland for me to study. Life as a cosmic imperative, de Duve says. I will read that book first, then do three pages of math. I have to learn math. My brain is only forty-four years old, for Christ's sake. Mother taught math. The gene's in there somewhere. It's just rusty. Before there was oxygen there was no rust. Iron existed in the prebiotic oceans in a ferrous state. My brain is like that. There are genes in there that have never been exposed to air. Now I will use them.

Nieman was trembling with the cold and the excitement of the ideas in his head. Proteins and nucleic acids, the idea that all life on earth came from a single cell that was created by a cosmic imperative. Given the earth and the materials of which it is created, life was inevitable. Ever-increasing complexity was also inevitable. It was inevitable that we would create nuclear energy, inevitable that we would overpopulate the earth. It was not as insane as it had always seemed. And perhaps it was not as inevitable once the mind could recognize and grasp the process.

Nieman heaved a great happy sigh. He left watching the snow and turned and climbed the ladder to the sleeping loft. There, on that bed, in that corner beneath the skylight, on a freezing night ten years before, Freddy and Nora Jane's twins had been born, his surrogate children, his goddaughters, his angels, his dancing princesses. Nieman lay down upon the bed and thought about the twins and the progress of their lives. Not everything ends in tragedy, he decided. My life has not been tragic, neither has Freddy's or Nora Jane's. Perhaps the world will last another hundred years. Perhaps this safety can be stretched to include the lives of Tammili and Lydia. So what if they are not mine, not related to me. All life comes from one cell. They are mine because they have my heart. It is theirs. I belong to them, have pondered over them and loved them for ten years. How can this new knowledge I want to acquire help them? How can this new birth of curiosity and wonder add to the store of goodness in the world?

Well, Nieman, don't be a fool. It isn't up to you to solve the problems of the world. But it might be. There were ninety-two people in that lecture room but I was the only one who had this violent a reaction to what the professor was saying. I was the only one who took what he was saying as a blow to the solar plexus. This might be my mission. It might be up to me to learn this stuff and pass it on. It is not inevitable that we overpopulate and destroy the world. Knowledge is still power. Knowledge will save us.

Nieman was crying. He lay on the bed watching the snow falling on the skylight and tears rolled down his face and filled his ears and got his fringe of hair soaking wet. He cried and he allowed himself to cry.

I had thought it was art, he decided. Certainly art is part of it. Cro-Magnon man mixing earth with saliva and spitting it on the walls of caves was a biochemist. He was taking the elements he found around him and using them to explore and recreate and enlarge his grasp of reality. After the walls were painted he could come back and stare at them and wonder at what he had created. Perhaps he cried out, terrified by the working of his mind and hands. I might stare in such a manner at this house we built. I could go outside and watch the snow falling on those primitive solar panels we installed so long ago. It is all one, our well and solar panels and the cave paintings at Lascaux and microscopes at Berkeley and this man in Belgium writing this book to blow my mind wide open and Lydia and Tammili carrying their backpacks to school each morning. The maker of this bed and the ax that felled the trees that made the boards we hammered and Jonas Salk and murderers and thieves and Akira Kurosawa and Abraham Pais and I are one. This great final truth, which all visionaries have intuited, which must be learned over and over again, world without end, amen.

Nieman fell asleep. The snow fell faster. The flakes were larger now, coming from a cloud of moisture that had once been the Mediterranean Sea, that had filled the wells of Florence, in the time of Leonardo da Vinci, and his royal patron, Francis, King of France.

The young man was wearing long robes of dark red and brown. His hair was wild and curly and his feet were in leather sandals. His face was tanned and his eyes were as blue as the sky. He had been knocking on the door for many minutes when Nieman came to consciousness and climbed down the ladder to let him in. "Come in," Nieman said. "I was asleep. Are you lost? I'm Nieman Gluuk. Come in and warm yourself."

"It took a while to get here," the young man said. "That's a kind fire you have going."

"Sit down. Do you live around here? Could I get you something to drink? Coffee or tea or brandy? Could I get you a glass of water? We have a well. Perhaps you're hungry." The young man moved into the living room and looked around with great interest. He walked over to the window and laid his palms against the glass. Then he touched it with his cheek. He smiled at that and turned back to Nieman.

"Food would be nice. Bread or cheese. I'll sit by the fire and warm myself."

Nieman went into the kitchen and began to get out food and a water glass. The young man picked up the book by the biochemist de Duve, and began to read it, turning the pages very quickly. His eyes would move across the page, then he would turn the page. By the time Nieman returned to the fireplace with a tray, the young man had turned half the pages. "This is a fine book," he said to Nieman, smiling and taking a piece of bread from the tray. "It would be worth the trip to read this."

"You aren't from around here, are you?" Nieman asked.

"You know who I am. You called me here. Don't be frightened. I come when I am truly called. Of course, I can't stay long. I would like to finish this book now. It won't take long. Do you have something to do while I'm reading?" The young man smiled a dazzling smile at Nieman. It was the face of the Angel of the Annunciation in Leonardo's painting. It was the face of David. "You knew me, didn't you?" the young man added. "Weren't there things you wanted to tell me?"

Nieman walked back toward the kitchen, breathing very softly. The young man's face, his hair, his feet, his hands. It was all as familiar as the face Nieman saw every day in the mirror when he shaved. Nieman let his hands drop to his sides. He stood motionless by the ladder while the young man finished reading the book.

"What should I call you?" Nieman said at last.

"Francis called me da Vinci."

"How do you speak English?"

"That's the least of the problems."

"What is the most?"

"Jarring the protoplasm. Of course, I only travel when it's worth it. I will have a whole day. Is there something you want to show me?"

"I want to take you to the labs at Berkeley. I want to show you the microscopes and telescopes, but I guess that's nothing to what you've seen by now. I could tell you about them. Did you really just read that book?"

"Yes. It's very fine, but why did he waste so many pages pretending to entertain superstitious ideas? Are ideas still subject to the Church in this time?"

"It's more subtle, but they're there. The author probably didn't want to seem superior. That's big now."

"I used to do that. Especially with Francis. He was so needy. We will go to your labs if you like. Or we could walk in this snow. I only came to keep you company. It's your time." He smiled again, a smile so radiant that it transported Nieman outside his fear that he was losing his mind.

"Why to me?"

"Because you might be lonely in the beginning. Afterward, you will have me if you need me." The young man folded the book very carefully and laid it on a cushion. "Tell me how cheese is made now," he said, beginning to eat the food slowly and carefully as he talked. "How is it manufactured? What are the cows named? Who wraps it? How is it transported?"

"The Pacific Ocean is near here," Nieman answered. He had taken a seat a few feet from the young man. "We might be able to get out in the Jeep. That's the vehicle out there. Gasoline powered. I don't know what you know and what you don't know. Do you want to read some more books?"

"Could we go to this ocean?"

"I guess we could. I have hiking gear. If we can't get through we can always make it back. I have a mobile phone. I'd like to watch you read another book. I have a book of algebra and a book that is an overview of where we are in the sciences now. There's a book of plays and plenty of poetry. I'd be glad to sit here and read with you. But finish eating. Let me get you some fruit to go with that."

"Give me the books. I will read them."

Nieman got up and collected books from around the room and brought them and put them beside the young man. Then he brought in firewood and built up the fire. He took a book of poetry and sat near the young man and read as the young man read. Here is the poem he turned to and the one he kept reading over and over again as he sat by the young man's side with the fire roaring and the wind picking up outside and the snow falling faster and faster.

> . . . Still, if love torments you so much and you so much need
> To sail the Stygian lake twice and twice to inspect
> The murk of Tartarus, if you will go beyond the limit,
> Understand what you must do beforehand.
> Hidden in the thick of a tree is a bough made of gold
> And its leaves and pliable twigs are made of it too.
> It is sacred to underworld Juno, who is its patron,
> And it is roofed in by a grove, where deep shadows mass
> Along far wooded valleys. No one is ever permitted

To go down to earth's hidden places unless he has first
Plucked this golden-fledged growth out of its tree
And handed it over to fair Proserpina, to whom it belongs
By decree, her own special gift. And when it is plucked,
A second one always grows in its place, golden again,
And the foliage growing on it has the same metal sheen.
Therefore look up and search deep and when you have found it,
Take hold of it boldly and duly. If fate has called you,
The bough will come away easily, of its own accord.
Otherwise, no matter how much strength you muster,
You never will
Manage to quell it or cut it down with
The toughest of blades.

"Now," the young man said, when he finished the biochemistry textbook. "Tell me about these infinitesimal creatures, amoebas, proteins, acid chains, slime molds, white cells, nuclei, enzymes, DNA, RNA, atoms, quarks, strings, and so on. What an army they have found. I could not have imagined it was that complicated. They have seen these creatures? Many men have seen them?"

"We have telescopes and microscopes with lenses ground a million times to such fineness and keenness, with light harnessed from electrons. They can magnify a million times. A thousand million. I don't know the numbers. I can take you to where they are. I can take you to see them if you want to go."

"Of course. Yes, you will take me there. But it must be soon. There is a limited amount of time I will be with you."

"How much time?"

"It will suffice. Will your vehicle travel in this snow?"

"Yes. Perhaps you would like to borrow some modern clothes. Not that there's anything wrong with your clothes. They are very nice. I was especially admiring the cape. The weave is lovely. They're always worrying about security. I want to take you to the laboratories at Berkeley. I can call the head of the department. He will let us in."

"You may have the cloak since you admire it. It can remain

here." He removed the long brown garment and handed it to Nieman.

"I'll give you a parka." Nieman ran for the coat rack and took down a long beige parka Freddy had ordered from L.L. Bean. He held it out to the young man. "I guess I seem nervous. I'm not. It's just that I've wanted to talk to you since I was ten years old."

"Yes. You've been calling me for some time."

"I thought you would be old. Like of the time when you died. Did you die?"

"I thought so. It was most uncomfortable and Francis wept like a child, which was not altogether unpleasant." He laughed softly. "It is better to come with my young eyes. In case there is something to see."

"Where are you when you aren't here?"

"Quite far away."

"Will it matter that you came here? I mean in the scheme of things, as it were?"

"It will matter to me. To read the books and see these instruments you are describing. I have always wished to have my curiosity satisfied. That was always what I most dreamed of doing. Francis never understood that. He could never believe I wouldn't be satisfied to eat and drink and be lauded and talk with him. It kept me from loving him as he deserved."

"I meant, will it change the course of anything?"

"Not unless you do it."

"I wouldn't do it. Could I do it by accident?"

"No. I will see to that. Do you want to go out now, in the vehicle in the snow?" There it was again, the smile that soaked up all the light and gave it back.

"Let's get dressed for it." Nieman led his guest upstairs and gave him a warm shirt and socks and shoes and pants and long underwear. While he was changing Nieman banked the fire and put the food away and set the crumbs out for the birds and locked the windows and threw his things into a bag. He forgot to drain the pipes.

"Well, now," he said out loud. "I guess I can drive that Jeep in this snow. Let's assume I can drive. Let's say it's possible and I will do it." He turned on the mobile phone and called the department at Berkeley and left a message saying he was bringing a senator to see the labs. Then he called the president of the university at his home and called in his markers. "Very hush-hush," he told the president. "This could be very big, Joe. This could be millions for research but you have to trust me. Don't ask questions. Just tell the grounds people to give me the keys when I come ask for them. I can't tell you who it is. You have to trust me."

"Of course, Nieman," the president answered. "After everything you and Freddy have done for us. Anything you want."

"The keys to everything. The electron microscopes, the physics labs, the works. We could use one of your technical people for a guide but no one else."

"There'll be people working in the labs."

"I know that. We won't bother anyone. I'll call you Monday and tell you more."

"Fine. I'll look forward to hearing about it." After he hung up the phone the university president said to his wife. "That was Nieman Gluuk. Did you know he's quitting writing his column? Took a leave of absence to go back to school."

"Well, don't you go getting any ideas like that," his good-looking wife giggled. "All he ever wrote about were foreign films. He'd gotten brutal in his reviews. Maybe they let him go. Maybe he just pretended that he quit."

There was a layer of ice beneath the snow. Nieman tested it by walking on it, then put Leonardo into the passenger seat and buckled him in and got behind the wheel and started driving. He drove very carefully in the lowest gear across the rock-strewn yard toward the wooden gate that fenced in nothing since the fence had been abandoned as a bad idea. "Thank God it's downhill," he said. "It's downhill most of the way to the main road. So, when was the last time you were here?" He talked without turning his head. The sun was out now. Birds were beginning to circle above the huge fir trees in the distance. "Have you been to the United States? To the West Coast?"

"Once long ago. I saw the ocean with a man of another race. I walked beside it and felt its power. It is different from the ocean I knew."

"We can go there first. It won't take long once we get to the main road. I'm sorry if I keep asking you questions. I can't help being curious."

"You can ask them if you like. I was visited by Aristotle in my turn. We went to a river and explored its banks. He was very interested in my studies of moving water. He said the flow of water would impede the mixture of liquids and we talked of how liquid forms its boundaries within a flow. He had very beautiful hands. I painted them later from memory several times. Of course everyone thought they were Raphael's hands. Perhaps I thought so too finally. After he left I had no real memory of it for a while. More like the memory of a dream, bounded, uncertain, without weight. I think it will be like that for you, so ask whatever you wish to ask."

"I don't think I want to ask anything now. I think we should go to the ocean first since we are so near. I forget about water. I forget to look at it with clear eyes, and yet I was watching the snow when I fell asleep. Also, I was crying. Why are you smiling?"

"Go on."

"I was thinking that when I was small I knew how to appreciate the ocean. Later, I forgot. When I was small I would stand in one place for a very long time watching the waves lap. Every day I came back to the same spot. I made footprints for the waves to wash away. I made castles farther and farther up the beach to see how far the tide could reach. I dug into the sand, as deep as it would allow me to dig. I was an infatuate of ocean, wave, beach. Are you warm enough? Is that coat comfortable?"

"I am warm. Tell me about this vehicle. What do you call it?"

"Automobile. Like auto and mobile. It's a Jeep, a four-wheel drive. We call it our car. Everyone has one. We work for them. We fight wars over the fuel to power them. We spend a lot of time in them. They have radios. We listen to broadcasts from around the world while we drive. Or we listen to taped books. I have a book of the Italian language we could listen to. You might want to see how it's evolved. It might be the same. It might be quite similar to what you spoke. Would you like to hear it?" Nieman shifted into a higher gear. The road was still steep but lay in the lee of the mountain and was not iced beneath the snow. "We'll be on the main road, soon," he added. "We're in luck it seems. I wouldn't have driven this alone. One more question. How do you read the books so fast?"

"I'm not sure." Leonardo laughed. "It's been going on since I quit the other life. It's getting better. At first it was not this fast. I'm very fond of being able to do it. It's the nicest thing of all."

"Where do you stay? When you aren't visiting? I mean, going someplace like this."

"With other minds."

"Disembodied?"

"If we want to be. Is that the main road?" It was before them, the road to Willits. Plows had pushed the snow in dirty piles on either side of the road. In the center two vehicles were moving in one lane down the mountain. A blue sedan and a white minivan were bouncing down the road in the ripening sunlight.

"I believe this," Nieman said. "I'm in my red Jeep driving Leonardo da Vinci down from the house to see the ocean. My name is Nieman Gluuk and I have striven all my life to be a good man and use my talents and conquer resentment and be glad for whatever fate dumped me in Northern California the only child of a bitter woman and a father I almost never saw, and I never went into a movie theater expecting to hate the movie and was saddened when I did. Maybe this is payback and maybe this is chance and maybe I deserve this and the only thing I wish is that my friend, Freddy, could be here so it won't destroy our friendship when I am driven to tell him about it."

"You won't remember it." Leonardo reached over and touched his sleeve. He smiled the dazzling smile again and Nieman took it in without driving off the road and took the last curve down onto the highway. "You will have it," Leonardo added. "It is yours, but you won't have the burden of remembering it."

"I want the burden." Nieman laughed. "Burden me. Try me. I

can take it. I'll write a movie script and publicize intelligence. *Nel mezzo del cammin di nostra vita mi ritrovai per una selva oscura, che la diritta via era smarrita. Ahi quanto a dir qual era e cosa dura esta selva selvaggia e aspra e forte.* That's the beginning of *The Divine Comedy.* That's what I went back to Berkeley to take. Instead, I'm in this forest of biochemistry. I'm dreaming the things I'm reading. They put literature into a new light. The artist intuits what the mind knows and the mind knows everything, doesn't it? Past, present, and forevermore."

"Some wake to it gradually. Some never know."

"I've worked for it," Nieman said. "I have worked all my life to understand, to see myself as the product of five hundred million years of evolution. You seem to have known it always."

"I was taken from my mother's house when I was four years old. On the walk to my father's house, the fields and the wonder of the earth came to console me. But I worked also. I always worked." He laid his hand on Nieman's arm. Nieman steered the Jeep across a pile of snow and turned onto the road leading down to Willits. Around them the snow-covered hills with their massive fir trees were paintings of unspeakable complexity. Neither of them spoke for many miles.

It was past noon when they drove through the small town of Willits and turned onto Highway 20 leading to the Pacific Ocean. "I'm going to stop for gasoline for the automobile," Nieman said. "We collect it in foreign countries. The countries of the Turks and Muslims, although some of it is under the ground of this country. We store it underneath these filling stations in large steel tanks. Steel is an alloy made of iron and carbon. It's very strong. Then we drive up to the pumping stations and pump the fuel into our tanks. Even young children do this, Leonardo. I don't know what you know and what you don't know, but I feel I should explain some things."

"I like to hear you speak of these phenomena. Continue. I will listen and watch."

Nieman spotted a Conoco station and stopped the Jeep and got out. He took down one of the gasoline hoses and inserted it in the fuel tank of the Jeep. Leonardo stood beside the tank watching and not speaking. "Don't smile that smile at anyone else," Nieman said. "We'll be arrested for doing hallucinogens."

"They never explode?" Leonardo moved in for a closer look, took a sniff of the fumes, then put both hands in the pockets of the jacket. There was a package of Kleenex in one pocket. He brought it out and examined it.

"It's called Kleenex. We blow our noses on it," Nieman explained. "It's a disposable handkerchief."

"Could one draw on it?" Leonardo held a sheet up to the light. "It's fragile and thin."

"Wait a minute." Nieman pulled a notepad and a black felt-tip pen out of the glove compartment and handed them to Leonardo. Leonardo examined the pen, took the top from it, and began to draw, leaning the pad against the top of the Jeep. Nieman put the hose back on the pump, then went inside and paid for the gasoline. When he returned, Leonardo had covered a page with the smallest, most precise lines Nieman had ever seen. Leonardo handed the drawing to him. It was of the mountains and the trees. In the foreground Nieman was standing beside the Jeep with the gasoline hose in his hand.

Nieman took the drawing and held it. "You are a microscope," he said. "Perhaps you will not be impressed with the ones we've made."

"Shall we continue on our way?" Leonardo asked. "Now that your tank is full of gasoline."

They drove in silence for a while. The sun was out in full violence now, melting the snow and warming the air. "The air is an ocean of currents," Nieman said at last. "I suppose you know about that."

"Always good to be reminded of anything we know."

"You want to hear the Italian tape? I'd like to hear what you think of it."

"That would be fine."

Nieman reached into a pack of tapes and extracted the Beginning Italian tape and stuck it into the tape player. "This Jeep doesn't have very good speakers," he said. "We have systems that are much better than this one." The Italian teacher began to teach Italian phrases. Leonardo began to laugh. Quietly at first, then louder and louder until he was shaking with laughter.

"What's so funny?" Nieman asked. He was laughing too. "What do you think is funny? Why am I laughing too?"

"Such good jokes," Leonardo answered, continuing to laugh. "What questions. What news. What jokes."

It was thirty-six miles from Willits to the Pacific Ocean. The road led down between mountains and virgin forests. They drove along at fifty miles an hour, listening to the Italian tape and then to Kiri Te Kanawa singing arias from Italian opera. Nieman was lecturing Leonardo on the history of opera and its great modern stars. Long afterward, when he had forgotten everything about the day that could be proven, Nieman remembered the drive from Willits to the ocean and someone beside him laughing. "Are you sure you weren't with me?" he asked Freddy a hundred times later in their lives. "Maybe we were stoned. But Kiri Te Kanawa didn't start recording until after we had straightened up so we couldn't have been stoned. I think you were with me. You just don't remember it."

"I never drove in a Jeep with you from Willits to the ocean while listening to Italian tapes. I would remember that, Nieman. Why do you always ask me that? It's a loose wire in your head, a precursor of dreaded things to come." Then Freddy would smile and shake his head and later talk about it to his psychiatrist or Nora Jane. "Nieman's fixated on thinking I drove with him in a Jeep listening to an Italian tape," he would say. "About once a year he starts on that. It's like the budding of the trees. Once a year, in winter, he decides the two of us took that trip and nothing will convince him otherwise. He gets mad at me because I can't remember it. Can you believe it?"

Outside the small town of Novo, Nieman found a trail he had used before. It led to a beach the townspeople used during good weather. He parked the Jeep in a gravel clearing and they got out and climbed down a path to the water. The ocean was very dramatic, with huge boulders jutting into the entrance of a small harbor. The snow was melting on the path. Even now, in the heart of winter, moss was forming on the rocks. "'The force that through the green fuse drives the flower,'" Nieman said.

"Dylan is happy now," Leonardo answered. "A charming man. I go to him quite often and he recites poetry. It makes the poetry he wrote when he was here seem primitive. I should not tell you that, of course. We try never to say such things."

"Look at the ocean," Nieman answered. "What mystery could be greater. Shouldn't this be enough for any man to attempt to understand? This force, this power, this place where land and air meet the sea? '. . . this goodly frame, the earth . . . this most excellent canopy, the air . . . this brave o'erhanging firmament, this majestical roof fretted with golden fire . . .'"

"Will loved the sea and wrote of it but had little time for it. Plato was the same. He talked and wrote of it but didn't take the time to ponder it as we are doing. Of course, in other ages time seemed more valuable. Life was short and seemed more fleeting."

They were walking along a strip of sand only ten to twenty feet wide. It was low tide. Later in the day it would have been impossible to walk here and they would have had to use the higher path.

"We could just stay here," Nieman said. "We don't have to go to the labs. I just thought you might want to see the micro-scopes."

"We have all day."

"They're leaving the labs open in the biochemistry building. We can go to Berkeley or we can stay here. I saw you looking at the atlas. Did you memorize it? I mean, is that how you do it?"

"I remember it. It is very fine how they have mapped the floor of the oceans. Is it exact, do you think?"

"Pretty much so at the time of mapping. The sand shifts, everything shifts and changes. They map the floor with sound-ings, with radar. When you leave here, where do you have to be? Is there some gathering place? Do you just walk off? Where do you go?"

"I just won't be here."

"Will the clothes be here? I only wondered. That's Freddy's coat. I could get him another one but he's pretty fond of that one. He took it to Tibet."

Nieman moved nearer to Leonardo, his eyes shifting wildly. The day had a sort of rhythm. Sometimes it was just beating along. Then suddenly he imagined it whole and that made his heart beat frantically. "I don't care, of course. You can take it if you need to. You can have anything I have."

"I will leave the clothes. It would be a waste to take them."

"When will you go? How long will it be? You have to understand. I never had a father. No man ever stayed long enough. I was always getting left on my own. It's been a problem for me all my life."

Leonardo turned to face him. "This is not a father who leaves, Nieman. This is the realm of knowledge, which you always longed for and long for now. It is always available, it never goes away, it cannot desert you, it cannot fail you. It is yours. It belongs to whoever longs for it. If you desert it, it is always waiting, like those waves. It comes back and back like the sea. I am only a moment of what is available to you. When I am gone the clothes will be here and you can wear them when you are reading things that are difficult to understand. You will read everything now. You will learn many languages. You will know much more than you know now. Tell me about the microscopes."

"I haven't used one yet. But I can tell you how it works. It concentrates a beam of electrons in a tube to scan or penetrate the thing you want magnified. It makes a photograph using light and dark and shadow. The photograph is very accurate and magnified a million times. Then a portion of that photograph can be magnified several million more times. It's so easy for me to believe the photographs so I think it must be something I know. My friend, Freddy, thinks we know everything back to the first cell, that all discovery is simply plugging into memory banks. Memory at the level of biochemistry. Which is why I can't believe it took me so long to begin to study this. I had to start in the arts. My mother is a frustrated actress. I've been working her program for forty-four years. Now it's my turn. But this is plain to you. You're the one who saw the relationship between art and science. It never occurred to you not to do both."

"I am honored to be here for your birth of understanding. Where I am, the minds are past their early enthusiasms. I miss seeing the glint in eyes. I miss the paintbrush in my hand and the smell of paints. If you wish to show me this microscope we can go there now. The sea is very old. We don't have to stay beside it all day."

It was a two-and-a-half-hour drive to Berkeley. They drove along the western ridge of the Cascade Range, within a sea breeze of the Mendocino Fracture Zone. Beside the Russian River. They drove to Mendocino, then Littleriver, then Albion. At Albion they cut off onto Highway 128 and drove along the Navarro River to Cloverdale. They went by Santa Rosa, then Petaluma, then Novato, and down and across the Richmond–San Rafael Bridge and on to Berkeley.

It was six o'clock when they arrived at the campus. It was dark and the last students were mounting their bicycles as they left the biochemistry building. Nieman nosed the Jeep into a faculty parking space and they got out and entered the building through iron doors and went down a hall to an elevator.

"Have you been on one of these?" Nieman asked, holding the elevator door with his hand. "It's a box on a pulley, actually. It's quite safe. When they were new sometimes they would get stuck. Some pretty funny jokes and stories came out of that. Also, there were tragedies, lack of oxygen and so forth. This one is thirty years old at least, but it's safe."

"Arabic," Leonardo said, touching the numbered buttons with his finger. "I thought it would continue to be useful."

"The numbers? Oh, yes. Everyone uses the same system. Based on the fingers and toes. Five fingers on each hand. Two arms, two legs. Binary system and digital system. We run our computers on the binary system. It's fascinating. What man has done. There's one playwright dealing with it, a man named Stoppard." Leonardo stepped back and stood near Nieman. Nieman pressed 2 and the box rose in space on its pulley and the door opened.

Waiting for them on the second-floor hall was the head of university security. He was wearing a blue uniform with silver buttons. "Hello," he said. "If you're Mr. Gluuk they have a lady waiting for you. President Culver said to tell you she'd show you the machines."

"Oh, that wasn't necessary. We only wanted to look at them." He took Leonardo's arm. So he looks like a genius who has spent a thousand years on a Buddhist prayer bench. So the smile is so dazzling it hypnotizes people. No one would imagine this. No one would believe it.

"Don't I know you from when I was a student?" Nieman asked. "I'm Nieman Gluuk. I used to edit the school paper. In the seventies. Didn't you guard the building when we had the riots in seventy-five?"

"I thought I knew you. I'm Abel Kennedy. I was a rookie that year and you kept me supplied with cookies and coffee in the newspaper office. I'm head of security now." Captain Kennedy held out his hand and Nieman shook it. He was trying to decide how to introduce Leonardo when a door opened down the hall and a woman came walking toward them. She was of medium height with short blond hair. She was wearing a pair of blue jeans and a long-sleeved white shirt. Over the shirt was a long white vest. There were pencils and pens in the pockets of the vest. A pair of horn-rimmed glasses was on her head. Another pair was in her hand.

"I was wondering if one could wear bifocals to look into the scope," Nieman said. "I was afraid I'd have to get contact lenses to study science."

"It's a screen." She laughed. "I'm Stella Light. My parents were with the Merry Pranksters. Some joke. I meant to have it changed but I never did." She held out her hand to Nieman. Long slender fingers. Nails bitten off to the quick. No rings. She smiled again.

"I'm Nieman Gluuk. This is our distinguished guest, Leo Gluuk, a cousin from Madrid. I mean, Florence. Also from Minneapolis."

"Make up your mind. Nice to meet you. I've read your stuff. I'm from Western Oregon. Well, what exactly can we do for you?"

"Just let us see the microscopes. Leo is very interested in the technology. It's extremely nice of you to stay late like this. I know your days are long enough already."

"I was here anyway. We've had an outbreak of salmonella in the valley. We're trying to help out with that. It gets on the chicken skin in the packing plants or if they are defrosted incorrectly. Well, I'll let you see slides of that. They're fresh."

They walked down a hall to a room with the door ajar. Inside, on a long curved table, was the console. In the center, covered with a metal that looked more like gold than brass, was the scanning electron microscope. The pride of the Berkeley labs.

They moved into the open doorway. Leonardo had been completely quiet. Now he gave Stella the smile and she stepped back and let him precede her into the room. She and Leonardo sat down at the console. She got out a box of slides and lifted one from the box with a set of calipers. She slid it into a notch and locked it down. Then she pushed a button and an image appeared on the screen. "To 0.2 nanometers," she said. "We can photograph it and go higher."

Nieman leaned over their shoulders and looked into the screen. It was a range of hills covered with cocoons. "A World War I battlefield," he said. "Corpses strewn everywhere. Is that the salmonella?"

"Yes. Let's enlarge it." She pushed another button. The hill turned into crystal mountains. Now it was the Himalayas. Range after range of crystals. Nieman looked down at his own arm. In a nanometer of skin was all that wonder.

Leonardo began asking questions about the machine, about the metal of which it was made, about the vacuum through which the electrons traveled, how the image was created. Stella answered the questions as well as she could. She bent over him. She put pieces of paper in front of him. She put slides into the microscope. She asked no questions. She had been completely mesmerized by the smile. She would remember nothing of the encounter. Except a momentary excitement when she was alone in the room at night. She thought it was sexual. She thought it was about Nieman. There I go, she would scold herself, getting interested in yet another man I cannot understand. The daddy track, chugging on down the line to lonesome valley.

They stayed in the laboratory for half an hour. Then they wandered out into the hall and found a second microscope and Stella took the thing apart and let Leonardo examine the parts. Then she let him reassemble it. She stood beside Nieman. She sized him up. He was better looking than his photograph in the paper. His skin was so white and clear. He was kind.

"You really quit your job?" she asked.

"A leave of absence. I was burned out."

"Who is he?" she asked. "I don't think I've ever met anyone I liked as much."

"We all love him. The family adores him. But it's hard to keep track of him. He travels all the time."

Leonardo put everything back into its place. He laid Stella's pencil on top of the stack of papers and got up from the chair. "We are finished now," he said. "We should be leaving. We thank you for your kindness."

Stella walked them to the elevator. They got on and she stood smiling after them. When they had left she went back into the laboratory and worked until after twelve. Two children had died in the salmonella outbreak. Twenty were hospitalized. The infected food had reached a grade school lunchroom.

When they left the building there was a full moon in the sky. There was so much light it cast shadows. Leonardo walked with Nieman to the Jeep. "I am leaving," he said. "You will be fine." He kissed Nieman on the cheek, then on the forehead. Then he was gone. Nieman tried to follow him but he did not know how. When he got back to the Jeep, the clothes Leonardo had been wearing were neatly stacked on the passenger seat. On top of the clothes was a pencil. A black and white striped pencil sharpened to a fine point. Nieman picked it up and held it. He put it in his pocket. I might write with this, he decided. Or I might draw.

He got into his Jeep and drove over to Nora Jane and Freddy Harwood's house and parked in the driveway and walked up on the porch and rang the doorbell. The twins let him in. They pulled him into the room. "Momma's making étouffée and listening to the Nevilles," Tammili told him. "She's having a New Orleans day. Come on in. Stay and eat dinner with us. Daddy said you'd been in Willits. How is it there? Was it snowing?"

They dragged him into the house. From the back Freddy called out to him. Nora Jane emerged from the kitchen wearing an apron. It was already beginning to fade. Whatever had happened or almost happened or seemed to happen was fading like a photograph in acid.

"Come on in here," Freddy was calling out. "Come tell us what you were doing. We have things to tell you. Tammili made all-stars in basketball. Lydia got a role in the school play. Nora Jane got an A on her first English test. I think I'm going bald. We haven't seen you in days. Hurry up, Nieman. I want to talk to you."

"He's your best friend," Lydia giggled, half whispering. "It's so great. You just love each other."

The Brown Cape

TAMMILI AND LYDIA were supposed to be cleaning up the loft.
Their father was working on the well. Their mother was cooking
breakfast and it was their job to make the beds and straighten
up the loft and clean the windows with vinegar and water.

"Why can't we clean them with Windex like we do at home?"
Lydia complained. "Just because we come to Willits for spring
vacation they go environmental and we have to use vinegar for
the windows. The windows are okay. I'm not cleaning them."

"You shouldn't have come then. You could have stayed with
Grandmother. You didn't have to come if you're just going to
complain."

"Why can't we have a ski lodge or something? Why do we
have to have a solar house? We can't bring anybody. It's too little
to even bring the dogs."

"It's a solar-powered house, not a solar house, and I don't
want to take dogs everywhere I go. There're wolves and panthers
in these woods. Those dogs wouldn't last a week up here. Dooley
is so friendly he'd let a wolf carry him off in his teeth."

"You clean the windows and I'll get all this stuff out from
under the bed. Everyone's always sticking stuff under here. I
hate piles of junk like this." Lydia was pulling boxes and clothes

out from underneath the bed where she and Tammili had been sleeping. It was the bed on which they had been born, in the middle of the night, ten and a half years before. Their father had delivered them and a helicopter had come and taken them to a hospital at Fort Bragg. Sometimes Lydia felt sentimental about that and sometimes she didn't like to think about it. It was embarrassing to have been delivered in a snowstorm by your father. Not to mention they had almost died. That was too terrible to think about.

"What are you thinking about?" Tammili asked, but she knew. She and Lydia always thought about things at the same time. It was the curse and blessing of being twins. You were never lonely, not even in your thoughts. On the other hand there was no place to hide.

"Who put this here?" Lydia dragged a long brown cloak out from underneath the bed. It had a cowl and a twisted cord for the waist and it was very thick, as thick as a blanket. It smelled heavenly, like some wonderful mixture of wildflowers and mist. She pulled it out and spread it on the bed. Then she wrapped it around her shoulders.

"I've never seen this before." Tammili drew near the cape and touched it. "It smells like violet. I bet it belongs to Nieman. No one but Nieman would leave a cape here. Let me wear it too, will you?" She moved into one half of the cape. They wrapped it around themselves like a cocoon and fell down on the bed and started laughing.

"Once upon a time," Lydia began, "there were two little girls and they were so poor they didn't have any firewood for the fireplace. All the trees had been cut down by ruthless land developers and there weren't any twigs left to gather to make a fire. They only had one thing left and that was their bed. We better cut up the bed and burn it, one of them said, or else we won't live until the morning. We will freeze to death in this weather. Okay, the other one said. Pull that bed over here and let's burn it up. Then they saw something under the bed. It was a long warm cape that their father had left for them when he went away to war. There was a note on it. 'This is for my darling daughters in case they run out of firewood. Love, your dad.'"

"Tammili." It was their mother calling. "You girls come on down. I want you to help me with the eggs." Tammili and Lydia put their faces very close together. They giggled again, smothering the sound.

"We're coming," Lydia called. "We'll be down in a minute." They folded the cape and laid it on the bed by Tammili's backpack. Then they climbed down the ladder to help their mother with the meal.

That was Wednesday morning. On Wednesday night their father decided they should go on an expedition. "To where?" their mother asked. "You know I have to study while I'm here. I can't go off for days down a river or in the mountains. One-day trips. That's all I'm good for this week."

"I thought we might overnight up in the pass by Red River," Freddy Harwood said. "Nieman and I used to camp there every spring. It might be cold but we'll take the bedrolls and I'll have the mobile phone. You can't go for one night?"

"I should stay here. Do you need me?"

"We don't need you," Tammili said. "We can take care of things. I want to go, Dad. We've been hearing about Red River for years but no one ever takes us. We're almost eleven. We can do anything."

"Get another adult," Nora Jane insisted. "Don't go off with both of them and no one to help."

"We are help," Lydia said. "Is it a steep climb, Daddy? Is it steep?"

"No. It's long but it's not that steep. Nieman and I used to do the trail to the top in three hours. Two and a half coming down. There's a bower up there under thousand-year-old pine trees. You don't need a sleeping bag. We'll take them but we could sleep on the ground. I haven't been up there to camp in years. Not since I met your mother. So, we'll go. It's decided."

"Tomorrow," they both screamed.

"Maybe tomorrow. Maybe Friday. Let me think about it." They jumped on top of him and started giving him one of their famous hug attacks. They grabbed pillows and hugged him with them until he screamed for mercy. "Tomorrow, tomorrow, tomorrow," they kept saying. "Don't make us wait."

"Then we have to get everything ready tonight because we have to leave at sunup. It takes an hour to drive to the trail. Then three hours to climb. I want to have camp set up by afternoon."

"What do we need?"

"Tent, food, clothes, extra socks. Vaseline for blisters, ankle packs for sprains, snakebite kit, Mag Lites, sleeping bags."

"We're going to carry all that?"

"Whatever we want we have to carry. We'll have extra water in the car. We'll take small canteens and the purifying kit. Go start pumping at the well, Tammili. Fill two water bags."

"Can't I fill them at the sink?"

"No, the idea is to know how to survive without a sink. That's what Willits is for, sweeties."

"We know." They gave each other a look. "So no matter what happens your DNA is safe." They started giggling and their mother put down the dish she was drying and started giggling too.

Freddy Harwood was an equipment freak. He had spent the summers of his youth in wilderness camps in Montana and western Canada. When he graduated to camping on his own, he took up equipment as a cause. If he was going camping he had every state-of-the-art device that could be ordered on winter nights from catalogs. He had Mag Lites on headbands and Bull Frog sunblock. He had wrist compasses and Ray-Ban sunglasses and Power Bars and dehydrated food. He had two lightweight tents, a Stretch Dome and a Lookout. The Lookout was the lightest. It weighed five pounds, fifteen ounces with the poles. He had Patagonia synchilla blankets and official referee whistles and a Pur water purifier and drinking water tablets in case the purifier broke. He had two-bladed knives for the girls and a six-bladed knife for himself. He had stainless-steel pans and waterproofing spray and tent repair kits and first aid kits of every kind.

"Bring everything we think we need and put it on the table," Freddy said. "Then we'll decide what to take and what to leave. Bring everything. Your boots and the clothes you're going to wear. It's eight o'clock. We have to be packed and in bed by ten if we're going in the morning."

The girls went upstairs and picked out clothes to wear. "I'm taking this cape," Tammili said. "I've got a feeling about this cape. I think it's supposed to go to Red River with us."

"Nieman saw baby panthers up there once," Lydia added. "The mother didn't kill him for looking at them she was so weak with hunger because there had been a drought and a forest fire. Nieman left them all his food. He got to within twenty feet of their burrow and put the food where she could get it. Dad was there. He knows it's true. Nieman's so cool. I wish he was going with us."

"He has to study. He's going for a Nobel prize in biochemistry. That's what Dad told Grandmother. He said Nieman wouldn't rest until he won a Nobel."

The girls brought their clothes and backpacks down from the loft and spread the things out on the table. "What's this?" Freddy asked, picking up the cloak.

"Something we found underneath the bed. We think it's Nieman's. I was going to take it instead of a sleeping bag. Look how warm it is."

"I wouldn't carry it if I were you. You have to think of every ounce." Tammili went over and took the cape from him and folded it and laid it on the hearth. Later, when they had finished packing all three of the backpacks and set them by the kitchen door, she picked up the cape and pushed it into her pack. I'm taking it, she decided. I like it. It looks like the luckiest thing you could wear.

In a small, neat condominium in Berkeley, the girls' godfather, Nieman Gluuk, was finishing the last of twenty algebra problems he had set himself for the day. His phone was off the hook. His flower gardens were going wild. His cupboards were bare. His sink was full of dishes. His bed was unmade.

He put the last notation onto the last problem and stood up and began to rub his neck with his hand. He was lonely. His house felt like a tomb. "I'm going to Willits to see the kids," he said out loud. "I'm going crazy all alone in this house. Starting to talk to myself. They are my family and I need them and it's spring vacation and they won't be ten forever."

He went into his bedroom and began to throw clothes into a suitcase. It was three o'clock in the morning. He had been working on the algebra problems for fourteen hours. When Nieman Gluuk set out to conquer a body of knowledge, he did it right. When he had studied philosophy he had learned German and French and Greek. Now he was studying biochemistry and he was learning math. "If my eyes hold out I will learn this stuff," he muttered. "If my eyes give out, I'll learn it with my ears." He pushed the half-filled suitcase onto the floor and turned off the lights and pulled off his shirt and pants and fell into his bed in his underpants. It would be ten in the morning before he woke. Since he had quit his job at the newspaper he had been sleeping nine and ten hours a night. The day he canceled his subscription he slept twelve hours that night.

"The destination," Freddy was saying to his daughters, "is the high caves above Red River. They aren't on this map but you can see the cliff face in these old photographs. Nieman and I took these when we were about twenty years old. We developed them in my old darkroom in Grandmother Ann's house. See all the smudges? We were experimenting with developers." He held the photograph up. "Anyway, we follow the riverbed for a few miles, then up and around the mountain to this pass. Four rivers rise on this mountain. All running west except this one. Red River runs east and north. It's an anomaly, probably left behind from some cataclysm when the earth cooled or else created by an earthquake eons ago. It's unique in every way. If there was enough snow last winter the falls will be spectacular this time of year. Some years they are spectacular and sometimes just a trickle. We won't know until we get there. Even in dry years the sound is great. Where we are camping we will be surrounded by water and the sound of water. It's the best sleeping spot in the world. I'll put it up against any place you can name. I wish your mother was going with us. She doesn't know what she's missing." He took the plate of pancakes Nora Jane handed him and began to eat, lifting each mouthful delicately and dramatically, meeting her violet-blue eyes and saying secrets to her about the night that had passed and the one she was going to be missing.

Tammili and Lydia played with their food. Neither of them could eat when they were excited and they were excited now.

"Is this enough?" Lydia asked her mother. "I really don't want any more."

"Whatever you like. It's a long way to go and the easy way to carry food is in your stomach."

"It weighs the same inside or out," Tammili said. "We're only taking dehydrated packs. In your stomach it's mixed with water so it really weighs less if you carry it in the pack."

Lydia giggled and got up and put her plate by the sink. Tammili followed her. "Let's go," they both said. "Come on, let's get going."

"I wish you had a weather report," Nora Jane put in. "If it turns colder you just come on back."

"Look at that sky. It's as clear as summer. There's nothing moving in today. I've been coming up here for twenty years. I can read this weather like the back of my hand. It's perfect for camping out."

"I know. The world is magic and there's nothing to fear but fear itself." Nora Jane went to her husband and held him in her arms. "Go on and sleep by a waterfall. I wish I could go but I have to finish this paper. That's it. I want to turn it in next week."

"Let's go," Tammili called out. "What's keeping you, Dad? Let's get going." Freddy kissed his wife and went out and got into the driver's seat of the Jeep Cherokee and the girls strapped themselves into the seats behind him and plugged their Walkmans into their ears.

Nora Jane went back into the house and stacked the rest of the dishes by the sink and sat down at the table and got her papers out. She was writing a paper on Dylan Thomas. "'The force that through the green fuse drives the flower / Drives my green age;'" she read, "'that blasts the roots of trees / Is my destroyer. . . .'"

*　　　*　　　*

Freddy took a right at the main road to Willits, then turned onto an old gold-mining trail that had been worn down by a hundred years of rain. "Hold on," he told the girls. "This is only for four miles, then we'll be on a better road. It will save us hours if we use this shortcut." The girls took the plugs out of their ears and held on to the seats in front of them. The mobile phone fell from its holder and rattled around on the floor. Tammili captured it and turned it on to see if it was working. "It's broken," she said. "You broke the phone, Dad. It wasn't put back in right."

"Good," he said. "One less hook to civilization. When we get rid of the Jeep we'll be really free. The wilderness doesn't want you to bring a bunch of junk along. It wants you to trust it to provide for you."

"Trusting the earth is trusting yourself. Trusting yourself is trusting the earth. This is our home. We were made for it and it for us." The girls chanted Freddy's credo in unison, then fell into a giggling fit. The Jeep bounced along over the ruts. The girls giggled until they were coughing.

"You have reached the apex of the silly phase," Freddy said, in between the bumps. "You have perfected being ten years old. I don't want this growing up to go a day further. If you get a day older, I'll be mad at you." He gripped the steering wheel, went around a boulder, and came down a steep incline onto a black-top road that curved around and up the mountain. "Okay," he said. "Now we're railroading. Now we're whistling Dixie."

"He hated that mobile phone," Tammili said to her sister. "He's been dying for it to break."

"It's Momma's phone so she can call us from her school," Lydia answered. "He's going to have to get her another one as soon as he gets back."

Nieman woke with a start. He had been dreaming about the equations from the day before. They lined up in front of the newspaper office. Gray uniformed and armed to the teeth, they barred his way to his typewriter. When he tried to reason with them, they held up their guns. They fixed their bayonets.

"I hate dreams," he said. He put his feet down on the floor and looked around at the mess his house was in. He lay back down on the bed. He dialed a number and spoke to the office manager at Merry Maids. Yes, they would send someone to clean the place while he was gone. Yes, they would tell Mr. Levin hello. Yes, they would be sure to come.

I'm out of here, Nieman decided. I'll eat breakfast on the way. They know I'm coming. They know I wouldn't stay away all week. I'll go by the deli and get bagels and smoked salmon. I'll take the math book and do five more problems before Monday. Only five. That's it. I don't have to be crazy if I don't want to be. An obsessive can pick and choose among obsessions.

He put the suitcase back onto the unmade bed. He added a pair of hiking shorts and a sun-resistant Patagonia shirt he always wore in Willits. He closed the suitcase and went into the bathroom and got into the shower and closed his eyes and tried to think about the composition of water. Hydrogen, he was thinking. So much is invisible to us. We think we're so hot with our five senses but we know nothing, really. Ninety-nine percent of what is going on escapes us. Ninety-nine percent to the tenth power or the thousandth power. The rest we know. We are so wonderful in our egos, dressed out in all our ignorance and bliss. Our self-importance, our blessed hope.

Freddy went up a last long curve, cut off on a dirt road for half a mile, then stopped the Jeep at the foot of an abandoned gold mine. "Watch your step," he said to the girls. "There are loose stones everywhere. You have to keep an eye on the path. It's rough going all the way to where the trees begin."

"It's so nice here," Lydia said. "I feel like no one's been here in years. I bet we're the only people on this mountain. Do you think we are, Dad? Do you think anyone else is climbing it today?"

"I doubt it. Nieman and I never saw a soul when we were here. Of course, we have managed to keep our mouths shut about it, unlike some people who have to photograph and pub-lish every good spot they find."

"Feel the air," Tammili added. "It tastes like spring. I'm glad we're here, Dad. This is a thousand times better than some old ski resort."

"Was a ski resort a possibility?" Freddy was trying not to grin.

"No. But some people went to them. Half the school went to Sun Valley. I don't care. I'd lots rather be in the wilderness with you."

"I'm glad you approve. Look up there. Not a cloud in the sky. What a lucky day."

"There's a cloud formation in the west," Tammili said. "I've been watching it for half an hour." They turned in the direction of the sea. Sure enough. On the very tip of the horizon a gray cloud was approaching. Nothing to worry about. Not a black system. Just a very small patch of gray on the horizon.

"Gather up the packs," Freddy said. "Let's start climbing. The sooner we make camp the sooner we don't have to worry about the weather. Those trees up there have withstood a thousand years of weather. We'd be safe there in a hurricane."

"What about a map check?" Tammili asked. She was pulling the straps of her pack onto her strong, skinny shoulders. Lydia was beside her, looking equally determined. This will never come again, Freddy thought. This time when they are children and women in the same skin. This innocence and power. My angels.

"Daddy. Come to." Lydia touched his sleeve, and he turned and kissed her on the head.

"Of course. Get a drink of water out of the thermos we're leaving. Then we'll climb up to that lookout and take our bearings." He handed paper cups to them and they poured water from a thermos and drank it, then folded the cups and left them in the Jeep. They hiked up half a mile to a lookout from where they could see the terrain between them and the place they were going. "Take a reading," Freddy said. "We'll write the readings down, but I want you to memorize them. Paper can get lost or wet. As long as the compass is on your wrist and you memorize the readings, you can find your way back to any base point."

"The best thing is to look where you're going," Tammili said. "Anyone can look at the sun and figure out where the ocean is."

"We won't always be hiking in Northern California," Freddy countered. "We'll do the Grand Canyon soon and then Nepal."

"Momma's friend Brittany got pregnant in Nepal," Lydia said. "She got pregnant with a monk. We saw pictures of the baby."

"Well, that isn't going to happen to either of you. I'm not going to let either of you get pregnant until you have an M.D. or a Ph.D., for starters. I may not let you get pregnant until you're forty. I was thinking thirty-five, now I'm thinking forty."

"We know. You're going to buy a freezer so we can freeze our eggs and save them until we can hire someone to have the babies." They started giggling again. When Lydia and Tammili decided something was funny, they thought it was funnier and funnier the more they laughed.

"Maps and compasses," Freddy said. "Find out where we are. Then find out where we're going, then chart a course."

"Where are we going?"

"Up there. To that cliff face. Around the corner is the waterfall that is the source of Red River." He watched as their faces bent toward their indescribably beautiful small wrists. The perfect bones and skin of ten-year-olds, burdened with the huge wrist compasses and watches. I could spend the day worshiping their arms, Freddy thought, or I could teach them something. "This is the Western Cordillera," he added. "Those are Douglas fir, as you know, and most of the others are pines, several varieties. Are the packs too heavy?"

"They're okay. We can stash things on the trail if we have to."

"In twenty minutes, we'll rest for five. All right?"

"I think I hear the waterfall," he said. "Can you hear it?"

"Not if you're talking," Tammili said. "You have to be quiet to get nature to give up its secrets."

"Stop it, Tammili. Stop teasing him."

"Yeah, Tammili. Stop teasing me." They walked in silence then, up almost a thousand feet before they stopped to rest. The path was loose and slippery and the landscape to the east was barren and rough. To the west it was more dramatic. The cloud formation they had noticed earlier was growing into a larger mass.

"A gathering storm," Freddy said. "We'll be glad I put the waterproofing on the tent last night."

"I am glad," Lydia said. "I don't like to get wet when I'm camping."

"Let's go on then," Tammili said. "That might get here sooner than we think it's going to."

They shouldered the packs and began to climb again. Freddy was drawing the terrain in his mind. He had planned on camping at a site that was surrounded by watercourses. It was so steep that even if there was a deluge it would run off. Still, there was a dry riverbed that had to be crossed to get to the site. We could make for the caves, he was thinking. There wouldn't be bears this high but there are always snakes. Well, hell, I should have gotten a weather report but I didn't. That was stupid but we'll be safe.

"He's worrying," Tammili said to her sister.

"I knew he would. He thinks we'll get wet."

"I don't know about all this." Freddy stopped on the path above them and shook his head. "That cloud's worrying me. Maybe we should go back and camp by the Jeep. We could climb all around down there. We can go to Red River another time."

"We're halfway there," Tammili said. "We can't turn back now. We've got the tent. We'll get it up and if it rains, it rains."

"Yeah," Lydia agreed. "We'll ride it out."

In the solar-powered house Nora Jane was watching the sky. She would study for a while, then go outside and watch the weather. Finally, she started the old truck they kept for emergencies and tried to get a station on the radio. A scratchy AM station in Fort Bragg came on but it was only playing country music. She was about to drive the truck to town when she saw dust on the road and Nieman came driving up in his Volvo. "Thank God you came," she said, pulling open the door as soon as he parked. "Freddy took the girls to Red River and now it's going to storm. I could kill him for doing that. Why does he do such stupid things, Nieman? He didn't get a weather report and he just goes driving off to take the girls to see a waterfall."

"We'll go and find them," Nieman said. "Then we'll kill him. How about that?"

*   *   *

The adventurers climbed until they came to a dry riverbed that had to be crossed to gain the top. It was thirty feet wide and abruptly steep at the place where it could be crossed. The bed was a jumble of boulders rounded off by centuries of water. Some were as tall as a man. Others were the size of a man's head or foot or hand. Among the dark rounded boulders were sharper ones of a lighter color. "The sharp-looking pieces are granite," Freddy was saying. "It's rare in the coastal ranges. God knows where it was formed or what journeys it took to get here. Hang on to the large boulders and take your time. We are lucky it's dry. Nieman and I have crossed it when it's running, but I wouldn't let you." He led the girls halfway across the bed, then let them go in front of him, Tammili, then Lydia. They were surefooted and careful and he watched them negotiate the boulders with more than his usual pride. When they were across he started after them. A broken piece of granite caught his eye. He leaned over to pick it up. He stepped on a piece of moss and his foot slipped and kept on slipping. He stepped out wildly with his other foot to stop it. He kept on falling. He twisted his right ankle between two boulders and landed on his left elbow and shattered the humerus at the epicondyle.

"Don't come back here," he called. "Stay where you are. I'll crawl to you."

"Don't listen to him," Tammili said. She dropped her pack on the ground and climbed back over the boulders to where he lay gasping with pain. "Cut the pack strap," he said. "Use the big blade on your knife. Cut it off my shoulder if you can."

"What time did they leave?" Nieman asked. He had called the weather station and gotten a report and put in a preliminary request for information on distress flares in the area.

"They left about six-thirty this morning. Maybe they're on their way back. Freddy can see this front as well as we can. He wouldn't go up the mountain with a storm coming. All they have is that damned little tent. It barely sleeps three."

"They could go to the caves. I'm going to try to call him on the mobile phone. If they're driving, he'll answer." Nieman tried raising Freddy on the mobile phone, then called the telephone company and had them try. "Nothing. They can't get a thing. We are probably crazy to worry. What could go wrong? The girls are better campers than I am. They're not children."

"Tammili only weighs eighty pounds. I want to call the park rangers."

"Then call them. We'll tell them to be on the alert for flares from that area. I know he has flares with him. He loves flares. He always has them. Then we'll get in the Volvo and go look for them. I guess it will go down that road. Maybe we better take the truck."

"We have to make a stretcher and carry him to the trees," Tammili was saying. Freddy was slowly moving his body but he wasn't making much progress. He couldn't stand on his left ankle and he couldn't use his right arm and he could barely breathe for the pain. There were pain pills in the kit but he wouldn't take them. "At least I can think," he kept saying. "I can stand it and I can think. We have to get a shelter set up before the rain hits. I want you to go on over there and wait for me. I can make it. I'll get there." Then he went blank and the girls were standing over him.

"Let's go over to that stand of trees and tie down the supplies and get the tent cover and drag him on it," Tammili said. "If you start crying I'll smack you. What do you think we went to all those camps for? This is the emergency they trained us for. Come on. Help me drag his pack to the trees. Then we'll come back and get him. Nothing's going to happen to him. We can leave him for a minute."

They pulled Freddy's pack to the stand of pine trees where they had left their own. They tied the straps around a sapling and then found the tent cover and went back for him. The sky was very dark now but they did not notice it because they were ten years old and could live in the present.

They laid the tent cover down beside their father and tried to wake him. "You have to wake up and help us," Tammili was saying. "You have to roll over on the cover so we can drag it up the trail. Come on, Dad. It's going to rain. You'll get washed down the river. Come on. Move over here if you can." Freddy came to consciousness. He rolled over onto the tent cover with his left shoulder and tried to find a comfortable position. "Clear the rocks off the path," Lydia said. "Come on, Tammili. Let's clear the path." They began to throw the rocks to the side. Working steadily they managed to clear a way from the riverbed to the trees. Freddy lay on the cover with the pain coming and going like waves on the sea. He rocked in the pain. He let the pain take him. There was no way to escape it. Nora Jane will call for help, he was thinking. I know her. This is where her worrying will come in handy. The truck runs. She will drive it into town and call for help. The rain was beginning. He felt it on his face. Then the pain won and he didn't feel anything.

Lydia and Tammili came back down the path to the unconscious body of their father. They folded the tent cover around his body and began to pull him along the path they had cleared. Every two or three feet they would stop and try to wake him. Then they would scour the next few feet for branches and rocks. Then they would move him a few feet more. The rain was still falling softly, barely more than a mist. "It's good to get the ground wet," Tammili was saying. "It makes the tent slide."

"You aren't supposed to move wounded people. We could be making him worse."

"We aren't making him worse. His ankle's right there. We aren't moving it and his arm isn't moving. We're just going to that tree. We have to get away from the riverbed, Lydia. That thing could turn into a torrent. Keep pulling. Don't start crying. Nothing's going to happen. We're going to pull him to that tree and stay there until this storm is over."

"I don't believe this happened. How did it happen to us? We shouldn't have come up here."

"We only have a little more to go. Keep pulling. Don't talk so much." Tammili dug in her heels and pulled the weight of her father six more inches up and to the right of the path. Wind came around the side of the mountain and blew rain into their faces. She went to her father and pulled the tent cover more tightly around his body. She looked up at her sister. Their eyes met. Lydia was holding back her tears. "We only have one move," Tammili said. "We take the king to a place of safety. I'm a bishop and you're a rook. We're taking Dad to that tree, Lydia. We can do it if we will."

"I'm okay," Freddy said. "I can crawl up there. I'm okay, Lydia. Help me up, Tammili. This is just a rain. Just a rain that will end."

He half stood with Tammili supporting his side. He managed to hobble a few more feet in the direction of the tree. Lydia dragged the tent cover around in front of him and they laid him back down on it and pulled him the rest of the way.

Nora Jane and Nieman climbed into the Volvo and started across the property toward the old gold-mining road that Freddy and the girls had taken earlier that morning. "It's too low," Nieman said, after five minutes of driving. "It will never make it down that riverbed. Let's go back and get the truck."

"The truck barely runs."

"Well, we'll make it run."

"Let's call the ranger station again. I don't think we can overdo that. My God, Nieman, what's that noise?"

"I think it's a tire. It feels like something's wrong with a tire." He stopped the car and got out and stood looking at the left front tire. It was almost completely flat and getting flatter.

"You have a spare, don't you?" Nora Jane asked. She had gotten out and was standing beside him.

"No. I left it months ago to be repaired and never went back to pick it up. We'll have to walk back and get the truck."

"Call the ranger station first, then we'll get the truck." Nieman didn't argue. He got the ranger station on the phone. "No, we don't know they're lost. We just know they didn't know this weather was coming. You can put it in the computer, can't you? So if anyone sees a warning flare in that area they'll report it? He always has flares. . . . Because I know. Because I've been camping with him a hundred times. . . . Okay. Just so you're on the alert. We're going there now. It's the old gold-mining camp below Red River Falls. The waterfall that is the source of Red River. Surely you have it on a map. . . . All right. Thanks again. Thank you."

"Insanity. Bureaucrazy. Okay, my darling Nora Jane, let's get out and walk."

Halfway to the house it began to rain. By the time they reached the house they were soaking wet. They changed into dry clothes and got into the truck and started driving. This time they didn't talk. They didn't curse. They didn't plan. They just moved as fast as they could go in the direction of the people that they loved.

Tammili and Lydia had managed to drag Freddy almost to the tree. There was a reasonably flat patch of ground there and they surveyed it. "Let's put the tent up over him," Lydia suggested.

"We'd have to move him twice to do that. We haven't got time and besides we shouldn't move him any more than we have to."

"So what are we going to do?"

"We'll cover up with the tent and put all the packs and some rocks around to hold it down."

"Water's going to run in."

"Not if we fix it right. Get it out." Tammili was pulling things out of the packs. "We'll get him covered up, then I'll set off flares."

"You better set them off before it rains any more."

"Then hurry." They dragged the tent over to their father and draped it over his body. Lydia took the cape and wrapped it around his legs and feet. They pulled the tent cover up to make a rain sluice and set rocks against it to hold it in place.

"Finish up," Tammili said. "I'm going over there by the river-bed and set off flares." She had found a pack of them in the bottom of Freddy's pack. She pulled it out and read the directions. "Keep out of the hands of children. This is not a toy. Approved by the Federal Communications Commission and the Federal Bureau of Standards. Remove plastic cap carefully. Point in the direction of clear sky. Da. Pull down lever with a firm grasp. If three pulls does not release flare, discard and try another flare. Okay, here goes." She walked over to the cleared place. She pulled the lever down and a huge point of light rose to the sky and spread out and held.

"Do some more," Lydia called to her. Tammili set off four more flares. Then waited. Then set off two more. Rain was beginning to fall in earnest now. She went back to the pack and put the leftover flares where she had found them. Then she buckled up the pack and put the smaller packs on top of it. Then she dragged the synchilla blanket underneath the tent and she and Lydia lay down on each side of their father. The rain was falling harder. They arranged the synchilla blanket over Freddy's body and then covered that with the cape. They found each other's hands. The fingers of Lydia's right hand fit into the fingers of Tammili's left hand as they had always done.

A volunteer fire lookout worker was in a fire tower ten miles from where they lay covered with the cape and tent. He was a twenty-year-old student who had always been good at every-thing he did. He prided himself on being good at things. Every other Thursday when he spent his three hours in the tower he was on the lookout every second. He didn't go down and fill his coffee cup. He didn't read books. He kept his eyes on the sky and the land. That was what he had volunteered to do and that is what he did. Earlier, before he began his stint, he had pulled up all the local data on a computer and read it carefully. He had especially noted the memo about Red River because his mother was a geologist and had taken him there as a child. He saw the first flare out of the corner of his eye just as it was dying. He saw the second and the third and fourth flares, but lost the last two in the approaching storm. "I will be damned," he decreed. "I finally saw something. It finally paid off to stay alert." He called the ranger station and reported what he had seen.

Nora Jane and Nieman were driving the four miles of rocky trail between blacktop and blacktop. They were driving in a blinding rain. Nieman was at the wheel. Nora Jane was pushing back into the seat imagining her life without her husband and her daugh-ters. I don't know why we built that crazy house to begin with, Nieman was thinking. I hate it there. Grass doesn't grow. You can't take a hot shower half the time. It's a dangerous place. We should have been down in the inner city building houses for people to live in. Not some goddamn, lonely, scary, dangerous trap on a barren hillside. He shouldn't have taken them up there, much less to Red River. As though they are expendable. As though we could ever breathe again if anything happened to them. But what could happen? Nothing will happen. They'll get wet, then we'll get them dry. He steered the old red truck down onto the blacktop and pushed the pedal to the floor. "I'm gunning it," he said to Nora Jane. "Hold on."

"Don't worry, Daddy," Tammili was crooning. "Momma will send someone to get us. Remember when Lydia broke her arm and it got all right. Her hand was hanging off her wrist like nothing and it grew back fine."

"It sure did," Lydia said. "It grew right back."

"Get behind the rocks," Freddy said. "Don't stay here. I'm okay. I'm doing fine." A sheet of lightning blazed a mile away. It seemed to be beside them. "It's okay," Freddy said. "Cuddle up. Rain always stops. It always stops. It always does."

"Sometimes it rains for two days," Lydia put in. She snuggled down into a ball beside her father. She patted her father's chest. She patted his ribs. She patted his heart. Another burst of lightning flashed even closer. Then the rain began to fall twice as hard as it had before. The earth seemed to sink beneath the force of the rain, but they were warm beneath the cape and the tent and they were together.

"These are Franciscan rocks," Tammili said. "The whole Coast Range is made up of the softest, weirdest rocks they know. Geologists don't know what they are. They used to be the ocean floor. Where we are, right now, as high as it seems, used to be stuff on the floor of the ocean."

"That's right," Lydia added. "Before that it was the molten center of the earth."

"The continents ride on the seas like patches of weeds in a marsh," Tammili went on. "Fortunately for us it all moves so slowly that we'll be dead before it changes enough to matter. Unless the big earthquake puts it all back in the sea."

"Who told you that?" Freddy tried to rise up on his good arm. The pain in the other one had subsided for a moment. He was beginning to be able to move his foot. "When the storm subsides we'll put up the rest of the flares. They'll be looking for us. Someone's looking for us now."

"We could drive the car," Lydia whispered. A third network of lightning had covered the mountain with clear blue light. Far away the thunder rumbled, but the lightning seemed to be only feet away. "One of us could stay with you and the other one could get in the Jeep and go for help."

"They'll find us," Freddy said. "Your mother will be right on top of this. If we don't come back, she'll send for help." The rain was harder now, beating on the flattened tent. Still, they seemed to be warm and dry. "This cape wicks faster than synchilla," Freddy added. "Just like Nieman to find this and leave it lying around." The pain returned full force then and Freddy felt himself going down. Don't think, he told himself. Turn it off. Don't let it in.

"Hold my hand," Lydia said and reached for her sister. "Tell more about the coast and the ocean. Tell the stuff Nieman tells us."

"It was a deep trench, the whole coast, the whole state of California. And the ocean and the hot middle of the earth keep churning and pushing and hot stuff comes up from the middle, like melted fire, only more like hot, hot honey, and it's very beautiful and red and gold and finally it turns into rocks and mud and gets pushed up to make mountains. Then the trench got filled with stuff and it rose up like islands and made California. Then the Great Plains got in the middle of the Coast Range and the Sierra Nevada and the Cascades. They are real thick mountains and all crystallized together with granite. But not the Coast Range. The Coast Range is made of strange rocks and there is jade left here by serpentine. And maganese and mercury and bluechist and gold and everything you could want."

"Serpentinite," Freddy said. "Manganese."

Nieman was saying, "You stay in the truck and wait for the rangers. Work on the phone in Freddy's Jeep. You might get it working. I'm going up."

They were standing at the base of the path. It was still

pouring rain. Nieman was wearing a foul-weather parka and was laden with signal devices, everything they had found in the house and cars.

"Go on then. Start climbing. I'll do what I can."

"Do whatever you decide to do." He looked at her then, this beautiful, whimsical creature whom his best friend adored, and he understood the adoration as never before. Her whole world was in danger and she was breathing normally and was not whining. Nieman gave her a kiss on the cheek and turned and began to climb. The rain was coming down so fast it was difficult to see, but he knew the path and he was careful. Maybe we should have gone for help instead of coming here. Maybe we should have done a dozen things. The rangers know. Surely to God they are on their way.

The ranger helicopter had turned back from the lightning and now a truck carrying a medic was headed in their direction but the road had been washed out in two places and they had had to ford it. "Plot the coordinates of the flares again," the driver said. "Are you sure twenty-four is the nearest road?"

"There's an old creek bed we might navigate, but not in this weather. An old mining road leads to within a mile. I'd rather take that. Here, you look at the map."

"Jesus, what a storm. A frog strangler, that's what we call them where I come from."

"Two little girls and their father. I'd like to kill some people. What the hell does a man want to go off for with kids this far from nowhere? It kills me. I used to teach wilderness safety at the hospital. What a waste of breath."

"Land of the free. Home of the foolhardy. Okay, I think I can make it across that water. Let's give it a try." He drove the vehicle across a creek and made it to the other side. As soon as they were across, the medic put on his seat belt and pulled it down tight across his waist and chest.

"Four hundred and three," Nieman was counting. "Four hundred and four. Four hundred and five."

*   *   *

Nora Jane sat in the passenger seat of the Jeep and worked on the phone. Once or twice she was able to hear static and she kept on trying. She took the batteries out and wiped them on her shirt and put them back in. She moved every movable part. She prayed to her old Roman Catholic God. She prayed to Mary. She made promises.

The storm was moving very slowly across the chaos of disordered rocks that is the Coast Range of Northern California. The birds pulled their wings over their heads. The panthers dreamed in their lairs. The scraggly vegetation drank the water as fast as it fell. When the sun came back out it would use the water to grow ten times as fast as vegetation in wetter climates. Tammili and Lydia held hands. Freddy slept. An infinitesimal part of the energy we call time became what we call history.

"Six thousand and one," Nieman counted. He wanted to stop and wipe his glasses but he could not bring himself to waste a second. Some terrible intuition led him on. Some danger or unease that had bothered him ever since the night before. He had come to where he was needed. It was not the first time that had happened to him. That's why I hated those movies, he told himself. When no one believed what they knew. When no one learned anything. The beginning of *Karate Kid* was okay. The beginning of it was grand.

He had come to a creek bed that was now a torrent of rushing water. I know this, he remembered. But how the hell will I cross it now? He stood up straight. He pushed the hood back from his parka and reached for his glasses to wipe them. A huge bolt of lightning shook the sky. It illuminated everything in sight. By its light Nieman saw the pile of tent and figures on the ground on the other side of the water. "Freddy," he screamed at the top of his lungs. "It's me. It's Nieman. Freddy, is that you?"

The rest was drowned by thunder. Then Nieman saw a small figure rise up from the pile. She came out from under the tent and began waving her hands in the air.

"I'll get there," he yelled. "Stay where you are." The rain was slacking somewhat. Nieman found a flat place a few yards down the creek and began to make his way across the rocks. Lydia met him on the other side. "Dad's broken his arm and foot," she told him. "We need to get him to a doctor."

The medic spotted the Jeep and the truck. "There they are," he yelled at the driver. "There're the fools. Let's go get them."

An hour later Freddy was on a stretcher being brought down the mountain by four men. The clearing was filled with vehicles. The brown cape was thrown into the back of an EMS van. It would end up at the city laundry. Then on the bed of a seven-year-old Mexican girl who had been taken from her mother. But that is another story.

Ten days later a party gathered at Chez Panisse to eat an early dinner and discuss the events of the past week. There were nine people gathered at Freddy Harwood's favorite table by the window in the back room. The young man who had seen the flares, the medic, the driver, Nieman, Freddy, Nora Jane, Tammili, Lydia, and a woman biochemist who was after Nieman to marry him. Her name was Stella Light and this was the first time Nieman had taken her out among his friends. It was the first time he had taken her to Chez Panisse and the first time he had introduced her to Nora Jane and Freddy and the twins. Stella Light was dressed in her best clothes, a five-year-old gray pant-suit and a white cotton blouse. She had almost added a yellow scarf but had taken it off minutes after she put it on.

"We had this magic cape we found under the bed," Lydia was telling her. "The minute we say something's magic, it is magic, that's what Uncle Nieman says. It's probably his cape but he can't remember it. He leaves his stuff everywhere. Did you know that? He's absentminded because he is a genius. Do you go to school with him? Is that how you met him?"

"Well, I teach in the department. Tell me about the cape."

"It kept us warm. Dad thinks it was synchilla. Anyway, it was raining so hard it felt like rocks were falling on us."

"It was lightning like crazy," Tammili added. "There was lightning so near it made halos around the trees."

"Tammili!" Freddy shook his head.

"You don't know. You were incoherent from pain."

"Incoherent?" Stella laughed.

"She always talks like that," Lydia said. "It's Uncle Nieman. He's been working on our vocabularies since we were born."

"I'm having goat cheese pie and salad," Nieman said. "I think he wants to take our orders. Menus up, ladies. Magic cape, my eye. Magic forest rangers and volunteer distress signal watchers." He stood up and raised his glass to the medic and the driver and the young man. "To your honor, gentlemen. We salute thee."

"To all of us," Freddy added, raising his glass with his good hand. "My saviors, my family, my friends."

Nieman caught Stella's eye as they drank. A long sweet look that was not lost on Tammili and Lydia. We could be the bridesmaids, Lydia decided. We never get to be in weddings. None of Mom and Dad's friends ever get married. Pretty soon we'll be too old to be bridesmaids. It will be too late.

"Stop it," Tammili whispered to her sister, pretending to be bending over to pick up a napkin so she wouldn't be scolded for telling secrets at the table. "Stop wanting that woman to marry Uncle Nieman. Uncle Nieman doesn't need a girlfriend. He's got everything he needs. He's got Mom and Dad and you and me." When she sat up she batted her eyes at her godfather. Then, for good measure, she got up and walked around the table and gave him a hug and stood by his side. Oh, my God, Stella was thinking. Well, that's an obstacle that can be overcome. Children are such little beasts nowadays. It makes you want to get your tubes tied.

"Go back to your chair," Nora Jane said to her daughter. "Let Uncle Nieman eat his goat cheese pie."

The Affair

NIEMAN GLUUK WAS finally going to be taken to bed. Not that he hadn't had love affairs before. He had had them but they hadn't meant to him what they mean to most of us. They hadn't thrown him to the mat. They hadn't given him a taste of what men kill and die for, dream about. One Stella Light of Salem, Oregon, was going to be the one to do it. Thirty-seven years old, five feet six inches tall, dark haired and dark eyed, a physicist, a biochemist, and a distance runner. A control freak. An expert on viral diseases of poultry. The only child of a high school science teacher and a librarian. A small-breasted woman who had dyed her hair platinum blond the week before she met Nieman and begun wearing a devastatingly expensive perfume called Joy. Her clock was ticking and her hours staring at photographs taken by electron microscopes had not given her any reason to put off doing anything she wanted to do.

It is dawn. Stella gets up and makes the bed. She puts on a white T-shirt and a pair of cutoff blue jeans and some high-tech Nike running shoes. She rubs sunblock lotion on her arms and face. She pours a cup of coffee that was made automatically at five o'clock by her combination clock radio and coffeemaker.

She walks out onto her porch. She surveys the mist that has

come in the night before. She imagines the coast of California swaying on its shaky underpinnings. She goes down the stairs and begins to run. In five minutes the endorphins kick in. In five minutes the blood is in her legs instead of her cerebral cortex, and for the only time during the day she is free of thinking, thinking, thinking.

She runs uphill for a mile, then cuts over to the Berkeley campus. She runs the length of the campus three times, back and forth, and back again. She stops once to pick up a curled leaf that has fallen from a tree. It has been infested with a bole. She scratches the bole open and squints at it, then puts it in the pocket of her shorts. She has been inspecting leaves since she was three years old.

Nothing surprises Stella. And everything interests her. Of late, she has found herself musing on reproduction more than she thinks is healthy. Leaf, bole, tree, nuts, seeds, eggs. Not to mention the terrible viral splittings on the screens of the microscopes. As Stella runs through the campus she forces her mind to stay in the realm of vertebrates. I should use one of my eggs, her mind keeps repeating. No one else carries Grandfather Bass's genes. No one else carries Mother's or Aunt Georgia's. I am the last. I should go deeper into life. Life is dangerous and awful. Still, it is all we have. I am tired of being perfect. Perhaps I am tired of being alone. Perhaps this is true. Perhaps it is a trick the hormones play.

Nieman had been laid before. He had slept with prostitutes and he had slept with a girl from Ohio for five months in 1973. He had slept with a French girl one summer when he and Freddy went to study French at the Sorbonne. What he had not done was fall in love. All he had seen around him were the ruins of love. His parents' marriage had been a disaster. He barely knew his father. The hundreds of movies he had reviewed and all the books he had read taught him that love was a wasteland, a tornado, an earthquake, a fire. Men and women in love were like children, given over to childlike jealousies and self-loathing and despair.

*   *   *

When he ran into Stella late one afternoon as they were both leaving the biochemistry building and knocked her papers out of her hand, he had no idea that his life was being changed. He had a premonition, a terrible sense of déjà vu, and so did she, but Nieman thought it was the weather and Stella thought it was because she was about to begin her period.

"They weren't numbered," she said, as she knelt to pick up the papers. "Well, that's not your fault, is it?"

"Oh, God, oh, please let me pick them up. Don't do that. I'm so sorry. Let me help you?"

"Have we met?" She was kneeling only feet away from him. She was wearing a blue denim skirt, a soft blue shirt, little blue sneakers like you see on sale at the grocery store. She smelled of some heavenly perfume, some odor of divinity. Underneath the shirt was a soft white camisole with lace along the edges. In the center of the camisole was a small pink flower. "I'm having a déjà vu," she added. "It's such an odd sensation. I'm probably hungry. I get crazy when I don't eat. Blood sugar. Oh, well."

"That's dangerous. Let me feed you. Please. Come with me." He had gathered up the rest of the papers. He stood up. He took her hand and pulled her up beside him. "Please. Come have dinner with me. I'll help you straighten up the papers. I'm hungry too."

"Well, if you'll go someplace near. How about the Grill across from the library?"

"Great. I like it there. I go there all the time. I'm Nieman Gluuk. I'm a student."

"I know who you are. You're the talk of the department. Did you really quit the paper to study science?"

"I wish that story hadn't gotten out. I'm a neophyte. A bare beginner. It's pitiful how far I have to go."

"Oh, I doubt that."

Twenty minutes later they were sitting in a booth at the Grill eating French fries and waiting for their omelets. They were telling each other the stories of their lives.

"So when they quit the Merry Pranksters, they moved back to Salem and had me. They were worried they had fucked up their DNA with all the acid they had done so they had me tested all the time. It turned out I test well. Then they decided I'm a genius. I'm not. I just learned to take the tests. So, out of their relief that I wasn't an idiot, they turned into the worst bourgeois you can imagine. They collect furniture. You wouldn't believe the furniture my mom can cram into a room. Danish modern, English antiques . . . Anyway, I like them. They leave me alone, considering I'm an only child. They work for environmental groups and they have a lot of friends. They're pretty people. Both of them are a lot prettier than I am. I look like my maternal grandfather, who invented dental floss, by the way. He was a dentist in New Orleans."

"You're very pretty. You're as pretty as you can be. You don't think you're pretty?"

"I'm okay. You ought to see them. They look like early-retirement poster people. So, what set of events made you?"

"An undependable father and an unhappy mother. No wonder I started going to the movies. She's a frustrated actress. I grew up thinking the theater was real life."

"Well, I'm a fan. I always read your column. I loved the things you wrote. I can't believe you just quit doing it."

"Twenty years. It got so unpleasant at the end. I couldn't please anyone. Even people I praised didn't think the praise went far enough. Now I want to know the rest. The things you know. I can't wait to use an electron microscope."

"They haven't let you use it?"

"They were supposed to last week, then the class was canceled."

"Oh, I know what happened. The Benning-Rohrer was down and we had to double up on the SEM. I'll show them to you. We can go there after dinner if you like."

The waiter appeared and put plates of steaming omelets in front of them. This is not what I thought would happen, Nieman was thinking. Always what you least expect. I already feel the air getting thin. Freddy told me someday this would happen to me but I thought he was projecting.

Look at that forebrain, Stella was thinking. The cerebral cortex. The verbal skills. I could breed with that, if I am being driven to breed. She sat very still. She picked at her food. She lifted a hand and touched her mouth with her finger.

"Are you left-handed?" Nieman asked.

"Yes."

"I am too."

When they had finished eating they walked back across the campus to the biochemistry building and went up to Stella's office and left the papers, which they had forgotten to put in order, on her desk. Then they went into the laboratory and sat down in the chairs before the scanning electron microscope. "How much do you know?" Stella asked.

"'The scanning electron microscope . . . a beam of electrons is scanned over the surface of a solid object and used to build up an image of the details of the surface structure. There are also several special types of electron microscope. Among the most valuable is the electron-probe microanalyzer, which allows a chemical analysis of the composition of materials to be made by using the incident electron beam to excite the emission of characteristic X radiation by the various elements composing the specimen. These X rays are detected and analyzed by spectrometers built into the instrument. Such probe microanalyzers are able to produce an electron-scanning image so that structure and composition may be easily correlated.'"

"My heavens. How did you do that?"

"My brand-new Encyclopedia Britannica, Macropaedia, volume twenty-four, page sixty-six. Do you want more?" Nieman was leaned back in the chair. He was smiling. He was almost laughing. He was wearing thin khaki pants. His legs were strong and spread out on the chair.

"Go on."

"'Fundamental research by many physicists in the first quarter of the twentieth century suggested that cathode rays (i.e., electrons) might be used in some way to increase microscopic resolution. Louis de Broglie, a French physicist, in 1924 opened the way with the suggestion that electron beams might be regarded as a form of wave motion. De Broglie derived the formula for their wavelength, which showed, for example, that, for electrons accelerated by sixty-thousand volts, the effective wavelength . . .' What? Why are you laughing?"

"Photographic memory?"

"Of course. It's selective, and I have to be interested in something to imprint it. I've seen movies I can't remember at all. That was a test. If I couldn't remember them, I didn't review them."

Stella was looking at his pants. He sat up straighter in the chair. He pulled his legs together. He coughed. "'The electron image must be made visible to the eye by allowing the electrons to fall on a fluorescent screen. Such a screen is satisfactory for quick observations and for focusing and aligning the instrument. A low-power binocular optical microscope fitted outside the column allows the flower on the screen, I mean the image on the screen, to be inspected at a magnification of about ten magnitudes. . . .'"

"You want to see the AIDS virus?" Stella asked. She pulled a box of slides from a drawer and inserted one into a locked compartment at the base of the instrument. "This is the virus on a human T-cell. I really hate this slide." She pushed a button and the lights came on the screen. Then an image appeared. Long tubular cells covered with watery stars of death.

"I've been to one hundred and seven funerals since this thing started," Nieman said. "Have you been tested?"

"Dozens of times. This job has its drawbacks. I essentially hate viruses. I'm not one of those biologists who love nature. Nature is not on our side. It's always trying to take us back. I'm for the higher mammals straight out. How about you? Have you been tested?"

"My dentist tested me. He never called me back so I assumed I was all right. How accurate do you think the tests are?" Nieman leaned forward to study the screen. It was terrible to behold. "Cut it off," he said and went back to looking at the flower in the center of the camisole under Stella's blouse.

Stella pressed a button. The screen went blank. The room was quiet. The overwhelming sense of déjà vu returned.

"I keep thinking I've been here before," Nieman said. "In this room with you. It's the damnedest thing."

"I feel it too," she answered. "I'm thirty-seven. I keep thinking about breeding. It's probably hormonal. We are primates, don't forget that." She turned around on the swivel chair and looked at him.

"Should we resign ourselves to that?"

"We could welcome it."

"You think so?" Nieman stood up. "There it is again," he said. "It's the damnedest thing. Déjà vu, it means *already seen*. Of course we must have met somewhere. Then, of course, the gene pool is wide. These things might be chemical. See, I'm beginning to think like one of you." He smiled down at her and she reached up and touched, first his sleeve, then his hand. She didn't take his hand or grab it. She brushed her fingers across the back of his hand, then left them only inches away from him. "I don't have much experience with women, sexually, that is." Nieman kept on smiling at her and at himself, at the strangeness of the moment, the silliness and divinity of it. "But I haven't given up on myself. I'd like to have an affair with someone, something that mattered, that might matter to them also. Am I out of line here? You can hit me or dismiss me."

"I haven't had a lover in three years. If I had a love affair I'd be the inexperienced one. I always start thinking what I'm doing is funny. Not the sexual part, per se, you know, but the thing entire, as it were. Well, what are we talking about here?"

"I think we are saying we like each other more than ordinary. I am saying that. I am saying, would you imagine some day, in your time, on your terms, having me as a candidate for a lover?"

"We could get an AIDS test in the morning and have the results back in a day. Then, if we still wanted to, we could explore this further. I have some time after my nine o'clock class." She went on and put her hands on his hands. "I'll admit this is partly about your verbal skills."

"For me it's the flower on your undershirt and your Ph.D." Nieman laughed. "Or the electrical systems in this building are affecting our brains. Tell me where to meet you. I'll be there."

"Would we really do this?"

"I think we are doing it. In my old life I always maintained that thought was action. So the question is: Would we actually carry it out?'"

"It's what the young people do, but not the first time they knock the papers out of someone's hands."

"How long do they wait?"

"I think three days. I heard three days from someone who was confessing something to me. I'm a student adviser part time."

"Then grown people only have to wait one day because we have a shorter time to live."

"That's a theory? Shall we leave now?"

"I suppose we should. Let me help you turn things off."

"All right. The switches are on the wall." They turned off the lights in the laboratory and walked to the elevator holding hands. They went down on the elevator and Nieman walked her to her car. "What time in the morning?" he asked.

"You're serious?"

"More than I've ever been in my life."

"Do you know where the student health center is now?"

"Yes."

"Meet me there at quarter past ten." It was very still in the tree-bordered parking lot. The earth smelled like birth and death and love. There were stars in the sky and a new moon above the physics building. Luckily they were both intuitive, feeling types. A sensate might have swooned.

At ten-fifteen the next morning they met at the student health center and asked to be tested for the AIDS virus. They filled out forms and sat in the waiting room reading magazines and were called in and blood was drawn and the nurse told them to call that afternoon for the results. "Sometimes it takes a couple of days if they're backed up but it's been slow this week. I'll tell them it's for you, Doctor Light. I think you'll get these back by five." She smiled a professional smile and Nieman held open the door for Stella and they walked back out into the waiting room and out the door onto the blooming spring campus. "Are you free tomorrow?" he asked.

"Pretty much. I have some papers to grade."

"I was thinking we could drive up Highway One to Mendocino and spend the weekend together. I mean, no matter how the tests come out. I want to talk to you. I want to be with you some more. I don't know how to say all this."

"I would love to go to Mendocino with you."

"Will you have dinner with me tonight?"

"Yes. Yes I will."

"I don't know where you live."

"Then you'll find out, won't you? Call me at six. If we're positive, we'll get drunk. If we're negative, we'll, I don't know."

"We'll be negative. Perhaps all we are supposed to do about that is be grateful. I'll call then. I'll call at six."

A young technician named Alice Yount put the slides underneath the microscope and watched the fine, free T-cells swim in their sea. She called the health center and made the report and then sent the papers over. It was a good morning. Only one test had come back positive and that was a man who had known it already. Some happiness, Alice was thinking as she took off her apron and washed her hands. Some good news.

At seven o'clock that night Nieman appeared at Stella's door. He was wearing a blue shirt he bought in Paris. He was wearing his best silk socks and seersucker pants and he had taken off his watch and ring. I am putting myself in the path of pain and suffering and life, he told himself. I am a Mayan sacrifice. I have seen this movie but I have never played in it. I can't believe it is this exciting and terrible and irresistible. I want to burn every word I've ever written. What did I know?

Then she was there and they walked into her kitchen and poured glasses of water and sipped them and were shy. They walked around her house looking at the books, the bare stone floors, the clean windows, the stark white walls, the wide white bed.

It was not silly when it happened and neither of them was afraid. "Nice scar," he told her later, examining her knee.

"Bike wreck when I was ten," she answered. "What do you have to show me?"

"Navel?" he asked. "Appendix scar? Cut on eyebrow?"

At two in the morning Nieman went home to pack for the weekend. "I forgot my sleeping pills," he explained. "There are limits to what the psyche can take. I might keep you up all night."

"Go on," she answered. "We're pushing the envelope. I'd like to be alone for a few hours. What do you take?"

"Ambien. Benadryl. Xanax if I travel. If I'm at home I usually just stay awake."

"Distressing, all the people who can't sleep. Do you think it's the modern world?"

"No. I think it's always been that way. Neurotic from the start. That's how I view our history. Short lived and neurotic. Now we're long lived and neurotic. I call that progress, any way you look at it."

"Me too."

At ten the next morning Nieman picked her up in Freddy Harwood's Jeep Cherokee and they drove out over the Golden Gate Bridge and took the Stinson Beach exit and began the 1,500-foot climb into the coastal hills. At Muir Woods they got out of the car and held hands and looked at the ocean for a long time. Already their bodies were joined at the hip. Already there was nothing that could keep them apart.

"Where's Nieman?" Nora Jane was asking. "What did he want the Cherokee for?"

"I think he's in love," Freddy answered. "It's the damnedest thing you've ever seen. He's trying to keep it a secret."

"Who is she?"

"I don't know. He wouldn't even look at me."

"He's getting laid. My God, imagine that."

"He had on a brand-new polo shirt."

"You're kidding."

"I am not. May lightning strike me if I am. It still had the creases in it. He hadn't even washed it."

"My folks drove this highway on the bus," Stella was saying. "I wish they didn't disavow that so much. They were just kids. Everything is in a state of anarchy, Nieman. Every single thing we see about us. Our universe is a nanosecond, the blink of an eyelash, and yet, we are here and this experience seems vast. Last night, after you left, I fell asleep giggling. I kept seeing us marching into the student health center to be tested. That will be all over the campus by the time we get back. Technically I can't date you, you know. Since you are a student."

"We aren't dating." Nieman slowed down. He drove the car to a wide place that overlooked the sea. He turned off the motor and turned to her and took her hands. "I am in love with you. That's been clear since Friday afternoon at six o'clock. I have waited all my life for you. I want to marry you, or live with you, or do whatever you want to do. I have three hundred and forty-seven thousand dollars in assets and no responsibilities I can't get rid of in an hour. I will go anywhere you want to go. I will live any life you want to live."

"My goodness."

"I wrote that down several times this morning. There's a draft of it in my jacket pocket. You can have it."

"Let's get something to eat first. I can't get engaged on an empty stomach."

"This is real, Stella. This is deadly serious on my part."

"I know that. I'm serious too. Don't you think I know a miracle when one slaps me in the face?" Then Nieman was extremely glad he had borrowed Freddy's Cherokee, because it had an old-fashioned front seat and Stella slid over next to him and stayed there all the way to Stinson Beach.

Which is how Tammili and Lydia Harwood finally got to be bridesmaids in a wedding. "I thought it would never happen," Lydia told her friends. "The last person I thought would give us this window of opportunity was Uncle Nieman. I am wearing pink."

"And I am wearing blue," Tammili would add. "It's going to be at our beach house. There will be two cakes and lots of petits fours and Jon Ragel from *Vogue* is going to take the photographs."

"Uncle Nieman will never get a Nobel now," Lydia would sigh. "Dad says Nieman has forgotten all about wanting a Nobel prize for biochemistry."

Design

GABRIELA WAS FIRST in line when the truck from the Salvation Army pulled into the driveway of the orphanage and unloaded the boxes. The older girls tore open the first box and began to sort through the clothes. The nun who was in charge had gone inside to finish a book she was reading.

Gabriela was only seven years old but even the older girls wouldn't tangle with her. She had come to the orphanage three months before and quickly established a reputation as a dangerous adversary. She would kick and bite and never back down. Also, she had an ally. An enormous eleven-year-old named Annie who had red hair and was listed as an incorrigible. An incorrigible was the best thing you could be at Santa Ramona del Río in Potrero. Even the nuns didn't cross the incorrigibles.

Gabriela let the older girls open the first two boxes. Then she went up to the third box and tore it open and took the first garment in the pile. At first she thought it was a blanket but when she shook it out she saw it was a cape. A long brown cape of some very soft, very fine material. She threw it over her shoulders and walked off down the long covered walkway to her room. She took the cape into the room and laid it across the bed. Something about it appealed to her. It reminded her of a lighter, warmer world. Not the house with many children where the food was nasty. Not the thin man with the ugly nose. Not the time before that in the truck. Someplace that was warm and sunny, where women with soft bosoms were laughing in the sun. Gabriela lay down upon the cape and wrapped the edges around her arms and fell asleep. It was Saturday morning. There was nothing she had to do until noon, when the bells would ring to call her in to lunch.

"They want a little girl. Someone who needs a family," the social worker from Oklahoma was saying on the phone to Sister Maria Rebecca. "They lost their child in an accident. They're fine people. Good, stable, attractive people. They speak Spanish, although the child would need some English to start school. Any age. Their child was four. They told me in Los Angeles you had the ones no one else will take."

"We have seventy girls," Sister Maria Rebecca answered. "Perhaps they would like to come and see them."

"They want a child who needs them. Someone you can't place elsewhere. Anyone in Oklahoma City will vouch for them. They're devout. There wouldn't be a problem with that."

"I might know the child for them," Sister Maria Rebecca said. "Yes, there is one I was worrying about this morning. She bit the last two people who tried to keep her."

"I know this couple personally. She's capable and kind. They could come any time."

"They have to understand we can't guarantee adoption. We don't know where she came from. She's been in the system two years since she was abandoned in San Diego. She's a pretty little thing, healthy and strong. Yes, they should come and meet her. We call her Gabriela."

"I'm sure they'll come soon. They're determined about this. They're not looking for a child to save them, you know, they just want to be of use."

"Send them on. I will look forward to talking to them."

That was Saturday morning. On Saturday afternoon, the social worker, whose name was Denise, got into her car and drove over to Allen and Jennifer Williams's house and got out and walked up the path to the door. Jennifer was on her knees by a bed of flowers. She got up when she saw Denise and walked toward her. She pulled off a yellow glove and used the free hand to shove her hair out of her face. She was a beautiful woman. Even in sweat pants and an old shirt. Even with grief written on her face as if forever. "What's happened?" she asked. "Could you find out anything?"

"There's a place in California that has children no one wants. The sister who runs it said there's a child you can meet. A little girl. Are you sure you want to do this, Jennifer?"

"Yes. I have to be of use in some simple, clear way. Just to feed and dress a child. Keep it safe. Nothing more complicated than that."

She pulled off the second glove and put them in the pocket of the pants. "Come inside. Tell us what you know."

They found Allen Williams in the kitchen. There were untouched newspapers on a table. He was sitting beside them looking out the window. It was very quiet in the house. Everything was in its place. No disorder anywhere. Not a sound.

"I should have called," Denise said. "But I wanted to see your faces. There's a little girl in California you can meet. This is going to be expensive, Allen. Are you sure you're up for this?"

"There's plenty of money." Allen got up and held out a chair for her. "We can go whenever you want us to go."

"How about Monday?"

"Monday's fine. The office doesn't care. They'll do anything to help."

"It could be a wild goose chase. It's a home for girls they don't know what to do with. They don't have records for some of them. And it wouldn't be a final adoption. Maybe couldn't ever be one. You'd just be volunteering to be out-of-state foster parents. I don't think there's a chance of losing one of these children once you have one, though. It's never happened. I researched this for days, Allen. Several people I trust told me about this place. The child would be healthy and free of disease. That's about all I could guarantee."

"We'll go." Jennifer came around and sat beside Denise. "Thank you for this. For all this trouble. You don't know what it means, to have this hope."

"You may not thank me a month from now."

"We're going to do this," Allen said. "And we're going to see it through. If we bring a child up here we'll keep her no matter what. My brother's a child psychiatrist. Our parents know."

"Allen said if all else failed he'd teach the child to ride," Jennifer said. "He says we'll move to the country if we have to and be cowboys."

"Okay." Denise opened her briefcase and got out a sheet of paper. "Get the airlines on the phone. Here's where we're going. I'll go with you if you want."

"We can do it." Allen took the paper from her and began to dial the phone. "If we need you, we'll call and you can come out later."

Jennifer put her hand on Denise's shoulder. The refrigerator began to hum. A child's drawing on the refrigerator door moved in the breeze from the air-conditioning vent. It was a drawing of a house. There was a setting sun. A moon, some stars, a cloud. In a corner, rain was falling on a tree. Adelaide had brought it home from the day-care center the day before she died.

After Denise left Allen and Jennifer went for a long walk to talk things over. "If we go and meet this child and we don't like her, what do we do then? Will she know we came to look her over? What are we doing, Allen? Do we know?"

"I thought we were going to like any child they gave us. That's what we said we'd do."

"I meant it. As long as the child isn't mean. I don't want someone who's mean. Or mentally handicapped. I couldn't handle that. Well, I couldn't."

"We're going to see what happens. I'm willing to take a chance on that, on anything. I want to fill our lives with life again, Jennifer. Remember when Mother said we should get some dogs. Can you imagine us filling this hole with dogs? Not that I don't like dogs. Christ." They had stopped on a corner by a building project, a huge house on a small corner lot. "Look at that," he continued. "Maybe we'll be like that. They didn't know what they were doing. They just started building and now they have this monstrosity on their hands. We could be like that. We could end up with some terrible problem we can't handle. But I have one now. Our house is so empty and quiet. We've gotten quiet. We have to fight back if we're going to live."

She was beginning to cry and he reached out and pulled her into his arms.

"We can't replace her," Jennifer said.

"We aren't trying to. We're going back into life. Dickie's a child psychiatrist, for God's sake. You used to be a teacher. I used to barrel race. Do you think there's a reasonably healthy child on the planet we can't save?"

"We'll find out." She held on to her husband for dear life, right out on the street at six o'clock in the afternoon. For the first time in months she felt desire, real desire, and she was going home and do something about it.

At three that morning she woke and went into the kitchen and took the drawing off the refrigerator and put it in her desk.

"So what did you do then?" Gabriela was asking. She and her friend Annie were sitting out in the yard talking. It was late in the day and they were trying to find something to do until supper. There wasn't much to do, but you could always sit on the boards by the fence and talk about things.

"I kicked him in the balls and ran for it. What do you think I did? I've told you about this before. Then he gets up and starts chasing me but he can't catch me. I used to be so fast I could outrun everyone. I'll probably get all soft and fat living with a bunch of girls. There's nobody in this place who could whip me."

"I know there's not, but Sister Felicia might hit you if you don't do your homework. She might not have been kidding about that. I heard she beat the shit out of some girls."

"I never saw her do that."

"Well, how long have you been here?"

"Two months before you came. I can't remember what month it was. I was glad to get here, I can tell you that. I was about

worn out by the time they took me out of Doris's place. She was
on the scam. She had six kids and she didn't give any of us a
thing. I didn't have a pair of shoes that fit."

"Don't talk about it. I don't like to think they were mean to
you."

"It was okay. I'm glad it happened or I wouldn't have met
you." Annie put her hand on Gabriela's black curls and patted
them down. Gabriela was the best kid she had ever had for a
roommate and gave her half her food. Anything with sugar in
it, Gabriela saved half of it for her. "My mother was fat," she
added. "I guess I'll have to get fat too."

"You might not." Gabriela put her hand on top of Annie's
hand and left it there. "You look great, Annie. You're the strong-
est-looking girl I've ever seen."

"Let's go in." Annie squeezed the small hand. "Let's go see
what they have for dinner."

On Monday Jennifer and Allen Williams boarded a plane and
flew to San Diego. They rented a car and drove to Potrero and
found the orphanage. It was a stucco and brick building that
had been a school. It sat on a flat brown patch of land that
turned to mud when it rained and a dust bowl when it was dry.
The only redeeming architectural feature of the place was the
covered walkway that led from the main building to the wooden
dormitory.

Jennifer was wearing a batik skirt and a soft pink blouse. She
had put on makeup very carefully. "We shouldn't look sad," she
said to Allen. "We have to try not to look sad."

"We are sad," he answered. "But maybe we won't always be."
It was one of the things he had begun saying. He didn't believe
it yet but he kept saying it as though to trick it into being so. In
many ways Allen was more shaken than his wife by what had
happened. He was the one who had dropped their child off at
the day-care center. He had identified the body. He didn't care
what happened now. If Jennifer wanted a child, he had made
up his mind to follow her and do what she wanted. At least she
had an idea. Allen had run out of ideas. The one thing he
believed was that he would sleep again. He no longer believed

in God but he believed in the future more than Jennifer did. She had an idea and she was willing to follow wherever it led, but he believed that things would get better.

"When did you decide to adopt?" Sister Maria Rebecca had served them tea and crackers. She was seated behind her desk. They sat before her on the matching rattan chairs.

"A month ago. At least a month. We called Denise, the woman you talked to, about two weeks ago. We're not chasing some whimsical idea. Anyone in Oklahoma City will tell you who we are. Father Matthew sent you a letter. If you want to read it." Jennifer got the letter from her purse. "We want to be of use to a child. That's it. That's the only thing we know. If you can help us."

"I'm an attorney," Allen put in. "I was taking depositions at the Social Security Administration. That's why our daughter was there. It was only for that week, as Jennifer had to be gone. Jennifer doesn't need to work. She could stay home with the child. We would never leave another child at a day-care center, or anywhere. We aren't unlucky people. We think this is a good decision, a wise, planned idea." He sat up straighter, took a breath. It was very hot in the room. Sister Maria Rebecca had not moved a muscle. She didn't look as if she believed anything they were saying. He took a deep breath, he went on. "I have five brothers. I know all about children. We would have had more children than Adelaide but they never came. We aren't trying to replace our child."

"Denise said there was a little girl named Gabriela," Jennifer added. "She said she was healthy. I don't care about anything else but I guess I hope she will be healthy. We have cold winters but our house is warm. We're healthy people."

"I must make sure you totally understand this situation. Gabriela has had a bad time. Frankly, we don't know much about her life before she came to us and she won't talk about it. She is, how shall I say it, sometimes fierce. She bit the last two people who tried to keep her. She tears things up."

"She can tear things up where we live," Jennifer said. "We don't give a damn. Excuse me, Sister. We have a swimming pool.

Allen makes a hundred thousand dollars a year. We don't drink. We have a good life. Does she speak English?"

"As well as Spanish. She likes to talk. I told her some people from Oklahoma were coming to meet her. That she might want to go stay with you if she liked you. She said she wanted to see your car." The sister smiled. Allen began to laugh.

"We have a red one that we rented. And we have two at home."

"I'll get her," Sister Maria Rebecca said. "Wait here."

In a few minutes she returned, bringing Gabriela by the hand. Gabriela was wearing her blue uniform and the long brown cape trailing behind her on the dusty floors. She stood in the door-way and waited, her hair a messy crown above the turned-up collar of the dress.

Jennifer moved across the room and knelt beside her. "We need a little girl to come and live with us," she said. "Will you try us out? Will you try to get to know us?"

"Well, I can sing for you," Gabriela said. "I know a bunch of songs."

"I play the piano and the guitar." Allen moved across the room toward them. "I love music. I love to sing."

"Okay. Here's the song." Gabriela spread the cape back with her elbows. She raised her head and began to sing:

> *Turkey in the oven. Tinsel on the tree.*
> *Something in the chimney. Sounds like a squirrel to me.*
> *Oh, there is a time of year that I love the best.*
> *Christmas is the name of it. Time of Jesus' birth.*

"I can sing it better than that if I want to. We learned that at Wallace's house. They had bad food there. Do you have good food where you live?" She pulled her arms back under the cape and turned her eyes on Allen.

"We sure do. If you don't like what we have we'll go to the store and buy something else. We heard you were interested in cars. We have a new blue car and an old black car."

Gabriela took a long deep breath that was almost a sigh. Then she walked across the room and stood by Sister Maria Rebecca's desk. "Could we take Annie with us?" she asked. "Annie wants to go to a house."

"Who is Annie?" Jennifer asked, but Sister Maria Rebecca was shaking her head.

"She's this girl who sleeps by me. She's my friend. You want to see her?"

"Sure we do," Allen said. He hadn't asserted himself in so long he was surprised by the sound of his own voice.

"Okay," Gabriela said and turned and left the room. Sister Maria Rebecca stood up. She had decided to let chance have its way. Before she became a nun she had been a large, homely girl from Lincoln, Nebraska. Sometimes she knew how to step back and let things go.

"They form attachments," she said. "Annie is a lazy girl. She doesn't work at school. She's a big lazy girl and she fights. But not mean. I don't think she's mean." She sat back down. Allen and Jennifer looked at each other and began to laugh. They didn't want to laugh. They were trying not to laugh. Allen gave in to it but Jennifer resisted. She felt like she was on a roller coaster ride. She had set out to do a Christian act and now she was sitting in a rattan chair getting ready to be introduced to a big lazy girl who fights.

"We believe Annie's father was Australian," Sister Maria Rebecca went on. "A merchant marine. The agency has tried to find him but to no avail. Her mother died in an automobile accident in San Diego and the relatives couldn't take her. She's been in several foster homes. Would you want two girls? It might be easier in many ways if you could afford it."

"We knew when we came down here we were going to a world we couldn't imagine," Allen said. "It is amazing, Sister. The work you do. How do you carry all their stories in your head?"

"I don't think of it. I'm only the instrument. I get up in the morning and try to do my work. We are always short of money, of course. Every month is a struggle. Then, sometimes, a miracle happens. It would help if you took two girls. That would leave room for two more. This is a paradise compared to many of the places they are living."

"I hadn't thought of two." Jennifer looked worried. "But we have room for two. Gabriela is a precious child, Sister. She's more than I could have imagined. She's so pretty."

"She's a riot," Allen added. "We could get her in a children's theater. Oklahoma City is big on theater. There are all sorts of classes and groups. I can't believe she just started singing. And what's with the long brown cape?"

"She's always dressing up in something," Sister Maria Rebecca said. "She ties things around her waist."

Gabriela returned with Annie. They had washed her face and combed part of her hair. She was a big girl with wide shoulders, just at the most awkward age for girls. Gabriela brought her into the room and stood beside her holding her hand. "Here she is. What do you think?"

"I think we should all go for a drive in the car," Allen said. "If that's all right with Sister. We could go into Potrero and get some dinner. Would you trust these young women with us, Sister? I'm hungry after all this traveling."

"Have them back by nine." Sister Maria Rebecca began to hope. This had the makings of a minor miracle. She was hungry too. For the stew she knew the kitchen was making and for something good to come of something. Why shouldn't these four forlorn human beings come together, she asked God. I will pray on this and you will be merciful, I am sure.

Annie and Gabriela climbed into the backseat of the rented car. They rolled the windows up and down. They pulled up the floor mats and looked underneath them. They moved the ashtray up and down.

"Where would you like to go?" Allen asked as he drove back out onto the street. "What would you like to do?"

"Annie likes food," Gabriela said. "If we go get some food Annie will eat it."

"Shut up," Annie said. "Why'd you say that?"

"What kind of food do you like?" Jennifer asked. "There's a whole strip of restaurants in Potrero. We'll drive by them and let you pick one out."

"Not Tex-Mex," Annie said. "I'd like something different for a change."

"We might find someplace that has music," Allen suggested. "Do you like music too, Annie?"

"Do I like it? Fucking-A I like it. Me and Gabriela sing all the time. That's how we stand this place. This one place I lived, this guy had so many CDs you couldn't find a place to sit. He worked in a record store before he lost his job. That's where I learned all the songs. I taught a bunch of them to Gabriela, didn't I?"

"Let's just go get some hamburgers before we starve to death," Gabriela said. "We can save the music for later. I'd rather just get a hamburger and some French fries and not mess around."

"You want to put on your seat belts." Jennifer turned around and faced them. "I really think you ought to put them on. Do you know how?"

"Oh, sure, we'll take care of that." Annie reached over and strapped Gabriela in. She smelled of mildew, as if her hair had not been washed in weeks. Jennifer was having to work to even like the child but she wanted to shampoo her hair and she had forgotten the headache she had had for months. There seemed to be so much going on that she felt like she might have to run to catch up with it.

"Go to McDonald's, Allen," she said. "Let's eat and then we'll find a mall. I might get my hair done at a beauty parlor if they have one. Anyone else want to do that?"

An hour later they were eating hamburgers. Then they were in a mall beauty parlor taking turns getting their hair shampooed. Annie panicked while the shampoo was on and had to be held down to get it rinsed. Only the promise of cookies kept her still while she was combed out and dried.

Then they were in a shoe store buying shoes. Gabriela bought some red patent leather shoes with straps and Annie bought the most expensive running shoes in the store. No one argued with either of them. The girls picked out shoes and Allen paid for them and they wore them out of the store.

On the way back to the orphanage the girls fell asleep in the car. Annie was on the bottom, with Gabriela curled on top of her. "What will we do?" Jennifer whispered. "Do we just take them home and say we'll see you in the morning?"

"What do you want to do?"

"I want Gabriela to come home with us."

"And Annie?"

"I don't know. I don't know if I'm up to it. She's almost a teenager."

"We don't have to decide tonight."

"Where is Denise when we need her? We should have brought her with us."

"I want Annie." He said it very quietly. "She tugs at my heart. And Gabriela needs her. They're a pair. How could we split them up?"

"Be quiet. They might hear you." Jennifer undid her seat belt and turned around on the seat to look at the girls. They were so sound asleep they seemed to be dead. Annie's right hand was on one of her new shoes. Her left hand was around Gabriela's shoulder.

They were late getting home to the orphanage. Sister Maria Rebecca was waiting for them at the door. "How did it go?" she asked, taking the sleepy girls into the foyer. "Did you get along all right?"

"We'll come back tomorrow," Allen said. "As soon as we have breakfast."

"Are you going to take us to your house?" Gabriela asked. "You think we're the girls you want or not?"

"Oh, darling girl." Jennifer went to her and hugged her. Then she hugged Annie. "Tomorrow we'll talk about it and see if you want to come."

"So what's the deal?" Annie asked but the sister handed them to a younger nun who took them off down the hall.

"Think it over," Sister Maria Rebecca said. "Come back tomorrow while they're in their classes. We will talk about it then."

"Could we have them both?"

"Annie's far behind in school. Very far behind. Think it over and we'll talk tomorrow. God speed."

*   *   *

"They won't take us anywhere," Annie was saying. "I've seen that look before. Once some people kept me a couple of weeks. They looked like that the whole time."

"What'd you do?"

"I just ate everything I could get my hands on and watched their television set. He beat her up the day before they took me back. I was glad to leave. He'd be beating on me next."

"I think they want us to go with them. They've got a horse and a trampoline and a piano. I was being as nice to them as I could be."

"I was too. I couldn't help it when they got that shampoo on my face. That was about to kill me."

"You want to sleep over here with me?"

"Sure. Why not. I like this cover you got out of the box. This is warm as a sweater."

"Pull it up around your neck. Doesn't it smell good? I think it smells like some kind of flower."

"Fucking-A. Well, go to sleep. At least we got some shoes."

Jennifer and Allen got into the rented car and drove very slowly back to town. "I think we ought to take them both," Allen said. "We didn't come all the way down here to end up feeling guilty and harming some eleven-year-old girl. The little one doesn't want to go without her."

"She's a dream, isn't she? All that life and spirit after God knows what kind of life. Picking out those red dancing shoes. I couldn't believe that was what she wanted."

"Annie walked around the store reading the price tags. She got the most expensive shoes in the store. Did you see her looking at the insoles? She was inspecting them like they were diamond bracelets. She isn't dumb, Jennifer. She's as bright as she can be. Think where she might end up."

"I don't know, Allen. She's so coarse, so crude."

"She's alive, Jennifer." Allen speeded up. "She's a living, breathing child. I could teach her to ride. You could teach her to read. We'll catch her up. Or she won't catch up and I'll teach her to rodeo. You know why I am insisting on this, besides not hurting them? Because the whole time we were in that mall I didn't think about Adelaide. I think that's the first time since the bombing that I've been free of pain. All I could see was their pain. How hard they were trying to please you. She was scared to death in that beauty parlor. She might never have seen one, much less been in one."

"That bothered me when she picked out those expensive shoes. I saw her reading all the tags."

"Think of how she's been cheated all her life. She was trying to make sure she got something back for the night. Hell, I liked that about her more than anything either of them did. They're survivors, both of them. We could do it, Jennifer. We can take them out of here and make a life for them. I feel it in every bone in my body."

"This was my idea," she said, sliding back into the seat. She had not seen Allen acting powerful in a long time. It took her by surprise. "And now you've taken it over. Okay. Let's go over there in the morning and throw ourselves into this. Let's get ready for the worst. They'll bite us or tear something up."

"They won't bite us." Allen pulled her over close to him and held her there. "They will eat us out of house and home or teach us to live on junk food. Actually I like junk food, Jennifer. Did I ever tell you that? Have you forgotten that?"

"Have them take everything out of Adelaide's room," Jennifer told her mother on the phone that night. "Everything. Take every single thing and give it away. Have someone come in and paint. Yellow and white. Yellow. Bright yellow. Then order some twin beds. Can you do that in five days? Call Dan Mahew. He'll get it painted. One is seven and the other one is almost twelve. Don't worry about it. We'll tell you when we get home. And some bicycles if you have time. And food. Get a lot of food. I don't care. Good food. Things that taste good. Don't ask me a lot of questions, Mother. Just do the best you can and call me back tomorrow night. I have to go. We're taking them to San Diego to buy some clothes to wear home on the plane.

". . . I don't care. I don't know. It doesn't matter. Don't worry about it. If they can't finish painting don't let them start. Just clean it up. We'll be there in a few days. As soon as we get the paperwork in order. This is what we're doing, Momma. And Allen said if you can, call Mr. Harrod to tune the piano. Leave him a key.

". . . A key. A key to the door. . . . Of course he can be trusted with it. He lives a block down the street. Don't talk about money. Money doesn't matter. It has nothing to do with this. And get ready to like them, Momma. Get down on your knees and pray for understanding. Because you might need it. I'm not telling you another thing. You'll have to wait and see."

We all have to wait and see, she decided, when she hung up the phone. That's all anyone is ever doing anyway, only most of the time we don't know it.

A Wedding by the Sea

THE WEDDING HAD been planned for June. Then for August. Now it was the tenth of September and at last Nieman Gluuk and Stella Light had set a date they wouldn't break.

"We are mailing the invitations today," Stella told Nora Jane. They were having tea on the patio of the Harwoods' house on the beach. It was Friday morning. Stella was missing a faculty meeting about grants for the graduate students, but the dean had let her go. No one was expecting much of Stella or Nieman this year. The world will always welcome lovers. This is especially true on the Berkeley campus, where many people have thought themselves almost out of the emotional field. "We have set a deadline. Every invitation in the mail before we sleep. Are you sure you want to have it here? This close to the baby coming?"

The women were sitting on wicker chairs with a small table between them. The table held cheese and crackers and wild red strawberries and small almond wafers Stella had brought for a gift. "I told the department head I had to have a week and he said, Take two weeks." Stella shook her head. "I think we'll just go to the Baja and lie in the sun and read. I have never imagined myself being married. It seems like such an odd, old rite of passage. Are you sure you want to have it here?"

"Freddy Harwood would die if he couldn't have this wedding here. He is fantastically excited about it. So are the girls. Did you bring a list?"

Stella fished it out of her jacket pocket and handed it over. "It's seventy names. This one is my cousin in Oklahoma City. The one who lost a child in the bombing. They have two foster children they're trying to adopt. So I think they will bring them. Two little girls they found in a Catholic home down on the border. One's eleven and the other's seven. My mother's been very involved in it. She specializes in children with learning disorders. They had to round up all sorts of counseling. They were kids no one else wanted to adopt. Anyway, they are coming to the wedding."

"Maybe they should be bridesmaids. Tammili and Lydia would love some help." Nora Jane stretched her legs out in front of her. She was eight months pregnant. Sometimes she forgot about it for hours, then the baby would start moving and remind her.

"I should have thought of that. Of course they can be in the wedding. But how will we get them dresses? Don't the dresses all have to match?"

"That's easy. Bridesmaids' dresses are big business. I'll have a shop here send them things or they can send measurements and we'll have dresses waiting for them. Where are they going to stay?"

"I made reservations at the Intercontinental."

"Let your cousin's family stay with us. The guest house is just sitting there. Four little bridesmaids. This is starting to sound like a wedding."

"I'll call Jennifer tonight. Momma said they were nice little girls. She said it's working out a lot better than anyone thought it would. It's been a godsend to me. It kept Momma off my back while Nieman and I decided what to do."

That was Friday morning. By Monday afternoon a bridal shop in San Francisco and one in Oklahoma City were deep in consultation on the subject of four pink bridesmaids' dresses that must be ready by October the sixteenth. The four little girls had been introduced on a conference call and Nora Jane Harwood and Jennifer Williams had gone past discussing dresses and hats and shoes and flowers and were into the real stuff. "You just went down there and got them?" Nora Jane asked. It was the fourth time they had talked.

"We had to live. When I saw them, my heart almost burst. They aren't a thing alike. Annie looks like she belongs in Minnesota. We still haven't figured out how she ended up in Potrero. But Gabriela is a little Mexican Madonna. Her ambition is to be a singer and get rich. She is very interested in getting rich."

"Can you adopt them?"

"We don't know yet. It's pretty certain we can have Annie but there aren't any papers on Gabriela. We're just living from day to day. I think if anyone tried to take them Allen would run away to Canada with them. Actually, the people here seem to think it will be all right. We're trying not to worry about it."

"This wedding is going to be amazing. It keeps growing. Freddy and Nieman found a string quartet and it's been in the papers twice. 'The famous iconoclastic bachelor Nieman Gluuk,' that's what they're calling Nieman."

"What are they calling Stella?"

"'Brilliant, reclusive scientist' was in the *Chronicle*. Freddy's teasing them to death about it."

"We will be there," Jennifer said. "I don't think either of them have ever been to a big wedding."

It was several weeks before eleven-year-old Annie started worrying about going to California to the wedding. Once she started, the worry fed upon itself. She began lying on her bed in the afternoon pretending to be asleep. Also, she started eating everything in sight.

"Don't you want to jump on the trampoline?" seven-year-old Gabriela asked her. "Don't you want to do anything?" She had known something was wrong with Annie for several days but this was the first time she had felt like doing anything about it. It was nice living in Oklahoma City, but Gabriela was getting worn out with all the things she had to do to keep it together.

Keeping Jennifer happy, letting Allen teach her to play the piano, trying to learn the arithmetic at school, talking Annie into taking her pills. The doctor had given Annie some pills that were supposed to keep her from getting mad at people, but she was afraid they would poison her and Gabriela had to help talk her into swallowing them. Sometimes Annie was afraid she would choke to death swallowing them and sometimes she just thought they might be poison. Gabriela would get on one side of Annie and Jennifer would get on the other side and Gabriela would say, "Would I let you get poisoned? Jennifer got them at a drugstore, Annie. She knows the guy who sold them to her. You swallow food all the time and it doesn't choke you, does it? It would take a lot of pills to make a French fry." Then Gabriela would take a piece of cereal or bread and demonstrate swallowing it and in the end they would usually get Annie to take the pill.

"You better let us keep them in our room," Gabriela advised Jennifer and Allen. "That way she'll know nobody's trying to slip her something."

"I'll take her to the drugstore to get the prescription filled," Allen suggested.

"Yeah, well, I knew a guy who worked in a place where they made pills." Annie was backed into a corner of the living room sofa. They were all around her. "He said they threw in rat shit when they got in a bad mood. He said you wouldn't believe what all was in pills you buy at the store."

Allen and Jennifer looked at each other. Both of them sort of half believed it. It was not the first revelation these girls from the lost half-world of the Mexican border had brought them.

Allen sat down on the floor. "Well, look at it like this," he began. "We have a system of trust in our culture. We all eat and drink things all day long that other people have handled and we have to believe that our inspectors, the people who go into factories where pills are made, are doing a good job of seeing that the things they sell us are clean and made out of the right things, not out of rat feces. Most of the people who make things for us do a good job of it, just like we would if we worked there.

I'll find out where the pills come from, Annie. I'll find out where the factory is and I'll call them and see if they're doing a good job before you take any more of them."

"That's right," Gabriela added. "I guess you got to think of it as getting lucky. If your luck's good, you don't get poisoned or raped or anything. If your luck runs out, you're fucked." She looked at Jennifer. She was trying not to say *fuck* around Jennifer. Jennifer smiled and went to her and touched her shoulder.

"It's okay," she said. "Say anything you want to say. So, Annie, what should we do? Should we trust the doctor and this druggist and take these pills or not? I don't want you to be scared every day when you have to take them."

"She'll take them." Gabriela went to her friend. "You're going to take them, aren't you? Look at me, Annie. Say something about it."

"I'm taking her to the drugstore to see where they come from," Allen said. "We'll find out where they're made. Maybe we can call the company and check on them."

"Okay. Give it here." They handed Annie a pill and watched as she swallowed it.

"Okay," Gabriela said. "Now let's talk some more about what we're going to get for our birthdays."

The next afternoon Allen took Annie to the drugstore and they talked to the druggist about where the pills were made and looked them up in the *PDR* and the druggist let Annie watch him put them in the bottle.

"You can keep them in your room," Allen said. "In a safe place. Every morning when you take one you can write it down in a notebook." They found the stationery department and picked out a pink notebook with a pencil attached. When they got home Annie put the pills and the notebook on a shelf in her closet.

"Tell us that again," she asked Allen that night. "That part about everybody trusts everybody else not to poison them."

*   *   *

"You think it's wise to let her keep them in her room?" Jennifer asked later.

"She needs to learn to write down dates. It will serve several purposes. I don't want her taking that stuff for long, Jennifer. The warnings in the *PDR* are pretty scary. It's just a form of Dexedrine. Why did Doctor Cole think she needed it?"

"Just to calm her down until we can get her settled in school. He says she's plenty bright. He just wants to make sure she doesn't get further behind and get the idea that she's dumb. Thank God for the sisters. She's going to stay in the fifth grade no matter what we have to do."

"She liked the notebook. I don't think she's had much of her own. Did you see the way she arranged her things in the room? She touches my heart, Jennifer. I can't believe how much I am attached to her already."

"Gabriela wants a savings account. She asked me to take her to my bank. Where did she find out about banks?"

"I'd be afraid to ask." They shook their heads in disbelief at what they had brought into their lives. Neither of them said Adelaide and neither of them had to. She was there, alive in their hearts and in every moment. World without end, amen.

On top of everything else she had to do, when Annie started acting funny about going to the wedding, Gabriela decided it was up to her to fix it. "I'll talk to her," she told Jennifer. "I can always get her to say what's wrong with her."

"How do you do it?" Jennifer asked.

"I just keep after her until she tells me. She's never afraid of anything except stuff that isn't true. She gets ideas in her head. She may be worrying about the airplane. She didn't like flying here too much but we didn't want to tell you."

That afternoon after school Gabriela cornered Annie in their room while she was changing clothes and started in on her. "Are you afraid of going on the airplane?" she asked. "You think it's going to crash or something?"

"I think they won't bring us back. I think they'll leave us there. They'll take us back to the home."

"No they won't. Jennifer says we're the reason she and Allen are alive."

"It's costing too much money. They have to pay the doctor and they have to buy me those pills. They cost twenty-four dollars. When I went to the drugstore with Allen to meet that guy that bottles them up I saw the bill. Twenty-four dollars for that little bottle that wasn't even full. They have to buy us all that food. They're going to get tired of that. They'll send us back."

Gabriela moved over and began to stroke Annie's hair. "They don't want to get rid of us. Would they buy us all these clothes if they weren't going to keep us? Not to mention that saddle Allen got you. Listen, you were so cute in that play last week. I bet Allen and Jennifer think you're the cutest girl they could ever get in the world. Come on, don't hide your face." Annie was starting to smile, thinking about the applause at her school play. Gabriela pressed her advantage. "If you'll stop worrying about going on the plane, I'll tell you what we'll do."

"What?"

"We won't be taking any chances. Wait a minute." Gabriela walked over to a painted chest at the foot of her bed and opened it and took out the brown cape. She arranged the cowl. "All right. Here's what we'll do. We will take this cape with us. This cape has been very lucky for us. The day we got it Sister Maria Rebecca told me about Allen and Jennifer coming to meet me. And it made you remember your lines last week when I made you sleep with it, didn't it? Admit it. Say something, Annie."

"Where do you think it came from?"

"I think some old monk had it in Nevada or somewhere, or else it's real old. Lucky stuff doesn't have to come from somewhere. You know when something's lucky for you."

"Okay. It's lucky for us."

"Then we'll take it to California to keep our luck going. Those girls we talked to on the phone are waiting for us. They're rich as they can be. They're going to make their dad take us to an amusement park. This is going to be a vacation, Annie. I never went on a vacation in my life. I want to go on one."

"All right," Annie said. "I'll go to this wedding. If I get to carry the cape."

"You can carry it. But if you lose it, I'll kick your butt. Do you get that?"

"I'd like to see you try." Annie stood up and grabbed her smaller friend around the waist and wrestled her to the bed. They fought for a minute, then they started laughing. The cape had gotten tangled around their legs. Besides, it was hard to fight without making any noise and it scared Jennifer to death if they punched each other. They had almost given up having fights, which was a shame because they were beautifully matched, despite the difference in their sizes. Annie was a wrestler, who liked to get holds on people and then sit on them or twist their arms. Gabriela was a stomach puncher and a shin kicker and a biter. She was also a good spitter and had won several battles at the home by spitting on people at crucial points in a fight.

The bridal shop in San Francisco mailed the dresses to the bridal shop in Oklahoma City. They were dresses by Helen Morley, who had also designed the dress Stella was going to wear. Stella's dress was elegant and simple, thick white silk with embroidery down the back and capped sleeves and a high neck.

The dresses for the girls were made of pale pink lace over satin slips. There were tiers of lace ten inches wide going down to the ankles and high-waisted bodices and full soft sleeves. When the owner of the shop in Oklahoma City pulled the first dress from the box a sigh went around the room. "Well," she said. "California always has to outdo everybody."

"They have all those Asian ideas," a saleslady comforted her. "Plus Hollywood."

"Yeah," said a third. "What do you expect?" Then the ladies recovered from their moment of jealousy and one ran off to comb the neighborhood for shoes. Another ran out to a rival store for gloves. A third began to work on the veils, which had been crushed in the mail.

At five that afternoon Jennifer and Annie and Gabriela arrived at the store and were ushered into a huge dressing room with golden chairs and a golden sofa. The girls took off their school clothes and were dressed in the pink lace costumes.

"I wasn't expecting this," Annie said. "How much does this dress cost?"

"This is for the Queen of Sheba," Gabriela agreed. "How are we going to wear this on a sandy beach?"

"Shit," Annie added, turning to see the back in the three-way mirror. "We look like a bunch of hibiscus flowers by the well."

"Fucking merde." Gabriela went to stand by her taller friend in the mirror. Even then the dresses looked perfect.

"Fucking-A," Annie agreed.

"Well, let's try on the gloves and shoes," the owner said. "We sent Roberta all over town to find shoes. We think white patent sandals since it's by the water."

The saleslady named Roberta began to open the shoeboxes that were stacked in the corner. "Every size they could possibly wear," she said proudly. "I looked all over town. We aren't going to be outdone by anyone in California. They will arrive with everything they need." Except mouthwash, she was thinking, and then chastised herself for being mean. Everyone in Oklahoma City knew the Williamses' story.

Annie sat down on the sofa and allowed Roberta to try the shoes on one by one. "You might consider shaving her legs," Roberta said. "I started shaving mine in the sixth grade."

Annie bent over and looked at the elegant little sandals on her feet. She examined the small, light-colored hairs showing along her bones. She pursed her lips.

"Her legs are perfect," Jennifer was saying. "She doesn't need to shave her legs."

"She's right," Annie muttered. "That looks like shit. I know how to shave it off. I seen a girl in the home doing it. You get me a razor and a bar of soap and I'll take care of that."

"Do you like the shoes? Is that pair comfortable? Get up and walk around in them."

Annie got up from the couch and began to parade around in front of the mirrors. What would it be like, being in a wedding? The priest would be fixing the wine. The altar boys would be swinging incense. Everyone would be looking at her. She stood very still, lost in thought. Gabriela moved across the room and took her arm. "Don't start getting moody," she said in a whisper. "Ask them if we're just going to wear these dresses, or if we're going to get to keep them."

"I need the shoes with the heels on them," she said in a louder voice to Jennifer. "If I wear those little ones I'll look like a midget."

It was seven that night when Jennifer and the girls got home from the store. They had gloves and hats and shoes in an assortment of sacks and boxes. The dresses had been left to be altered and hemmed. "So now do you think they would get rid of you?" Gabriela asked Annie, when they were alone in their room getting ready for bed. "After they got you a dress that cost about two hundred dollars and all that other stuff that matches it?"

"I've got to get me a razor," Annie answered. "I've got to shave these fucking hairs off my legs."

It stormed in the night. A huge thunderstorm that roared in about twelve o'clock and woke up the town. Jennifer and Allen lay in bed listening to the hail hit the roof. Then they went into the kitchen and got out food. They got out potato chips and sliced chicken and mayonnaise and lettuce and tomatoes and chocolate chip cookies and Gatorade. Since the girls had been there they had completely altered their diet and gone back to eating things that tasted good. "Something's bothering Annie," Jennifer said. "She's worrying about something and I don't know how to ask her what it is. I don't know if I should wait for Doctor Cole to find out or ask her. I don't know how far to pry into her mind. What would it be like, to be here with us, to think you were on probation, whether you were or not? What else can we do?"

"She's been knocked around from pillar to post all her life. How could she keep from worrying? If she's breathing, we're ahead. But I don't like her taking Ritalin, Jenny. That's a class four drug. Ever since we went through that business with going

to the drugstore I've been reading up on it. I don't think they
ought to be giving her drugs for anything, even to make her do
better in school."

"Did you ask your brother?"

"He agrees it isn't the best idea but Cole is the only child
psychiatrist he could find us on short notice. He said it would
be all right to let her take it for a month or so until he can find
another doctor."

"It seems to help."

"Drugs are for sick people. She's not sick. I thought we
weren't going to care if they didn't act like normal children. I
thought they were going to tear things up. I was hoping they'd
break some of that bric-a-brac of Mother's in the living room. I
hate that bric-a-brac. I was looking forward to seeing it in piles
on the floor." Allen brandished his chicken sandwich. He added
more mayonnaise and took a bite.

"I didn't know you hated the bric-a-brac. I hate it too. If you
hate it, let's go take it down. We have those boxes the encyclopedia came in. We'll take it down and put it in them."

"Okay. Let's do it." Allen ate one last bite of his sandwich,
grabbed a couple of potato chips, and led the way into the living
room. There, behind the sofa, was a wall of shelves holding the
remnants of his childhood, little cups and saucers and figurines
and glass statues and vases and bookends. "I used to be late for
baseball practice because I had to dust that stuff on Saturdays,"
he said. "Now I shall have my revenge." He began to take the
things from the shelves. Jennifer brought in a bag of newspapers they were saving to recycle and began to wrap the pieces
and put them in the encyclopedia boxes. They were almost finished removing every piece when Annie appeared in the door.

"That rain woke me up," she said. "You guys have the noisiest
weather I ever heard in my life."

"No mountains," Allen said. He went to her and put his arms
around her shoulders. He pulled her with him over to where
Jennifer was packing a kneeling Cupid into the last box. "Jennifer thinks you're worrying about something," he began. "So
we're worrying about you worrying. If you worry, we worry. We
know something's worrying you because we love you and we are

thinking about you. You want to tell us what's wrong, so we can worry about the right thing?"

"Why are you taking all this stuff down?" she asked.

"Because I'm sick of looking at it. We're going to put it in the garage. You don't want to talk about if something is worrying you?"

"I'm worried about going on that plane," she answered. "I don't see what holds it up."

"I'll show you what holds it up." Allen hugged her tighter, then let her go. "You have come to the right place with that question, Miss Annie. Did you know that I just so happen to know how to fly airplanes? Did you know that I also know how to fly a helicopter and flew them for three years in the United States Air Force?" He took the little girl to a table and opened a volume of the new encyclopedia which was still stacked in a corner waiting for him to get around to assembling the bookshelf that had come with it. He spread the encyclopedia down on a table and began to teach her the principles of aeronautics.

Two weeks went by. In Berkeley, everyone was busy getting ready for the wedding. The guest list kept expanding as friends Nieman and Stella hadn't heard from in months kept calling and asking where to send gifts. The gossip columns were full of the news. Also, the story of the girls from the home in Potrero had leaked out, adding to the public's interest.

In Salem, Oregon, Stella's mother was working out at a gym every afternoon hoping to lose weight so she wouldn't embarrass Stella by being fat. Stella's father was reading back issues of the *National Geographic* and pretending to ignore the whole thing. Nieman's mother was so mad she couldn't sleep. She had intended Nieman to marry a wealthy Jewish girl, preferably from New York City, and instead he had chosen this thirty-seven-year-old woman who didn't even wear eye makeup. "You can barely see her eyes," Bela Gluuk told her friends. "I doubt if she'll have her hair done for the ceremony. . . . No, of course not. No rabbi, not even a minister or a priest. Some woman judge, just to make me miserable, no doubt. What else has Nieman ever done?"

*　　　*　　　*

In Oklahoma City the day finally arrived to board the plane and fly to San Francisco. Annie clutched Allen's hand and climbed aboard the plane. She had the cape slung across her shoulder. "Why are you bringing that?" Jennifer asked. "They have blankets on the plane."

"It's something lucky we have," Gabriela explained. "I let her carry it for luck."

"Fine with me," Allen said. They found their seats on the DC-9. Allen and Jennifer were together with a seat in between them and Gabriela and Annie were across the aisle. "There is nothing to fear on this plane but the food," Allen whispered. "Don't lose that sack with the sandwiches and cookies."

"Allen," Jennifer said. "Keep your voice down. Don't let the stewardess hear you."

"At least I know it's my lucky day." Gabriela reached underneath the cape and took Annie's hand. "At least I lived long enough to have a vacation."

Annie squeezed the hand Gabriela had put in hers. She pushed the sack with the lunch around until she was holding it with both her feet. Allen and Jennifer tried not to laugh out loud. "She lived to go on a vacation," Jennifer whispered to him. "I have to start writing down the things she says."

Stella and Tammili met the Williams family at the airport. Lydia had not been able to come as she had a class on Friday afternoons. "So, how was your flight?" Tammili asked. She picked up Gabriela's backpack and carried it. Gabriela picked up Annie's pack and carried that. Annie carried the cape.

"I threw up," Annie said. "Allen told me why the plane stays up, but I stopped believing it when we were halfway here."

"I made her look out the window at the mountains. That's when it happened," Gabriela added. "I thought you had a twin sister. Where's the other girl?"

"She's at an acting class. We have to take a lot of classes so we'll have different interests. I don't do it anymore, but Lydia does everything they think up for her. So, how are things going in Oklahoma? You all getting along all right?"

"Except for storms," Gabriela answered. "Just when I thought

I was going to live someplace that doesn't have earthquakes, I get adopted by some people who live in Tornado Alley. That's what they call it there. It's okay, though. People wear a lot of colored clothes. Like all these old ladies have these pink outfits they wear to the mall. Do you all have malls around here?"

"We have Chinatown. Did you ever go to it when you lived out here?"

"Are you kidding? The nuns never took us anywhere. So, where's this wedding going to be anyway?"

"At our house. That's the best part. We don't have to ride in a car in our dresses and get them wrinkled. All we have to do is put them on and walk out to the patio." They had come to the baggage carousel and were standing beside the grown people, waiting for the luggage to come. Tammili moved nearer to Annie. She reached up and touched the cape. "That's weird," she said. "My sister and I had a cape like that. We lost it on a camping trip when Dad broke his arm. Where do you get those capes? Did you buy it in Oklahoma?"

"It's magic," Gabriela said. "It's got powers in it."

"So did the one we had. Listen, it stayed dry in this terrible rain. This synchilla blanket we had that's supposed to wick faster than anything you can buy, got wet, but that cape was still as dry as a bone."

"She thinks some monks in Nevada probably make them." Annie moved the cape until it was around both of her shoulders. "Gabriela thinks they make them and sell them to people to give them luck. We seen some monks in Potrero. A bunch of them came and stayed with us on their way to Belize. We had them there for a week but that was before Gabriela came. She never got to see them."

"I saw them. Where'd you think I saw monks if it wasn't for that bunch that came and stayed at the home? I got there the day they were leaving. I saw them all sleeping on the ground. This cape is just like the stuff they were wearing."

"We're Jewish," Tammili said. "We don't have any monks."

The bags arrived and a man in a uniform appeared and helped them carry the bags outside to a limousine.

"The limo's just for fun," Tammili said. "My dad thought

you'd like a limo, so we got you one. There're things to drink inside. Get in. See how you like it. Lydia and I adore limousines but we never get to get them because Dad usually says they're for movie people and Eurotrash."

The grown people got into the back and the girls got into the seats facing backward. Tammili was sitting next to Annie. She reached out and touched the cape again. She felt the softness of the weave caress her hand. "This is going to be the best wedding anyone ever had," she said. "I've been waiting all my life to be a bridesmaid. I don't care if it's bourgeois or not. I think it's the best."

"Well, I've never been in a wedding. I never even gave it much thought. I just hope I don't do something stupid."

"My parents' friends almost never get married. They just cohabit and have serial monogamy. So we are lucky this happened. You see, the groom is our godfather. He means a lot to us."

Annie and Tammili were deep in conversation, their heads turned to each other. Gabriela started getting jealous. "Did you take your pill this morning?" she put in, leaning toward them. "Where are they, Annie? Where did you put them?"

"I don't know," Annie answered. "I don't know where they are."

"Dad found this article in the *New York Times* about these people who have been getting orphaned babies from China," Tammili was saying. "We saved it to show you. Lydia and I are begging Mom and Dad to adopt some to go with the baby we're having. They said if we both made the honor roll for a year they'd think about it. Anyway, we saved the article for you. I mean, what you're doing is not that unusual. Well, this is San Francisco. That's the Golden Gate Bridge up there. We have to cross it to get to our house."

"She forgot her pills," Gabriela said to Jennifer. "Annie forgot her Ritalin."

"Good," Allen said. "She doesn't need any pills. I think that doctor's crazy to give pills to that child."

"She's taking Ritalin?" Stella asked. "I didn't think they still prescribed that to children. What are they giving her Ritalin for?"

"To get her adjusted to school," Jennifer answered. "Why? What do you know that we don't know?"

"It's just a very old-fashioned drug. Primitive, compared to the things we have now. How long has she been taking it?"

"A month. Almost a month. What's wrong with it, Stella?"

"I took a couple of them," Gabriela put in. "It didn't do anything to me but make me talk all the time. And, yeah, that day at school I did all that arithmetic so fast. I was wondering if that had anything to do with that."

"You took one?" All three of the adults leaned her way.

"I sure wasn't feeding them to Annie without knowing what she was taking. I seen, saw. I saw that happen with a girl in this place I stayed once. She took some pills this guy gave her and she ended up almost dying."

"You took a Ritalin?" Allen took both her hands in his. Stella began to breathe into a Zen koan.

"I cut one in two. I know about drugs. I used to help out at the home when kids got sick. Sister Elena Margarite said she might make a nurse of me."

"Where are they now?" Stella asked. "I'd like to see these pills."

"She left them at home. She wouldn't ever take them if I didn't remind her."

"It's all right," Jennifer said. "Forget about the Ritalin. When we get home we'll find another doctor."

"Was this my mother's doing?" Stella asked. "Is this some of Momma's old hippie connections she put you on to? Damn that woman. She and Dad are at a Ramada Inn waiting to hear from us. I've been praying for weeks they wouldn't come."

"Stella, how can you talk like that about your parents?"

"I'm an unnatural child. Nieman is too. That's why we're marrying each other. I finally met a man who isn't interested in meeting my family."

Annie had slid back into the seat, listening. These were the strangest adults she had ever encountered. All these days and weeks and they kept on acting just like they had the day she met them. As if life was funny, an adventure, something amazing to be watched and commented on. As if some light was in them that did not go out. She raised her eyes and they were smiling on her. Stella was looking at Gabriela.

"You got any crabs on this beach where your house is?" Gabriela asked Tammili. "I went to the beach a couple of times. These old birds were pecking for food in the sand and there were crabs underneath a log. I'd like to catch one in a bucket and get a good look at that if I could."

"We're almost there," Tammili told her. "We are almost to our house."

As soon as they arrived at the Harwoods' house, Stella excused herself and got into her car and drove to her office in the biochemistry building and started making phone calls and pulling things up on her computer. In an hour she had talked to child psychiatrists in New Orleans and New York City and Pittsburgh. She had researched recent antidepressants and had missed her appointment for a haircut. She stopped on her way home at a walk-in beauty parlor and let them even up the back and sides of her very short, severe haircut. She shook out the navy blue dress she was wearing to her rehearsal dinner and got into the shower still running the statistics on antidepressants through her head. Not good, she decided. Feeding Ritalin to a perfectly healthy child. She probably needs a shrink and Stella and Allen need to find out where she's been and what happened to her but I could figure that out if I had her alone for a week. Anxieties are like fingerprints but they are easily traced. What a fantastic cousin I have to think up something this crazy and wonderful and brave. I really like that girl. And the other one, the small one, is as pretty as a picture. What a lovely, ancient face. She looks like she's thirty years old inside. She took one of the pills! God, the human race. You can't see that underneath a microscope, Stella. There is nothing in RNA and DNA to account for our behavior, except the attachments we form are in the pattern, aren't they? Each of us has our receivers, what the old Jungians called the anima and animus, and someone comes along that fits the pattern and we meld. I am getting married in the morning to Nieman Gluuk. I am going to be his wife and make a home with him and be with him when we are old. Scary and wonderful, I guess.

She turned up the water in the shower and decided to stay there until the hot water ran out. The phone started ringing as soon as she got comfortable. She got out and answered it. "Stella," Nieman moaned on the telephone. "Where are you? I can't be alone waiting to get married. I'm coming over right this minute."

"Then I won't get dressed," she giggled. "Come on. Let's see what terror does to the parasympathetic nervous system."

"I'm in the car. I'll be there in ten minutes."

The living room of the Harwoods' house at the beach was an inspiration of the movers. They had moved all the musical instruments into one room while they waited for someone to arrive and give them orders. The Harwoods had left it that way. The room contained two baby grand pianos and a harpsichord and a harp. That was it. Except for a long thin table holding a Bose music system the size of a book.

"Fucking-A," Gabriela said when she saw it, forgetting her vow not to curse at the wedding.

"We had to get this house because my dad's bookstore keeps getting bombed," Tammili said. "My grandmother bought it for us. Don't worry about it being big. Most of it is wasted space. It was a wreck when we got it. We had to have the roof replaced and all the plumbing and the windows. The windows were so loose they rattled when it rained. So, there's the ocean. I guess that makes up for everything. And the guest house is nice. You'll like it there."

"What do you do with all these pianos?" Gabriela asked.

"We play them. Go ahead, try one. Come on. You can't hurt it. Momma's got a piano tuner who used to work for the symphony. He comes out every other month. Go on, play it. See how it sounds."

Gabriela walked over to the harpsichord and ran her fingers soundlessly across the keyboard. Nora Jane watched them from the doorway. "Would you like me to show you how?" she asked. "I have all these pianos because I was an orphan too. I have these pianos so I won't have to put up with feeling bad in case I ever do. I just come in here and start making noise. Come on, sit down by me." She sat down at one of the baby grand pianos. Gabriela sat beside her. Annie came and sat on the other side. She was still holding the cape over her shoulder like a shawl. Tammili stood behind her and laid her left hand very lightly on the cape. Nora Jane began to play show tunes, songs from Broadway musicals.

Tammili moved away from the piano. She began to dance. Gabriela got up and danced beside her. When Lydia came in the front door she found them dancing and joined them.

The wedding of Nieman Gluuk to Miss Stella Ardella Light began with children dancing.

The day of the wedding dawned bright and clear. By nine in the morning all four of the bridesmaids were dressed and wandering around the house getting in the way of the caterers. "Dahlias," Freddy Harwood declared. "The house is full of dahlias." Freddy was dressed in his morning suit and was videotaping everything in sight. He videotaped the bridesmaids in the music room and on the patio and in the kitchen. He videotaped the judge arriving with her twenty-six-year-old boyfriend. He videotaped Nieman and Stella getting out of Nieman's car and walking up the pathway to the back door. "He's scared to death," Freddy said into the microphone. "He's terrified. He can barely walk. He's making it. He's opening the door for her. It's nine-fifteen. Forty-five minutes until ground zero."

Nieman's mother arrived in a limousine. Stella's parents came in their Mazda van. The guests were crowding in. The driveway became packed with cars. The cars spread out across the lawn. The string quartet was playing Bach. Between nine-thirty and nine-forty-nine, a hundred and fifty people made their way up the front steps and filled the house. Someone handed bouquets to the bridesmaids. They formed a semicircle around the altar. The judge stepped into the middle. Nieman appeared. The quartet broke into a piece by Schubert. Stella joined her groom and the judge read a ceremony in which the bride and groom promised to do their best to take care of each other for as long as they lived and loved each other. Nieman kissed his bride. The audience heaved a sigh of relief and Champagne began to be passed on silver trays.

"That's it?" Annie said.

"I guess so," Lydia answered. "You want to get some petits fours and go play in my room?"

"We had a cape like this," she was saying later. She and Annie were lying on her bed with a plate of petits fours and wineglasses full of grape juice on her dresser. "We found a cape like this in this house we have that's in the hills. We took it on this hike with us and then we lost it."

"Your sister said the same thing. She said your dad broke his arm."

"We thought it was a lucky cape. Then we lost it."

"This one's lucky. As soon as Gabriela got it we got adopted. Just like that."

"I wish we could get another one. Do you know where to get them?"

"No. But I can't let you have this. It's Gabriela's. She just let me borrow it to fly on the airplane. So, is your dad going to take us to this amusement park?"

"He said he would if he could. If it opens before you have to leave tomorrow. I wish you could stay a few more days. There're a lot of things we could show you. We could take you on BART." Lydia lay facedown upon the cape, smelling the wonderful smell of wildflowers. "I think they make these out of some kind of flowers they grow somewhere. Like linen is made of flax. Where do you think they make them?"

"I think, Italy." Annie had no idea how she had decided to say Italy, but as soon as she said it she felt it was true. "I think they have this town in Italy and all they do is grow the flowers to make these capes."

*   *   *

"They think the cape is magic," Jennifer was saying. "They think they have a magic cape."

"What?" Nieman asked. "What are you talking about?"

"Like Michael Jordan wearing number twenty-three," Allen put in. "They believe in it, but they don't know we know they think it's magic. They just keep dropping hints."

They were on the side porch of the Harwoods' house. The wedding was winding down. The guests had nearly all gone home. The string quartet was in the kitchen talking to Freddy and Nora Jane. Jennifer and Allen Williams and the bride and groom were on the porch. It was the first time the Williamses had had a chance to be alone with the pair. Nieman had been commenting on how well the adopted girls had managed to fit into a scene they could not possibly have imagined. "Perhaps they saw it on a film," he had been saying. "I've written several times about how film teaches manners. Not just the obvious bad things, like violence, but also niceties, like how to hold your wedding bouquet. Do you think they were exposed to many films?"

"I don't know about that," Allen said. "But they have a cape they think is magic."

"They found the cape in a box of Salvation Army things a few days before we came to the home and met them. So they think it brought them luck. Technically, it's Gabriela's cape, but she lets Annie share it. She let Annie carry it on the plane. They pretended they wanted it for a blanket."

"I'm having a déjà vu," Stella said. She took Nieman's arm. She pressed herself into his side. "What is this all about?"

"I have it too," he said. "Just then. When Jennifer started talking about the cape. You have to understand," he said to Jennifer and Allen. "The first time we met we had this huge mutual déjà vu. Is this part of love, do you think? A harkening back to the mother–child relationship?"

"It's probably blood sugar," Stella said. "A magic cape. Well, that's a wonderful thing to believe you have. I found a really fine psychiatrist in Oklahoma City who will see her, Jennifer. I had to beg, but he'll see her once a week. Don't take her back to that man who gave her Ritalin. Promise you won't go back to him."

"Whatever you say, brilliant cousin," Jennifer answered. "It's unbelievable how much you learn to love a child, any child." She looked at Allen. "It's hard enough to suffer when you're old. Eleven years old should be a happy time and we want to make it one for her. If you found someone, we'll go and see him. I believe in psychiatry. I always have."

"I've thought of going into it," Stella said. "Sometimes I think I've taken molecular biology as far as it will go. Maybe I'll abandon the field to Nieman and get myself a new career." She closed her eyes, then opened them. "A dog runs across the street in front of your car. In a nanosecond the entire chemistry of the body changes. There are Buddhist monks who can regulate their heartbeat, control pain, choose when to die. There is so much to learn, so much to know." She turned to Nieman and kissed him on the lips. Jennifer clapped her hands, then kissed Allen long and passionately. It was the best kiss they had kissed in many months. A storm was brewing on the ocean. The negative ions were thick in the clean, sweet air.

"We'll come see you in August," Tammili was saying. "And you'll come here at Christmas when it's snowing where you live. We'll do that every year as long as we live and always be friends."

"We swear by the cape to be friends," Lydia added. The four little girls were sitting on the floor in their dresses. The cape was spread out between them. They were each holding part of it.

"Every time we see each other we'll get your dad to take videos of us," Gabriela put in. "In the meantime if he meets any movie people he can show them the videos and see if they want us to be in movies. Give them Jennifer and Allen's phone number if they do."

II

Stories

New Orleans

Nora Jane was hiding in the goldenrain tree waiting for her mother to go back in the house. "Nora Jane, come in here. I'm warning you, if you don't come back in this house you will regret it. This time I'm not kidding."

Nora Jane had been hiding in the laundry room drawing on her drawing pad when the phone began to ring. She knew it was the school. The sisters always called the minute they knew someone wasn't there. As soon as Nora Jane heard the first ring she slipped out the back door and went up into the tree. The cat had followed.

"She'll give up in a minute," Nora Jane whispered to the cat. The cat was cradled in her arms. They were lying on the platform in the top of the tree. "She's too hung over to look for me. She'll go back to bed in a minute." The cat wiggled out of her arms and took a position about a foot away. She raised a paw to her mouth and licked it clean.

"That's it, you know," Nora Jane continued. "It's final. I'm never going to school on Wednesday as long as I live. I'm not going over to that damn old Home for the Incurables and read to those people. That old man was spitting on me. If God wants those old people to have some company, he can go himself. It's not my fault they're in there." Nora Jane rolled over on her back and stretched out her legs until they touched the branch that held the platform. It was turning out okay. As soon as her mother went inside she'd go over to the park and find something to do. She might end up getting her fortune told, or meeting some interesting people, or taking her money and buying a snowball at the zoo. Except she had left her money inside. Not to mention her shoes. "That's okay," she told the cat. "She was so drunk last night she'll sleep all day. If she doesn't call Grandmother and get her worried. Well, she won't call her. They hate each other. Maybe after she goes to sleep I'll take the kitchen phone off the hook. Then the sisters won't keep calling and getting her stirred up."

Her mother slammed the back door and the yard was quiet. Nora Jane took off her top shirt and used it as a rag to clean the debris off the platform. It was an old uniform shirt with the Sacred Heart seal on the pocket. Underneath it she was wearing a white undershirt stained with red from the time her mother put all the clothes in the washer with a red sock. Nora Jane couldn't think about that. It had ruined all her white uniform shirts and a pair of Chinese pajamas her grandmother had given her for Christmas.

"You won't always live in that mess," her grandmother had consoled her. "As soon as you're old enough we'll get a court order and you can live with me."

Nora Jane thought about that a lot. The court was the portrait of her grandfather in his robes, but he was dead now. She didn't see how he was going to come order Madelaine around.

"You need to clean up this house," Lydia always said to Madelaine if she had to come inside to wait for Nora Jane. "This house is a disgrace. What happened to the maid I arranged for you?"

"Nora Jane leaves her clothes and things all over the floor," Madelaine protested. "How can I clean up with all her stuff thrown all over the place?"

"Shame on you to blame this on the child," Lydia had said to her one day. She had grabbed Nora Jane and taken her off for four days that time. Since that day Lydia and Madelaine were really at war.

"She's trying to turn you against me so she can collect your father's government check," Madelaine told the child. "I know you like her, honey, but you don't know how she is. She's a bitch to everyone but you."

"I didn't put all this stuff on the floor," Nora Jane answered. "Most of this stuff belongs to you."

Nora Jane cleaned every twig and leaf and cobweb off the platform. Then she rolled back over on her stomach and let her head drop down to look at the earth beneath the tree. There were deep gulleys in the dirt and Nora Jane imagined they were the Mississippi River going down to the Gulf. If she came out here when it rained she could make little boats and see where they went. "I'm about to starve to death," she told the cat. "I could go over to Grandmother's house and get her to make some poached eggs, but she'd make me go to school. We'll go back down in a minute. She couldn't catch me anyway. She won't run out in her nightgown."

Some time went by. The sun moved higher in the sky and the patch of light that had been on the platform faded into darkness. A line of ants moved across a board and Nora Jane let them go. It might be unlucky to kill those ants. You couldn't take a chance on things like that.

When the shaft of light was completely blocked by the canopy of leaves, Nora Jane climbed down out of the tree and walked into the house and found her shoes and a clean shirt and stopped in the kitchen to get a dollar out of her mother's purse and then found two cold biscuits on a plate and a jar of honey and a spoon and went back out into the yard. She put the honey on the biscuits and ate them. Then she put on the shirt and shoes and walked out the front gate. The sun was high now. People had gone in off their porches. It must be ten o'clock. She had the day to herself. Anything could happen.

*   *   *

The first thing that happened was a lady in her yard on Henry Clay Avenue. A lady as old as her grandmother, standing on a stone porch watering her azaleas. She was as beautiful as a picture and her long thin fingers were covered with diamond rings. She looked like someone from another world. She didn't look like anyone from New Orleans.

"Good morning," the lady said. "Are you all out of school today?"

"I am," Nora Jane said. "I'm going to the zoo." She stopped by the side of the yard and examined the lady more closely. She was wearing a long white negligee and robe like a bride would wear. The rings were so big you could see them from the sidewalk. It was hard to tell if the lady was young or old but she had a beautiful smile and she didn't look like someone who would yell at you. Besides, Nora Jane never told a lie to anyone but her mother. No matter what happened, she never lied about a thing she did.

"I didn't know they had a zoo," the lady answered. "I'm not from around here."

"When did you come here?"

"Two days ago. I am from California. I married Doctor Monroe and moved here. I don't know a thing about this place." The lady started laughing. She put the hose down on the porch and stepped over the hedge and walked over nearer to Nora Jane. "Is that a uniform you're wearing?"

"Yes ma'am. It's the Academy of the Most Sacred Heart of Jesus. My name is Nora Jane Whittington. I'm in the fifth grade. Are you doing okay? Since you moved here."

"My name is Sally Ladner Monroe. I just got married and I'm sixty-two years old. Isn't that outrageous? It's the most outrageous thing I've ever heard of, don't you agree?"

"Where's your husband?"

"He's at the hospital."

"Did you bring anyone with you?"

"Like who?"

"Any children you have or cats or anything?"

"I brought my dog. I'm afraid to let him out. I'm afraid he'll run away."

"He could run around the park. What kind is he?"

"A sheltie. He's very nervous about being here. He isn't used to being on a leash but I guess I'll have to get him one so I can take him walking."

"Bring him on out. Let's look at him." The woman began to laugh. She laughed a beautiful long laugh that made her look very young and funny.

"I'll do it," she said. She went back into the house and returned in a few minutes with the dog. She had put on a pair of white shorts and a white silk blouse and was carrying a pair of little sandals. She sat down on the steps and put on the sandals, and the small sheltie dog ran all over the yard in circles.

Nora Jane moved nearer to the steps. "He's cute," she said. "He's a very attractive pet. I'm glad you brought him with you."

"Why is that?"

"I would take something with me if I moved away from my home."

"Why are you going to the zoo?"

"Because it's Wednesday. I don't go to school on Wednesdays anymore. They make us go to the Home for the Incurables and read to them. This old man was spitting on me. I won't put up with that."

"Well, I don't blame you for that. There." She had buckled the last buckle on the sandals. She stood up. "Shall we walk the dog for a while? Will you accompany me?"

"Sure. If you want me to." They walked along together with the sheltie running in circles in front of and behind them. They walked along the tree-lined street and arrived at the park and began to walk the dog along the sidewalk of Exposition Boulevard.

"What's it like in California?" Nora Jane asked. "Did you like it there?"

"I liked it until my husband died. Then it was very lonely and I met Doctor Monroe at a party and he asked me to marry him and so I did. I've only been here two days. But I told you that."

"You won't need to get a leash," Nora Jane said. "Look at him. He's doing fine. He isn't running away. Well, there's the turn to the zoo. I'm going up that way. You want to go that way with me?"

"I'd better be going back. I have to get dressed for a lun- cheon." They stopped on the sidewalk. Nora Jane stood a few feet away, looking at the woman's rings. One was a big square diamond with small diamonds on the side. The other was a band of diamonds, each one as large as her mother's ring. There was a third ring, but the stone was turned into the palm of her hand.

"I'll probably see you again," Nora Jane added. "I hope you have a good time in New Orleans. I never moved anywhere. I don't know what it would be like."

"It's very odd really. The furniture in the house isn't mine. It's not what I'm used to. There is a great deal of furniture in that house. I don't know how I'm going to get rid of it." She laughed delightedly at the thought and Nora Jane imagined her squeezing through the heavy rooms.

"Well, I hope it turns out all right. It was nice meeting you. I'll probably be seeing you again." Nora Jane was moving off in the direction of the curve at Magazine Street. The lady stood for a long time staring after her.

"That was an interesting adventure," Nora Jane said to herself as she crossed Magazine and began to work her way back toward the zoo. She was moving toward the shell road between the levee and the back of the zoo. "I guess when you get old you have to do anything you can to have fun. At least she can go for a walk. Grandmother can't even go for walks anymore. I don't want to get old. It looks like a really horrible thing to do."

She walked along Magazine on the river side, walking as straight as she could so no one would wonder why she wasn't in school. Two ladies in tennis dresses pushing baby carriages walked by. Their heads were turned to each other. "So I said, Then it will never be my turn, will it?" the shorter lady was saying. "It has always been your turn and it always will be." Nora Jane pretended not to hear. She stopped at a water fountain and got a drink of water. She turned onto the shell road and walked along it until she came to the back of the zebra cage. She could see the zebras' heads sticking up above the fence and she spoke to them. "I'd be glad to turn you loose," she said. "But you wouldn't have anywhere to go."

She turned and took a shortcut past the biggest live oak tree in New Orleans. It sat out in the middle of a clearing and the roots were wonderful natural benches. She stopped and patted the tree for luck and then she went on across the clearing and hurried down the street to the front of the zoo. It was deserted except for a man in uniform behind a ticket counter and two black men painting a fence. Nora Jane decided she didn't want to go in after all. All I'd be doing is feeling sorry for the animals, she decided. I have better things to do than that. She walked by the ticket cage as though she were on an errand of great importance. The edge was wearing off her feeling of adventure.

I'd better go to Grandmother's, she decided. If Momma calls and tells her I'm gone she might get worried. I don't want her worrying about me. I'm all she has. The thought brightened up the day. The thought was full of light and seemed to make a space before Nora Jane as she walked. No matter what happened, her grandmother Lydia loved her with all her heart. I am her heart, Nora Jane said to herself. I am the dearest thing on earth to her. She wouldn't know what to do without me. She began to walk faster until she was almost running. The heat had settled down upon the park and the joggers were slowing their paces but Nora Jane walked faster and faster. She moved past the golf club and past the curve to the flower clock and crossed Saint Charles Avenue and moved along in front of Tulane and Loyola and found Story Street and she was running now.

Her grandmother was in the living room writing letters. When she saw Nora Jane come up onto the porch her heart lifted and she forgot the terrible ache she had borne in her back all morning and went to the little girl and held her in her arms. "What happened?" she asked. "Has anything gone wrong?"

"She got drunk last night and I didn't get any sleep. I need to eat something, Grandmother. What do you have to eat around here?"

Twenty minutes later they were seated at the dining room table. Nora Jane had a toasted pimiento cheese sandwich on a gold-banded plate. She had an ironed linen napkin on her lap. She had a plate of carrot and celery sticks and a tall glass of milk with ice. Her face and hands had been washed and her underwear removed and replaced with some her grandmother kept in a drawer.

"I met a lady this morning who has a dog from California," Nora Jane said, when she had finished half the sandwich. "I want to get a dog, Grandmother. A dog would walk around with me when I go out to the park. It would bark if anything tried to get me. Do you think I can get one someday?"

"That's what you want, a dog?"

"I've been wanting one for a long time. I guess she wouldn't let me have it, would she?"

"You can have a dog. I will get you one. If she won't let you have it, I'll keep it here. I have a friend who raises short-haired fox terriers. I'll call and see when he's going to have some puppies."

Lydia Whittington stood up. Nora Jane wanted something that was within her reach to give and she was going to give it. It soothed Lydia to think of getting Nora Jane a dog. It made her forget her dead husband and her dead son and her drunken daughter-in-law and her lost fortune and the plight of this child, who was her reason to live. My one and only reason to live, she thought. She went around the table and caressed the child's dark curls and kissed her beautiful ivory cheek. "Finish eating that and drink the milk. I'm going to call Judge Bass." She went into the kitchen and dialed the number of a retired federal judge who had been one of her admirers in her youth. "Joe," she said. "I am in need of a puppy. When are you going to have a puppy for a little girl?"

By the time Nora Jane had finished eating it was settled. The judge had a litter that was two months old and he was coming in his car to pick up Nora Jane and her grandmother and take them to his house to see the puppies. "You better call my momma and tell her where I am," Nora Jane suggested. "Before she calls the police like she did that other time."

Lydia dialed the phone. She opened a box of vanilla wafers

and put some on a plate while the phone rang ten, then twelve, then fourteen times. On the fifteenth ring Nora Jane's mother answered it.

"She's with me," Lydia said. "I'll send her home this afternoon for some clothes. She's staying here for a while. If you argue with me, I'll call the court. This time I mean it, Madelaine. She looks like an urchin. Her hair wasn't even combed. Go back to bed. I'm hanging up.

"Have a cookie," she added, holding out the plate. "We're going to pick out a dog. You need to have plenty of energy for that."

"She combs my hair," Nora Jane answered. "She always combs it every night."

The phone was ringing. It was Madelaine calling back. "You are the worst bitch in New Orleans," Madelaine said. "I'm the one who's calling the police, Lydia. You're turning her against me. I know what you're up to, you know. You aren't fooling me."

"You're drunk every night and everyone knows it. That house looks like a pigpen. Judge Bass is on his way over here right now to talk to me about it. Go back to bed, Madelaine. She's staying here. I'll have you committed if I have to. You can't threaten me. Every derelict on Magazine Street will testify for us."

"That's my child, Lydia. Nora Jane belongs to me. You're going to be sorry for this. You'll regret this day." Madelaine hung up the phone and went into the kitchen and opened a can of beer and took it with her to the bed. It was going to be one of those days when life was as black as the coffin in which her husband's remains were lying in the ground not a half a mile away. She lay in the bed and cried into the pillow. After a while she fell asleep.

Nora Jane and Lydia were waiting on the porch swing when the judge's chauffeured Lincoln pulled up to the curb. The driver opened the door and the judge got out and walked up onto the porch and spoke to Nora Jane and offered Lydia his arm. They proceeded across the porch and down the stairs and the driver held open the door and Lydia and the judge got into the backseat and Nora Jane sat up front with the driver. They drove down

Saint Charles Avenue to the Garden District and the driver turned into a driveway on Philip Street behind a huge gray house with porches and towers and beautiful flower gardens in full bloom. It was very hot and the judge was sweating in his seersucker suit and Lydia was sweating in her pale blue and white striped dress and Nora Jane couldn't believe her luck. All the other girls in the fifth grade were at the Home for the Incurables reading to the old people and she was at Judge Bass's house getting ready to pick out her dog.

The puppies were in a pen by the shade garden. There were four of them. Brown-and-white fox terrier puppies, their faces looked up at her. They scrambled over each other to lick her hands and arms.

"Which one do you like?" the judge asked, when she had been with them ten minutes or more, sitting on the ground with the puppies all over her and climbing on her legs.

"I don't know if I should take one away," she said. She lifted her face to his. "Won't it be lonely if I take it away from its brothers and sisters?"

"You could take two." The judge laughed and looked at Lydia to see if she was going to kill him. "Which two do you like the most?"

"I have to decide. I want a boy and a girl. I want the one with the most black on his face and the one with brown paws." She turned her face to the judge's again. She gave him a smile so huge and terrible and beautiful that he would have given her his house, would have signed it over. "This one and this one." She pulled two puppies into her arms. She moved their faces toward each other.

"That child will lead a charmed life," Judge Bass told Lydia later, while the butler was helping Nora Jane settle the puppies in a kennel for transporting them to Lydia's house. "You were almost that beautiful, Lydia, but not quite. But then, I didn't know you when you were a child."

"She is the dearest thing on earth to me. I may have to try to take her from Madelaine again. Will you help me?"

"There's nothing I can do. The courts won't take her from

her mother unless she physically harms her. I'll call around this afternoon, but it won't do any good."

"Never mind. She won't desert Madelaine even though she wants to. She is beautiful, isn't she? It will protect her, I suppose. She met Alston Monroe's bride in the park this morning. They went for a walk."

"She is very special, charismatic. I've only seen her once before, when you brought her by the office. How old was she then?"

"Five."

"I've never forgotten the face. Will the pups be all right over there? I wouldn't want them neglected." He leaned forward. He was sitting on a chair. Lydia was on the settee.

"I'll keep them at my house. I'll keep her for a while. After one of her bad episodes, Madelaine lets me have her. I think last night was bad. The child didn't get any sleep."

Nora Jane folded the blanket and laid it on the bottom of the kennel. She arranged the edges flush up against the bars. "I don't want them feeling any steel around them," she said to the butler. "It will make them cold. They might think it's a knife or something."

"They won't mind. Just to ride in the car awhile."

"They might. You don't know what dogs think. You have to read their minds."

"If you say so." He held the kennel door open while Nora Jane picked up the male puppy and laid him on the blanket. Then she picked up the female puppy and laid it beside its brother. Then she shut the kennel door and locked it. "This is only for a little while," she said. "After that you will never have to be in a cage again. I promise you that."

The butler picked up the kennel. The chauffeur appeared. They all walked back out onto Philip Street and loaded up the car. The puppies went in the trunk. Nora Jane was in the front seat. Lydia and the judge got in the back. "Hurry up," Nora Jane told the chauffeur. "I don't want them in the trunk for long." They drove back down Saint Charles Avenue. They passed the Academy of the Most Sacred Heart of Jesus, where the girls were filing out to catch the streetcar and their rides. Nora Jane barely glanced their way. She was worrying about the oxygen in the trunk. "Hurry," she said to the driver. "They could suffocate back there. They could have nightmares the rest of their lives from riding in the trunk."

"They'll be okay," he said. "There's plenty of air."

"That's easy for you to say. You aren't in a cage back there." She smiled her dazzling smile at him and he drove as fast as he dared all the way to Story Street. As soon as the car stopped, Nora Jane jumped out and ran around to the back of the car. "I'm coming," she was calling. "Don't worry, angels. Heart of my heart. I'm coming to get you out of there. You're home now. You're home with me."

The chauffeur hurried out of his side and opened the trunk with the key and lifted the kennel from the trunk and carried it up onto Lydia's front porch. Nora Jane sat down beside it. She opened the door. She put her arm into the cage, talking and stroking the puppies' backs. "You are all right now. You are with me. Nothing can hurt you now. I'm going to take care of you. You are my darling, darlings, heart of my heart."

"Is that what we say to each other?" the judge asked. He put his arm around Lydia's waist and hugged her to his side. When he was twenty years old he had loved her enough to die for her. On the day she married he had gotten into his car and driven five hundred miles without stopping. Now they were as old as the hills and nothing had changed.

"Come in," Lydia said. "Send the chauffeur home. I'll make you a cup of tea."

"You are my own little dogs," Nora Jane was saying. "You will never have to do anything you don't want to do. You can just run around with me and sleep when I'm in school."

The puppies began to walk out of the cage. They shook their legs. They shook off the ride in the trunk. The sun was shining. The voice was sweet and soothing. There were good smells in the air. Mice and squirrels and roots and vines, shoes and tables and the undersides of swings. They began to tumble around the painted porch. There was nothing to be afraid of here.

*   *   *

Nora Jane's mother came over about seven o'clock that night. She was dressed up and she was sober and she was contrite. "Come see my dogs," Nora Jane said to her and took her by the hand and led her to the kitchen where the puppies were playing in a cardboard box. "They don't have names yet. I just call them boy and girl. Do you like them? Do you think they're cute?"

"Lydia, you didn't do this to me?"

"She's staying here until the school year is over. You are welcome here at any time as long as you are sober. That's it. It's final, Madelaine. Don't talk about it anymore."

"You want to stay here? You want to leave me alone in that terrible house?" Madelaine turned to Nora Jane. Tears were beginning to run down her face.

"You could clean it up if you hate it so much," Nora Jane said.

"Don't do this, Madelaine," Lydia said. "It's almost her bed-time. Don't do this now."

"I'll come over there whenever I can," Nora Jane said. "But I have to stay here and take care of them. They wouldn't like it with the cat. So I have to stay here for a while." Madelaine was backing up. She thought about grabbing Nora Jane and drag-ging her out the door. But the little girl turned her back to her and lay down on the floor beside the cardboard box.

"Goddamn you, Lydia," she said. "You don't care about any-thing but yourself. You think you can break into my house and steal my child. No wonder your son was such an egotist. He learned it from you, didn't he?" She kept on yelling various insults, and Lydia followed her to the front porch.

"You are a mean old witch is what you are," Madelaine said. "You can't have her, Lydia. I'll get a court order to keep you from ever seeing her again."

"Calm down, Madelaine. Please don't yell out here in the front yard."

"I'll yell all I goddamn well please. And I'm going to sue you for everything you own for this day's work." Madelaine got into the car and started the motor and drove off down the street. Nora Jane came out onto the porch holding the puppies in both arms. "She'll just go find her friends and talk to them," Nora Jane said. "She probably won't be back tonight."

"I hope not, sweetie." Lydia sat down in the swing and the dogs began to tumble around the porch and Nora Jane tumbled with them. The first stars were showing in the sky beyond the porch. Even though there was still light, the moon and several stars were showing. Nora Jane rolled over on her back and laid her head upon her grandmother's soft leather shoes. The puppies licked her face. It had been a long long day.

A long time later Lydia woke her up and took her into the house and bathed her and washed her hair and cut the ends of it and found her a toothbrush and cleaned her teeth and examined all the mosquito bites and bruises on her skin and cleaned behind her ears and put her into a long white cotton gown and tucked her into a beautiful four-poster bed with clean peach-colored sheets and big soft pillows. When Nora Jane was asleep, Lydia drew her own bath and prepared herself for bed. Twenty years, she was thinking. If I can live twenty years or even ten. Give me ten, God, and I will make her safe before I leave. Please give me twenty. Give me twenty or give me ten. I will take whatever you allow me to have. Lydia was crying then, thinking of the child alone in the world. Then she stopped her tears and gave herself a lecture on courage and climbed into her own clean high bed and went to sleep.

A Man Who
Looked Like Me

THE MAN I should have married drove two hundred miles the other day to come and hear me lecture. Fortunately, he was late. Fortunately, he only saw me later at his sister's house. Fortunately, I didn't know he was coming or I wouldn't have been able to say a word. I suppose I could have read a story out loud and answered the well-intentioned questions from the audience. But I couldn't have been my self-assured, sparkling self, the person people drive long distances to hear on those rare occasions when I become greedy or generous enough to pack my suitcases and climb aboard germ-infested airplanes and sleep in strange beds and let the public see me. I like the people who come to hear writers read. I just don't like to travel and I don't like to be the center of attention.

Who are you? is the question they want answered, but I never seem to be able to answer to their satisfaction. He probably could have told them, this man who drove two hundred miles and missed the lecture and came running across his sister's lawn with his wide-open smile to see me. To forgive me. I'm the one who broke our engagements. But it wasn't really me. It was my father and my mother and my fear. Ugly, mean old fear. Teach your children not to be afraid. Make safe homes for them and don't make them move around and go to ten different schools. Don't built nests like robins build, out on crazy limbs that wouldn't hold up a tennis ball. I watched just such a nest fall last Saturday. The first rain washed it down. "You fool," I told that robin. "That wasn't a branch. That was a place where two limbs fell across one another." All my life I have found robin's eggs on the ground in spring. That unforgettable, marvelous blue. Sometimes the eggs are whole. Sometimes they are broken and the yolk is spilled. Once there was a chick. I thought all those years it was because robins are unlucky birds. No, it is because they build stupid nests that are not anchored properly.

I am not blaming my parents for what happened between Farrell and I. Farrell and me, whatever. I could live somewhere where people speak the English language properly but I cannot leave this nest I've made. I have made a home that's strong and safe. Nothing can harm me here. Here I can dream and create. Here I can sleep. I was fifty years old before I learned to sleep.

I was engaged to Farrell twice and both times I broke the engagement. I was afraid to marry him because my parents turned their noses up at his parents. His father was a social worker. His mother taught the second grade. These are professions I admire above all others now. These are the sort of people I surround myself with in my safe and lovely sleeping nest. But then I could not make such judgments. If my parents thought he was not good enough for me, I had to think so too. I was in the third high school I had attended. I had lived in three different towns in five years. I could barely hold on to a stable personality. I held on by reading books. Wherever I went, my books went with me. My books were my nest. Even later, when I was quite old, I had to have those books near me, in the bedroom where I slept. Later, when I became allergic to old books, I finally threw them away. I threw them away as a gesture. I had them memorized. I knew what they said and how each page looked and my name written in the corner of the first page. *Jane Martin, 1951*, or some such date. This was all so long ago and is still imprinted on my brain. The past is not dead, it is not even past, Faulkner wrote. My analyst says, The past is a swamp where we wander at our peril.

There was no peril in the time I spent with Farrell. Our days were filled with laughter. Our nights were filled with a strange hilarity and goodness. He looked like me. He had blond hair and a big, soft, generous body like my body would have been if I had ever let it go. His hands were wide and freckled and his intelligence was full of humor. These are the people I love in the world. People who know the world is funny.

He came into my life at a Demolay dance in the basement of the Seymour, Indiana, library. The Demolays were a club of young men whose mothers aspired to have them grow up to be gentlemen. Four times a year these same mothers cleaned up the library basement and made lemonade and cookies and brought in flowers and invited the young women of the town to come and dance with their sons. The record player was playing "Deep Purple." "When the deep purple falls. Over sleepy garden walls. And the stars begin to flicker in the sky."

That's when I think of you, sweet Farrell, tall and smiling, not afraid to glide across the floor and dance with me. Not afraid to put your hand around my soft waist and pull my pretty soft bosoms into your blue suit and two-step me around as though you were Fred Astaire, or at least a grown man. Which you were not. You were eighteen years old and I was sixteen years old and you had heard about me, way over in Taylorsville, Indiana, where you lived.

"I heard you were writing for the newspaper. I heard you got a day off from school to help put out the paper every week."

"I do."

"How did you arrange that?"

"I don't know. They asked me to write them a column and I did. I wrote about my niece being born and everybody liked it so they let me have a job. I have a Social Security number. So you heard about that?"

"My mom showed it to me. She thought it would inspire me to do the same." He pulled me closer to him. It was hot in the basement of the Seymour Public Library. We were sweating and our bodies were pressed against each other in heat and terror. This was an age of innocence. Everyone was innocent. No modern sixteen-year-old can imagine the world in which we lived. Sex was never discussed, never written about, it was taboo. If you did it, you got pregnant and your life was ruined. That was that. The entire message we received, and we believed it. Only girls who had bad mothers *who did not believe the message when they delivered it* had sex despite the taboo and suffered the consequences. I was lucky, as luck went back then. My mother believed it when she said it.

"Will you go to a movie with me?" Farrell asked. "Or I could take you to this place on the river, Carlo's, everyone goes there to drink beer. It's great. It's real rustic, built out over the water. Will you go?"

"When do you want to go?"

"Saturday night. I'll come get you at seven."

"You don't know where I live."

"Yes, I do. You live in the old Trane mansion on Elm Street. I heard your dad had it restored."

"He always buys old houses and rebuilds them. It drives my mother crazy. She's always in a building project."

"Will they let you go?"

"They don't tell me what to do. I do anything I want to do." I laughed my most sophisticated laugh. It was so hot on the dance floor. He was so intense, he was a darling boy, a tall, blond dancing boy who looked like me.

My father immediately began to make fun of Farrell. "How's your old country boy?" he would ask me. "Your big old country boy." It was himself he was describing. Of all the boys I ever dated, the one who resembled my father most was Farrell. My father's hair had faded and his freckles had faded too and he wore glasses now and worried all the time about making money. So he had lost the thing that would have allowed me to see the resemblance. In just this way he had come into my mother's richer world and whisked her off to be his companion on his

lifetime search for riches. Farrell was not the last one of my
boyfriends whom he would ridicule and belittle, but there was
a special gaiety to his taunts about Farrell. How clear it all seems
to me now. Farrell looked like him and Farrell looked like me
and it was ourselves we were rejecting. You think that's simplis-
tic? You think we have learned that lesson, that we don't need
to know that, here, in the last years of the millennium, in the
United States of America, in our rich and fertile land, with our
constant food supply and time on our hands?

Farrell came to get me on that Saturday night and put me in
his mother's Oldsmobile and we drove out of Seymour, Indiana,
and took the highway to a country road. We bumped over the
ruts and got to Carlo's just as it was getting dark. I think we
talked on our way, but I'm not sure. I think we told each other
the stories of our lives and all our plans and who we were and
what we knew. It was still light while we were driving. When we
got to Carlo's it was almost dark and we walked up the wooden
steps to the dance floor and bought a beer and sat at a table
trying to look like people on a date and then we put some money
in a jukebox and began to dance. "Give me a kiss to build a
dream on, and my imagination will thrive upon that kiss." This
was the man my father should have wept on his knees to dream
of finding for me. This was a young man who would never be
mean, never fail at anything, never be cruel, never stop knowing
life was funny. This was a man who knew how to love. A man
from a safe, loving, secure nest who wanted only to love a
woman and make a nest for her and love and protect her until
the day he died. I could have had that. That was offered to me
that summer, in Seymour, Indiana, in 1953, by a boy who looked
like me.

I must have fed twenty quarters into that jukebox. That was a
lot of money back then. Some of the quarters were Farrell's.
Some of them were mine. We played love songs and slow-
danced to them and the river ran beneath the dance floor and
the tables were damp and the foliage on the trees above the
place was as thick as a jungle. The air was so clean back then.

No one can imagine how clean and sweet the world used to seem to be. This is not an exaggeration or some sort of nostalgia. This is the truth of what you missed if you are the children and grandchildren of that time. Perhaps somewhere in the genes is the memory of that time of innocence. Perhaps you can smell its freshness in your dreams.

Like our aquatic memories when we are in water. Farrell and I went swimming in the river later that evening. We swam in our underpants without looking at each other. I don't believe we let our bodies touch in the soft, brown water of the river. I don't think we did that on that night. But we did it later. At Calhoun Lake, on the Fourth of July. That night I allowed him to bring his body so close to mine that the next day I decided I was pregnant. He did not penetrate me. I don't think I took off my underpants. But the next day I decided I was pregnant and he was so innocent, because I believed it, he believed it too.

For three days and nights we believed it and talked about it. "I was supposed to start menstruating and I didn't start." That's what we told his younger sister when we went to see her to tell her our terrible and thrilling secret. "It's been four days," I added. "I'm sure I'm pregnant."

"You'll have to get married." She was thrilled and excited too. It was the most exciting thing that had happened all summer. She was my age and I had not met her until we took our secret to her. "I'll go with you. We'll run away and find a justice of the peace."

"Yes," Farrell said. A man of eighteen, a man who accepted his responsibilities without question. "We'll do it tomorrow."

"I can't go tomorrow," I said. "My mother's taking me to Evansville with Sue Smythe to buy some clothes. I have to go. She'll be suspicious. You get us a marriage license while I'm gone. Where do you get them?"

"I'll ask my uncle. He's a lawyer. He won't tell. He'll help us, won't he, Sally? Don't you think he'll help me get a license?"

"I don't know," Sally said. "That's dangerous. Telling Uncle Bill. He might think he has to tell our mother."

"He's a lawyer. He's sworn to secrecy."
"I don't know."

We were on the rug in their den in their house in Taylorsville.
It was a lovely house, old and painted white and full of things
that had been there for fifty years. It was the sort of house where
my grandmothers lived, a house where people had been for a
long time. It was not filled with carpenters and new sofas and
newly bought antiques like the houses my mother kept creating.
It was not a house to impress the neighbors. *It was where they
lived.*

The old green rug on which we were lying on our stomachs
with the oscillating fan blowing from Sally to Farrell to me, the
wicker rockers, the radio on its table, the open windows with
their white organza curtains; it could have been either of my
grandmothers' houses. I was lying on the floor with two people
who could have been my siblings or my cousins, in a room that
was comfortable and sweet, in a home where people loved each
other, thinking I was pregnant, in the presence of a boy with an
imagination as wild as my own who was ready to marry me and
work for me until the day he died, and the fear my father had
put into my head would not let me accept it.

"I love her with all my heart," Farrell said, and reached over
and took my hand in his and held it strong and tight and looked
deep and straight into my eyes and pledged himself to me.

"I love you too," I said. "We'll get married Wednesday."

Tuesday afternoon, in Evansville, Indiana, which is the nearest
large city to Seymour, Indiana, in a dressing room in a department store, with my mother sitting primly on a chair and my
best friend, Sue Smythe, trying on winter suits, I reached down
to pull a dirndl skirt up around my waist and felt and then saw
the blood begin to run down my legs. The salesladies scurried
off and returned with sanitary napkins and I pinned them to
my underpants and dressed and went into the bathroom to
wash my body. My mother stood guard outside the ladies' room
so no one would come in and catch me in my shame.

Later, I got Sue Smythe alone and told her the whole story.

"I knew something was going on," she said. "You looked terrible this morning when we picked you up."

"I think I had a miscarriage," I whispered. "I don't know what I'll tell Farrell. I bet it will break his heart. He wanted me to have his baby."

I told him that night. I rushed in the house at five that afternoon and called Taylorsville and told his sister to find him and tell him to come over as quickly as he could. I hung up the phone and went into my room and took my new blouses and skirts out of their boxes and hung them in my closet. I put my new underpants and bras into my underwear drawer. I put my new socks in the hamper to be washed. I got into the bathtub and took a long hot bath, washing my body with lots of soap and bubble bath, examining my navel, lost in thought of the time I had been hooked up inside my mother and the little girl or boy I had lost while bleeding. I was almost in tears at the thought. My mother came into the bathroom and stood watching me. How must I have looked to her? So young and perfect, so strong of will and limb, so powerful and like my daddy. My thick, short hair curling around my head, my legs sticking out of the bubbles in the water, my crazy ideas and energy and talents. "What is wrong with you?" she asked. "You've been acting funny all day."

"Nothing's wrong. I love the stuff we got. Why do you think something's wrong?"

"You aren't worrying about, well, what happened, are you?"

"Menstruating? Of course not. Who cares. You better get out of here, Mother. I'm getting out. Farrell's coming over to see me."

"You didn't tell me that."

"We're going to listen to records. He brought back some new ones when he went to Chicago to see where he'll live next fall. I have to give them back to him. Well, I'm getting out." I stood up in the water, bubbles dripping from my thick, sixteen-year-old skin, my miscarriage tragedy forgotten as I was trying to decide what to wear. "I might wear that new blue skirt tonight," I said. "And that off-the-shoulder blouse. I love that blouse, Momma. You were so sweet to give it to me." She handed me a towel. I used it to cover my nakedness and laughed and went with wet feet into my room.

I dressed in my new clothes and put on white patent leather sandals and went back into the bathroom and covered my skin with Revlon pancake makeup and covered my lips with Revlon Firehouse Red lipstick and put on some of my mother's perfume. Then I went downstairs and ate two crackers and drank a Coke and went out onto the porch to wait for Farrell.

"Aren't you going to eat dinner?" my mother asked me several times.

"Please don't make me eat," I answered. "I don't want to eat anything. It's too hot and I can barely button this skirt as it is."

"Leave her alone," my father put in. "Let her do anything she wants to do. Old bigfoot is coming over from Taylorsville. How could she eat?"

Then he was there, wearing a fresh blue shirt and freshly shaved and with his hair combed down tight and his strength and energy and goodness at my service. I waited for him on the porch. He got out of the car and ran up the steps to me. I took his hand. "I lost the baby," I said. "It's so sad and they're just in there eating dinner. Let's get out of here." He took me in his arms and I think he cried. I am almost sure he cried, but I made him stop and we got into his car and drove out of town to a lovers' lane and held hands and kissed and basked in the light of our drama. "Now we'll get married correctly in a church," he said to me. "As soon as we can. I won't take a chance on this happening again. I love you too much for this to happen."

"Don't worry," I said. "I'm changed of course, but not hurt by this. 'I too beneath your moon, almighty Sex, Go forth at midnight crying like a cat, Leaving the lofty tower I labored at For birds to foul and boys and girls to vex with tittering chalk . . .' That's Edna Millay. I'm memorizing the book."

I should have been quoting: "If in the years to come you should recall. When faint at heart or fallen on hungry days. Or full of griefs and little if at all from them distracted by delights or praise. . . . How of all men I honored you the most. . . . Indeed I think this memory, even then, must raise you high among the run of men."

Because that is what the memory does for me. The knowledge that Farrell considered me worthy of his love, that he threw his love down before me like a gallant's cloak.

He came running across his sister's lawn, as lanky and smiling and full of goodness as he had been forty years before. In no way a disappointment, and the three of us went into the kitchen and talked for an hour and told the story of when we thought I was pregnant when I hadn't even been penetrated. We said no one now would believe such a story and we sat close to each other and loved each other for not growing old, not yet.

Some other lucky woman got to have this man for a husband and I do not regret that. My destiny was someplace else. Another man, sons, grandchildren. Rivers run in one direction. Never look back except to praise. May goodness and mercy follow us all the days of our lives. Amen.

Paradise

WHEN THE SWEETEST stockbroker in Harrisburg married his childhood sweetheart and moved into his dream house it cheered us up. Everyone in town was excited about it. His first wife had gone crazy and started screwing the carpenters. Then she divorced him and took his home and half his money. Then he drank for a year. Then he went up to Chicago and brought back the girl he should have married thirty years before. The one he took to the prom. The one he laughed with when he was young.

They bought an old house out on lovers' lane. We all thought it must be where they necked when they were young. Anyway, they tore it to pieces and built a dream house on top of the shell. They planted roses everywhere. They put up a flagpole and flew a different flag every day. The American flag, the state flag of Illinois, the flag of the United Nations, the Australian flag, the Betsy Ross flag, the flag of the forty-eight states before we added Hawaii and Alaska. When the town stopped talking about them getting married, it started talking about the flags. Some people thought it was unpatriotic to fly other flags. Others thought it was "cute."

I live a mile from the dream house. I pass by there every day taking the cocker spaniels for a walk. Suzanne Smith was the bride's name before she became Suzanne Mayfield. She was a tall blonde who had been the drum majorette, always twirling, twirling, twirling, wearing her boots, carrying her baton. She had gone to Chicago when she finished high school and had not come back. There was rumor she was involved in some sort of problem at a savings and loan up there but none of us pushed that rumor. We were glad to see something good happen in the world. This isn't a mean town. We were pulling for them. I'd be pulling for them still if I thought it would do any good. I don't blame other people for things I do. If I ended up at an orgy right here in Harrisburg, it's my own fault. No one made me go to that party. No one made me stay. It's not the first time I have strayed from my decision to live an orderly life and only serve Athena.

I first learned about the marriage of Davis and Suzanne when the sound of machinery woke me at dawn. By the time I had gathered the dogs and gone out on the road it sounded like the whole woods was being razed. As I drew near the house I could see it was two bulldozers tearing off the porch and clearing the back lot. "What's going on here?" I asked the dozer driver. "You've woken the whole neighborhood."

"Davis Mayfield's bringing home a bride," the man answered. "We have to rebuild this house in a hurry."

By the end of the week every carpenter and plumber in town was at work. Even some of the carpenters who had hastened the demise of Davis's first marriage were out there. This is a small town. You can't worry about things like that if you want to get anything done around here.

"He's trying to outdo the other house," everyone said. "He's going to show her how to get a restoration done."

"She never has finished that other house," others agreed. "After the divorce she just let it go to pot. She's living like a pig."

*   *   *

Davis and Suzanne went off to California to get married. They stayed four weeks, driving around the West, getting used to each other and letting the house be finished and the town get over the shock. Then they came home and started having parties. First they had a benefit for the Handicapped Bus. They had it on the lawn before the roses even started blooming. I baked three cakes for the benefit and dressed up in my best lavender slacks and top and went over to see how Suzanne had fared. She looked pretty good for fifty years old. Pert and not half as crazy as she had been in high school. Davis runs to crazy women because his mother drank herself to death when he was thirteen.

"Hey, Suzanne," I called out as I came walking up the new brick sidewalk. "We are all so glad to have you back here."

"Hello, Anne," she answered. "Davis told me you lived down the road."

"I walk by every morning. I have these cocker spaniels my daughter left with me two years ago. I am waiting for them to die. In the meantime they must be walked."

"William died?" She was speaking of my late husband.

"His heart stopped last Christmas Eve. It's all right. We had a good life."

"What happened to you and Bras?" She was talking of my old boyfriend.

"He's drinking himself to death. He's around town. You'll run into him."

"He was a beautiful man. Is he still pretty?"

"I suppose he is. I try not to dwell on it. What a waste."

"Well, you're looking very well."

"So are you. You've made Davis a happy man."

"It's mutual." He came walking toward us and put his arm around her waist.

"Come upstairs," Suzanne said. "I'll show you our rogues' gallery." So the next thing I knew I was up in their bedroom looking at about four hundred photographs of them when they were young and them with their separate children and her grandchild and her old house in Chicago and a blown-up photograph of them at the prom.

"I really can't stay too long," I said at last. "I just came to bring the cakes and put in an appearance."

"What do you do with yourself?" she asked. "Come and see me. Let's be friends."

"Of course," I answered. "I'd like that. Well, I really have to go." I made my escape, and it felt like one. What was there about her that bothered me? I chastised myself. Harrisburg is too small for petty discriminations. Still, I hurried past the flagpole and the gardens. I hurried back to my car and drove home. Why hadn't I answered her questions? Why didn't I want to help?

She called the next morning and wanted to go to lunch downtown at the hotel. "I can't today," I answered. "I have to go to work."

"Oh, where are you working?"

"Here. At my house. I'm writing a dissertation. I'm taking anthropology at Carbondale. I went on a dig last year in Missouri. I have to write it up."

"That's fascinating. Davis said no one ever sees you anymore, except when you walk the dogs."

"Well, of course they see me. I'm right here where I've always been. I'm getting a degree in anthropology. I've been busy." I was bristling. What was wrong with me? Why couldn't I be nice to people?

"Well, you always were a loner."

"You don't know what I am, Suzanne," I answered. "Well, I have to go now. Thanks for asking me. We'll do it another time." I hung up. My problem, I decided, was that Suzanne was noticing me. In a small town, if you are quiet, people forget you are there. They leave you alone. Whoever you decide you are, you are free to be. When someone new comes along and starts asking questions, it stirs things up. We are not sessile like trees, but we depend on roots as they do. A root system needs to be left alone. It needs to do its work in the dark, find its boulders, suit itself to the terrain. Suzanne wanted to shake me up, but I wasn't in the mood for it. And what of poor old Davis? He needed to make a happy home so much that he would keep on marrying crazy women and letting them stir up his life. What he was really doing, of course, was trying to recreate his child-hood and fix it up. Make a world where his mother did not die. Except the only women he could love were ones who reminded him of the one he had lost. Doomed to repeat our failures. Doomed to sacrifice the present to the past.

Not me, I decided. I will learn from this not to love another running back no matter how much they remind me of my father. I will get my degree in anthropology. By then, maybe these dogs will have died. I will go to France. I will bribe people until I get to go into those caves and see those paintings.

Meanwhile, I have been playing the market and taking scuba diving lessons at the Y. My father left me two hundred thousand dollars in blue chip stocks. I have turned that into five. When it reaches seven I will leave. The underwater cave is the one I really want to see. I have a theory about those handprints with the missing fingers. I am writing my dissertation on it. I had a life and I had a plan. I just wasn't talking about it or letting it show. And I sure wasn't going to let Suzanne Mayfield in on it.

She tried to draw me out. She fixated on me. She couldn't leave me alone. Finally I relented and told her to meet me at the gate and she could walk with me. "Be waiting," I told her. "I don't want to slow down. Do you have some walking shoes?"

"I think so. I'll do the best I can."

She was waiting at the gate and I picked her up and we started down toward the creek that runs into the Morgans' land. "I used to park by that creek with William," I began. "Did you and Davis ever park there?"

"His daughter's coming to spend the winter with us," Suzanne replied. "What's she like? I'm scared to death of what this will mean."

"Why doesn't she stay with her mother? Her mother's right over there on Willow Street in the big house."

"She doesn't like her mother. Davis says we have to let her stay. What's she like, Anne? You've got to help me out. I have to be prepared."

"She used to be into drugs. Then they sent her off to school. I don't know. She isn't pretty. Sallow-faced and thin. She doesn't smile much. Can't you get out of it? Get her an apartment. That's my advice."

"Oh, God. That sounds terrible. I don't want to be involved in this."

"You married him. You're involved in his life. Didn't you ask any questions before you married him?"

"I didn't even sleep with him. He wanted to wait. I thought he had enough money to make up for whatever happened."

"It won't make up for Livingston. That's what they call her. Well, maybe she's changed. She might be better now."

"I should have slept with him." We were almost to the dirt path that led to the creek. I turned on the path and walked deep into the woods. Suzanne followed me. "If I'd slept with him, I wouldn't be here. He hardly ever makes love to me. He says he's going to but he never does. Then he says he's too worried or too sad or he doesn't feel like going to bed."

"Why are you telling me this?" I turned and faced her. I held a branch out of her way. This town is too small to know things like this. We have to maintain our secrets. We have to believe in one another. We have to leave our sadnesses in our rooms.

She moved nearer to me. She moved too close. "I thought you might want to kiss me," she said. She reached out a hand and put it on my shoulder. She looked at me. I took her hand and removed it from my shoulder. "I don't kiss girls," I said. "I only kiss running backs and I'm about to quit kissing them."

"Yes. Go on."

"I'm fifty years old. I'm trying to find out how to be useful in the world. I'm not going to start kissing girls at this late date."

"Have you ever tried it?"

"Look, Suzanne. If you like to kiss girls, it's fine with me. But don't get me in it."

"If you change your mind, let me know. You and Davis and I could have dinner, drink Champagne, get in bed and have some fun. We got some girls in Las Vegas and really had a party. Made all our dreams come true."

"Suzanne. This is a small town. My dream is to get a degree in anthropology. Also, I do business with Davis. I don't want to be privy to the sex lives of people I do business with." I turned

Notes

seen, heard, noted & qu

talk show

"Any guy who has a problem with feminists is signaling a shortage in his pants." —*Singer Bonnie Raitt*

"We've always told our children that if they can articulate why they want us ... we'll do it."

ore

before she could answer and plunged deeper into the woods. I had been walking slowly so she could keep up but now I walked as fast as I could go. If she was so brave and could think up doing threesomes in Harrisburg, she could get her heartbeat up. Let her get bit by chiggers, I decided. She is welcome to all the excitement she can generate. As for me, I'm out for a walk. The dogs were ahead of me now, running madly into the bushes. They are very crazy, city dogs. I would never have picked these dogs in a million lifetimes to be my own.

I came to the creek. I bent over and tasted the water. I took off my shoes and socks and set them on a rock. I waded into the water, walking along on the clean white stones with the sunlight coming down between the leaves making patterns on the water. I could hear her behind me. She followed me into the water. "Just remember I asked you," she said. "If you change your mind, call me up."

"Don't worry, Suzanne, I won't change my mind about that."

"You have beautiful shoulders," she said. "From the back you look like a goddess." I turned around. She had taken off her shirt and bra. She stood in the water in a pair of faded blue jeans. Her breasts hung down like a native's in the *National Geographic* magazine. Was I suppose to think that was funny? Was I supposed to say something?

"What do you think?" she asked. "Pretty sexy, huh? Do you like what you see?" I waded back to where my shoes were sitting on a stone. I put them on. I walked back to the road and ran the rest of the way home. I could feel her laughing after me. I could hear her laughing even after I bolted my doors and threw myself on my bed and covered my head with my pillow.

I started walking the cocker spaniels in the other direction in the mornings. You must change your life, Rilke said, and I am always willing to change mine when I have to. I figured out a route that led down past the old junior high, which is now a sixth grade. I went past the street where Dixie Lee Carouthers had lived. In that house I shaved my legs for the first time. It was the night of the first football game when Dixie and I were seventh-grade cheerleaders. Later that night two of the players sneaked in the door and I stood guard while Dixie necked with them. Story of my life, I decided. I'm always watching while some hot girl gets laid. Why don't I ever get to be part of the hot, fast life? Why do I always run away or turn everyone down? Except for Bras and William, the doomed backfield of the Harrisburg Panthers. One deceased, one drunk, leaving me alone. Why don't I ever get to marry my childhood sweetheart on the spur of the moment or kiss women or take my shirt off at the creek? Not my role, I decided. I'm the girl who makes good grades. I'm the one at the library looking up seven-syllable words in the *OED*. I'm the one who gets excited about ordering a new magazine. I'm the one who is going to get a degree in anthropology. I'm the one who makes money in the stock market. It's not a bad life. It's mine. I'm in charge of it and it's going to stay that way. At least I'm not married to Davis Mayfield and getting ready to spend the winter with his crazy daughter.

I began to see Livingston Mayfield's truck coming and going on the road. She drives a green pickup and wears black and looks like she hasn't done anything with her hair since the last ice age. She didn't wave when she passed my house. She looked straight ahead. Driving sixty-five or seventy, as fast as the truck would go. Windows down, even though fall was here and it was getting colder every day. Windows down, arm hanging out the window. Cigarette burning.

The second week she had a passenger when she would drive past the yard, coming and going, going and coming. It was Suzanne. They were both smoking now. Wearing old sweaters, headbands, tennis shoes. Good God in Heaven, I decided. The neighborhood is starting to look like L.A.

I ran into Davis about that time. He was at the drugstore picking up a prescription. He looked terrible. Worse than he had after the divorce. I guess he's drinking again, I decided. Well, who could blame him? Imagine being in that house with Suzanne and Livingston and both of them smoking.

"What's wrong?" I asked him. "Why do you need a prescription?"

"Something to sleep," he answered. He held the bottle out to me. "Do you think this will kill me?" It was Ambien. I had read about it in *Scientific American*. I studied the printed warnings on the label.

"It looks all right. You could just hypnotize yourself. That's what I do. Prescription drugs are systemic. I try to stay away from them."

"Livingston's here," he added. "She's come to stay awhile."

"I heard about that and I've seen her truck. Walk with me to the car. I want to talk to you. I've been thinking about you. How are things going, with Suzanne? with your work? with your life?" It was the most intimate conversation I had ever had with Davis. I had always just been his distant friend although we had gone to school together for twelve years and to the same church and walked the same paths all our lives.

"It's all right. We covered the roses for the winter. I hope they make it. I especially liked those white ones. You are still going to Carbondale to school then?"

"Four days a week. I'll graduate in May. Then I might go to France to see those caves."

"Oh, the painted caves. I think about those hands in the underwater cave. The ones with missing fingers. I have a theory about them." We had reached my car. He held his hands up in the air, bent down two fingers to make a shadow hand on the hood. The moon was very bright. The shadow was lovely.

"That's my thesis. That's what my dissertation is about! That's why I'm going to France. I'm taking scuba diving at the Carbondale Y. In December I'm going on a dive in Belize to get certified. Imagine going down into the sea to arrive at thirty thousand years ago. I'm going to bribe officials if it comes to that. I'm going to see those hands for myself. I might come by the office and get you to figure out how I should carry the money. I don't care what it takes. It's my dream, my principal obsession and goal."

"I understand entirely. I could do that with my life. It's abso-

lutely worthy. Good for you." He stood beside my car. He was
wearing a black cashmere coat over a white shirt and business
slacks and shoes. A darling man. A man I had overlooked in my
life of running backs. Civilized, that's what Davis is. A gentle-
man.

"I hope everything works out for you," I said. "I'm sorry we
don't know each other better, Davis. Sorry we don't see each
other more. I'm thrilled you adore those hands. Not many
people understand about them." I paused, then looked at him.
"Crisis is to be expected in the world right now," I added. "The
world is changing very rapidly. It speeds up good and bad alike.
It's all one can do to stay in orbit."

"Please come out for dinner," he answered. "Livingston
would like to see you. She admires you so much. She asked
about you the other day."

Subject to flattery just like every other member of my species.
I guess I had forgotten about when I was famous. Well, not very
famous, but in Southern Illinois I had had my moment. I had
been the first woman state senator from my district. I had been
elected when I was thirty-two years old and served two terms
before I quit in disgust. While in the senate I had led the
pro-abortion forces and had some triumphs. Anyway, if Livingston admired me it could only be for that. The remainder of my
life had been quiet. Will be quiet, I thundered in my brain. No
one will disturb the peaceful passage of my days.

Suzanne called the next afternoon to ask me to dinner and I
said yes. I had been sucked in by curiosity, flattery, and kindness.
Not to mention having Davis understand about the hands
painted on the caves. Do you know they used saliva for moisture
when they painted them? This was when the cave was not
underwater, of course. They mixed pigment, then put it in their
mouth and spit it on the wall. Can you imagine a more intimate
art? No, you cannot. Although hand-thrown pottery is close. Van
Gogh probably died from the yellow pigment on the brushes
he held in his mouth and Van Gogh painted the great paintings
of his late life only miles from the painted caves. Is it something

in the soil, the air, a magnetic field? You can't rule out anything in human life. You can't leave a stone unturned if you are truly curious. So of course I put on my new white wool pants and a dark green turtleneck and walked at dusk the mile to the dream house. Why did I walk? you well might ask. I think I felt it gave me some control over the situation. I should have known it was going to snow. I have lived in this climate all my life. I should be able to smell snow clouds coming our way across the plains but I was busy planning how to swim into the dangerous deep waters of the Mayfield craziness and look around and swim right out carrying my satisfied curiosity in my teeth. Only the water was deeper than I had predicted and I needed a regulator and a tank.

"Darling Anne," Suzanne said, opening the door. "Where's your car? Don't tell me you walked?"

"I always walk in the evenings. In the morning I walk the cocker spaniels and in the afternoons I walk without them to bother me. It's a compromise I make with the universe. Where's Livingston? I've been seeing her driving by." She appeared in the hall, wearing a long embroidered robe, looking like a person who had just come back from some exotic port.

"Hello, Mrs. Watson," she said. "We're mighty glad you came to have dinner with us. I'm making dinner. Come in the kitchen and watch me cook." I followed her into the kitchen. Suzanne and Davis were drinking wine but Livingston appeared to be sober and not under the influence of anything worse than the music that was playing. Some plaintive American Indian chant, something played on a flute.

"I hope you like Indian curry?" Livingston said. "That's what I'm cooking. If you hate it, I'll make you some soup and a salad."

"Curry's fine. I'm fond of curry. Where did you learn to cook it?"

"In New York City. I lived in Manhattan last year with a girl from Cincinnati. Her dad has an apartment there and he let us have it for a year. We lived a block from Jackie Onassis. We were there when she died. Anyway, I learned to cook by running out of money and asking questions."

"What did you do when you were there?"

"Nothing. Hanging out. Talking to people. Going to museums. Seeing plays." She poured boiled rice into a bowl. It steamed beautifully. She put the bowl on a tray. "We're almost ready to eat," she said. "Did someone get you a glass of wine?" Davis was holding one out to me and I took it although I almost never drink. Davis and Suzanne were standing in the doorway to the dining room. The night was Livingston's. We were letting her have it.

"I stopped being a dope addict," she said. She was grinning now and I could see all four of her grandparents in that face. This is the reason to stay in Harrisburg. To watch the generations form. To see what happens next to people I have been watching all my life. Here was Livingston, a girl I had completely written off, cooking Indian food and smiling huge smiles that made her absolutely pretty. She poured the curry into a second bowl, added it to the tray with the rice, and led the way into the dining room.

We had a feast. I was feeling so guilty about the bad report I had made to Suzanne over Livingston that I drank too much. At least four glasses of wine. I must have been on the fifth when my old boyfriend, Braswell Carter, knocked on the door and Suzanne let him in. He is the best lover that has ever lived, in all probability. Three other women in Harrisburg will attest to that. Georgia Blake, who dated him after I broke up with him our senior year. Lucy Morrow, who married him the year after that. And Tera Thompson, who drank with him for five years. In between them I was coming and going in and out of his bed. I slept with him on and off until I was forty-five. I had written him off also. After the tenth rehabilitation program failed and after he threw a gin bottle through my bedroom window one Friday night when I wouldn't answer the phone or let him in. I called the cops that night and since then we have only nodded when we met.

"The best." That's what all four of us say. "The best in the world, in all probability." I have talked to them about it, here and there across the years. We don't know why he is the best. It's not his physical beauty. It's something else, some rhythm, some deep humanity, some tenderness, some keen desire or drive or timing. Anyway, you don't forget it.

"Hello, everyone," he said. "Hello, Annie. I've been missing you."

"How have you been?" I asked, wondering if he was drinking. This is the main question you ask when you see Bras. Is he drunk? Is he drinking? Will he throw something at me?

"It's snowing outside," he said. "Did you all know it's snowing?"

That was the beginning of the night. He was not drinking, having just come back from dry-out program number eleven. The snow piled up. The snow covered the trees and the cars and the roads and the hills and the streetlights. The snow was magical and pure. We all went outside and caught it in our hands and giggled and ate flan for dessert and drank black coffee. Bras and I held hands on the sofa. Someone called. In a few minutes a four-wheel-drive vehicle came sliding into the yard and a young man who coaches the high school football team was there for Livingston and we turned off the lights and watched the fire and listened to Whitney Houston and Carly Simon and something else.

"Well, you can't go home now," Suzanne said at last. "No one should drive in this snow. There are four bedrooms empty. Everyone take your pick. Davis and I are in the new suite."

"There are plenty of blankets in all the rooms," Livingston said to me. "Suzanne's a bedding freak."

Suzanne left the room and returned carrying robes and slippers and handed them to me. I was drinking brandy but I was still the one studying anthropology. So here we are back where we started, I decided. A snowy night in Harrisburg, Illinois. Nothing to do. An empty house the adults have abandoned. We are getting to use the beds and we will use them. I had a memory of a night at Dixie Lee Carouthers's when her mother was out of town and six of us were necking together on her mother's bed. Suzanne had been at that party. Come to think of it she might have been one of the ones on the bed. All the lights had been out that night and afterward I was so guilt stricken I had erased the memory.

"Suzanne," I said. "Do you remember one time when Dixie Carouthers's mother was gone and we had a party there after a football game? Were you at that party?"

"I thought that party up, honey," she said to me. "It was the first blanket party in Harrisburg. Then we went inside."

"That's right, I remember now. I was carrying a blanket on my bike all the way down Elm Street. I was feeling like a criminal with that blanket."

"Well, we aren't criminals now," she said and handed me the robes. "We are grown people and can have all the blankets we want."

Livingston started laughing at that and Bras slipped his hand around my waist and started caressing my ribs as though not a day had passed since the last time I told him I wouldn't see him anymore.

Davis banked the fire. Someone turned off the lights. Bras and I found a room upstairs and opened the heat vents and got into bed with our clothes on and started kissing. We kissed and kissed and kissed. The rest is private.

We all had breakfast watching the still falling snow and acted like normal people and helped Suzanne pick up all the glasses from the night before. Bras drove me home in his truck and stayed a couple of days until the snow melted.

So what was the problem? you might well ask. There should be some happy endings here. Not the same old unhappy patterns. Not snow turning into rain, as it says in the country-western song. Bras going back to drinking. Livingston continuing her work of breaking up her father's marriage. Davis always getting rid of his crazy women before they can get rid of him. Prophecies and patterns. There should be a happy ending here. Not a dark and empty dream house with the roses dead as doornails and the people in separate apartments talking to their lawyers. That's how it ended up. Davis got tired of the parties and Suzanne packed up and moved back to Chicago. Livingston moved in with the football coach for a while, then disappeared and hasn't been heard from since. I guess she went back to New York. Bras went back to drinking. He was good for three weeks this time. It was a nice three weeks and worth the two rounds of antibiotics I had to take to cure cystitis.

It makes me sad to pass that empty house when I walk the cocker spaniels. I refuse to look at it. I look up into the trees. I see squirrels and birds and visions. I see the dark architecture of the winter. I see the buds of spring. I see the lush, hot foliage of summer. Our oxygen factories. Our true and faithful lovers. I think about calling Davis and seeing how he's doing but I never do it. I've run the money up to six hundred and fifty thousand as of last week. I have the degree in anthropology on my wall. I'll be in France before too long. I'll be diving down into the cold blue waters of the Mediterranean Sea. I'll be breathing oxygen from a tank. I will have taken the stuff the leaves give us out of their love, and contained it in a tank and carried it down beneath the water to feed my blood while I swim past the French guards and along the passageway and when I surface I will see the hundreds of hands painted by their owners on the walls. I don't believe the theory of ritual mutilation. They didn't cut their fingers off on purpose. They lost them to cold or bears or spiders or snakes. Then they went into the cave and painted them to get the lost parts back. I know what people want. They want to be whole. Perhaps we were whole that night we all spent together in the snow. Like a family ought to be, but who can bear that burden, that Procrustean bed? Who can bear to fight off all those other needs, neuroses, and obsessions? Not me. Not Anne Watson, age fifty-one and on her way to France.

Fort Smith

THE SMALL BEAR woke in his nest of oak leaves and rolled over onto his back to attend the sky. The great ball of fire burned down between the leaves, warming his stomach and his snout. He sniffed the air, searching for food. He had not eaten anything of value in two days. Since the day when the large bear ran him off, cuffing him over and over with his paws until finally the small bear gave up crying to his mother for help and loped off into the strange woods. Which became stranger the longer he traveled. The place where he was now was a long wooded hill that ran down to a creek, then to a long white line that smelled gritty and strange, a smell that made the small bear grind his teeth and swallow. He kicked his feet up into the air, he closed his eyes and concentrated on finding food. A smell of something fine and new came to him, distant and alluring, and he rolled over onto his feet and followed it down the hill and across the creek and found the source of it beside the water. A crackly, ugly exterior he had trouble swallowing and then, a lovely salty taste. It was the small bear's first potato chip. An unopened sixty-nine-cent bag of chips a lady on a diet had flung from the window of a GMC Jimmy on her way home from a camping trip. That's it, she had decided. Out of sight, out of mind. A minute on the lips, forever on the hips.

The bear finished the bag and the chips and stood up to look around for more. On the white line huge animals went by at such a speed it seemed there was nothing to fear from them. Their smell was very bad, however, and he climbed back down into the creek to think it over. Mixed with the bad smell were other smells, good things to eat, fine new things to eat. He would wait until dark, then travel along the line to trace the smells. He crouched beside the water. He drank of it. He waited.

Minette had married Dell one May. The next May she had graduated high school. In between she had DuVal. Then she had two abortions. Then she got smart. Now she was a checkout girl in the Wal-Mart and her mother took care of DuVal and Dell was still good to her but he was depressed. He was working at the chicken-plucking plant and he hated the work. He had never intended to marry Minette and have DuVal and be stuck in a job, but here he was and the only relief he got was when he was drunk. He only got drunk on the weekends. He never touched a drop from Monday to Friday afternoon.

"There's a bear loose in town," he told Minette when they met by the garage after work. They had come driving up within a minute of each other. Minette hadn't even had time to take off her apron or go and get DuVal.

"One comes in every spring," Minette told him back. "Don't you remember that black bear we had last spring and they treed him by the bakery. It was on TV. You didn't see it?"

"Of course I saw it. Come here to me. What's that on the front of your dress." Dell moved in on her and she almost gave in and let him make her laugh. Then at the last minute she fought it off. "I got to go get DuVal. Momma said if I was late one more time she'd stop taking him. She's been down in the back. He's driving her crazy."

"He's a crazy little boy. Got a crazy momma." Dell pressed her against the hood of the Chevrolet. He nuzzled her with his chin.

"You need a shave, Dell. Go take a shower and get the chicken feathers off of you. I'll be right back. I'll fry you a chicken if you'll get it out of the freezer while I'm gone." She pushed him away and walked out past the car to the Jeep and got into it and drove off to get DuVal.

The small bear was getting very unhappy. There was food everywhere but he couldn't find it. When he found it the bark wouldn't come off. He had broken a claw trying to break open one of the shiny containers with the food inside that sat beside the clearings. He had found some food but no more of the fine, salty things he had found beside the creek. Deep in his brain a signal kept going off calling for more of that ambrosia. He loped along behind the line of trees he had found that morning. It seemed a very long time since he had been playing with his mother and his brothers. It seemed as if he were on a search that might never end. Go on, his brain told him. You can find it if you look.

DuVal was packed and ready and standing on the porch. He had his things in his little backpack and he was holding a package of Lay's potato chips his grandmother had bought on sale at the IGA. They had eaten part of them in the swing. The rest were still in the sack, secured by a long green and red clip his grandmother had attached to it. "Don't eat any more of those chips until after dinner," she had said. "I'm lying on this sofa resting my neck. You wait on the porch if you like, but don't go down them steps."

Minette drove up waving and DuVal ran down the steps and got in. He was very coordinated for a three-year-old. One good thing about Dell, Minette was always saying. He takes DuVal off to play ball. "Got you some chips," she said, leaning over to give him a hug. She fastened his seat belt. "Sit down then. Let's go home and cook some dinner for your daddy. Momma," she called out. "We're going."

She waited a minute, until her mother came to the door and waved. "She's all right," Minette said to DuVal. "She always thinks there's something wrong with her. It's just her way."

Minette did a U-turn on the street in front of her mother's

house and drove fifty miles an hour down the side road and over to the housing development where their blue house stood on its acre and a half of ground. Dell had inherited it from his aunt. Someday that house and land would be worth some money, they were always saying to each other. If we just keep the taxes paid and hold on and wait, this house will put us on easy street. It was true. Fort Smith was growing so fast no one could keep up with it. Every year the outskirts of town grew nearer to the development, which had been way out in the country when Dell's aunt had spent her salary as a nurse to buy the blue house. Some people in the family said she never married because she had seen too much death. Others said it was because she was ugly. Dell's mother said she didn't like men. Anyway, out of all her nieces and nephews she had picked Dell to get to have the house. Of course he was the only one who was a father when the aunt died. Maybe it had been because of DuVal. Now they had the house and except for having to keep all that land cut in the summer it was a nice little nest. The taxes on it were three hundred dollars a year but they could pay it. DuVal loved the big yard with its trees. Practically the only thing he talked about when he learned to talk was about trees and birds and squirrels.

While Minette was frying chicken, DuVal walked out the back door and began to play around in the cleared place where they kept his toy trucks and his wagon and the tricycle he never rode because he was too small to ride it but Dell had bought it anyway one night when he was about half drunk. He couldn't wait to have a child who could ride a bike and he had gone on and bought this tricycle that only a four- or five-year-old could even reach the pedals.

The small bear lay in the curve of the cherry tree. There were small bitter berries on the tree and he had eaten several pawfuls of them, then chased the taste away with a pawful of grass. He lay back against the smooth bark. There were other fruit trees in the area and something about the place reminded him of better times. His stomach was small and flat again. Tonight he must try again to batter the bark of the shiny containers. Now he would rest in the heat of the late afternoon. Time had no meaning for the small bear. There was only heat and cold and smell, only pain where the big bear had scratched him on the shoulder and the smooth curve of the tree limb and the hot white ball in the sky. He lay back and closed his eyes, and slowly at first, and then more surely, he barely sensed and then smelled the potato chips. He sat up and reveled in it.

DuVal was taking the potato chips out of his pocket and putting them along the edge of the road he had built for his tractors. He lined them up. Every piece that was left in his pocket.

"Dell, bring the baby on in here and get him cleaned up," Minette called out. "Go on. I read in the paper that fathers never spend more than thirty minutes a day with their children. That's why so many of them go bad."

Dell got up from the television set and walked out the back door and scooped up DuVal and rode him on his back. "Your momma is frying a chicken, son. Proving once again that wonders never cease."

The bear sat for a long time smelling the fine, rare smell. It was mixed with other smells now, each one finer and rarer than the last. He shook his head and stood up on his hind paws and scratched at the tree. Then he began to move in the direction of the feast. The last rays of the sun moved down between the leaves. He squinted his eyes against the light and followed the smell.

A little brackish creek ran behind Minette and Dell Tucker's place. Dell had built a stile over the backyard fence so DuVal could climb it and think he was going somewhere. That had proved to be a mistake as Minette couldn't turn her back on DuVal without him starting climbing. In the end they had to put a little gate on the top and put a lock on the gate. "It makes the yard look like a prison," Minette said, when all the work and the additions were done. "I don't know why we started this in the first place."

"Because he needs to think he's going somewhere," Dell said. "When I was little we went anywhere we wanted to. We weren't all walled in all the time like he is. I was dreaming the other night about him trying to get out of the yard. That's why I built it."

"You are the craziest man I could have married," Minette said. "That's why I married you."

"Oh, yeah," Dell answered. "We'll see about that. I'll show you crazy." And he tackled her and laid her down on the sofa and started pretending to tickle her. "If I get knocked up I'm getting an abortion," she told him. "You just be prepared for that."

Now the small bear moved along the side of the brackish creek. The lovely smell was getting closer. He was lost in it. It smelled of ten good things all mixed together. He warmed in the smell. He moved happily along the ground, bringing his stomach with him.

On the back screened-in porch with the patched and ratty screens and the old painted table with its wobbly legs and the green chairs with the tall backs, Minette and Dell and DuVal feasted on the fried chicken. There was a platter of it on the table. Plus fresh boiled corn and butter and mashed potatoes and the blue and white dish of green peas and carrots. There was also a round loaf of Hawaiian bread, which was Dell's favorite and Minette's downfall. Tonight neither of them was paying much attention to the bread. The chicken was hot and crunchy and had been prepared by a combination recipe of the way both their mothers had fried chicken. It was dipped first in egg the way Dell's mother insisted it be done and then shook up in a brown paper bag with flour and salt the way Minette's mother did it. The deep hot fat boiling in the thick pan was agreed upon by everyone they knew who knew a thing about frying chicken. The fat was on the back of the stove where DuVal could never reach it. The table was set. The Tucker family was at dinner.

"I might make him a little baseball diamond," Dell was saying. "Back where we had that garden last year. It won't be long, Minette, he'll be playing T-ball."

"He won't play T-ball for three or four years. You got to quit rushing him into everything. He won't like it when he gets there."

"I wish we could have another one." Dell looked right at her when he said it.

"Another what?"

"Another one. A little boy or a girl. I think all the time what if something happened to him. Where would we be? It's too big a chance. Only having one."

"And how would we live then? On just our salaries? We can't do it, Dell. We wouldn't even be able to pay the taxes or for the roof. What if I got sick? What would happen then? I don't think Momma would take care of two of them. She complains enough as it is."

"I only said I wished we could. I didn't say to do it." Dell reached for a third piece of chicken. He brandished it before he took a bite. He ate it with lovely manners. He was just a lovely man, Minette thought. But that didn't mean she was having any babies. A breeze stirred from the south. Beyond the fence the clouds were gathering. A front was coming up from Texas. It would be there by midnight. She helped herself to corn and ate it daintily. He wasn't the only one who could have manners.

DuVal was making a dam in his mashed potatoes. He had two sides built up but the melted butter kept dripping out of the other sides. He put his finger in it and sucked it off. "Get down," he said. "Getting down." He squirmed down out of the high chair and moved around the table to the door.

"Let him go," Dell said. "He's had enough. He was only playing with his food."

"Momma gave him potato chips," Minette said. "I told her not to, but she does it anyway."

DuVal had forgotten about the potato chips. Now he went into the kitchen and retrieved the bag where his mother had put it on the counter and carried it out the kitchen door to the backyard. They watched him going down the stairs carrying the bag. "Let him go," Dell said. "He looks so cute. What do you say, honey, is he the cutest child that ever lived?"

"He might be," she answered. They watched him moving out into the yard, the bag of chips dragging along in his hand.

The small bear arrived at the stile at precisely the moment that DuVal moved past the circle of toy trucks. The smell was now so overpowering that the bear ran up the steps of the stile and beat on the gate with his paws. When it wouldn't budge, he climbed around it and fell down the steps into the yard. DuVal froze. He had never seen a bear. He didn't know a bear from a hole in the ground but something in him knew to scream. The first scream was low-pitched. The second was bloodcurdling. The third was so terrible it stopped the bear in its tracks. By then Minette was out the door. "Oh, God," she screamed. "It's the bear. Get the gun." She ran toward her child. She ran twenty feet in a second. She grabbed him up and started toward the house. Dell was behind her with a 12-gauge shotgun in one hand and a pistol in the other. Minette reached the circle of toy trucks. Dell pulled her behind him. He drew a bead on the bear, which had moved toward them across half the yard.

"Don't shoot it," DuVal screamed. Minette had made it to the porch with him now.

"He hates that noise," Minette yelled. "Let me get him inside. Then shoot up in the air. It said on TV to shoot up in the air."

Dell wavered. The bear had stopped moving. Then, as they watched, he picked up the bag of potato chips and began to devour it. He bit into it, plastic bag and all, and chomped it down in five bites. Then he glanced their way, shook his head, bent over, and began to lick up all the crumbs.

"Throw him some chicken," Minette suggested. "Throw him the corn."

"Call the police, Minette," Dell answered. "Get the police on the phone." He moved back into the porch. He put down the pistol and picked up the plate of chicken and moved it to the end of the table near the door. He took a bite of a wing, then

sailed it out over the bear's head toward the stile. Behind him
Minette got the Fort Smith police on the phone.

Later, after the police had shot the bear with the tranquilizer
and the photographers had been there and the television cameras, and Minette's mother had shown up at just the wrong time,
Minette and Dell wrestled DuVal to bed by promising to tape
the photos of him on the ten o'clock news and after they did
that they got into their four-poster bed and made love two and
a half times before they finally fell asleep. It almost tied the
record they had the time they went camping by Lee Creek. "Now
everyone will know where we live and come and rob us blind,"
Minette said, cuddling down into her almost sleeping husband's
arms. She was pretending to be helpless and dumb. "I'm going
to be afraid to be alone a minute after this."

"No, you won't," Dell muttered, trying not to fall right asleep
after the article she had made him read in *New Woman* magazine
about women hating you to go to sleep after you made love to
them. "You never are afraid of anything."

"Yes, I am," she said, but he was all the way asleep by then.
She kept on saying the rest of what she had to say just the same.
"I'm afraid of dying and I'm afraid I'll lose my job and I'm afraid
of getting bit by spiders. I'm afraid something might happen to
DuVal and I'm afraid you might start liking someone at the
plant." Since he was definitely asleep and the moon was bright
outside the open window and they had had such a narrow
escape, she decided to let it all hang out. "I'm afraid of getting
pregnant and I'm afraid if we wait too long I might never have
a daughter. I'm afraid Fort Smith is getting too big or if it gets
smaller we might both be out of work. I'm afraid we looked
stupid on that television story and everyone will tease me to
death tomorrow. I was afraid you'd shoot that little bear. As soon
as you aimed at him I was about to cry thinking he'd be all
blown up and bloody like people in Bosnia or somewhere. Well,
to hell with it. We're the ones who caught him. If it wasn't for
us he'd still be on the loose. What would you have done if you
were me, that's what I'll say to them. We had DuVal to protect,

for goodness' sake. To hell with it. What-a day." Minette moved her body back over onto her own side of the bed and went dead to sleep. The moon moved across the sky. So did the earth we're riding on. Not that anyone notices it anymore what with all that stuff there is to keep up with on television.

Desecration

I DID NOT KNOW they were going to paint swastikas on the church. I did not know they were even in the church. I did not know where they were taking me.

My name is Aurora Harris and I have been an extremely good and reliable person most of my life and in Gifted and Talented since they tested me in second grade. My father is the head of the English department at the university and my mother is a housewife and former painter. I am the oldest of two children. My little sister is not in Gifted and Talented because she has no self-esteem, which is not my fault, and doesn't test well. She is spoiled rotten, to tell the truth, and one reason I ended up on that altar is because my mother is so busy spoiling Annie she never has time for me. All she does is drive Annie around to art classes and acting classes and ballet classes and everything they can think of to develop her potential. Meanwhile, *I did not get elected cheerleader* and if you think it's possible to go Webster Junior High School and not be a cheerleader you have another think coming. I was conditioned to think being cheerleader was the main reason to go to junior high. Is it my fault I tipped over into the criminal element when I did not get elected? Not to mention I got fat. First I did not get elected and then I got fat and then I fell in with Charlie Pope and the next thing I knew I was lying on an altar in a nightgown.

Thank God for my dog, Queen Elizabeth. She may be little and she may be handicapped but she will bite and everyone in Fort Smith knows it. She bit the mailman and because of that we do not have our mail delivered to the house. She bit a woman who came by selling cosmetics and almost cost my father all his money in a lawsuit. She has snapped at half the people at the junior high when she follows me to school. I wish she would bite most of them. Not that the student body got to vote, as if we were in a democracy or something. No, the teachers vote and it is based on who is sucking up to them the most and I do not suck up to people, no matter what.

It was four days after I did not get elected that I met Charlie for the first time. I had seen him in the halls, wearing his leather jacket and with his hair dyed blue and six earrings in each ear. You had to notice him but that was when I was still trying to get the popular kids to like me so I just nodded to him and passed him by. Now it was four days after my three best friends went off to their first cheerleading practice and all I'd been doing for those four days was moping around and walking home by myself about three blocks an hour. I even threw up one day. I swear I did. I just walked into the house and threw up several times. I could tell I was on my way to having an ulcer from only three months at Webster Junior High, but I didn't tell my parents. They are very nervous about me as it is. I didn't want to get them thinking about taking me back to the psychiatrist who gave me those drugs last year. So I kept my mouth shut and ate some crackers and peanut butter for supper and played with my dog. She is a mutt we saved from death at the pound and she loves me when all else fails.

Here's what happened next. It was Autumnfest, when all the stores downtown block off the streets and have carnival games and everyone is supposed to walk around admiring the maple trees and buying cotton candy and cookies from the AIDS Task Force and the Humane Society and the Women's Shelter. I've been going every year for years. Except now my three best friends are going with the other cheerleaders and I'm left out. I wandered on down there on my bike. They are all still talking to me. They are trying to act like nothing's happened. But the minute I saw them I thought, ride on by, don't even talk to them, and that's exactly what I did. I rode around behind the Bank of Fort Smith to where they had some games. Someone had come in from Fayetteville with this huge mattress made of Velcro and for twenty-five cents you could run at it and stick yourself to it. It was against the back of the brick bank building and you had to wear these filthy-looking jackets covered with Velcro so you'd stick when you hit the mattress.

Three or four boys I knew were forking over quarters as fast as they could fish them out of their pockets. Charlie Pope was standing off to one side with his hands in his pockets looking contemptuous. As soon as he saw me watching him he got out a package of cigarettes and lit one and started smoking. I have been taught that contempt for human frailty is a cardinal sin. That's my dad's strongest indictment. Pride, Greed, Ignorance, Fear, Desire, the five daughters of Maya, King of Darkness, that's what it says over my mother's kitchen stove. My father moves the sign around and sometimes he changes it. For a long time underneath the five main cardinal sins, it said: Contempt for human frailty is self-hate.

What does he know about how it feels to not get elected cheerleader when you were the smartest girl in second, third, fourth, fifth, and sixth grade? Now they are going to make you a second-class citizen by a system you never agreed to be part of. I looked Charlie Pope in the eye. Obviously, he was running his own show. I guessed I could get used to the earrings. I walked over to his side of the parking lot and said, Hello, how you doing?

"You want to throw yourself at the Velcro?" he asked. "I'm paying."

"Sure. Why not? Have you done it?"

"Are you kidding? Here, have a turn." He fished a quarter out of his pocket and held it out to me. His hands were not that clean and I could see the end of the snake he had tattooed on his wrist curling down to meet the inside of his palm. At any other time this might have grossed me out, but not today.

"I have plenty of money," I said. I turned my back to him and walked over to the guy selling tickets and bought four of them and put on one of the jackets and hurled myself against the wall. At the last minute I jumped as high as I could and ended up stuck to the wall about five feet off the ground. The crowd roared its approval. I did it a couple of other times but never managed to get that high again. I gave the last ticket to a kid I knew and put my own jacket back on.

"You want to hang out?" Charlie asked. "Let's walk up to the square."

"Sure," I said, and walked along beside him. Now that I was nearer I could tell he was pretty strong and tall for a boy in the ninth grade. He started to pique my imagination. I have an extremely active imagination. It has always been difficult to keep me from being bored if there isn't plenty for me to do. That is what the psychiatrist told my parents last year. They sent me to him to get over my trauma after one of Dad's students killed himself and we had to have the funeral.

"Did you read about that bear that got loose?" Charlie asked. "It's the same one who came to town last spring. They stapled a tag to his ear when they caught him last year. I think it sucks to staple things to animals' ears. He probably came back to get revenge."

"You should talk. With all those earrings in your ears. God, doesn't that hurt?"

"No. You ought to do it. You're a big enough girl to have your ears pierced. Why don't you do it?"

"Because my grandfather is a biologist. He would go crazy if I put holes in my ears. He is paying me two thousand dollars a year not to smoke until I grow up."

"What's that got to do with piercing your ears?" We had arrived at the corner of the square and there were my parents, coming along the street in my direction. I told Charlie good-bye and walked on over to meet them. They're good people. Don't get me wrong. They understood that the cheerleading failure had an effect on me. They just never could understand the breadth of it. They didn't have to go to Webster Junior High every single weekday of their lives and pass their three best friends in their white and green uniforms. It was intolerable. It has ruined my life.

I was in that church when the cops came and my name was in the papers and now I am going to have to go to Lausanne in Memphis which will cost all the money I could have had for college and even there the story will be known. I am a marked woman. There is nothing left to do but go on and try to get into medical school and go to Zaire and try to save some kids from dying of Ebola. I mean it. That's the only thing I think of now. I will finish high school and college. Work my way through medical school. Stay up all night being an intern and then go to some foreign country that needs me and save lives. My life is finished in the U.S.A. There is nothing left for me here.

I didn't get involved with Charlie right away after the Velcro incident. I was too busy having my life go from bad to worse. My grades got lower and lower. I sank so low that I even got a D in science, my favorite subject. I lost my will to live after the cheerleading contest. I really did. I used to have nightmares about it. I would be sitting there at my desk and Mr. Harmon would get up and read the list of girls who made it and my name was not there. That's it. The day my life ended.

I've been trying not to think like that. This friend of Dad's who's always been nice to me, this English teacher, gave me a copy of a new translation of Rilke and I read that for a while, then I just started reading Stephen King and Anne Rice and crap like that. At least I could talk to the other kids about Anne Rice. You think there's anyone at Webster Junior High who wants to talk about Rilke? There aren't even any teachers that know Rilke. Well, I guess I shouldn't say that. So I started reading Anne Rice and you know I told you I had a very active imagination and I think it was because I sort of halfway started believing in vampires that I started talking to Charlie Pope. He looks like a vampire. I was running into him when I'd go downtown on my bike. He wasn't at Webster Junior High anymore when I started talking to him. He'd been kicked out for skateboarding in the halls and was going to this school called Uptown where they put kids who are too wild for the regular schools. Except he never even goes to Uptown. His parents are divorced. Neither of them wants him so they gave him an apartment near the school and he lives there with these three other guys and a couple of dogs his parents were getting rid of too.

It's really not that bad a place. I mean, Charlie keeps it clean. He's a nut about cleanliness. We have that in common. So I think it was the apartment being clean and him being nice to the dogs that made me think it was all right to go over there. In spite of the posters on the wall. There were some naked girls on motorcycles and some other gross stuff I don't want to talk about.

So first I went over there a few times. Then I started believing the weird things he said. Then I said I'd go to the meeting. Then I let them blindfold me and got into the car and then I was at the church. I don't deserve to live for being dumb enough to even talk to Charlie. Much less believe it made me somebody to have him like me.

Days and weeks and hours have passed since I learned my cruel, costly, bitter, crushing, stupid lesson. I am alone in my room writing this in longhand on a legal pad. I have given up on the computer. He surfed it at night and slept all day. It was there he met other members of the cult he started. It was right there on the computer screen, where the CIA or the FBI could have read every word, that he got the idea to break into the Silas Mills Methodist Church and paint swastikas all over the walls and other stuff I don't want to write down and then put thirteen-year-old virgins on the altar and initiate them into the cult with sex.

I was not the first girl to be drugged and put upon that altar. I was the third and the main thing you must know about my dog, Queen Elizabeth, is that she bit him. They had brought her along in the car. I guess they were going to cut out her heart or something. Anyway, when they brought me into the church I started trying to get away. They'd given me some kind of pill Charlie stole from his mother's bathroom but it quit working when I saw that mess on the walls. "Get me out of here," I said.

"Calm down," Charlie says, and his stupid friend, Lamont, tries to get a half nelson on my arms, forgetting that my father wrestled in college and has taught me everything I need to know to protect myself. I elbowed him and when he reached for my neck I kicked him you know where — where it really hurts. About that time Queen Elizabeth broke free and bit Charlie on the shin. Not some tiny little bite that will heal in a few days but a real bite from the wildness that resides in even the most domesticated animal.

Then the cops broke in. They were coming in every door and they were not in the mood to think anything was funny. It would have been better for me if I had been tied up or handcuffed but that's water under the bridge.

I am still a virgin, you'll be glad to hear. Not that it matters after my name was in the papers. Well, not my name because that's against the law, but enough so that everyone knows it was me. Not to mention my parents told everyone they knew. I hate that in them. They think the unexamined life is not worth leading and that you must live so that you can admit everything that happens. That was okay back in the sixties when they were young but it doesn't work anymore. There are too many people now and most of them don't think it is a cardinal sin to sit in judgment or be contemptuous.

I have to wash the windows at the church every Saturday afternoon for the rest of my life. I owe them five hundred and sixty-two dollars for my part in the desecration of their paint job. I am paying it back out of my allowance and baby-sitting money until I go off in the fall to Lausanne or Saint Stephen's in Austin or maybe All Saints in Vicksburg, Mississippi.

Several times I have tried to make a list of the things that led up to me being on that altar. I have changed the order several times. I have left out a couple of events I do not think it's good to dwell upon. This is the best I can do and I am going to put this on the Internet as a warning to other young girls like me. Here it is.

1. Thinking I wanted to be a cheerleader and spend my afternoons jumping up and down and saying mindless, boring, repetitious cheers.
2. Being told by my grandmother how she was the cheerleader in Pine Bluff and was also the homecoming queen.
3. Being told by my mother that she was the cheerleader in Greenville and how popular she was.
4. Ever reading or saying the word *popular,* which only means you are so dumb or stupid or easily influenced that you want a lot of people you don't know to like you and vote for you for anything.
5. Getting sucked into trying out for cheerleader.
6. Not getting elected cheerleader by the panel of teachers who included an English teacher who had it in for me because I corrected her in class one day. She said T. S. Eliot was an Englishman when anybody knows he was born in St. Louis, Missouri.
7. Losing interest in school and starting to make bad grades. Only how could I help it under the circumstances?
8. Continuing to go to Webster Junior High School after I didn't get elected. I should have made my dad put me in college. I should have taken the Graduate Record Exam. I bet I could have passed it. I am a lot smarter than many people who get into the University of Western Arkansas. Many people my father teaches can barely read English, much less Rilke.

Well, that is all water under the bridge. That is spilled milk. I am going to be shipped off to boarding school with other girls who didn't fit into the scheme of things. Well, I have to go now. I have to study biology for about three hours to make up for the two weeks I was running around with the cult and didn't crack a book. Wish me luck. Don't believe everything you hear about disturbed teenagers. Most of us are sadder than you know. Very, very sad. And I'll tell you something else whether you want to believe it or not. It's not our fault. I didn't invent cheerleading.

I didn't dump it right down in the middle of junior high school to totally ruin the lives of everyone except the fourteen girls who make the squad. I'll tell you something else. It ruins the lives of some of them. They peak too soon and are never that happy again.

Update

FROM AURORA HARRIS to anyone who received my parents'
incredibly stupid Christmas letter and believe anything it says
about me. In the first place I do not look anything like that
picture and did not know they were sending it out. I have never
been as embarrassed as when I saw that photograph. Can you
just see me sitting under a Christmas tree with a red hat on my
head? That was one moment last Christmas Eve and Granddaddy made me let him take the picture. He is extremely rich
and is leaving most of his money to me so I have to indulge him
when he gets into something like buying a camera. He used to
be a four-star general and people still call him General Drake.
He is my mother's father. My father's father is an intellectual
and a college professor and a noted biologist who once worked
with Crick. It is sort of hilarious to have them in the same room
since they are both egomaniacs and don't like to share the
spotlight. Mother is always thinking they should come and visit
at the same time and show solidarity.

Back to me. I have changed my whole outlook on life. I am
still planning on going to medical school but I have decided
now to be a psychiatrist. I have been talking to this woman
psychiatrist and because of her I am not going to have to go off

to school next year after all. She went to Johns Hopkins Medical School and has been through two training analyses and is so smart it blows my mind to even think about her much less talk to her about my family and the cheerleading crisis last year and being dragged onto that altar by Charlie Pope and almost initiated into a satanic cult. Dragged, my ass, she might say. You went gladly. Anything to escape the middle-class values my mother is espousing in order to save herself from worrying about the real fear and terror of every living human being, which is death and decay.

You see, there isn't any reason to spend your life dreading the inevitable. You might as well go on and live very fully in the present moment and get as much done as possible to help your fellow humans and sop up all the good karma you get from being useful and sleep like a baby.

Her name is Diana Voss, this angel of enlightenment, and she is making me into a freak by teaching me all this stuff. Can you imagine talking to her for almost an hour three times a week and then walking into Fort Smith High School and looking around you at the pitiful insanity of most of the teenagers in the United States? Our dopey principal says we are the elite who will run the country one day. Can you just imagine these idiots trying to make the laws?

I don't think half of them can read the newspaper with any comprehension. Diana thinks I should go on and go to college and just skip high school but we haven't told my parents yet. I think I'll tell my grandfather Harris and let him arrange it. I could just go live with him in Fayetteville. It's only forty miles away and there is a good enough science department there for me to stay interested.

The tree in that photograph you got sent by my mother isn't even the tree that I remember from last year. The real tree is the one Dad brought home that shed all its needles by December 14 and we had to take it down and drag it out the door and who do you think had the job of vacuuming up the needles? Who do you think had to get blamed and feel guilty when the needles broke the Electrolux and we had to go to Wal-Mart at nine o'clock at night and buy a new vacuum sweeper? The tree in that photograph is a fake Christmas tree we ordered from the florist shop. It cost one hundred and ten dollars, money that could have been used to help Habitat for Humanity or Saint Jude's. It is made out of the same petrochemicals that are responsible for the mild winters and terrible storms we have been having. If I have to explain that statement, don't read on.

Now that Christmas is over we are going to have to store that tree in the attic where it takes up all the room. Think of that tree stuffed into our attic with the boxes of Dad's textbooks from college and the trunk with Mother's old cheerleading and home-coming queen costumes and the daybed that belonged to my great-grandmother that no one wants but no one can bear to throw away. If you want to think Christmas, think about that tree up there all alone eleven months of the year, a completely useless, frivolous, retrograde symbol of a tribal ritual whose real purpose is to give people an excuse to wear red when the days are short and sunlight is in short supply.

If you want to think about something good think about me, Aurora Harris, walking down the street disguised as a teenager, on my way to talk to the smartest woman I have ever met who is going to see to it that I escape enough of my conditioning to be able to move on out into the future. I'll probably marry someone like Bill Gates or be someone Bill Gates will come to when he gets in trouble. I'm going to have a happy life and take as many people with me as I can save. Happy New Year.

The Dog Who Delivered Papers to the Stars

WHEN COPEY CULP'S wife stole his children and went home
to her people, the first thing he did was take her dog out in the
woods and shoot it. Fortunately for the dog, Copey was so mad
he didn't finish the job. He drove the dog to the outskirts of
Harrisburg, parked by an old borrow pit, walked the dog to the
edge of the woods, took aim with a four-ten, and shot it in the
neck. The dog stared at Copey in surprise, shook for a moment,
and fell to the ground. Copey felt awful about it. The minute he
pulled the trigger he was sorry he had shot that dog. What if
Sally Sue came back? He would have to lie to her about the dog
and she could always tell when he was lying.

He straightened up. He turned his back on the murder scene
and walked back to the car with the gun broken over his arm.
I had to do it, Copey was thinking. That goddamn dog has kept
me awake for the last night. Plus, bit holes in all the newspapers
and cost me hundreds of dollars in vet bills. If she wanted that
dog she should have taken it with her.

Sally would have taken it with her but she had to fit four kids
and all their clothes into a 1986 Mazda station wagon and
there wasn't any place for a dog. She had thought she could
send for it later when Copey settled down. She knew he didn't

like the dog. She even knew he might not be good to the dog and feed it right. But it never occurred to her that he would shoot it.

The dog's name was Dan. He was a golden retriever who already had a history when Sally Sue acquired him. He had come to Harrisburg with a crew who came to town to shoot background scenes for a movie about Frank and Jesse James. He had come with the truck that carries the dead horses for the shootout scenes. Whenever there is going to be a battle or a shootout in a movie they send this van full of dead stuffed horses to lie around the field after the shooting is done. Dan was the driver's dog. "He has delivered papers to the stars," the driver told Sally Sue. Sally Sue was on the set because her twin boys were extras in the film. Sally Sue was smart and kept her ear to the ground for ways to earn extra money so Copey wouldn't have the whole burden on his shoulders. The twins had made two hundred dollars a day for five days. It was a huge windfall and Sally Sue was in an elated mood when they fell in love with the dog and the driver said they could have it.

For two years Dan lived on Valley View with the Culps. Too many nights to mention he had awakened Copey by barking at passersby or squirrels. Also, if the Culps slept late and the door wasn't open when the newspaper boy delivered the morning papers, Dan sometimes messed them up in his desire to deliver them. "Who all did he deliver to?" Sally Sue had asked the driver. "What stars?"

"Sharon Stone for one," the driver lied. "Brad Pitt. Winona Ryder. They all lived in my neighborhood. He'd collect the papers from the street and take them to each door." It was true that Dan had been in the habit of delivering papers in the driver's neighborhood. Some of the young people in the houses probably would end up being stars. Besides, the driver had to get rid of Dan. He had work waiting in New Jersey and it was winter. No one was going to rent him a decent room with a dog in the deal.

"So where did you get him to begin with?" one of the twins asked.

"Elizabeth Taylor owns the mother," the driver said. "I heard the father belongs to Michael Jackson, but I can't prove it."

A month later the movie crew packed up all the dead horses and dusty clothes and headed for New Jersey. The Culps were left with Dan. As I said, Sally Sue would have taken him to Kentucky if he had fit into the car. As it was he stayed on Valley View and wailed all night while Copey was mourning for his wife leaving him. Then Copey took him out and shot him.

When Dan awoke it was the middle of the night. A badger had come by and nudged him. Then a shorthaired sheepdog had stopped and licked him on the face. After the sheepdog left, he opened his eyes and looked around. His neck felt like it was encased in a huge iron collar. It was all he could do to hold his head up long enough to limp over to a tree and lean against it while he licked the blood from his leg and paw. The blood was fresh and gave him new courage and he began to move in the direction of the road. He made it almost to the borrow pit before he collapsed again. The secretary to the president of the Bank of Harrisburg found him there on her way to work. She was dressed in a new, pale peach outfit, but she put vanity in its place and managed to get Dan into the backseat and drove him to the Harrisburg Animal Shelter. The young man and woman who ran the shelter took him inside and found a vet and by two that afternoon he was resting in a cage, heavily sedated and with a large piece of neck muscle missing, but alive. Morphine affects golden retrievers differently than it affects human beings. It takes their minds straight back to the past, to a place where they were happy. As his body healed, Dan dreamed he sat on the steps waiting for the paperboy to deliver the *Los Angeles Times* to the neighborhood of stucco cottages. The sun warmed the steps. The sound of a motor vibrated in the ground. It came nearer. A young boy leaned out the window and threw the papers in a pattern on the ground. One by one Dan picked them up and took them to the painted doors. It was Saturday and smiling faces opened the doors and petted him and thanked him for his help. When the driver woke he came out the door and took the paper Dan offered him and said so the neighbors all could hear, "Elizabeth Taylor gave me this dog. She trained him when he was a puppy to deliver the paper to her in the morning. He's the goddamnedest dog to deliver a paper I ever saw in my life. I shouldn't leave him outside like this. Someone's going to steal him before it's over. But what the hell, he can't live if he can't be out when the paper comes."

It was these Saturday mornings that Dan dreamed of now. When he woke it was harder and harder to move his neck or jump or even walk but the young man and woman had taken a liking to him and coaxed him along and petted him. He looked all over the cage and the floor and the yard for a paper to deliver but there was none to be seen. He delivered them in his dreams. Even after they stopped giving him shots, he could dream the Saturday mornings. Sometimes a door shut in his face without a smile. Then he woke and tried to lift his head.

"We want to come out and shoot some video of the dogs," a local television anchor told the boy who ran the shelter. "You know, feature a dog a week and see if we can get you some business. Run a voice-over, something like, This dog has seven days to live unless a home is found."

"Come on out," the boy replied. "We have some nice fox terrier puppies. And we have a really pretty golden retriever but it's been shot in the neck. I don't know if anyone will adopt it."

"We can try." That afternoon the television crew arrived. The cameras reminded Dan of better times. Perhaps the driver was coming back to take him to the Saturday mornings when he lived where there were many papers to deliver.

He shone for the camera crew. He valiantly lifted his head and walked around the room. He sat on the sofa with the girl who ran the shelter and looked into the camera as if it were his friend.

The video was on the five o'clock news, the six o'clock news, and the ten o'clock news. William Hagedorn saw it at five and was moved. He saw it again at ten and decided it was fate. At noon the next day he got into his car and drove to the shelter to look Dan over. He had a hard time finding the shelter as he was not from Harrisburg originally. He was from Champaign-Urbana, where his father was the head of the physics department at the university. He had come to Harrisburg because he had AIDS and he was trying to find a cheap place to live until he died. It might take a long time to die, he had decided. I want to go someplace small and quiet where no one knows me and no one will ask me questions. I want somewhere out of the way but near enough to home so that if I have to be hospitalized I can charter a plane and get back in a hurry. William had several hundred thousand dollars his grandmother had left him in her will. His grandmother had been born in Harrisburg and knew about the house where Frank and Jesse holed up in their last months of life. I guess if it was good enough for Frank and Jesse, it will be good enough for me, William decided. "Let me go," he told his parents. "It's not that far away. Grandmother always told me stories about Harrisburg. I think it's fated that I go there to live."

"Why won't you stay here?" his mother asked, but there was relief in her voice and William heard it.

"Because I'm tired of the way people look at me. I want to go somewhere where it isn't known."

"It will be known," his father said. "It will be suspected. If you go away, go to San Francisco, somewhere where there are other people of your persuasion." His father was angry because his mother had left the money to William instead of him. It was a slap in the face from his own mother. She had known William's lifestyle and still she had left it to him. It was because he had gone out to the nursing home every afternoon and talked to her. At least she hadn't had to know about the disease. William's father sighed, thinking of the one good thing about his mother's death. At least she didn't know her only grandchild had the plague.

"I don't know how this happened to me," William told Dan when he had the dog in the car and they were driving home.

"That's the best thing about it. I don't know who gave it to me so I'm not tempted to hate someone. And I don't think I infected anyone, but I might have. I think about that a lot. Well, mostly I think about dying. That's what I think about. If dogs live ten years we might die about the same time. So, how old are you? They said about three or four so maybe I won't have to live for ten years. What do you think about that, Gold. Maybe I'll call you Gold. And don't worry if I talk too much. I'm hypermanic. It runs in my family." Dan moved his body closer to William's body. The sun was coming in the windows of the car. The tape player was playing a tape by the Gipsy Kings.

William had been able to buy a fine house for his dying-in. It was small but very pretty. An old Harrisburg cheerleader on her third divorce had built it for a love nest. Her lover was an architect, so it was perfect in every detail. By the time the house was finished she and the architect had decided to get married and live in his house so they put the little house on the market in pristine condition. It was the first thing the real estate agent showed William and he bought it before they reached the bedrooms. It had twenty-two hundred square feet, a large bathroom with a hot tub, a patio, a fenced yard, beautiful landscaping on an acre lot, and two bedrooms, a large one and a smaller one. William bought it for one hundred and thirty thousand dollars, a huge bargain it seemed to him, since he had lived in a city all his life. He made a twenty-thousand-dollar down payment and settled down to live as well as he could while he died.

"I am twenty-five years old," he told Dan as he drove up and parked by the front door. "So I drive on the grass if I want to. I guess I'll have to get a different sort of car to take you riding in." Dan lifted his head and looked at William. "Well, you're probably right. You don't want to ride around in a sports vehicle in the back behind a wire barrier, do you? Still, I've been wanting a Jeep Cherokee. You're right, we ought to get a sports car and you can sit up front with me. Are you all right, old boy? This is the house. What do you think?"

Dan spotted the paper. It was in the bushes where it had been since dawn. The one from the day before was beside it. The day before William had been too depressed to go out and get the paper. The day before he hadn't even bothered to get dressed.

Dan ran to the bush and retrieved the paper. It hurt to run with his neck still stiff but he hurried to the paper and took it in his mouth and ran back to William and held it out to him. William took it and reached down to pat him. Dan flew back to the paper from the day before. It was wet and part of it came off in Dan's mouth but it didn't register with him. He flew back to William and held the second paper out. "Good work, Angel," William said. "I should call you Angel. You look like an angel when you run. Don't worry, your neck will get better. Maybe I'll find you a masseur."

A few days before William saw Dan on television, Copey Culp had driven to Kentucky to bring his family back. Only it didn't work. Sally Sue's brothers told him if he ever showed up in Franklin, Kentucky, again, he was dead. They had seen Sally Sue's bruises and been told what he'd done to the twins. Copey Culp was history with his wife and children. That was plain to see. "And another thing," the brothers told him. "She wants her dog back. You get that dog and ship it down here and the rest of that furniture Mother gave you. We mean it, Copey. We ought to kill you this afternoon but we told Mom we'd give you a chance. Your chance is to get that dog here in good shape and the dining room table and chairs and the chifferobe that belonged to our granddaddy." That was the oldest brother talking. He was six feet six inches tall and redheaded. Copey felt like a bug under his brother-in-law's shoe. In about a minute he'd be dead and he knew it. The younger brother stood back a few feet and finished him off. "She wants you to send some child support. I mean, serious money, Copey. We're going to take care of her but you're the one who kept knocking her up and you're going to pay for it. We've got seven years to get the police in on this. Daddy wants them in on it now but Sally Sue is afraid it'll reflect on the kids so we're holding off on that for now. I can't believe you drove down here and just thought you'd take her back. You must have gone crazy, Copey."

"I don't make that much money to begin with, Arthur. Work's been thin in the building trades. There's nothing being built."

"Find somewhere where there is work, then. We're going to be waiting to see if you send the money, Copey. You remember that." The older brother moved back. He let the younger brother talk.

"Get the dog here by next week. The kids miss it. The furniture can come by van, if you don't want to bring it yourself. You can have a few weeks for that."

Copey got in his truck and started home. It was two in the afternoon. The low point in his life. He had beaten up Sally Sue and hit the twins with a chair and he had killed the dog. Now he was going to have to turn his paycheck over to a woman he didn't even get to fuck and he was never going to see his kids again and if he didn't come up with the dog there was a good chance Arthur would use it as an excuse to whip his ass. Copey was scared of Arthur. He had played football with a big red-headed man like that and there was something there that couldn't be reckoned with. That was that. He'd have to make up a lie about the dog. Say it ran away while he was in Kentucky. Then he'd pack the furniture tomorrow and send it by van and then he'd go out to the woods and see if the dog was still there.

"I could call the pound and say I'd lost my dog," he said out loud. "That's it. I'll report him lost, then wait a few days and call and tell Sally Sue. She really liked that dog. If she forgave me she could get around her brothers. She'll come back sooner or later. She's getting old. She'll be thirty next year. She won't be finding any new boyfriends, as old as she is and with all those kids."

She had already found one. Recycled an old one. She hadn't been home in her parents' house in Franklin two days when she ran into an old boyfriend at the grocery store and invited him over to see her kids. "He didn't beat them at first," she told the old boyfriend. His name was Edgar Delafayette Royals and he had just mustered out of the air force and was home looking for something to do with his life. He had been in military intelligence in the Gulf War and had seen all he wanted to see of the desolation of the world outside the United States. He had studied bacterial warfare. He shuddered every time he thought about how simple it was to kill millions of people. He had been on the debate team at Franklin High School as well as on the football and basketball teams. "If I knew then what I know now," he told Sally Sue, "I could have won the state debating."

"Anyway, he'll never touch one of them again," Sally Sue added. "It's going to be thin for a while. I might have to work in Nashville if I can't get work here. I'll commute or stay there in some cheap place and come home on the weekends. Momma's going to keep them for me. We'll adjust."

"Is he working?"

"He works for a builder. He builds the cabinets in houses. He's a smart man. You just can't trust him if he has a drink. Only he was sober when he beat the twins. He did it with a chair."

"I'll beat the shit out of him if you want me to," Edgar said. "I hate a bully. God, Sally Sue, to think you went through that. I've thought of you a thousand times. I'd give anything if we'd gotten married. So none of that would have happened to you. You could have been in Hawaii with me the time I was there."

"But I wouldn't have my kids. Or my dog. You're going to love this dog when you see it. Some movie people gave it to me. Its mother belonged to Elizabeth Taylor. They think the father belonged to Michael Jackson but they aren't sure. Do you think Michael hurt that kid, abused him, or not?"

"I don't know anything about it. I didn't keep up."

"Well, our dog, Dan we call him, used to deliver newspapers to movie stars. It's this trick he knows. He loves newspapers. He lives for a paper to be delivered so he can bring it to you. I meant to teach him some more tricks but I never had time. Maybe you and me will teach him some." Sally Sue took the hand that was around the back of the swing and brought it down to rest on her shoulder. She had known Edgar a long time before she made the mistake of meeting Copey Culp. She could let him put his hand on her shoulder if he wanted to. Or on my breast, she decided. Or someplace else. What the hell. I'm on the pill.

*   *   *

At that same moment Copey Culp was returning to the scene of the crime. He parked half a mile away, sauntered past the borrow pit, and circled around to the woods. The collar was there, cut in two by the shell, but there was no sign of Dan. No bones, no hair, no dog. Something must have dragged it off to eat it, Copey decided. Only there'd be something left. Maybe he dragged himself, but he was out cold, he was gone.

Copey looked around to see that no one was watching him. He stuck the collar into the pocket of his coat. He strode into the woods and began looking. He got two ticks and half a dozen different kinds of seeds on his pants but he didn't find anything about the dog.

In the beautiful small house in Harrisburg William and Dan were lying on the sofa watching the Learning Channel. Dan had just had his morning massage and William had just taken four of the sixteen different medications he took each day. The four he took in the morning were the worst. "Or else it's because I feel good in the morning and it's a shame to ruin it," William said. "I wish I could teach you to talk, Angel. I'll teach you to read. That's it. Of course your throat is made for barking. But that doesn't mean you can't learn our language. I know, your language is probably more sophisticated than mine. All smells and intuitions and fine hearing. Hunting sight. I wonder if your accident hurt your eyes. See, I need more information. I'll teach you to spell *murderer*. You can tell me who shot you and I'll have them brought to justice. Leave them to heaven, as it says in the movies and Shakespeare, or was it the Bible? Anyway, let's get off this sofa and go shopping. I want to get some groceries and I need to see if my pills arrived."

William was having his prescriptions filled in Champaign-Urbana and mailed to him by his parents. He knew better than to get prescriptions filled in Harrisburg if he wanted to keep his secret. "They know," he had told Dan several times. "It's written all over me. My awful father was right. They suspect. Ah, but my dearest canine, dearest friend. They don't know. Suspect is not to know. I'm okay here. And, besides, it brought me you." William cradled the dog's big body in his arms. He stroked the scars.

He felt the muscle with his hands. Yes, it was loosening. The body heals. It heals if it can.

Two hours later they were back at the house. With groceries, wine, a new imitation leather bone, a box of Purina Dog Treats, and a large net bag filled with alphabet blocks. William put the groceries away, set the Purina Dog Treats on the television set, and lay down on the floor with the blocks. W I L L I A M, he spelled out on the floor. L I V E, he put on one corner. In the other he spelled out D I E.

"When did you last see your dog?" the boy at the shelter asked Copey. He was looking at the photograph Copey had brought him. He was thinking how glad he was that he was alone. If Little Sugar had been there she might not have known what to do. She might have given it away.

"I saw him three days ago before I went to Kentucky to see about my wife. She's sick. She had to go stay with her mother. No, not three days ago. I guess I haven't seen him in about two weeks. That's right. I told a neighbor boy to feed him while I was off on a job in Marion. We keep him in the yard but I was getting home at midnight so I didn't see him in a while. But I thought the neighbor was taking care of him for me. Then when I got back from Kentucky three days ago I noticed he was gone. His name is Dan. You don't have him here, do you?"

"No, we don't. But we'll put out a folder on him and we'll be on the lookout. Was he wearing a collar?"

"No, he was not. He'd outgrown it and I hadn't had time to get him another one. What with my wife being sick and my having to get her to Kentucky. Well, if you see him, let me know. My kids miss him. He was their dog."

"Do you own a gun, Mr. Culp?" The boy stood up behind the desk. He wasn't afraid of this hairy redneck. He already knew everything he wanted to know. This son-of-a-bitch had shot that dog and now he was making an excuse.

"Well, of course I do. Who doesn't have a gun in this day and age? I wish I'd had one while that man was stealing my dog."

"You think someone stole your dog? I thought you said it was lost."

"It wouldn't surprise me. That was a valuable purebred dog. Those movie people that were here last winter gave it to my wife. My kids were in that movie, the one about Jesse James."

"You're going to have to fill out these forms, Mr. Culp. You can sit over there to do it if you like." He handed the papers to Copey and while Copey was sitting at the table working on them he went out the back door and out to the parking lot and began to inspect the truck. There was a four-ten in the rack behind the front seat. The boy opened the door to the truck. He was trying to figure out a way to get a shell out of the gun for evidence when he spied the dog's collar on the floor of the front seat. It was shot in two. He picked it up and stuck it in his shirt and walked back in the back door and put it in the desk and called the girl he worked with and told her to get over there and bring a camera. "If you get here before he leaves, take a picture of the truck," he said, "and a picture of the gun that's in the back."

"I'm scared of him," she said. "I think I'll bring my dad along."

"Don't do that, Little Sugar. Please don't do that. Don't get everyone in Harrisburg in on this before we even have proof."

Three miles across town from the pound William and Dan were on the floor pushing the blocks around. William had called a bookstore in Champaign-Urbana and ordered a book on dog intelligence. "It's the latest thing," the bookstore owner told him. "We just got them in a week ago."

"Send it by Federal Express," William said. "I need it today."

"You've got it. How's it going, William? How are you getting along?"

"I'm getting on fine. I just want to communicate with this dog I adopted and I think I'm going about it the wrong way. Are you busy, Howard? Are there people in the store?"

"Not many. What can I do for you?"

"Read me part of the book. Is there something about teaching them to speak?"

"Well, not to speak. Their mouths aren't formed like ours.

They can't make human speech. Even I know that and I haven't read the book."

"See what it says about sign language. I heard they taught chimps to talk with deaf language. Why not dogs?"

"Because they don't have free hands. Wait a minute. Here's something. Dog-Receptive Language. You want to hear this?"

"If you don't mind."

"'The so-called receptive language ability of dogs is quite good, as shown when dogs respond to spoken words appropriately. For example, consider this mini-dictionary of my own dogs' vocabularies. Each word is presented along with the actions that demonstrate' . . . William, I think you'd better read the book. It looks like they can understand but can't tell us things. . . .'"

"Get it in the mail."

"I will."

"Do you hear that, old Angel." William turned to the dog and gave him a huge extra-long hug. "You can listen, but you can't talk. No wonder dogs are man's best friend. Let's eat dinner early tonight. I want to walk you around town and see if I can figure out where you came from. I'm going to graph the town and we'll cover it together in the weeks to come." He sat down on the floor among the blocks and wrote some words. He wrote L O V E and D O G and S U N and L I S T E N. Then he sat back on his elbows and thought about the words. Dan came and laid his head in William's lap. He was feeling better every day. His neck still felt heavy but it no longer gave him pains. He lifted his head and thought about getting a newspaper out of the basket of them by the door and giving it to William, then decided against it. It was very nice with his head on William's leg. He decided to stay there for a while.

The phone was ringing. William let it ring. In a moment his mother's voice came on the speaker. "William, I know you're there. Answer the phone. Oh, well, I just wanted to tell you they're giving your father an award. I thought you'd like to know. Call when you get home. Oh, well." William had been almost asleep. Now he considered getting up and taking the rest of his prescriptions but he wasn't in the mood. It was too early in the day to be nauseated. He might just put it off until eight o'clock, he decided. One day can't matter. Don't dwell on it or my parents and the way they feel about me. Or anything else. Think about Dan. Thank the universe for that.

They were still asleep when Charley Boyd called from the shelter. "I think I know who shot your dog," he said. "I found the collar in his truck, shot right through. I told Little Sugar, the girl who works here. I guess she can be trusted. We are keeping this strictly under our hats. I need to see the dog to see if the collar fits. How's she doing?"

"He's a male dog. Don't you remember?"

"Oh, that's right. Look, I can't leave here. Will you drive down here and let me try it on him?"

"I don't want to bring him in. Not that it isn't nice. It's the best-run shelter I've ever seen. I just don't want to upset him."

"Okay. Stay in the car. I'll be watching for you. I'll come out. When will you come?"

"Right away. I'll be there in fifteen minutes." William got up and stretched his arms. Then he went into the kitchen and took all the pills at once. Then he drank a glass of Gatorade, then he ate a piece of bread. Then he started his breathing exercises and he kept them up while he loaded Dan in the car and drove down to the shelter. Charley came running out and they fit the collar around Dan's neck. It was a perfect fit. "He said he lost the dog three days ago. Then he said he lost it two weeks ago. He said he was off working and left the dog with the neighbors. I called his boss. They said he's only worked three days in the last two weeks. So, what do you want to do? Press charges? Sue for custody? Or just lay low and let it pass? He's just trying to make an alibi so no one will know he shot the dog."

"I don't want any commotion. I just want to live a quiet life."

"What do you do for a living?" Charley waited. "I forgot what you said you did."

"I'm studying the intelligence of animals," William answered. The chemicals were starting to work on the lining of his stomach. It was time to smother them in some pasta. "I need to go eat dinner, Charley. Thank you for doing all this for Dan." He suspects, William decided. I'm too thin. Too little hair. Too sad. He suspects.

But he does not know. William smiled his best smile. The smile that had won him rooms full of good-looking men in the days when that sort of thing was still in play. Men so handsome and polished and refined and accomplished they would never notice that Charley Boyd even existed. "You are a real human being, Charley. You saved this dog from death. You should be proud of that every day in your life. And you made me happy because I like having him in my home. He's a spectacular dog. He's one of the best dogs I've ever seen."

"He's not the first one I saved." Charley was beaming. He backed out of William's car and came around and stood by the open window. "We'll just keep all this under our hats and see what develops. How about that?"

"You did what?" Sally Sue was saying. "You lost my dog. You let my dog run away. He wouldn't run away. He never ran away a single time in his life. You gave him away or took him somewhere. You're not fooling me, Copey."

"Let me talk to the kids."

"No. I'm not going to. Get a court order if you want. I'm not letting them even remember what you did to the twins. If they talk to you, they'll think about it."

"Jesus Christ, Sally Sue. You've gone nuts down there in Kentucky. This is me, Copey Culp. Your husband. The one that's been sweating every day for years to earn your board and keep."

"You better find that dog, Copey," Sally Sue said. "Bobby's stuttering. That's what you did to him. We're having to take him to Nashville to a doctor. You made him stutter, Copey. You're not getting within a mile of him. Arthur will kill you if you come down here. You'd better start believing that."

Copey hung up the phone and decided to go down to the pool hall and shoot some pool. If he was going to be a bachelor he might as well start enjoying a bachelor's life. The pool hall in Harrisburg is next door to the old ice cream parlor, now a new ice cream parlor specializing in frozen yogurt and shaved-ice cones. Usually only people who had lived in Harrisburg all their lives patronized the old shops off the square, but William had discovered them on one of his walks with Dan and that's where he was headed now.

Copey parked the truck by the courthouse and got out and started tucking in his shirt. Dan spotted him half a block away. Dan didn't hold Copey responsible for the shot. Copey had been there but there was nothing in the shock of the gun that had a direct relation to Copey. Copey had never been good to him but he had never done anything more threatening than throw him out of the house and once into a lake. Dan was glad to see Copey. It reminded him of Sally Sue and the kids and the way they would roll around the floor with him. Dan moved a few feet in front of William, something he never did unless William said, Away.

William watched Copey. Everything about Copey spelled trouble. I don't like it, William decided and turned and began to walk back the way that he had come. But Copey had seen them now. Had seen the dog with its limp and its neck pressed to one side for eternity. He was putting it together but William turned and walked away and Dan went with him. In three minutes they were out of sight.

I must be wrong, Copey thought. No dog could have lived through that. But he wasn't there. There wasn't a bone. The collar was there and the dog was not. That fellow could have found him. It could happen. It might.

Copey went into the pool hall and bought a beer and found an old acquaintance and they began to shoot some pool. It worried him. Like a rock in his shoe. He kept seeing that dog start toward him and the man turn around and the two of them walking away. The thin man and the lopsided dog walking off down East Street as if they knew where they were going. "Who's this Charley Boyd guy who's running the pound now?" Copey asked. "Where'd he come from? I went down there to report my lost dog and he wasn't much help. Acted like he had some kind of attitude."

"The what?" his friend asked. "Runs what? Talk up, Copey, so I can understand what you're saying."

William had decided upon a plan. Get up at six, walk Dan for fifty minutes. Come home, eat breakfast, teach Dan language for an hour, then take the worst six pills and ride it out until noon. Then do exercises with weights, then read all afternoon. Eat, take the rest of the medications. By nine at night he'd be feeling good enough to work until midnight. William had sent for his cameras. He was photographing Dan learning things. It will be a book, William decided. A beautiful book called *The Wonder Dog*, no, *The Survivor.* With a photograph of a gun somewhere. Just a gun lying in the woods, broken. A shell beside it. No, don't get fancy.

He reached down, found the dog's head, began to massage the scalp and neck. "So far we are learning my language," he told the dog. "When we are finished with forty words, or phrases, I will begin to learn yours. I am learning it right now. There, there it is, the muscle we want to stretch. Yes, an accident occurred and changed your life. One changed mine. We have no choice. We can live or die. It's our only choice. This is all there is. This is all we have. It is a lot, Angel. You will teach me your joy at walking down across the fields, your joy at sun, your joy at squirrels, your joy at food. I was the cutest thing that ever walked into a bar on Chartres Street. You ask them. I had this baby blue silk shirt I used to tuck into my chinos. No socks. And this virus used our fun to invade our bodies. So what? So the fuck what?" William was crying now. Massaging the dog's neck and crying hard hot tears into his fur.

The phone was ringing. It was Charley Boyd. "I've been working on this case," he said. "Can I come over and talk to you about it?"

"When do you want to come?"

"How about noon?"

"Sure. Fine. Come on." William got up and began to straighten the house. Not that it was messy in any way. But he wanted it perfect. He looked at the clock and revised his medication schedule. He took the two most important ones and drank eight ounces of papaya juice and took Dan out and walked it off.

By noon he was waiting, wearing a blue and white checked shirt he had bought in Paris and enough makeup to cover the breaking out on his forehead. Dan had been brushed and combed and was waiting by the door. "We are expecting a guest," William said to him. "You will be the first dog in town to have that in your vocabulary."

Charley figured out that William was gay as soon as he was seated. No straight man could make a house look this good. Well, that just convinced Charley he should be in school so he could join the district attorney's office.

"I've been asking around town and I found out about this guy I think shot him. His name's Copey Culp and the tag is in his name. We've got him nailed. The point is, what do we do about it? His wife left him and went to Kentucky. It was the kids' dog. We might prosecute Copey but the wife might want the dog back. I've got to tell the police but I thought I ought to talk to you first. I know you're real attached to him."

"Let's call his wife and ask her about it. If she left him, she's probably mad at him. You don't think she shot him, do you?"

"No, she left about the same time it happened. I don't know if we can find her without the police getting in on it."

"I can find her. I have a friend who can find anyone. What's her name?"

"Sally Sue Anderson was her name. Now Sally Sue Culp. She's in Kentucky with her folks. I know a girl who knows her. She isn't sure but she thinks the town is Lexington."

William got on the phone. He called the library at the University of Illinois and spoke to his friend. In ten minutes he had Sally Sue's parents' name and was talking to Sally Sue on the phone.

"I hate to say this," he told her, "but we think your husband shot your dog. Is that possible?"

"My God. Of course. That's why he won't bring it here. He shot Dan?"

"Dan's okay. We got him fixed up. You called him Dan?"

"It was already his name. I got him from a guy in the movies. He's a very valuable dog. He was raised by Elizabeth Taylor. His father is owned by Michael Jackson. Well, we aren't sure of that. He's the best dog I ever saw in my life. Copey shot him?"

"We're pretty sure he did. Do you want him back? I hope not, because we're nursing him. His muscle is still not well. He's going to limp. Listen, Mrs. Culp. I think you better talk to Charley Boyd. He's the one who runs the animal shelter. I'm giving him the phone."

Charley got on the phone and talked to her and told her the rest of what they knew. "Put the guy back on. The one who has him," she said.

"Mr. Hagedorn?" she began. "I'm at my mom's with four kids. I couldn't take him now even if he wasn't hurt. I have to start work next week in Nashville. It's a two-hour commute. So if you want to keep him awhile, you can. I want to tell you about how I got him sometime. Did you ever see that movie called *Jesse's Girl?* That was the movie. This guy who drove the truck with the dead horses for battle scenes was the one who had him. When he was in Hollywood he delivered newspapers to movie stars. There's a long history in that dog."

"I'll call you every Sunday and let you know how he's getting along."

"I'm going to have someone shoot Copey, is what I'm going to do," she added. "Every Sunday afternoon go shoot Copey, is what you can do for me."

"Let me talk to her," Charley said. "We need some papers on this."

Much later that night William lay in his bed looking out the window at the spring stars. Dan was on top of the covers, his head on William's leg. The window was open. It was a nice night for that time of year, warmer than it should be. The nausea was coming and going but William had decided to just accept it and try to put his mind in the stars. "I'd like to get some shots of you at night," he was saying. "Just a shadow against the sky. Or maybe on a rise like a wolf. Oh, you don't like that? You reject your ancestry? All right. No wolf photographs then." The wave of nausea passed and William began to fall asleep. His brain shut the doors to Hades and began to open upon some scenes a man could bear to watch. Elizabeth Taylor and Michael Jackson at Neverland on a sunny day. A litter of puppies. Elizabeth falls to her knees and begins to cuddle the puppies against her breasts. She is wearing a pale pink cashmere sweater. Michael kneels beside her. He is wearing a uniform with epaulets. He takes off the jacket and puts it beside the puppies. Dan crawls over and lies down upon the silken lining of the jacket. Michael and Elizabeth begin to laugh.

Dan moved his big warm body closer to William's legs. He heard the earth's core and the blood coursing through William's veins and the distant call of a mourning dove. It was dark and warm in the room and he was safe. He closed his eyes and saw a line of newspapers on a sunny street. They were waiting for him. When he woke he would deliver them to their people.

An Ancient Rain Forest, or, Anything for Art

We were stuffed into the MG for four hours. The prize-winning poet, the Mormon she had vowed to save, and myself, a would-be poet trying to get away from my family. It was my dream come true. Being near the poet Simone Travist. Getting to talk to her about poetry, maybe even getting her to say she liked my poems. I had decided to become a poet after reading Simone's poems. She spoke to the soul within my soul. She had looked inside my head and said the things I never dared to say. Now, unbelievable as it might seem, I was in the back of a borrowed MG on the way to tour the rain forest with my idol.

An ancient rain forest on the Olympic Peninsula, the last one of its kind in the world. Then, at the last minute, Simone had invited the Mormon to come along on the trip. "Just think, Rhoda," she said to me. "It's our chance to save thousands of women. This Mormon is very influential in Salt Lake City. She is a direct descendant of Joseph Smith. If we free her, she will free others. I dreamed of it last night. Thousands of women in a burning barn and we saved them."

"I was in your dream?"

"You were indeed. You were an integral part of my dream. I'm going to turn the dream into a poem. You will be in it. I might even use your name."

"My God. I'm honored. I don't know what to say."

So now the Mormon was riding shotgun and I was stuffed into the small backseat. Simone was lecturing as she drove. "We love men. We aren't saying that men aren't nice or good to screw. Many of them are well intentioned, gentle, hardworking, and kind. But we still have a right not to be subservient to them. We are tired of always being the ones to run houses. It's boring work, repetitive. Women have other drives and talents and ambitions. They need to exercise those drives. They need to have a life outside the home. Abortion is about young girls finding out their full personalities before they are stuck in a rut being mothers. It's about timing."

"I've had two abortions," I lied. "I have three children and I had two abortions and I'm as happy as I can be. What's the big fuss about? It's just a piece of tissue. No different than using a rubber."

"Well." Simone set her lips into a line. Only the night before she had told me about her abortion. Now, just because the Mormon was here, she was acting like I'd said too much, stepped over a line.

I hated the Mormon. I wanted to shock her. I wanted to throw her out of the car so I could talk to Simone about my poems.

The Mormon's name was Mary Anne. She had told us about her ancestors having three wives and how much the children hated each other. She had told us about her years running a halfway house for girls who got in trouble. She told us how they cried for the babies who were taken from them whether they liked it or not. She told us about the girls who came back year after year begging for information about their babies. It was this recurring heartbreak that had caused her to sign up for the writing conference and travel to Washington State to meet Simone and talk to her.

"You can have a great influence on the women of your place," Simone was saying. "Think what an opportunity you have. Joseph Smith was the spiritual leader of the group. Anything you say will be listened to. Anything you do will be noticed."

"My husband was for me coming," Mary Anne said. "He wasn't born into the Faith. His family only joined when he was twelve. He's not as hot on it as he once was. We have to give them so much money. We have to pay tithing."

"Would he renounce it? Is there enough money to live in another state?"

"Oh, not renounce it. I'm a Mormon. I believe in it. Not the old ways, but the new ways."

"I'm an atheist," I said from the backseat. If you can call a place designed to keep luggage a seat. "I've been an atheist from the day I was born. One religion is as bad as another. They're all about control. Control, control, control. For God's sake, Simone. I'm about to die back here. Can we stop and let me walk around?"

"I could take a turn back there," Mary Anne offered.

"You wouldn't fit," I answered, and it was true. She weighed about a hundred and fifty and was five feet eight inches tall.

"I would get back there if my back would let me," Simone said, but of course I couldn't let her do that. After all, she was sixty years old, although she looked and acted like a girl. I struggled to bring my legs into a different position. We were on a two-lane blacktop road surrounded by tall trees. We were in the middle of nowhere.

"Well, for Christ's sake, stop."

Simone brought the MG to a stop at a wide place in the road and we all got out and stood by the car. "How can you believe that crap?" I asked, shaking out my legs, tucking my plaid shirt into my jeans. I had been starving for weeks before flying to Washington State to meet Simone at the conference. I was as thin as I get. I loved it. Being able to stuff a plaid shirt into blue jeans and still look good. I wasn't having much fun at the conference, but at least Simone had been reading my poetry. At least I had finally met some real writers even if they did turn out to have feet of clay.

One young San Francisco poet was writing long epic poems about the love he bore his wife and children. He was reading them to us at night. Curled up by his side was the Chinese student he was fucking afternoon and night.

There was a mad poet from Minnesota who wanted everyone to dance together at night. He was the life-affirming poet and on his fourth National Endowment grant. I liked his style if not his poetry.

There was a drunken fiction writer from the East Coast who showed up two days late and took me off to get drunk with him. I told him some lies about how much I loved Malraux and he was about to fall in love with me when Simone broke it up. "Quaaludes," she said. "That's all I have to say about him. Don't get mixed up in that."

Of course she turned out to be right. The next night I started to go to bed with him but then I found the bottle of pills in the bathroom and changed my mind. I put my shoes back on and told him another lie. "I can't sleep with you after all," I said. "I would only be doing it because you won a Pulitzer Prize. That's not a good enough reason. We'd be here for ten more days trying to figure out why we'd done this."

"Are you sure you feel that?" he asked. "Or is that something Simone told you to say?"

"What do you mean?"

"She's such a rabid feminist. I don't think she wants anyone to get laid."

"What do you mean? She's married and she has dozens of admirers. She's the sexiest woman her age I've ever seen."

"Are you leaving?"

"Yes. Forgive me. We'll have breakfast in the morning."

I left his cabin and took a long walk up and around the old naval base, which was the site of the conference. There was a full moon. The huge wildflowers that grow on the Pacific coast raised their faces to me in the moonlight. On top of a bluff overlooking the barracks I came upon a group of students sleeping in sleeping bags. They stirred when I came near and I said hello and went back down the path and went to bed.

But this was five days later and I was in the back of the MG. I had forgotten the help Simone had given me with my poems. I had forgotten the lunches we had shared, the long sunbaths on her porch, the good advice she had been lavishing upon me. All I thought about was this goddamn Mormon taking up the front seat and all of Simone's attention.

"It isn't all crap," Mary Anne said. Simone had gotten the thermos from the trunk. She poured coffee for the three of us. We stirred it with a plastic spoon. We drank.

"Okay," I said. "Tell me the part that's true. You know what you need to do, Mary Anne. You need to go back to school and learn some things. About biology and primate behavior and anthropology and chemistry. You need more facts. You know this polygamy stuff the Mormon men got into? It's just primate behavior. Men are herd animals. '. . . a hillocky bull in the swelter of summer come in his great good time to the sultry biding herds . . . ,' as Dylan Thomas wrote. Every male poet I know adores that poem. It's about fucking a lot of different women, and all alpha males want to do it. Most of them do do it. They want to fuck everybody, but they really want to fuck alpha females because chemistry or the unconscious or whatever tells them that will make the strongest children. Alpha females are better mothers. They want to impregnate you and let you spend the rest of your life taking care of their DNA. All this is true. This is real information. Religion is just a bunch of crap designed to get you to accept the status quo without complaining or shooting them. God, I can't believe the things that go on. The human race." I strode off down the road about twenty yards and then came back. Simone was leaning near Mary Anne. Probably telling her not to mind me or that I was right or that I was wrong. Who knows what she was saying.

"The Church is a force for good in our community," Mary Anne began. "It takes care of young girls when they get in trouble. That's why they take the babies. So the girls can have another chance. So they won't be stuck with it."

"But they're stuck anyway." Now I was getting mad. This was my main issue and the one I would eventually write about when I learned to write what I knew. "Listen, Mary Anne, you told us yourself the girls come back to see you, grieving for the children they relinquished. The children the Mormons took. You admitted they didn't really have a choice. They had to have the babies and they had to give them up. That's barbaric. Totally barbaric. Come on, let's go. If I have to ride in the back of the MG, I want to get it over with."

"I shouldn't have come along," Mary Anne began. I fit myself into my uncomfortable nest and Simone got behind the wheel and started driving.

Ten miles down the road it began to rain. Rain came out of nowhere just as we were passing a stretch of clear-cut forest. In the distance Mount Olympus was wreathed in clouds. You could see where the rain began and stopped. Once this had all been rain forest, hundreds of miles of mystery. Now we were going to visit what remained. Already it was making us sad and sober.

We pulled over and put up the top and now I was really crushed in the so-called backseat. "You tell me how to alleviate human suffering," I said. "You tell me what to do and I'll do it. Women having babies makes suffering. It does. For every time childbirth is a good idea, there are three times it's a bad idea. India, China, Africa, our slums, take a look. What do you see?"

Simone answered me. "You know that old story about the walled town where everything was perfect and the people were completely happy? The only thing that was wrong was that a little girl had to be kept all her life in a dungeon to maintain that happiness. No windows, no light. Once a year the towns-people had to file past the dungeon and look at her. After that, some of the people would always leave. Go out the gates into the desert. The ones who stayed would keep on being happy." Simone looked straight ahead as she spoke. The windshield wipers pushed against the pouring rain. "Who is that child in our culture?" she added.

"The ones who shouldn't have been born," I answered. "The ones who are born to helpless mothers. Jesus Christ, there are no answers, are there?"

"So what can we do each day?" Simone speeded up, pushing the MG through the rain. "Because nature doesn't care about us. Nature doesn't give a damn one way or the other. Only man cares for man. I don't hate religion as you do, Rhoda. Much of it has to do with goodness, kindness, charity."

"That's easy for you to say. You're Jewish. What does a Reform Jew know about indoctrination? Hell and damnation. You're right. I hate it. It's all madness."

"Not everyone is smart enough to do without a God." I couldn't believe the Mormon had said that. I might have to rethink the Mormon.

"You're smart," I offered. "Write a book about the home you ran. Tell the stories you told us. Publish it. Get some cards out on the table."

"She's going to," Simone said. "She has files, notes, letters. I'm going up there this winter and help her with it."

"How much farther is it?" I asked. "I don't know how long I can maintain this position."

"Fifteen minutes," Simone answered. "Hang on. The rain has almost stopped. If no one minds, now I'll drive this car."

She pushed the pedal to the metal. She floorboarded it. She drove that little car like it was meant to be driven. Heavenly to remember a time when we lived like that. When no one ever seemed to be afraid of a thing.

Then we were there. We parked in a lot with other cars and got out and walked into an enchanted forest. I have never been anywhere more beautiful in my life. It was a cathedral, a cool, green paradise. Trees as big around as houses, as tall as ten-story buildings, trees that are hundreds of years old. Moss and vine and brilliant flowers, capes of moss, silence, fabulous, ancient silence.

It is called the Hoh Rain Forest and it covers nine hundred thousand acres of land in the Olympic National Park.

We walked together across a wooden bridge and went deeper into the wildness, coolness, mystery. I had an overwhelming desire to be alone with it. I didn't want to speak. These trees were beyond language or human thought. They existed in a time of their own. I signaled to Simone that I was leaving. Then I hurried down a path. They had stopped to read a plaque beside a Douglas fir. I don't think they even saw me leave. I pushed on until I was out of sight of all the other tourists. A rope ladder was hanging from a Sitka spruce. I climbed it until I was in the branches of the tree. I hung there, swinging gently, thinking of the story Simone had told us. Who was that little girl? Not me. Certainly not me. I had had the best our culture has to offer since the day that I was born. How dare I not be happy? How dare I resent a human soul? How dare I be mean to the Mormon? Think of the courage she had shown, to come to a place like this among people who were bound to be contemptuous of her life. And yet, I cannot love her, I decided. What is wrong with me that I cannot learn to love? What good is Simone to me if I learn nothing from her?

I will burn my stupid poems, I decided. I will burn everything I've written and start again. If I cannot write with love, if I cannot know compassion, I will give it up and go back to playing tennis.

I climbed back down the ladder and started moving along a path. I was getting high on oxygen. The trees were so dense, the air so rich. There was so much to breathe, so much to learn, so much to understand. I would never do it. I would live and die an ignorant savage, a stick of protoplasm wearing borrowed leaves.

I walked for what seemed an hour. I wandered off the path and back onto the path. I was not worried that I was lost, and I didn't want to be found. Suddenly, the path opened out onto a rocky beach. I had come to the Hoh River, a shallow, fast-moving river fed by melted snow from the glaciers on Mount Olympus. I walked to the edge of the cobbled stones and reached down and felt the water. It was very, very cold. So clear it was like a mirror. Fish flashed by across the rounded stones. The sound was indescribable, without pattern, as random and chaotic as an electron dance, as hypnotic as a Bach fugue. The Glass Bead Game, I decided. Here is where I'll find it. I looked around me, at the cobbled beach, the mountains in the distance, the hovering forest. Then I lay down upon the stones and fell asleep.

It must have been an hour later when I felt a hand on my shoulder and looked up to see Simone's worried face. "We were afraid you were lost," she said. "We thought of finding a guide. Then I saw you. Are you all right?"

"I fell asleep," I answered. "Enchantment. Where are we, Simone? 'What is the time and the place?'"

"It's daunting." She sat down beside me. Mary Anne was thirty feet away, wading in the water. "I'm so glad you came. So glad you came with me."

"I was mad when you asked the Mormon. I want to apologize for that." I leaned back on my hands. "Let's move in," I said. "Let's live here."

"Someone did, I suppose," she answered. "Imagine their lives. So much has been lost. But other things are found."

"Like what?" I answered. I was waking up. "Name me one thing we have made to compare with this river."

"Smocked dresses for little girls," she offered.

"Why did you tell me that terrible story? I'll never forget that as long as I live."

"I wish I hadn't reminded myself of it." We looked down the river to where Mary Anne was standing in the freezing water.

"Let's put her on a diet," I decided. "Let's take her to Seattle to go shopping. Let's get her a lover, or a divorce."

"She can't leave. She has children. It's a world, a way of life. She can't escape."

"Can you?" I asked. "Can I?"

"We have. That's why we're here."

"If I could stop wanting things. Wanting more and more. These trees are greedy too, Simone. All that life in there. So beautiful, but each life form is trying to crowd others out. The capes of moss on the trees. Remorseless, unthinking. What if we are like that too? What if we are as cruel as the rest of nature?"

"Do you feel cruel?"

"Selfish. Mostly selfish. But I would go into the barn with you to save the women. And something else." I stood up. "I wouldn't stay in the town with the child in the dungeon."

"What would you do? Walk out into the desert and starve and die?"

"I would start a movement to let her out. I would tell the people that we didn't need to keep her there. That it was a lot of bullshit. A lot of lies we had been taught. Were there priests in the story? Who was in charge of putting her there? Who kept her there?"

"They would all be against you. Your father and your brothers. Maybe your mother and your sisters. Everything that made you safe."

"I'd overpower them or I would find someone who could and band together with them. Come on, let's collect the Mormon and go back into the forest. I'm starving. We need to find somewhere to eat." I stretched and yawned. "I will love her," I added. "I'll help her if I can."

"She's the little girl in the story." Simone stood back, giving me one of those goddamn politically correct looks that drive me completely up the wall. There's a smell to that kind of thinking that poisons the air for miles around.

"For God's sake, I know that. Except she's not in a dungeon. She's at the apex of power in that culture. She has money and possessions. It's not the same thing, Simone. I want her to escape, but you and I both know she can't. Well, it's hopeless, let's get going." Mary Anne was walking toward us, a big, sad-faced Amazon who could be thought of as a war criminal, or part of the burgeoning wonder of the physical world, or a recruit in a revolution, or just a big unhappy woman looking for a way to live.

"I have better things to do than run around with Mormons," I added. "But this is your trip. I'm just along for the ride. I will try to love her as I do air or light on the river, Simone. But you walk with her through the forest. I don't trust her not to say something stupid about the trees."

Excitement, Part I

EVERYTHING WAS GOING along just fine until the Frenchman came to town. Abby's brother was in the habit of taking care of the foreign students at Tulane and he's the one who met him. This Rugby-playing Frenchman who was six feet tall. I heard about it when Abby and I were out running in the park. "Phillip's got a Frenchman for me to meet," she said, when I asked her if she could come to dinner that night. "I have to stay at home because he's going to bring him over."

"A Frenchman," I said. "Well, that should be interesting. What kind of a Frenchman?"

"A tall one who plays Rugby. Phillip met him last Saturday at a Rugby match."

"I've never met a Frenchman. I never get to do anything. When is he coming over?"

"I don't know. About eight o'clock, I guess."

We ran in silence for a while. I was eaten up with jealousy. I'm the one who deserved a Frenchman. Only I was married so I didn't get to have anything, except an occasional poet who showed up or something like that.

"I might come over and meet him too. I'll come after dinner."

"Don't do that. Don't come over." We were running pretty fast and we were panting, so our conversation was turning into pants.

"Okay, I won't come over. Keep your Frenchman to yourself."

"Thank you, I will."

"Do you want to do another lap?"

"Sure, if you do."

"It's obsessive."

"I know. Let's do it."

We rounded the flower clock. We passed the swings on Saint Charles Avenue. We passed the pro shop at the golf course. We passed the chin-up bars. We passed the tree that was the first thing we ran around two years before when we had started running. It was a small circular walk around a huge old moss-covered oak tree.

"Remember the day we ran around that tree?" I asked.

"We could hardly make it a quarter of a mile."

"We've come a long way since then."

"We have, haven't we?"

"If I hadn't made you start running, there wouldn't be any Frenchman. You'd be so fat no Frenchman would look at you. I think you ought to let me come and meet him."

"Why do you want to meet my Frenchman?"

"Because I've never met one. Because I'm bored to death. Because I don't have anything to do."

"You have your husband. And you have the tennis player."

"Big, big deal. He won't even return my phone calls."

"Why not?"

"Because he says I'm married."

"You are married. Your husband's a great guy."

"He is that. And a wonderful father. So what?"

"I wish I was still married."

"What for? It's slavery. You have to tell them where you are every minute."

We passed the curve at Magazine Street. We passed the bicycle racks. We passed the volleyball court. "I'm turning off at Prytania," Abby said. "I have to go do something with my hair."

"Okay. Go on. I'm going to run another lap."

"Obsessive."

"Who cares."

Abby turned off at Prytania and ran in the direction of her car. A secondhand Volvo her father had given her a week ago. I watched her long legs and long brown hair disappear into the shade of the live oak trees. I ran alone. I was thinking about going over to the tennis player's house and leaving him a note. Then I thought better of it. What I really needed was a divorce, but I didn't know how to get it. I didn't know how to do anything and I had never had a job so I didn't know where to start to stop being married.

I kept on running. I ran another lap, and then, as luck would have it, the tennis player came by on his bicycle and began to ride along beside me.

"Why didn't you call me back?"

"Because you're married."

"But I don't want to be."

"But you are."

"So what? Put your bike down and run with me."

"I don't have a lock."

"Okay."

"I've been thinking about you."

"I started to leave you a note. It's my birthday tomorrow. I'll be thirty-one. I need to celebrate."

"By running around the park."

"I like to run around the park."

"Would you like to come over to my place?"

"Now?"

"Why not?"

"All right, I might. Don't you have to work?"

"Not for a while. Follow me home."

"Let me get my car."

I ran across the grass to where my car was parked on Prytania Street and the tennis player rode his ten-speed bike along beside me. It never occurred to me not to go over to his house and fuck him. It almost made up for Abby's Frenchman, but not quite.

That night my little girl had to play in a basketball game at the Jewish Community Center. After supper my husband and my little girl, Molly, and I drove down Saint Charles Avenue and parked a block away and walked to the center holding hands. The tennis player came riding his bicycle down the center of the streetcar track. He waved at me. I waved back. It was a coincidence that kept occurring. Three times after I had fucked him in the afternoon I had run into him later that afternoon or night somewhere in uptown New Orleans. He thought it was only because we lived so near each other. That was one thing wrong with the tennis player. He didn't believe in attraction or cosmic awareness or anything really good to talk about.

"Is Abby coming to my game?" Molly asked.

"She can't. She has a Frenchman coming over tonight to meet her."

"A Frenchman?" my husband said. "That's all she needs. Where did she find a Frenchman?"

"Her brother met him at Tulane. He plays Rugby. I have to go over there after the game and meet him. She wants me to see what I think of him." As I said it I knew it was true. There was no way I was letting Abby keep that Frenchman to herself. If it wasn't for me she'd be too fat for a Frenchman and so on and so forth.

Chapter two. We lost the game by twenty points. The other team had fourteen players and we only had five players. None of our bench showed up. "Benchless," my husband proclaimed. "We will have to go out and recruit again."

"Take Molly home," I said. "I have to go see about this Frenchman." My husband was glad to have his little girl to himself so he could lecture her about getting rebounds and not being discouraged when things didn't go her way. He kissed me on the cheek and said he'd come get me when I called. Abby's house was only a block from the center. I walked along in the lovely warm evening air thinking about the tennis player and

whether or not it would be worth getting a divorce from someone as nice as my husband just so I could sleep with him at
night. I decided against it. It put me in a sad mood to decide
not to get a divorce and I looked at my watch and saw it was
only fifteen after eight. It was too soon to go to Abby's house
and meet the Frenchman. It would be better to go somewhere
and get a drink and then go to Abby's house. After all, I hadn't
had a drink in twelve days. Surely I had stopped being an
alcoholic by now. Just one little drinkie-poo. Just one little vodka
martini and then I'd quit for the night. A double. Just one little
double vodka martini or maybe just a glass of wine.

But where to go? I could go by my cousin Ingersol's house,
but that was ten blocks away and I didn't have a car. I could go
to a pay phone and call him and tell him to come get me, but
then I'd have to take him with me to Abby's house. I could walk
back to Saint Charles Avenue and catch the streetcar to the
Pontchartrain Hotel. I could go in the elegant bar and sit on a
bar stool and pretend I was in Paris, France, and have a glass of
French wine or maybe a nice little double vodka martini in a
squat frosted glass with three olives, or maybe four.

What a night! Gorgeous stars above the live oak trees, soft
sweet air, one day from my fabulous, wonderful birthday. I had
hated being thirty but I loved being thirty-one already and it
was still four hours away. Yes. I would catch the streetcar and go
to the Pontchartrain Hotel and order a bottle of French Champagne and charge it to my husband. Maybe I would get another
one and take it over to Abby's. Maybe I would call Ingersol after
all and let him drive me around all night. After all, Ingersol was
crazy about me. He was my favorite cousin in New Orleans and
he could always be counted on to rescue me or take me somewhere.

I was running now in the direction of the streetcar stop at
the corner of Jefferson and Saint Charles. It was wonderful that
I was a practiced runner. Wonderful to think of myself showing
up at the Pontchartrain Hotel wearing my running shoes. It
would add to my legend. Alone at the bar drinking French
Champagne and then being rescued by my gorgeous, extrava-
gantly wealthy cousin, Ingersol Manning.

I arrived at the streetcar stop just as the streetcar was screeching to a stop. It was empty. No one rode the streetcars at eight o'clock at night. "Take me to the Pontchartrain Hotel," I told the driver. "It's three and a half hours to my birthday."

"That'll be fifty cents," the driver said, and I put a streetcar token in the slot and went back to the middle of the car and took a seat by the window. This is a night to love New Orleans, I decided. Tommy and Molly at home doing Molly's homework, probably thinking of something to buy me or wrapping up something they already bought for me. Mother calling from Laurel and me not there to answer the phone and all her stupid questions. Ingersol sitting at his house bored to death waiting to come rescue me. Abby and the Frenchman and Abby's brother probably talking about something boring. They'll be glad when I get there with French Champagne to liven up the party. "Way down yonder in New Orleans," I started singing sweet and low to the breeze coming in the window, "In the land of dreamy dreams. There's a garden of Eden, that's what I mean."

The streetcar arrived at the corner of Jackson Avenue and I thanked the driver and got down and walked to the hotel. I went into the lobby and through the wooden doors into the Bayou Room and walked up to the wide bar and ordered a martini. "And a bottle of French Champagne to go," I added. "The best one you have. It's almost my birthday. Is there a phone I can use?"

The bartender handed me a phone and I called Ingersol. Of course he was waiting for me. "My darling, darling," I said into the phone. "It's almost my birthday. Come get me at the Pontchartrain bar. I've got a plan."

"As soon as I get dressed," he answered. "I was half asleep."

"Abby's got a Frenchman," I told him. "We're going to crash the party."

The bartender was not impressed. He seemed unhappy. His white jacket could use some bleach. He was tall and gangly and his fingernails were dirty. It was not turning out to be a good idea to be in the deserted Bayou Room in my running shoes.

There was no one in the bar but a trashy-looking couple in a corner holding hands. The bartender put the drink down in front of me and I started not to even drink it. Alcohol turns into formic acid and formaldehyde in the brain, I could hear my psychiatrist saying. It puts holes in your liver. It gets you confused and sad. Why would you do something that stupid to yourself?

"Never mind it," I said to the bartender. "It's the nineties. I think this is an idea whose time has passed." I shoved the drink and a ten-dollar bill in his direction and got down off the bar stool.

"What about the Champagne?" he said. "Do you still want that?"

"I don't think so. I'm going outside and wait for my cousin." I left the Bayou Room and walked out through the lobby and stood on the corner by the newspaper stands waiting for my cousin to come and get me. THOUSANDS DEAD IN BOSNIA, the headlines read. HOUSE CUTS WELFARE PROGRAMS. NEW ORLEANS NUMBER ONE IN MURDERS.

What a night, I started humming. Sweet confusion under the moonlight. Maybe I should get into politics, or maybe adopt some abandoned children. Or study biochemistry or go to medical school. I'm only thirty-one. I could still go to medical school if I wanted to.

I leaned against a lamppost. I pulled one leg up and began to stretch my hamstrings. I saw Ingersol's Porsche coming down the street. The top was down and Ingersol's thin blond hair was flying all around. "Cousin Baby Sister," he said, when he had come to a stop beside me. "Get in the car. What are you doing out here all alone in the murder capital of the world? And what is this about a Frenchman? Have you had anything to eat? Let's go somewhere and pick up some crayfish." He got out of the car and took my arm and put me in the passenger seat and pulled out my seat belt and handed it to me.

"I almost had a drink but I stopped myself," I said. "Can you believe it, Ingersol? I haven't had a drink for almost thirteen days. Take me to my house. I want to see my husband and my child. There's tons to eat at my house. There's everything we need." I touched him on the arm and he turned the Porsche around and started driving to my house.

"I decided not to get a divorce from Tommy," I announced. "I'm going to stop fucking around on him and be a wife."

"Jesus Christ, cousin. You are having a birthday epiphany, aren't you now?"

"We're wasting our lives, Ingersol. How old are you now?"

"Thirty-eight. I'm not wasting mine."

"You ought to quit racing sailboats all the time and use your brain. You ought to quit dating half-wits."

"I'm going to Aspen next week. You want to go along?"

"The slopes are too crowded. I don't like it anymore."

We drove in silence for a while, down the long tunnel of live oak trees, past the mansions, past the yards where we had been to parties every day of our lives, past the streets that turned off to our schools, past a thousand lovers and boyfriends and girl-friends and walks and bicycle rides. "I love this town," I said at last. "I love my birthday. I love my life."

We turned off onto State Street and went down a block and came to a stop in front of the three-story blue house Tommy's mother had given us. Molly's bike was on the steps. The lights were on in every window. Music was pouring out the doors. There were cars lining the driveway. Ingersol started laughing. "Get out," he said. "It's a party. We thought we lost you for a while but we knew you'd call one of us if we waited."

I got out of the car and walked around Molly's bicycle and into my house, which was full of everyone I knew. My parents were there and my cousins were there and my neighbors were there and half the girls in my exercise class and Abby and her brother and the Frenchman, who turned out to be a dismal chain-smoking academic searching for a living. The cake was monstrous. A huge half-chocolate, half-lemon doberge tart with thirty-one candles in roseate holders. Molly had put on her best pink and blue flowered party dress and she lit them while my friends began to sing. WE LOVE YOU, GARLAND, it said on the cake, and the voice of my tribe bellowed out HAPPY

BIRTHDAY TO YOU and I hugged my child and my mother and my husband and blew those fuckers out.

"What did you wish?" Molly asked. She has her father's retentive mind.

"World peace," I answered. "You have to wish for that or all else fails."

"You could wish for more wishes," she suggested. "That's what I always do."

Later, after the guests and the caterers had left, I went into the kitchen and had a second piece of cake with my child and we lit some candles and collected a few more wishes.

"You took a big chance having this party after your ball game," I said. "Weren't you worried when I went off to meet the Frenchman?"

"We knew you'd call Ingersol if you were walking," Molly said. "We made him go over to his house and wait."

"What made you think I'd call him?"

"Because you always do. Daddy bet Abby's brother twenty dollars you'd call Ingersol before nine o'clock."

"In the future I may be less predictable," I said, and hugged her. "Now that I've quit drinking wine and become a serious thirty-one-year-old person. Well, it happens to be past eleven o'clock and you have to go to school in the morning. If you can't get up, it will be my fault."

"May I sleep with you tonight?"

"No. I am sleeping with your father. But I'll tuck you in. Go get ready."

After I got her to sleep I put on my best red nightgown and went into my bedroom to seduce my husband. He was waiting for me, reading a sexy foreign affairs article in the *Atlantic Monthly* and wearing his tight Brooks Brothers pajamas he has had for the nine years I've been married to him.

"I want our marriage to have a new birth of feeling," I told him. "I want you to take off your clothes and turn off the light and get me pregnant." It was an inspiration of the moment. Of course, there was no chance he could get me pregnant with my contraband IUD safely tucked up in my uterus but he was much too excited to remember that. He worked on pumping me full of sperm and I worked on pretending there really was a Frenchman and he was in the bed and all in all being thirty-one was turning out to be right on the money as far as good times were concerned.